THE B

CH00767252

Farrukh Dhondy was bo͟ȓ   ͏ȣ͏ graduating in
physics from Wadia Colle͟g͟͟e, ͟e won a scholarship to Cambridge
to train as a quantum physicist but ended up reading for a BA in
English. He has lived in England since and has worked as a teacher,
and as a commissioning editor at Channel 4 television.

Dhondy's first collection of stories, *East End at Your Feet*,
was published in 1977. His output is prolific and wide-ranging:
books for younger readers, such as *Come to Mecca* (1978) and *Run!*
(2002); the classic collection of stories about Indian small-town life,
Poona Company (1980); the Whitbread Award–nominated novel,
Bombay Duck (1990); *C.L.R. James: A Life* (1996); and screenplays
for film and television, including *Split Wide Open* (1999) and *The
Rising: The Ballad of Mangal Pandey* (2005). He also writes for the
stage, his latest production being *Karna: Warrior of the Sun* (2008).
He is currently working on a film adaptation of V.S. Naipaul's
A Bend in the River, among other things.

THE BIKINI MURDERS

A Novel

Farrukh Dhondy

HarperCollins *Publishers* India

First published in India in 2008 by
HarperCollins *Publishers*

Copyright © Farrukh Dhondy 2008

P-ISBN: 978-93-5116-046-5
E-ISBN: 978-93-5029-258-7

2 4 6 8 10 9 7 5 3

Farrukh Dhondy asserts the moral
right to be identified as the author of this work.

This is a work of fiction and all characters and
incidents described in this book are the product of the
author's imagination. Any resemblance to actual persons,
living or dead, is entirely coincidental.

All rights reserved. No part of this publication may be reproduced,
stored in a retrieval system, or transmitted, in any form or by any means,
electronic, mechanical, photocopying, recording or otherwise,
without the prior permission of the publishers.

HarperCollins *Publishers*
A-75, Sector 57, Noida, Uttar Pradesh 201301, India
1 London Bridge Street, London, SE1 9GF, United Kingdom
Hazelton Lanes, 55 Avenue Road, Suite 2900, Toronto, Ontario M5R 3L2
and 1995 Markham Road, Scarborough, Ontario M1B 5M8, Canada
25 Ryde Road, Pymble, Sydney, NSW 2073, Australia
195 Broadway, New York, NY 10007, USA

Typeset in 11.5/14.5 Elegant Garamond BT by
R. Ajith Kumar

Printed and bound at
Saurabh Printers Pvt.Ltd.

And voices in me said, If you were a man
You would take a stick and break him now, and finish him off.
Was it cowardice that I dared not kill him? Was it perversity, that
I longed to talk to him?

—From 'Snake' by D.H. Lawrence

PART 1

1

*E*duard du Monde wears dark glasses even in the dimly lit casino. He has trained himself to live at a remove from brightness. He is wearing a tweed jacket and green sweater, both bought in cheap Chinese emporia in Paris, as are his leather shoes.

He always plays blackjack because of a superstition about the number 21. It is a superstition with no roots in numerology or any other mumbo, but a personal and fanciful one. His father first got in touch with him on his twenty-first birthday. They hadn't even met before that and suddenly, out of nowhere, the man wanted his son to smuggle diamonds. Then there was the fact that he had counted twenty-one bodies in the streets of Saigon on the first day that he went walking to school with his mother. He must have been five.

Numbers. Luck.

A numerologist, one he met in jail, told him the numbers in themselves were lucky. The digits added up to three and the factors of twenty-one were seven and three, both numbers of fortune: one representing luck, the other the trinity. His certainties about these numbers aside, he thinks of himself as a Buddhist. It is the only religion he can believe in because in his mind it relieves him of the responsibility for his actions. Most of these, in his version of

Buddhism, are the result of deeds in past lives, deeds hidden from the intellect and memory, deeds in the records of God or whatever power it is that passes sentence on the life about to happen. Of course this life's good and bad deeds will determine the course of the next, but that has to be a contradiction, because the deeds of the last life determine the events and progress of this one – and so on backwards and forwards to both eternities. Everything is part of a chain…

He shrugs as he thinks about it all.

The chips by his side have grown into a formidable pile, and then, as his concentration wanes, dwindled again. He knows that the game of blackjack is part of the big game of luck, but then most humans believe that wit or cunning can beat it or influence it. He has lived riding on both all his life, and what has worked for life should carry him through the accumulation of petty sums of money at a gaming table, surely.

Around the poker tables, the lighting was deliberately designed to allow the reading of faces; around the blackjack tables one had to strain to catch the contours of and the expressions on the other players' faces.

The sofas at the sides were red velvet and the dim lighting hid the cigarette burns that dotted the upholstery. The bar was busy and crowded but it was a relatively sleepy night in North Face casino. The girls who strutted about in tights and short skirts wore caps, suggestive of both the ears of Playboy Bunny costumes and of the jewelled headwear of Nepalese women. But they were not Nepalese. They were almost all from Bangkok. The clientele preferred Thai women and the laws against trafficking natives and the freedom from harassment by

Nepalese feminist groups made it easier to import 'waitresses' and 'bar girls' from the East.

A man was looking at du Monde. An older Nepalese man, perhaps in his sixties. He stood directly in his line of sight and observed him holding his cards and steadily losing his stack of chips. du Monde couldn't see him and didn't notice him beyond the circle of light. Very many people, gamblers or idlers, came to the North Face to drink, to hang out, to stare at the fools who were losing, or the very rarely fortunate who were breaking the bank – and would perhaps return the next day to lose the fortune they had acquired.

The man either didn't find what he was looking for, or got bored observing other people gaming, and left.

Half an hour later, he returned, accompanied by two men in suits.

The North Face casino, with all its suggestions of the heights of the Everest plastered as tasteless wallpaper at the entrance, is in the basement of the Metropole hotel. The man, with a gaunt and lined leathery face and scant white hair above a tall but narrow forehead, came down its carpeted stairs and through the foyer before the cloakroom attendant could stop or question him. He strolled into the main gambling hall and towards du Monde, who was still where he had left him.

The man knew he'd still be there, because on the stairs and at the exits to the casino a squad of six uniformed policemen had been posted to detain him if he tried to leave.

'Johnson Thhat, we want to talk to you about the murder of Mary Ann Smolinsky.'

du Monde didn't bat an eyelid. His body gave not the slightest indication of acknowledging that another person had come and stood by him. He carried on placing his bet and staring at his cards and trying to see what the dealer was doing.

'You don't remember me?' the old man asked.

du Monde turned to look at him. 'Excuse me?'

'Inspector Ganesh Pradhan? You remember?'

'I beg your pardon?'

'So, no attempt to disguise the voice, Thhat? I am pronouncing your name right, aren't I? You taught me, remember? How to enunciate the first consonant by holding the tongue between the teeth and pulling it back while breathing quickly out through the mouth; and the fact that it rhymed with "fart" rather than "fat"?'

'I don't know what you are talking about, sir, I am Eduard du Monde and I…'

'Yes, I know you have a passport to prove that you are someone else, Johnson, but you know who you are and I know who you are. I am now back on temporary duty with the police. These are my colleagues. We want you to come with us.'

'There is obviously some mistake, Captain,' Thhat said in his lisping English. The words came out as 'Dey eez obvyosly some meesthake, Captain'.

'No, no mistake, M. du Monde. You should come with us now.'

'For what?'

'For questioning.'

'I weel of course cooperate with the poliss, Captain, but you have the wrong man. I don't know the name you are uzeeng. I am a tourist and a beeznessman.'

'And a murderer who has got away with it for too long,' said Pradhan. 'You should come. Or we will take you by force.'

The game had stopped while all this was going on. The bouncers, who relied on the meanness of their features rather than the size of their bodies to deter miscreants, hastily came forward and hovered around. One of the young men in civvies behind Pradhan showed them an identity card and the bouncers immediately became respectful.

One of them stepped forward. 'You should better go with them, sir,' he said.

'Can I see a superior officer?' du Monde protested. He remained seated.

'Yes, of course you can, now come on, Johnson.'

'Please, call me M. du Monde. It's my name and some terrible meesthake has happen here.'

He got up from his chair. Pradhan indicated to one of the bouncers that he should take his chips.

'Let them help you,' Pradhan said.

'I will fix thees and come back, just now – get me a credit note for the chips,' du Monde said to the bouncer.

'I hope these credit notes last a long time,' Pradhan said.

'I hope, Captain, I can estableesh my identity and then I shall return to my game.'

'If the casino is still here when you get out. The Maoists may not allow gambling and they are in the hills now. They'll be running the place tomorrow.' Pradhan wouldn't have said that if he had been a serving officer, but he wasn't. He had been summoned from his bed that night on this specific mission. He was not the type to frequent the North Face or, for that matter, any tourist spot.

The bouncer gave M. du Monde his credit slip as he had requested. The night duty security staff knew du Monde, or had seen him relentlessly winning and losing at blackjack for ten nights. He would arrive late each night and play through until the early morning, sometimes returning to his hotel in a taxi with a modest fortune and sometimes walking home after losing all his money. When he won, he was generous with tips.

du Monde was taken in a police car, not to the police station but to a house on the edges of Kathmandu, which is not so large a town. At that time of night, it was devoid of traffic.

'Do you know, Johnson,' Pradhan said to him as the car meandered through the streets, 'Kathmandu is the only Hindu town left in the subcontinent? Built according to the old Hindu architectural sciences laid down in the shastras. Very logical.'

His prisoner was in no mood for a discussion on town planning. He was cool, seemingly unworried, stonewalling all attempts to lower his defences. He was not going to admit to being anyone other than Eduard du Monde.

'I have my passport on me, Inspector,' he said. 'This could be very serious for you. I have connections with the French Foreign Office and the consul has to be told about this. Can I make a phone call?'

'Oh, sorry, I forgot to ask you for your mobile phones. All of them, please. And very sorry, you cannot make any phone calls.'

'What is this all about? Has Nepal become a fascist state?'

'You know I am not a political analyst, Thhat, I am a simple retired policeman. Stalinism, fascism – Nepal is older. But I expect you'll still be here when it's Maoist. Though you should pray it never gets that way. These fellows are not your Sartre-loving French intellectuals. They "liquidate the class enemy" and they hate criminals of different persuasions from themselves.'

'You will have to call the French consulate for me, then.'

'My feeling is you'll need more than connections in the Foreign Department of France. Have you any connection with the big man himself?'

du Monde ignored the taunt, looking straight ahead through his dark glasses.

'We know that you have connections with the fellow down below. Call on him. You don't need our phone, use your private line.'

du Monde said nothing.

'You didn't see the body of that girl after you left it half-burnt, did you? Well, I did. And my seniors asked me why you had chopped it up if you were going to burn it. I always meant to ask you that.'

'You have got the wrong person. This is a case of mistaken identity, officer, and you will be in some trouble when your superiors find that. So please take me to my hotel and you can complete your investigations tomorrow and confiscate my passport if you like.' He took his passport from his jacket pocket and handed it to Pradhan.

'Huh! Since when has the lack of one passport prevented you from travelling on another? I know you probably have five of them in your hotel room – or maybe not in your hotel room. Hidden somewhere. You bastard!'

'This will not do you good, I swear, I am noting this behaviour for your superiors,' du Monde said.

'I have lived with the fucking images of the murderous mess you left behind for twenty-five years,' Pradhan said.

'These superiors arrived yesterday, infants who can still remember their mothers' milk. What can they do to me? The dead and the retired have nothing to fear.' He grinned, taken by his own witticism.

When they got to the safe house, du Monde was conducted in, and taken to an interrogation room, done up like a cell with a sparse bed and a table with three chairs. A basin was fixed to the wall and there were metal bars on the window.

'Now take your jacket off and your glasses and let's see those famous snake eyes,' Pradhan said.

The prisoner took his jacket off.

'I have an eye condition, I can't take my glasses off,' he said.

Pradhan snatched them off his face. du Monde's eyes, slightly upturned at the corners, betrayed his Far Eastern genes.

'Still the same. Like Peter Pan,' Pradhan said. 'I don't blame you for not recognizing me, but then I think perhaps you do. Pity. If you did we could talk about old times.'

'I have never been to Nepal before in my life, Captain. You can search my hotel room. I have purchased the sample artefacts I came to buy – I am an arts and handicrafts dealer – and I have papers and proof of my company's business.'

'Ah, never been to Nepal. This is indeed a new Nepal. Since you were here, killing people. There are still hippies but now they are rich,' Pradhan said. 'They used to trek from India. Now they come by the planeloads. And they are less religious. But you have been between the hotel and the casino mainly, haven't you? We haven't noticed you investigating possible victims. Unless you are after the fat cats who gamble, Mr Thhat?'

'This whole thing is ridiculous. On what grounds are you holding me?'

'I wasn't even told to beat a confession out of you. Just to keep you safe, to make sure that you are you and to bring you to court tomorrow.'

'What am I being taken to court for? You are violating all international law. I have to be allowed to call the French consul. And you can't take my property from me. You haven't arrested me or anything.'

'Ah, you have dropped the accent, M. du Monde. You should really have practised harder. You know, I don't understand how criminals are so keen on the law – they are always quoting it. And it's your strong point, isn't it? I have followed your career. Diligently. Lots of people in Nepal have. And still no one knows the truth, eh? I doubt if you know the truth, though often when I think about you, I think you must have a clear, flowing mind, crystal clear. And you must feel proud of it, telling yourself that you are a sort of genius. Don't you?'

'Mr Inspector, you are making a big mistake.'

Pradhan didn't reply, and started walking towards the guarded door, but then turned back and sat down.

'Can I tell you, Thhat, that you changed my life? I knew when we first brought you in and you were young and disdainful. I knew about you and I saw you looking down on us poor policemen. Pig-ignorant, stupid, idiot policemen. That's what you said. I took it as a challenge. I did not have time to do much about my stupidity then, but I have spent all my years in retirement reading, studying. At least I won't die that ignorant, stupid policeman. Oh, forget it. I am going to leave you to sleep. I doubt if you will, but if it helps, I can tell you that we have no surviving fingerprint evidence. The bribes you paid destroyed all that. So tell me then, why did you run away? Why didn't you face trial and get yourself acquitted at the time? It would have been all over. The bribe you paid my superiors wasn't enough. The record of that murder still exists, so does my statement. No clean slates. Stingy fucker, you could have bought your way out. You wouldn't be here.'

Pradhan paused. He looked at du Monde's face and for once, du Monde looked back, expressionless.

'Slip out of things, back into your hole in the ground like a snake. That's the game, isn't it, Thhat? God help you.'

Pradhan got up and left.

✦

The prisoner was already wearing his dark glasses the next morning when Pradhan came to take him to the station in the city for fingerprinting. He still insisted that he was the Frenchman Eduard du Monde and that this was a nightmare from which he and the sadly deluded ex-inspector Pradhan would soon recover.

Pradhan was sure that they wouldn't. He was also sure that this was Johnson Thhat.

They were late getting to the city centre, twenty minutes later than they had expected, because of traffic at the outskirts. As du Monde was being ushered out of the police van into the station, another van drew up besides theirs in the yard. Four men in handcuffs, Afghans or Pakistanis, stepped out. They were wearing tourist clothes, T-shirts and jeans. One of the T-shirts had the pennant of an American football team. The men stared at du Monde as they were led out of the van and, Pradhan thought, attempted to disguise the fact that they recognized him. But as du Monde did the same and turned away, one of the men, the shortest and darkest-skinned of the four, spat. It was a contemptuous act, not just a casual bad-mannered shower of saliva.

Pradhan had seen this sort of gesture being made before. du Monde seemed to pay it no attention and they went into the station, but as he was being taken to be fingerprinted, Pradhan thought he detected the faintest sign of discolour in du Monde's face. He was thinking hard.

Pradhan chatted away, explaining that the fingerprinting had to be done using ink and pads because the wretched Kathmandu Police had not yet set up the electronic fingerprinting machines that had been bought and were waiting for the appropriate experts to arrive from the Chinese police force. China and Nepal were having one of their intermittent stand-offs and hence the delay.

The prisoner endeavoured to keep a poker face. Pradhan was watching him when he mentioned China. His police training had, he thought, given him the ability to read even the faintest flicker of the mind behind the eyes.

The damned dark glasses!

✦

A lawyer had been appointed by the court to defend du Monde. When the defence was called to present its case, he took charge, but there was nothing to take charge of. du Monde wouldn't speak to this lawyer. All he had to say was that he refused to be represented as a person he was not.

'So if you are du Monde, what did you come here for?' the prosecutor had asked him.

'I came to buy Nepalese handicraft samples and art pieces,' he answered.

'Why did you spend your days in the hotel and your nights in the casino?' his own lawyer asked du Monde.

'I am addicted to gambling,' du Monde replied.

The defence lawyer turned to the judge and said, 'Thhat, the supposed accused, spent twenty years in jail; therefore he couldn't be addicted to gambling. Gambling is not allowed in Indian jails.'

'This is a hopeless argument. I am not here to listen to lawyers' opinions,' the judge replied. 'Get on with the trial.'

'I have no more questions as my client is hostile,' the lawyer said. 'The defence is forced to rest on the grounds that sufficient evidence has not been produced to prove that this is the one and the same man alleged to have committed the murder twenty-five years ago.'

The prosecution took a few hours. du Monde was identified by Pradhan as Johnson Thhat, the man arrested for the murder of Mary Ann Smolinksy, an American who disappeared in Kathmandu nearly twenty-five years ago and whose body had been discovered chopped to bits.

She was a rich backpacker who had been convinced by Thhat to buy gemstones which he said he was selling cheap. He had charmed her and then, it was alleged, killed her to get back the stones that he had sold her.

From the dock, Thhat protested. He seemed used to sitting in the box and to court procedure, and said he wanted his contention of mistaken identity to be heard first.

How would Eduard du Monde have known about legal procedure, Pradhan thought. It confirmed to him that this was his man. He had file photographs and newspaper reports which said that Thhat, with another young man, a Bengali doctor who was travelling with him, were the alleged murderers of the American girl. There were descriptions of the mutilated body and speculation about how the young woman was killed.

Thhat was not yet ready to offer any defence to this parade of supposed facts. He remained adamant that he wasn't the man and every now and then stood up to protest. 'Can you call the embassy, your honour? I am the victim of legal kidnap. You are supposed to uphold the law, not violate it.'

The judge stated they would disregard Mr Thhat's outbursts and proceed as though they were trying Johnson Thhat and that he was satisfied that the defendant in this murder trial had been identified.

Thhat began to shout. 'I am Eduard du Monde! I must see the French consul. Call the United Nations' representative! You won't get away with this!'

The judge warned him that he would be removed from the court.

There wasn't much of a trial to follow. A photograph of Mary Ann Smolinsky standing in front of a Hindu temple with Thhat's arm around her, both of them smiling, was produced. It was established through old police records and the recollection of an ancient decrepit Gurkha who had been a cleaner at a cheap hotel then that Thhat and the Bengali doctor had indeed rented rooms there. He said that he had actually seen Mary Ann going into Thhat's room.

Other witnesses were brought onto the stand. A reporter who had covered the disappearance of Mary Ann said that he had been told about it by a jealous boyfriend who alleged that Thhat had charmed her away from him. Three days later, her body was found at the side of a highway, chopped to bits and partially burnt. The murderers, or those assigned to get rid of the body, had not even waited for the burning process to complete itself. The victim was identified by her teeth because a dentist in Delhi had attended to her in the weeks before she came up to Kathmandu.

No eyewitness accounts of anyone's doings or whereabouts were produced and there was no circumstantial or forensic evidence to link Thhat to the murder. Thhat had not even been identified at the time as himself. He was travelling even then under a pseudonym, had papers to prove it and was charged under that name.

Pradhan, in charge of the case at that time, had traced Thhat's criminal career through the papers in Thailand. Immediately after the Smolinsky murder, he was convinced that this fellow they were holding was not who he claimed, but Johnson Thhat himself.

Pradhan testified that the Bengali doctor had hired a car whose tyre marks were found near the burnt body. Those records were lost but the judge said he trusted Pradhan's memory. Pradhan also testified that there had been fingerprint evidence taken from the metal belt, which Thhat had removed from Mary Ann's jeans and taken to his room.

None of this evidence had survived the twenty-five years since the crime.

Where was the evidence? Pradhan was convinced that a

senior police officer had taken a bribe from Thhat and allowed the murderers to escape over the border into India. He must have destroyed the forensic evidence so that all that was left was gossip and hearsay, which would not stand up for a minute in any court in the world.

Had he been a fool all these years for trying to be an honest cop, when all about him were building houses and buying farms with the bribes they got from the organized mafias of Kathmandu, India and China?

And was Pradhan totally honest? The body of Smolinsky was charred beyond recognition. In Thhat's hastily abandoned hotel room Pradhan had found a small triangle of fire-resistant canvas fabric. Pradhan had kept the yellow, black-fringed shred and hadn't entered it in the register. Years after the murder investigation had been closed, Pradhan had discovered that the fabric was sometimes used in the manufacture of light tents and in sportswear. Sportswear! Swim wear. Of course! Mary Ann had been described by hotel staff as often wearing a bikini and sunbathing on the terrace or by the pool. Pradhan knew that the international press, latching on to a report from Thailand, had dubbed this man the 'Bikini Murderer', even though, from the record he had read, most of his victims were men.

It crossed Pradhan's mind that the fragment could still be subjected to DNA analysis. It would yield Mary Ann's DNA footprint, but probably not Thhat's. It wouldn't help to convict if any help was necessary. Besides, Pradhan would have to explain why he had not surrendered a vital piece of evidence when investigating the murder.

In the ensuing years Pradhan had followed Thhat's fortunes. He knew he had turned up in India and been convicted and imprisoned for offences other than murders, and also that fantastic legends had grown around him. The papers constantly referred to him as the serial killer wanted in Thailand for eleven murders, but he had escaped justice there. He was in the process of being tried for these murders, which held a sentence of death by firing squad, when he had escaped, in disguise, to India.

Then he had been jailed for drugging and robbing a group of French tourists. The Indian jails had been his home for twenty years. After his release, he had simply dipped below the horizon.

Yes, this would be the first time that Thhat would ever be convicted of murder. The judge had admitted evidence, which wasn't evidence at all.

Pradhan watched him, mongoose to snake.

Just from the sight and smell of the man, Pradhan knew that this was a killer, a man whose immediate reckoning of the world revolved around himself, where others were nothing but were 'patches of colour that made interpretable sounds'.

✦

Two days earlier, late at night, a very high-up civil servant from the Foreign Office had called at Pradhan's house with another official from the justice ministry. Why would they come to the house of a retired policeman at this time of night?

They immediately explained why they were there. His old antagonist was back in town and was in fact at the North Face casino at that very moment. They had had people trailing him and they wanted him put on trial for crimes past.

On the way to the foreign ministry, the senior official had felt obliged to explain himself.

'Nepal has been getting a bad press with the murders in our royal family and the Maoist insurrection. We can recover some ground by bringing a serious serial killer to trial for crimes he committed on our soil. The case will be widely reported. We know you were on his case at the time but the bugger escaped. Now's your chance, Pradhan.'

The next morning, as he was being driven to take Thhat to court, there were calls from the Indian newspapers. Had he got Johnson Thhat in custody? Would he be tried? Was there a death penalty in Nepal?

The reporters who now thronged in to follow the case had been told that it was Pradhan who had discovered Thhat; recognized him while he was on a private social occasion in town, cornered and arrested him, as a dutiful ex-policeman passionate about bringing the murderer who had once eluded him, to justice.

✦

At the end, a quick one for a murder trial, the judge sums up and pronounces the defendant, Johnson Thhat, guilty of the murder of Mary Ann Smolinsky.

'This court finds the defendant Johnson Thhat, also known as Eduard du Monde…'

'No!' shouts Thhat.

'We find him guilty and sentence him to life imprisonment in a place of safe detention.'

'Mr Prosecutor, can I see you below? Can I see anyone from the Nepalese government?'

Thhat, protesting, is bundled away by two policemen.

Pradhan, having sat through the entire trial, leaves his seat with a sigh. If the all-seeing gods had passed such a judgement, he could not be more content. He knows that no government, not even the Maoists if they come to power, would release a convicted serial killer. The Maoists had morality. They would release men found guilty of killing for terror, but not Thhat. He would never be released.

Thhat now turns round and addresses the court, fighting his attendants off briefly.

'You are sending me to death. Can you please send me to maximum security straight away? They will kill me! You know that.'

This is a startling request and the judge, who has not risen from the bench, shouts back at him.

'The prison authorities will look after you very well, Thhat.'

2

Two days after the sentence was passed and reported all over the world, Pradhan got a call at home. It was the defence lawyer.

Pradhan didn't know why the lawyer had called him. The lawyer explained apologetically, 'What could I do? The man was guilty as you said, but I had to do my duty. I applied to see him in jail to apologize and see if I could discover any contacts for him, but authorities would not let me. Thhat requested you go and see him.'

'Why should I see him?' Pradhan asked. 'I hope he rots in jail and his flesh falls off his bones. Did you see the way they had hacked up that poor girl? What about her life?'

'I was simply conveying message,' said the poor defence fellow.

Pradhan resisted for a day. But then his curiosity got the better of him. It was perhaps more than curiosity: he wanted to tell Thhat, face-to-face, that he had got what was coming. That justice was bigger than the law. He was striving to coin a proverb, but couldn't quite get it right: 'Hell is the hole you dig for yourself…' No, that wouldn't enter the *Oxford Dictionary of Proverbs* anytime soon.

'How calmly does the orange branch, Observe the sky begin to blanch,' he quoted to his wife as she served him tea before he set out.

She was not literary. She could read English but never bothered. He was reading the reprint of three of Tennessee Williams' plays and felt that his characters were recognizably Nepalese. Incredible.

His wife ignored him. She was used to him quoting meaningless bits from the books he was reading.

Pradhan was driven in a police jeep to the maximum-security prison inside Kathmandu, a little fortress of a place. The jail was built in Victorian fashion around courtyards. It looked primitive from the outside, but inside it had been rebuilt in crude steel and concrete. The governor himself conducted him down numerous tortuous corridors and to Thhat's isolation cell. He explained that the prisoner was there for his own protection. The other murderers might turn judgemental and do him harm.

Thhat was in prison uniform. It was a triple cell, built to house three prisoners, but Thhat was alone.

He was polite.

'Thank you for coming. They would not allow me to see anyone else.'

'I know why I wanted to see you. I wanted to tell you that justice has various ways… But why do you want to see me?'

'What happened to those Pakistani and Afghan fellows?' Thhat asked.

'They are no concern of mine,' Pradhan replied.

'Are they accused of anything? Are they going to be tried?'

'I have no idea. So, you think they will kill you?'

'They or someone else. And you say you have no idea. Well, I have a complete idea, Pradhan, and I will stop fooling around if you stop playing games with me.'

'Well, well, well. Playing games, eh? Who is playing games, Monsieur Eduard du Monde?'

'Forget about all that. You've got what you want. I am in jail. You were not sent by the police, you were sent by the Foreign Office to get me, right?'

How did this fellow know?

'Tell your masters that the best thing they can do is to deport those bastards straight away. No trial, no reporting. I am speaking as a friend of Nepal. There will be bad consequences if you people do anything else.'

Pradhan smiled.

'So you, a convicted murderer, are trying to take charge of the Nepalese government?'

'You know, Pradhan, you have a typical idiot policeman's mentality. That's what's got you where you are. Which is nowhere. You've been a stupid cop since we first met twenty-five years ago and you're still a stupid cop. Fuck your reading.'

'And you are a world-famous murderer. That's better, yeah?'

'I am at least a world-famous something.'

'I think dumb Nepalese cop is quite enough for me, Thhat.'

'Put aside your policeman's prejudices and get out of here and go to the American consul and say that you want to see him. Or if he is on tour or whatever, someone high up in the American consulate.'

'Why would they see me?'

'Use my name. Explain. They know all about it anyway.'

'Why should I do anything for you?'

'Because you have had me captured and convicted for something I didn't do. It will stay on your conscience for the rest of your life, which may be longer than mine. Think logically for once.'

'So you still insist you are not Johnson Thhat?'

'No, I don't insist. I am only saying you have to consider the possibility that I didn't kill that girl all those years ago, even though my fingerprints were on her belt. After taking into account my whole reputation as a criminal, you think I'd be stupid enough to leave my fingerprints on the metal belt of a murdered hippie girl? And what am I, some kind of amateur, setting out to buy a can of petrol to burn a body with?'

'The can of petrol wasn't mentioned,' Pradhan said.

'But it was there in the original files. Because this idiot ran out of petrol for the hired car and I had to walk to the pump with a can. It was for the car. If I really wanted petrol to burn a dead body I would have siphoned it out of the petrol tank of any car, not walked in broad daylight into a petrol pump, where anyone could identify me, and fill a can.'

'That's part of the technique, isn't it? Do the most brazen thing because that's what people least expect.'

'Spoken like a policeman who reads too much. That happens in crime books and books about psychopaths, not in the real world. If I was going to kill Mary Ann, I would be very careful that fools like you wouldn't find out who did it. I wouldn't hang around with her for five days before she was killed.'

'Why don't you say "murdered, chopped up and burnt"? In a yellow bikini? Squeamish?'

If mention of the yellow bikini startled Thhat, he didn't show it.

'Murdered, chopped up and burnt, okay? I spent twenty years in Indian jails; squeamish is not how you come out of that. Now will you do as I ask?'

'I still get letters from her relatives, you know. Her sister writes to me. Her father died four years ago, but he used to write. They weren't squeamish either. They wanted to see the police photographs, the burnt body, the site of the dumping, the hotel room where you presumably strangled her or put a pillow over her head after giving her sleeping pills. Everything. They wanted to see and know everything.'

'And you sent them the pictures?'

'Yes. And then they wrote to me at Christmas and whenever they thought of their Mary Ann. Maybe for you this girl's was one among many murders. It was over when you escaped the hangman. But for them it was a life left empty of the person who should have been living it. It was a vacant place at their table at Christmas and an absence of sound in the father's house in the other days of the year.'

'You read a lot of books?'

'I feel sorry for those people. A brute like you feels nothing for anyone, does he?'

'Will you call the Americans for me? I'll cut you a deal. I know why you answered my call. You want me to confess to the murder? Put your roving stupid policeman's mind at rest? I'll tell you everything I know about the murder, one way or the other, if you do me this favour. I swear.'

'You swear? On a holy book? On the heads of the dead you've sent to oblivion?'

'I can't convince you any other way. Maybe I can write it all down and then keep it and hand it to you when you fulfil your part of the bargain, because my dear fellow, you really don't know what happened to Mary Ann, do you? Not with a hundred per cent certainty. The trial was a farce and you know it. Nothing was established. The same will happen if they ever allow me to appeal. I know that, and you suspect it. I can tell you why. Now go and get me the American authorities.'

Pradhan left the jail wondering what he should do. He wandered around Kathmandu, sat in a tea shop and watched the tourists go by. Then he walked to the American consulate. He went to the reception and said he wanted to see the ambassador.

The Nepalese female receptionist with a distinctly American accent said there was no ambassador in this country, but perhaps he meant the consul to Nepal. Well, he couldn't see him, but one of his secretaries would consider the request if it was made in writing. She gave him a pen and a sheet of paper and told him how he could make such an application in writing.

Pradhan wrote out his note. It said:

To His Excellency the Consul of the United States of America.

Your Excellency,

I wish to convey to you a request from one Johnson Thhat who is now serving a life sentence for murder in Kathmandu Central Jail. He says he wishes to speak to you personally or to an authorized representative of yours as he has information to convey which is

of utmost importance to the security of Nepal and
of the United States of America. Please contact him
directly at the jail.
Yours sincerely,
G. Pradhan, Inspector (Retd), NPS

Five days later Pradhan went to the jail again. Thhat was
relaxed. He was still the sole occupant of his cell. He had a
desk and a stool and was writing in longhand in what looked
like a ledger. He was still wearing his dark glasses, but he took
them off when he sat on his bunk.

'These people are taking me seriously. They know who
I am, you see.'

'I put a request in writing,' Pradhan said. It was apparent
that there had been no response.

'No, they won't reply. I don't think so, now. They want
me to rot and die. But they will regret it. I have information
they can use. Maybe they don't think so. But if I was them, I
would make full use of someone like me. Ah! Do something
for me, Pradhan. I am writing the whole story for you. All of
it. I told you I would. But can you take a letter out of the jail
for me? Post it to the address…'

'They told me I was to take nothing in to you and nothing
out.'

'Look, this is my memoir. The beginning. I have nothing
to lose now. It's for you; and then when it's finished, to send
to a writer friend in England. I will give you the address. I
am going to write out everything. What my life has been and
what I thought of it – every step. As you are a cop you can see
it as a confession if you like.'

'Why would you want to confess?'

'People must know why I am here. That I shouldn't be in jail on a life sentence for murder here, whatever else I may have done and wherever else I should be prosecuted and punished. Not in this hellhole.'

He handed Pradhan the partial manuscript, a wad of paper.

'I'll continue and you can come back for the rest as I write it. You are the reader. When you finish each bit, send it to the address with the letter, the last sheet there, to England. The fellow Murad will know what it is. And bring me more paper.'

'If I come back,' Pradhan said. 'And anyway, how can I take this stuff in and out?'

'You are a policeman.'

'Ex-policeman.'

'Then bribe them. It's only pieces of paper,' Thhat said. 'They would treat me like a king if the Americans told them who I am... The most two-timing nation in the world.'

'That's funny coming from you, Thhat. So you are one-timing, are you? Okay. We made a deal,' Pradhan said. He didn't know what to expect. Would Thhat confess to the murder of Mary Ann now, just coldly, directly: 'Yes, I killed her'?

'I know we made a bargain and instead of feeding you a morsel, I have prepared this banquet. I wrote something else before, my story, but from a different angle – all lies actually. I tried to sell it, but it was rejected. I know something now: if I tell the truth it will be understood better than any story I can make up. You know, Pradhan, I see myself clearly, not like you fools who see only the shadows of yourselves. It's part of the fascination of risk. The risks that I take – risk that comes bang up against life and death. Those moments clean the vision, your head is light and you see clearly.'

'What happened to the first autobiography, the lies?'

'I threw it in the dustbin.'

'James Joyce threw his in the fire too,' Pradhan observed.

'Who is James? A killer? My first book was no good. It was boastful, you know, bragging. And I tried to sell it to the English but they don't like other people boasting.'

'Right,' Pradhan said.

'But when this one is finished, people will understand. It will take me a few weeks to write and then you take it out for me. Maybe piece by piece. It will be dynamite, I tell you, man. Nothing to lose now.'

'When all is told, we cannot beg for pardon,' Pradhan said.

'Exactly, old man,' Thhat said.

Pradhan was being pulled into Thhat's scheme. How easily. Now he thought to himself that he ought to step back. What was he doing, accepting small commissions and lying confessions from this fellow? And this sense of self-importance. Of course he had read about it in the criminology manuals. It was the paranoid importance of the delusional criminal.

But he smuggled the papers out in his pocket.

At home, he began to read.

His wife was, for once, curious and asked what it was as he went out to post the pages later.

'He is afraid the Americans will kill him,' he replied, turning around at the door. 'Why? I think he is going to tell me.'

PART 2

1

I counted the bodies. Nineteen, twenty, twenty-one. They lay awkwardly. A girl on the pavement, her head hanging onto the road as if in sleep. A man across a doorway, temples leaking blood. More – face down, face up, flies settling on ears and lips.

My mother gripped my hand and tried to hurry past. She had taught me to count to twenty and said I should be content with that. For now. However, I had discovered by myself what came after twenty.

There were a few rickshaws on the road and other passers-by. People couldn't stay out of sight forever. The bodies had lain in the road now for days but the firing had stopped and the armoured cars and jeeps were no longer roaring through the city. There were other sounds, the city waking to life again, human voices instead of the staccato of the guns.

I remembered it as my mother taking me to school that day. I thought I remember clutching my sketchbook in which I was practising writing numbers. But to tell the truth I can't recall going from the streets into any school.

It couldn't have been open. The school, the desk, the teachers, and we little ones sleeping on the mats all afternoon or lying awake waiting for the bell, must all have happened after that. My mother was probably taking me with her because she didn't want to leave me alone in the one room we called home. She was perhaps on the streets looking for somewhere to buy food or milk, or perhaps she was looking for some indication of a way out of the hell of Saigon. The French called it an offensive. They and their Vietnamese allies had left the city to the mercy of the enemy.

I had no idea who was killing whom or why. I heard the guns and the rumble of the rolling tanks or machinery outside but we stayed at home with the wooden shutters tightly closed and didn't venture out for days.

The stench has stayed with me. There is nothing worse than the smell of rotting flesh. My mother tied scarves around my face and hers and we went, picking our way through the bodies in the street, mostly soldiers, and some women. I presume now that there must have been communist guerrillas, who later called themselves Vietcong, among them. Even the enemy had not removed their dead, though they had a reputation of great care and respect for their soldiers, their own people's army.

I suppose the memories of when one is five are always overwritten by all that comes later, by perceptions and judgements that get laid over the sights and smells of those moments.

I remember asking my mother what comes after thirteen, and counting off the bodies we stepped over or saw till we reached twenty, the supposed limits of my mathematical knowledge at the time. And then there was the twenty-first one and I asked my mother what we should call the next one and she asked me to shut up.

No, of course I didn't go to school that day. I think I now recall returning home with some bananas and some bags of rice. Do I recall a market? Yes. Some of the bodies there and the beginnings of the clean-up of the city. Our government had returned. The enemy had swept over the city like a wave, left some of their dead and receded back into the jungles around. There were no Americans amongst the dead. If any had been killed, their bodies had been cleared away.

✦

I have another memory of my mother telling me about two men.

The first was a French soldier who had asked her to marry him earlier and with whom she had kept in touch by letter. They had been lovers while he was stationed in Vietnam. I don't think he made her a firm offer of marriage and migration when he left Saigon, even though she claims he lived with her in her room rather than in his barracks for weeks on end. He, Claude, was young and may have felt that he couldn't take on the responsibility of a Vietnamese wife back in France, and left her.

Then my mother, who worked in bars in Saigon, met my father. He was an Indian gem dealer. She discovered his real name only once he had moved in with her and was using her address as his own to receive letters and callers. Everyone called him John. His real name, Janimal Jaisinghani, was too complicated for the Vietnamese merchants.

When I was born, he named me Govind Jaisinghani, but everyone else, including my mother who used it both as a name and an explanation, called me 'John's son' or Johnson.

I grew up knowing that I could be an Indian citizen with the name my father had given me. But my mother would have to prove my parentage first, because he abandoned her when I was six months old. He went back to India and then to trade in the Middle East.

She was still in touch with Claude du Monde. He would write to her. He had discovered that his young love was and would be his only love. He had discovered that Frenchwomen were much more demanding in the fifties and sixties than Vietnamese women were. He had discovered that a woman who lives in the memory is more beautiful than the women one meets in the flesh.

She eventually confessed to having had a child. He said he didn't mind that; he too had a child but wasn't with the mother. He said he was sorry he had been so immature and abandoned her, something he never should have done because it was throwing away a jewel more precious than all his tribe. And now he was ecstatic that she would consider him again.

How could she not? She had nothing in Saigon, save a life of serving drinks and selling her body.

To leave, she had to have his name added to her old French passport. There was no French authority in Saigon any more to issue passports. She would have to fill in a form and get a pass from the government saying she was a French citizen by virtue of having been born in French Indochina.

An American man was advising the Vietnamese woman filling in passport and exit visa forms.

'What's the boy's name?' he asked.

'Johnson.'

'That's his second name?'

'No, that's his name. That is what we call him.' My mother was reluctant to submit the Indian name I had been given at birth. They may not want an Indian child.

'Fine, then what's his surname?'

'He don't have.'

'He has to have. Are you married to his father? Legally?'

The American could see what kind of girl she was. He knew precisely their look, their manner. He had used girls like this before and seen their bastard children. He didn't wait for her reply.

'Okay, what's your name?'

'I go to France to marry M. du Monde. I must have that name. But you can't call him that!'

'I think we can. I haven't got till Christmas. You can call him that.' He turned to the Vietnamese secretary woman. 'Write that down as his surname.'

He moved to the next desk. And that's what the secretary woman did. But she misspelled it and wrote down 'Thhat'.

Johnson Thhat.

It sounds Oriental enough. I lived with that name in France, and soon, without my noticing it, it became my name, like an awkward shoe that adapts.

But Claude du Monde never loved me. He paid for my schooling and I ate the food of his household where my mother was the Vietnamese slave, but as soon as I could, I fled.

Now you mustn't think that I am pleading a troubled childhood to explain my behaviour. I hate that shit, blaming one's childhood unhappiness for what you do later. Buddhists make their own happiness. This childhood Freud stuff may be a universal theory but it's the resort of fools.

The priests at the school were fools. They would warn us against stealing and disrespect to elders and to one's parents. They said masturbation was a selfish indulgence, using what God had given you for his purposes for your own. They would talk about violence, about street stabbings and how one should stay away from gangs who carried weapons. But none of them mentioned calculated murder. It seemed too obvious to mention. One didn't have to be instructed not to plan and plot to take someone else's life. And yet when the priests said 'sin' I didn't think of drugs or buggery or blasphemy. My mind moved to murder. Thou shalt not commit premeditated murder. A small addition to the sixth Commandment. Surely God did not literally mean 'Thou shalt not kill', because in the same bit of the book he tells Moses he is the God of War and that killing is necessary. He has himself killed the Pharaoh's armies, thousands upon thousands.

God doesn't contradict himself. So these commandments must have been made up by Moses. Logic. It was man's commandment, society's commandment. And Moses wouldn't have made it up if he believed in God. So, I concluded as I went to church with my mother's husband, there is no God, there is only the police.

In France, there are plenty of amateur psychologists. Like my probation officer. He would say that a damaged childhood leads to a damaged personality that can't differentiate between right and wrong. I used to tell him, I know what's right and wrong: wrong is profitable, right is not.

In Paris when I was a teenager my teachers told me that sex outside marriage, as the Catholic Church preached, was not wrong. But the female teacher said that sex without love was. It was a betrayal of the instinct. Which man, or for that matter confident woman, has not found that sex with one or even a group of strangers, without the idea of love ever entering it, is also pleasurable? So why did the teacher lie?

The stuff about drugs being damaging and one shouldn't go near them? In later life I found that drugs were fun and a source of income, that cocaine was about as dangerous as roller skating, which if done persistently and in traffic may lead to an early death. So why did they all lie?

Because society perpetrates these lies, sanctions them, excuses them and then builds many mansions on their foundation.

But I never let sex tempt me from my purpose and no drug ever caused me to stray. I am a consciousness addict. Even sleeping makes me uneasy, seems to me a betrayal, a holiday from the duty of the mind to stay awake and protect its cunning. Yes, of course, I sleep, but when I wake up the mind starts working again.

I am a Zen Buddhist, which allows me to be the opposite of what I am. I meditate, not to reduce my mind to a silent spot, but to expand its noisy thoughts. I want not peace, but more and more complex, worrying thought. My mind hungers for the opening. It is a dog watching a rat, a mongoose watching a snake, a spider that weaves the web and awaits the flies and unwitting moths that come wandering into its trap.

I came to realize that control was all. Those who controlled others controlled the world. You look at a colony of ants. Each of them carries a grain in a long line to a store. I always assume that there is one of these sitting inside the store receiving the grains they carry, one who has power over the others. A child's textbook will tell me that this is a queen who waits for the drones to bring her food and won't stir a leg herself. They do it because their natural conditioning is her power and – which is the same thing – her power comes from their natural conditioning.

Human beings in their evolution have almost shrugged off that conditioning. And yet you watch a building site and see a group of men and women constructing a building. The engineer tells the workers what to do. The architect stays at home. The conditioning has become social. I always wanted to be the architect. To make others feel that it would be to their advantage to behave in a particular way. And the way would lead to their being controlled by me.

This, I discovered at the age of fifteen, was a better religion than that of the Pope, the religion to which my stepfather du Monde seemed to be dedicated, at least on Sundays. The rest of the week he was dedicated to rum.

I took his gun; the one he had kept from his army adventures, making sure it was loaded. I went on the metro to a suburb of Paris, randomly chosen, one to which I had not been before and studied the route from the station to a block of flats. I chose one at random. I rang the bell and when a woman answered the door, I thrust the gun in her face and said, 'Give me any money you've got and the house keys.'

She gave me three hundred francs from a bag and I thanked her, yanked her phone wire out of its wall socket, locked her into the house from the outside, walked back to the metro and rode away. I threw the keys in a bin.

The next day I did the same thing in another suburb. And then again. Easy. The money was not all. I saw for the first time the fear in a random victim's eyes. They were never surprised. This was something they knew would happen. They were all subconsciously waiting for it.

I knew that it was the gun in my hand that compelled them to do as I asked, but I was working towards a time and a state in which there would be no gun, when there would only be contact, eye to eye, and the compulsion would be the same. They would do as I would say.

I didn't need the money. I bought fancy new shoes with some of it and my stepfather asked me where I got the money to buy them. I said I ran errands for the local priest. On Sunday he started up a conversation with the priest and said he was delighted that his good-for-nothing stepson was running errands for small tips. He was perhaps on the way to reform and would soon attend church. The priest of course said he hadn't seen me in years. My stepfather returned from church convinced that my mother had slipped me some of his hard-earned money and when she denied it, he beat her.

I was on one of my missions at the time in my new shoes. I returned home with a few hundred francs and the gun in my pocket and the bastard jumped me as I walked in the door.

He was short but bullish, a strong man. I fought back but he threw me on the floor and found the money and the gun. He found more money in a hole in the sponge mattress on my bed. My mother was crying. He was shouting. My little stepbrother and stepsister, who were still wearing their Sunday church clothes, began crying too.

I knew it was time to go. I knew he would beat me to extract a confession, so I ran. My stepfather went to the police. He was in his Sunday good-Catholic, loyal-French-civic-citizen mood.

The police had reports and descriptions of a boy who robbed households wielding a gun. Somewhere in some crime headquarters, they had pieced together my initial career in crime. I must have committed forty robberies and they had reports of fifteen.

I was on the run and decided to leave Paris. I had no money now and no gun. I had the vague idea that I should leave the country and make my way to some port. I knew that getting on a plane without a ticket and a passport would be impossible, but I could stow away on a ship if I could get into a cargo dock. Again, I had no idea which railway station to take out of Paris and thought it would sound suspicious if I went up to a stranger or a railway official and asked which train went to Marseilles. There might be an alert out for a boy of sixteen who looked Oriental.

There was. And in the end, being compelled to ask a porter at St Lazare where I could board a train to Marseilles, I was picked up by a squad car.

I was sent into juvenile detention and after two years transferred to an adult jail, locked up for four months and then released. I was allocated a room in a hostel for released prisoners but I wasn't going there. I went 'home'.

Neither my mother nor my stepfather had come to see me during my term of imprisonment. My stepbrother, now thirteen, didn't know who I was. I can't say I felt alone in the world. I had known nothing else.

My mother was surprised to see me. She asked me in. My stepfather was working away from home, she said. She would have come; yes, they knew where I was, but he had forbidden all contact. I must be treated as if I was dead. He had power over her. Had he stopped beating her, I asked, but she didn't reply.

She said I couldn't stay there, I mustn't be seen there. I said I had come to ask her where my real father was and whether she would give me the necessary papers for me to get a passport.

She could barely pronounce my real father's name. He had lived in a place called Poona and then in a city called Bombay where he had a business selling gems in the Far Eastern market. Beyond that, she knew nothing of him. She thrust some money at me. Tears wet her cheeks. She seemed to feel that the money was buying me off, and was ashamed. She was saying she had no love to give but my eyes should have told her that expecting love is the pastime of the weak and foolish.

I was wearing the denim jacket and dark blue denim trousers that the prison service had given me on dismissal. I had thrown away the suit they equipped me with. But jail had equipped me with much more. It had given me the passage out of France. I had the address and phone number of a man who would give me a false passport with a sailor's visa for any country except the United States of America stamped in it. Jail is a stock exchange, a university, a football club, an army in waiting, an employment exchange, a market, a battle on the high seas between ships that fly their own personal flags. It's a recruiting ground and always has been. Men thrown together tell each other their plans, and the hardest plan – the most risky or most profitable – wins universal admiration.

✦

La Sante, the prison, is on the Left Bank in Paris. It is surrounded by the housing of the rich and the powerful, but inside the concrete and stone and the steel gates, it is a small hell. You share the space with rats, lice and insects. Men go mad here. They swallow the laid-out rat poison. And it's hot, so hot, no ventilation. The smell of sweat hangs over the place because prisoners are only allowed showers once or twice a week.

I had no fear for my sanity when I was sent there, though others, including prison officials at the youth detention centre in Villefranche, told me what to expect. La Sante was a mixture of hardened criminals and those still on trial detained by examining magistrates for months and years while they looked into their alleged crimes. I was told to fear for my body. Young bodies are violated. The attractive and the very ugly, the small, the weak, the weak-willed become slaves to stronger prisoners. They are made to perform for them, at first as a seduction or rape and then to be the victims in acts of utter control. Prisoners compel their slaves to submit to their lust in the open. There is nothing they have to hide. They compel them to perform oral sex or to strip naked and submit to buggery in broad daylight when others from across the corridors can watch and cheer or jeer.

I was determined that I was not going to be a slave and neither was I going to be a slave-master. I would cultivate a detachment from the need for sex. But that didn't mean I would give up the need for control, for enforcing my will, for making clear to those around who was to be master. But I wanted no one as a personal servant. Needing someone's service is also a weakness and can become addictive. I wanted to stay free.

2

The sailor whose identity I took was called Jacques Lefevre. The man who sold me the passport, replacing the photograph with mine and forging the authentication that validated photographs, said Lefevre had 'disappeared'. I was not interested in my 'original', so to speak, and was assured that there was no chance of being traced by him. Dead men don't report lost property.

I had no money to buy an air ticket but was told by the contact of my contact in La Sante that I would be given a ticket to India and money to spend there if I took half a case of US dollars with me. I had to take them past Indian customs. Those were the days when India had no foreign exchange and the Indian underworld would buy dollars at exorbitant rupee prices. With the rupees I got I had to buy diamonds on the illegal Gujarati diamond market.

I had told them that my father was a diamond merchant, but not that I had never met him and wouldn't know him if we passed each other in the street. I could of course disappear with the dollar notes in India, but my contact dissuaded me from doing this. He said the notes were themselves counterfeits but very good ones and the Indians who bought them on the black market would never know, but I shouldn't run the risk of trying to spend them. I would be caught and they still had the whip hand of being able to report me as travelling on the forged passport they had supplied. And if I double-crossed them, I would have to stay far away from Europe.

I didn't want to meet my father. He had not only abandoned me, he had avoided me when my mother sent me to India to his sister's house. She was off to France to be with du Monde. She hadn't wanted me around. She had my father's sister's address in India. That too, she had stumbled upon by mistake. She had told du Monde that they could be rid of me. Something he dearly wished, and he encouraged her to take me to India on the way to France. Born of an Indian father, I should grow up Indian.

The French troop ship that carried us stopped in Bombay and she took me, aged seven now, to this town called Poona where this sister lived and turned up at her doorstep. My father's sister, my aunt, refused to take me in at first. She said she didn't know what this raving Vietnamese woman was claiming. But my mother must have sensed that she would relent in the end and she told me she would be back and left me sitting with an ice cream in a park adjoining the street of my aunt's house, while she went back to the station to catch her train to Bombay.

It was my uncle who came out, as it was getting dark, to look for the child in the park. They took me in, abandoned, frightened. I cried for days. My mother had lied to me. It was then that I resolved that I would never trust anyone.

I was told my father would come to get me. My aunt and uncle tried to find him. He never answered their letters or calls.

They spread the word among a network of relatives. He was a wanderer. They didn't even know if he knew that he had a son waiting for him there. I firmly believed, even at that age, that he knew and that he was avoiding me.

I played with my cousins. I went to school with them. I learned to swear in Hindi and to fight off bullies in the playground who would tease me for being 'the chink-eye boy'. Gangs of little kids would follow me in the street shouting 'Aayy! Chine-iss, Chine-iss!'

Then my uncle got the information that my father was in jail in Iran on a smuggling charge and that he wouldn't be out for some years. He and my aunt had too many mouths of their own to feed and I showed no love or gratitude to any of them. There were several phone calls to France to trace my mother and finally I was put on a plane to Paris.

I wasn't told that my father was in jail and couldn't have come to get me even if he had wanted. No, I didn't want to meet him, but my karma, as he was later to say, had brought me to him.

✦

I had delivered my bag with the hidden compartment full of counterfeit dollars to a shop that sold pots and pans in north Bombay, a most unlikely place for money changers. After being given several cups of tea and sitting on a wooden bench for six hours, I was summoned by the man who had disappeared with the suitcase into a car on the busy street. He gave me another suitcase. It was full of Indian banknotes. He shook my hand and drove me to south Bombay where the jewellery district was.

I carried the suitcase full of money with me. I dared not leave it in the dingy hotel room with the rest of my sparse luggage.

I had been pointed to a particular diamond trader in a very small shop in a crowded and narrow alley. The entire district was a warren of these alleys with ancient-looking showcases in the tiny shops. The shop I entered was ten feet deep, no more, with just room enough for one or two customers to stand before the counters, behind which were trapped two or three of the traders in their daily puppet show.

I had refused a guide from the moneychangers, wanting to put distance between them and me, knowing that these Bombay gangsters would be changing money illicitly and they would certainly not appreciate the fact that the dollars were not genuine – if they ever found out. I wanted to be far away if and when they discovered the fact.

But perhaps they already knew and were in on the venture, trusting to the fact that the buyers of the dollars who would purchase a few hundred or thousand at a time, to finance a trip or pull some deal abroad, would not know the real thing from the counterfeit. The retail customers would find out only at the point of contact or exchange with the West, by which time they would have parted with good Indian money at twice the market rate.

The dealers who had sold them would use several middlemen to get the dollars to them and would themselves be safely anonymous. No comeback. Only a hundred embarrassed Indians at banks in Geneva or in Harrods, Macy's or Bloomingdale's having to accompany security guards or police and answer questions about the origins of their counterfeit cash.

The jewellery merchant led me further through the crowded alleys to an adjacent district of the city where there appeared to be similar small dingy shops selling antiques. Most of it was British memorabilia with fragments of stone sculpture purportedly stolen from temples. The shop he led me into had a whole showcase of old brass instruments from a nineteenth-century naval vessel – old brass telescopes, navigating gear and models of sailing ships.

Inside the shop, the piece de resistance was an old harpsichord of which the beady-eyed proprietor was very proud. He seemed to know why we were there. He looked at my suitcase.

'He'll be here any minute,' he said.

They offered me a cup of tea and I sipped it sitting in the back of the shop. Some tourists walked in, English people looking through the bric-a-brac. They bought an old naval clock, a heavy cylindrical brass thing. The shopkeeper bargained with them and they beat him down to half the price he had at first asked. They went away triumphant.

A man in his late forties, already balding, wearing khaki trousers held up by a thick leather belt, and an Indian waistcoat, walked in. He ignored the shopkeeper and came straight to me.

'Johnson?' he asked.

'Jacques Lefevre,' I said, standing up.

'Yes, exactly,' he said and instead of holding out his hand he hugged me.

Was this some form of Indian mafia ritual?

'Happy birthday,' he said.

How did he know?

He must have seen the question cross my face even though I had always nurtured the conceit that my features would remain a blank and no one would ever have the art to know what flickered through my mind.

'I will make it a happy birthday. What a great day. What a turn of fate,' he said.

I looked into his face.

'The cheekbones, you have her high cheekbones,' he said.

And I knew.

'They always called you Johnson, but you know your name is Govind, don't you?'

I didn't reply, though I was sure by now that this wasn't a trick.

'You are a handsome boy,' he continued, standing back to survey me. The antique shopkeeper stood watching.

'Ay, Chintoo, come and meet my son. The French son,' he said. 'It should be his twenty-first birthday today. The stars work in wonderful ways. We are going out to celebrate.'

'I asked people for you but I didn't know...' I began.

'Shush! I wasn't part of your Paris people's plan. But everybody in the money-laundering business knows me. Someone sent me word that a boy from France was looking for me by name. I was suspicious at first but then I started calculating and then came to conclusions and then came to see. So now we are united. I have told your financial business parties that we will keep it in the family. I have bought one of the parties. You are now doing business with me, or we shall do business as Jaisinghani and Son. Eh? Eh? I came to see you but there is no mistaking. You have your mother's eyes and you have her exact colour. Chinky, eh?'

I felt like saying, 'You abandoned her, you son of a bitch, and now you come sniffing around me talking about the shape of her eyes and the colour of her skin?' I didn't.

'His mother started jig-jig with a Frenchie so I left her,' he announced to the shop.

I controlled a sudden impulse to hit him in the face and run. But giving way to impulse is the way to get caught, the loser's weakness.

'You must call me Jacques,' I said.

'No, no, no, no. Never. The days of hiding are gone,' he said.

Why was this slimy man so enthusiastic about seeing me, and playing the long-lost father?

'Let's get out of here,' he said. 'You can leave the suitcase with Chintoo. This shop is also part of my business. I am going to do the deal with you.'

'There is no deal. I was just supposed to deliver the suitcase, but not to you, to…someone else.'

'Yes, I know,' he said. 'That has all changed. I told you I bought the deal from them. We don't do things on paper here, so I don't have anything to wave before you. My word is my bond. You can phone your party in France and ask them. I have already done the needful.'

I was by now certain that this man was my father and of course that he was dealing straight. But I didn't want to leave the suitcase.

He sensed my doubt.

'Phone them now,' he said.

There was a telephone in the back of the shop and he left me to make the phone call. I held on to the suitcase and dialled Paris.

They were waiting for my call.

Yes, my contact said, I should hand over the suitcase to someone who would say he was my father. This person would explain what my further role would be if I wanted to stay involved in the game. There would be another consignment of money coming to me if I joined the game at this level, a higher level.

'Very high, hovering near the top,' he added in French.

My father was all grins when I got back.

'I am glad you don't trust anyone,' he said, as though he had taken a paternal interest in my development all my life.

The hypocrisy was towering. And yet I admired it, this ability to slip into a falsehood, which would enable a mutually profitable future. Recriminations about the past are, again, a sign of weakness to be avoided. Revenge is the feast of fools.

His chauffeur drove us to the Sea Lounge in the Taj Mahal hotel.

My father moved strangely. In his khaki trousers and thick white shirt and large, pocketed waistcoat, carrying an umbrella, he could have disappeared into the crowd that thronged the alleyways of the jewellery and antique district (called the 'thieves' bazaar', he told me). Until you looked at his shoes. They were crafted by personal Chinese shoemakers imitating the patterns from magazines featuring Italian designer styles. The most expensive leather, and imported, branded socks.

And then he was equally at home in the Taj where the concierge and bellboys greeted him by name. The Taj is the stylish hang-out of the rich. Its old, colonial, stone building overlooks the opening to the natural harbour of Bombay, where ships can shelter from the ten-foot-high waves of the monsoon that rock the Arabian Sea.

'This hotel is a fable whose moral is never leave a task unsupervised. Know all the facts,' he said. He was about to begin a story, in the way that father's tell sons moral tales. I listened.

'The architect designed the front to face the sea. The builders built it the other way round with the frontal façade facing the land and the back of the hotel towards the sea. The architect arrived when the building was completed. His heart was broken. He committed suicide.'

This is the kind of story that circulates around India, I later learnt, a story without a grain of truth but whose possibility has been suggested by one of the many liars of the race.

We sat next to an open window from where we could see the tourists heading out to sea in launches, towards the mainland and the distant hills bordering the great southern plateau of the subcontinent, now shrouded in what must still have been pure mist rather than pollution. No building or habitation had come to that part of the mainland. It was still the vast empty vessel while the little lifeboat of the island of Bombay heaved with people just across the harbour channel.

I told him I didn't drink so he ordered a gin with 'fresh lime soda' for himself and then 'just a cup of tea' for me. He was not going to let me forget that he had marked my birthday. He pronounced, sentimentally, that now that we had met, we were never going to part.

He seemed to have no curiosity about my assessment of him, about my life without him, about my mother's life, about what happened after he abandoned us. He seemed to have been informed that my mother had married a Frenchman and gone to Paris because, he said, he had enquired after me. He alluded to her once or twice when saying he thought I had taken the right decision in coming to India.

'I knew that one of these days, after your mother left me, and that bastard Frenchman of hers prevented you from knowing me, that we would meet. That you would grow up and come looking for me and I was waiting for the day and the day has arrived.'

He didn't want to take me to his home. I guessed that it was because he too had a wife and a family and it wouldn't be possible for him to acknowledge me, though we discreetly disdained to discuss it. He drove me back to my hotel, took one look at it and said he would book me in elsewhere; I couldn't live in such a hole.

He made a few phone calls from there and instructed his driver to take us to the Holiday Inn in Juhu, where some flunkey of his had booked a room for me.

I had one rucksack, which he looked at pityingly. He held my hand in the back of the car. He had dark and large eyelids, darker than the rest of his face, which one could observe when he blinked, because his eyes shut with great deliberation, giving his blinks the appearance of being executed in slow motion.

He said he would call me early the next morning and that I was not to worry about the suitcase, about business – or about the rest of my life. He was there to take care of it. I said I was sure he was there to take care of it and it had been a reassuring day for me.

He held my hand again in both of his and said he was so glad I had been restored to him, and I knew then that he was going to use me, that he intended to put me to some purpose of his.

He did call the next morning and we had coffee by the swimming pool.

'I lay awake all night thinking of you, Govind. God has been good to us to guide your footsteps here. I want you to go into partnership with me.'

I said that sounded good to me.

'We must get you a genuine fake Indian passport. I will take you to see Gol Singh, king of all passport-jobbery.'

Gol Singh turned out to be a superintendent in the Bombay Police. We phoned him and he came out of the police station and joined us in our car. He said he was very pleased to meet me and would fix me up straight away.

We drove to a building downtown and went up in the lift to the fifth floor.

There were patches of blood spattered in the lift and on the walls.

'How do you avoid getting TB?' I asked.

'Why are you afraid of TB?' Gol Singh countered.

'I would have thought that in a rich building like this, people wouldn't spit their blood in the lift. They can't help it?'

Both Gol Singh and my father started to laugh as we got out of the lift.

My father put his arm around my shoulder. 'This is not blood,' he said. 'Indians eat betel leaf with red colourations inside and spit anywhere.'

I thought it strange that a money launderer and a crooked policeman were both refusing to admit that most of their countrymen had TB and spat blood all over the city. It was an epidemic, so why were they trying to hide it?

A woman answered the door at the flat. Gol Singh walked in as though it was his house, not acknowledging her. He sat us down on the plastic-covered sofas, went into another room and came back with a pile of Indian passports.

'Completely authentic. You are now twenty-one years old? When is your birthday?'

'Yesterday,' I said.

'Oh, ho, belated birthday wishes, we must get cake,' Gol Singh said.

He leafed through the passports.

'This one will do. We will give your real name. Aaii!'

The woman in the flat, instantly obedient, came to his side and he handed her the passport.

'Take Master Jaisinghani and have all particulars done.'

She assented with the shake of the head that Indians use.

'Come, sir,' she said to me.

'I go with her?'

'Yes,' said my father.

In the street, we caught a taxi.

'What are the people spitting, this red stuff, all over the roads and even inside buildings?' I asked.

'Paan. We are calling it paan. It is like chewing gum but you have to spit it.'

'You can't swallow chewing gum either,' I said.

'Really?' she asked.

She took me to an office in what looked like the corporate district of Bombay with old colonial stone buildings. We went into a dingy, shuttered room up a long, filthy, old wooden staircase. She handed my passport to a little man who wore spectacles tied with string. A photographer took my photograph.

'You can go, sir. It will be delivered to Boss,' she said.

The next day I had my passport. I was quite happy then to travel as Govind Jaisinghani.

'Am I going somewhere?' I asked my father.

'Places, my son, you are going places,' the old dog said.

3

I only understood what my father meant when his 'partner' came to my hotel room in the Holiday Inn.

A few days after my twenty-first birthday, someone knocked at the door early in the morning. When I opened it, there was a woman in her late twenties outside.

'I'm Ravina,' she said.

I was in my underwear and wearing the previous day's sweaty shirt. I wouldn't have presented myself like that to her, but opened the door because I thought it was room service with my tea. She walked in boldly, unperturbed.

The thought that went through my mind was that I never expected a hotel of this quality to supply girls.

'Your father sent me on a very delicate mission,' she said. She deduced what I'd been thinking. 'Not that sort.'

She had black hair, which fell over her forehead in a tuft she kept pushing back, dark round eyes and a lot of bright red lipstick that was startlingly well chosen for her dark complexion.

She began to explain the delicate mission.

'Your father has bought you a little holiday in Bangkok. I have the ticket. Club class. And the hotel accommodation.'

She took a little travel folder out of her bag and opened it before handing it to me to show me the ticket, the hotel voucher, the map of the city and the passport.

'Why does he want me to go to Bangkok?'

'I want you to go too, because I am going with you. I am in business with your father. You can call me his partner.'

The room service came with the tea and knocked at the door. I asked for an extra cup.

She made the tea and declined the toast.

'I want to tell you about the business,' she said. 'Your father didn't want to do it himself and thought I would issue a more tempting invitation.' She smiled.

'I want to know,' I said.

'We deal in gems. We buy them cheap and sell them dear.'

'That makes sense,' I said.

'But we have to take them abroad to sell them because in the Far East there is a better market than in India. They cut diamonds in Gujarat and they are sold in Bombay, but no diamonds are mined in India. They all come from South Africa. It's a leftover trade from the Raj. The Gujaratis have been in the cutting business for generations.'

'I know that.'

'Of course you do, but what you don't know is that your father and I bring in the raw diamonds in bulk and then take out the cut gems in bulk too.'

I accepted the information in silence.

'Governments don't like diamonds crossing borders. Especially not the Indian government, which has to control foreign exchange. But we don't want to sell the diamonds and share the dollars with the socialist Indians. You wouldn't want to give up what you'd worked for and earned just because some blasted dhoti-wallah passed a law saying he wanted some of your loot. And what they collect in taxes doesn't go to the country, you know, it finds its way into politicians' Swiss bank accounts.'

'I see. So what about the holiday in Bangkok?'

'We go tomorrow for a few days. Today, after that toast, you shouldn't eat anything. Just drink orange juice or tea or something.'

She pulled what looked like a tiny metal purse out of her bag. It was made of woven aluminium thread or maybe stainless steel thread or the like. It was tightly clasped and she opened it and went over to the writing table. She took out a velvet cloth from her bag, spread it on the table and emptied the contents of the purse onto it.

Out tumbled a small collection of gems – diamonds mostly, with a few red, purple and green stones. I stared at them.

'We are to carry these,' she said.

Then she swept them – rather carelessly, I thought – back into the metal purse.

'How do we carry them?'

'That's the tricky bit. I have been sent to get you to practise,' she said. For the first time she smiled and I saw her looking at me, searching my face and taking in my body. I could see the reflection of myself, not in her eyes, but in her mind. She was comparing me to my father and I knew she was hungrily digesting the fact that while his skin had become flabby over his jaws, mine was taut. She looked away when she saw that I was watching her stare.

Again she went to her bag and pulled out packets of condoms and unwrapped one. She pushed the tiny metal bag into the condom and tied the end of it into a knot.

'Squeeze the air out,' she said.

Then she took another one and pushed the package into that, and tied it up again.

'A few of these will stop it being attacked by your intestinal juices,' she said.

'I can't swallow that,' I said. She was looking intensely at me.

'It goes in the other end,' she said. 'I am going to carry a bag myself, up the rear. It's not that uncomfortable once it's in. You can actually forget about it.'

She was anxious to reassure me.

'I've done it lots of times. You father said maybe I could assist you the first time, show you how it goes in and comes out.'

'He asked you to do that?'

'I don't mind. He knew I wouldn't mind. After all we are partners and you must think of it as just a body thing.'

I wanted to ask her if she thought that her other orifices were just a body thing too.

'I sometimes swallow them, but then they have to be tiny, different packaging,' she said and, reading my thoughts again, 'I have carried them in all sorts of ways into Europe, even Singapore where they're very strict. It's really safe. Otherwise your father, who has just found you, wouldn't ask you to take the risk.'

I had never shoved anything up my arse.

'Try it if you like, gently,' she said. 'But it's best to wait till after you have gone to the toilet and sure you're empty.'

She got out some lavender oil and some Vaseline and put them on the table. 'They are part of the kit,' she said. 'Look, Govind, your father was embarrassed to ask you, but he knows that you want to work with him – with us. Bangkok is lovely. We deliver and then we have fun.'

In prison, I had seen the most outrageous things done. People pushed things up themselves regularly. It didn't shock me as even she expected it to. My father was lending me this girl. I hoped.

Ravina, ravishing.

4

What Ravina didn't tell me was that Thailand was, at the time, run by a military dictatorship, a junta that had decreed, for instance, that the penalty for diamond smuggling was death by firing squad. Yes, I'd been a criminal, but I had never challenged a state to take my life by committing a capital offence. I had carried a gun and carried it loaded, but had made up my mind – locked the thought in with a mental safety catch – that I would never use it unless I was fired at. Then there might be the chance of pleading self-defence.

There were police and armed soldiers all over Bangkok airport. Ravina and I pretended we didn't know each other and went into separate queues for the passport check. We collected our luggage and then passed the officers waiting around in white naval-looking uniforms, checking people's luggage.

A customs officer stopped me and examined the camera I was carrying. He said it was illegal to sell cameras in Thailand. I said I had brought it for my personal use, I didn't intend to sell it. He asked me to go with him through a door at the end of the customs hall. As soon as he said it, a soldier stepped forward with a machine gun as though to enforce the officer's will. I was quick to obey and went where he pointed.

He took me into an empty room. The soldier stood guard.

'Take your glasses off and talk to me,' he said.

I took my sunglasses.

'You are walking in a funny way, my friend,' he said.

I said nothing. The room was bare except for two chairs, a bench and a tabletop on which they presumably emptied and examined suitcases. There was a grey door at the end of the room.

'You have things concealed about your person,' he said.

'I don't know what you mean,' I said in French. This startled him.

'Ah, Indian speaking French,' he said. 'Look, brother, I could call them and have you examined. Up the arse. I know you have hidden things. They will shoot you now. The army is not asking too many questions. Bang bang! Ttho ttho!'

He was grinning.

'Now you play balls with me. I play balls with you, mister. There is bathrooms there. No window. Go and do big shit and give me ten per cent.'

'How will you know it's ten per cent?'

'You are cheeky bastard. How much stone did you concealed?'

'Ten.'

'Then give two good ones.'

'That's twenty per cent.'

'That's life.'

I went towards the grey door.

He followed me and said, 'You see, I could take them all, but I want making good friends with mister. Then we for life. No good to me you dead or walking free even and hating me. Christopher Sien.'

He held out his hand, a little prematurely, I thought.

He took my rucksack from my back and my camera case.

There was no window in the bathroom, which was bare and smelt of antiseptic. I crouched and pulled the package out of my rectum. I had to cut it open with the end of a key in my pocket. I unclasped the metal bag and took out two diamonds for him. Then I put the metal bag in my pocket. I couldn't bear to push it back up again.

Outside, Sien was making a show of examining my rucksack. He had emptied everything on the tabletop and was now shoving it back in.

He opened one of my handkerchiefs and indicated with his eyebrows that I should deposit the payload there. I put the diamonds down and he stared at them. He folded the hanky looking towards the guard outside the door and put it in his pocket.

'Come on, mister, I will take you out and you will remember me and I will remember you. And we can meet in Bangkok and do more business, proper business, next time.'

He took me to the exit of the hall.

Ravina was waiting for me where the passengers catch their taxis. Touts were hanging around bargaining with tourists. I didn't tell her about my encounter. I was itching to get away from there.

'We need to get straight to Phuket,' she said. 'It's several hours by road.'

'Full Bangkok tour, miss,' said one of the touts, and Ravina went to bargain a price with him.

A boy, very effeminate-looking, approached me.

'You come with me, saar, I will make you forget woman forever,' he said.

'No, no, I don't want you to, but are you a cab driver?'

'All services,' he said.

Ravina came back and I told her I'd found a ride.

The boy walked us to his car in the park and we started off.

We stopped at a wayside stall and had some fruit juice about fifty miles down the road. In the cab, I told Ravina of my adventure and that I hadn't lost much. I spoke in Hindi, as much as I could manage to, so the boy-driver wouldn't catch on.

He pulled into a petrol station and when he came back and started the car he said, 'A man is coming behind you, sir.'

We were now on the highway on the narrow coastal strip that leads to Phuket. There, we were to meet the dealers who would take the gems off us. I turned round and saw a car close behind us.

'Every time we is stopping, he is stopping, you see,' the boy said.

Ravina looked nervous.

'Then stop by the side of the road and let him go past us,' she said.

The boy did as he was told and the black car slowed down and then decided to carry on at a slow speed. As it passed us, I looked out of the window. The driver was in military uniform and I could swear it was the soldier who was at the door when Christopher Sien was taking his 'ten per cent' off me.

'We've got to turn round. That's the military man from the customs hall. He suspects, if he doesn't know, and he's taken the trouble to follow us.'

'Turn the car,' Ravina said.

The boy started the car up and did as he was told.

'He will have stopped to wait for us and then he'll come after us,' Ravina said.

'Go faster,' I said.

The boy turned round. He had stumbled on two desperadoes and he may have guessed our secret. 'The military mens have walkie-talkie,' he said. 'You better go now from me. Please go. They can kill all.' He stopped the car by the side of the road. He wanted us to get out.

Ravina was very quick.

'Okay, but you better get our suitcases out of your car. They have smuggled goods in them and they'll catch you.'

The boy got out and, as he unlocked the boot, Ravina picked up a boulder from the side of the road and struck him hard behind the head. The boy collapsed immediately.

'Don't stand there! Shove the bastard in the boot,' she said. 'Come on, the army guy will come back and we'll get shot, man.'

She had made a deep gash in the boy's head and he was bleeding profusely, but his health wasn't our immediate problem.

I lifted him by the shoulders and Ravina held him by the feet and we bundled him into the boot of his cab.

I got in the driver's seat and we took off.

There was no sign of the black car behind us yet.

We tore down the highway and came to signs saying Prachap Kiri Khan and Maw Daung Pass.

'Turn left,' Ravina said. 'We are getting out of Thailand.'

I didn't question her and turned up the mountain road. The traffic had thinned out.

'Where is this?' I asked.

'We are on the border with Burma,' she said. 'The Thai army fellow won't follow us there.'

'But we'll have to get through checkpoints and customs.'

'Get two of your diamonds and a few dollars out,' she said. 'These guys can be bought for a hippie's pair of jeans.'

She was right.

At the head of the Maw Daung Pass there was a Burmese army checkpoint. They stopped the car and Ravina went out and took the officer aside.

He came back to the car with a huge grin and opened the car door for her. The barrier was opened and we went through.

The jungle around was dense and lush. Trucks passed us going the other way.

'Where are we going?'

'I think we should get as far as we can from this car, and then back into Thailand. I told the officer at the checkpoint that he might see us again.'

We drove maybe ten miles into Burma and then Ravina indicated that it was time to abandon the car. I found a clearing in the jungle and drove the car, revving the engine through the vines and undergrowth as far as it would go between the trees. When it stopped, we got out.

'What about the driver?' I asked, feeling for the first time that I was betraying my role as the callous tough guy. Perhaps I shouldn't have asked.

'What about him? He was trying to kick us out of his cab, get us executed. He was trying to kill us. We do unto others as they would do unto us. It's like self-defence.'

I opened the booth. Ravina stood by in the undergrowth. I pulled the boy out. I felt his pulse. His eyes stared at me.

'He's dead,' I said.

'What did you expect? Let's go, Govind. Is there anything in your rucksack with your name on it or any identifying marks?'

'Just clothes and junk,' I said.

'Nobody has your fingerprints to match them, do they?'

'The French police.'

'That means nothing here. Burmese jungle. Let's go. And hope this murder is not discovered for a long time.'

The word struck a chill in my heart. I had never killed anyone before. Strictly speaking, she'd done it. I looked at her. She was cool. A man was dead. She had killed him. We had killed him. She still had diamonds up her arse.

✦

She said we shouldn't take the road.

'Can you walk ten miles? We are going to cross the border through the jungle.'

In the end, crossing the thickets and swampy land, it seemed more like a hundred miles. We walked through the night and by the morning we thought we must have crossed the border. There were fields in the foothills and the going became easier. We both picked up dried wood for walking sticks as though we were tourists on a casual ramble.

We reached a side road and soon a truck came along and she thumbed a lift. Yes, he was going to the highway and then to Bangkok itself. The driver barely spoke any English but we made ourselves understood by repeating the city's name.

My first murder. I looked in the papers the next few days but I never saw a mention of a dead taxi driver though the local papers were filled, almost every day, with reports of murders, assaults and disappearances. No mention of a young, camp taxi driver found in the jungles of Burma across the border.

Perhaps no one ever found him, perhaps there was no one to miss him or report him missing.

'I will make you forget woman forever,' he had said. I would never forget him.

I had to put the fellow out of my mind, but Ravina? Had she seen corpses before? Had she killed anyone before? I didn't want to ask.

✦

We moved into an apartment in Bangkok. We had to wait till our buyers came to us from Phuket. 'Shouldn't we get out of the country? If they find that fellow…?'

'Look, Govind, forget about it. There's nothing you or I or God can do. People die all the time.'

'I am not worried about God, I am worried about the police.'

'The Burmese and Thais hate each other. They won't talk or exchange information or anything. We are safe.'

It was not reassuring, and that first time, I confess I desperately needed reassurance.

A day passed and we walked in the Bangkok market. We had been told to hang about for three days.

'Did my father ever kill anyone?' I asked.

'No,' she said, as though she had been expecting the question. 'Neither did I. But we are beginning to learn it's possible, eh?' she grinned, and it was only then that I saw that

Ravina had a gold-capped tooth in the top left of her mouth. There was something masculine about it, but that too was strangely attractive.

The buyers came. Ravina called them to the flat and showed them the gems. They haggled for a few hours. I was allowed no part in it. Ravina asked me to take a walk. When I came back, she said the deal hadn't been done.

'They were unreliable people. I can't deal with them. Your father has made a mistake. Which is extremely unusual for him. But these are the wrong people.'

'Where are the gems?' I asked.

She took out the velvet cloth and opened it. The entire collection, the ones I had saved and the ones she was carrying, were there.

'What was wrong with the buyers?'

She turned on me in a rage. 'You really want to know? Your bastard father double-crossed me. He told them he would accept payment for these gems in Bombay by transfer. He was using us, you and me, as mules. Which is not what he told me. He said we were partners and I could get a price for these gems and we'd share. He's now told them something else and they just came to collect. I told them I'm not a carrier, I own these. Your fucking father, he thinks he controls my pussy and so he controls me. Wrong on both counts.'

She picked up the entire lot of gems, crushing them in the velvet, and walked out.

She came back late that night. I heard the key turn in the outer door of the flat. We had spent three nights in this apartment in separate rooms.

I heard her go into her room and I lay awake in bed wondering whether to step out into the living room of the flat and knock on her door and ask her what the next move would be.

Before I could do that, I heard her rustle down the corridor. My room was dark but the standard lamp in the front room threw a dim light into it and I could see her silhouetted against the door. She was naked.

'Govind, Johnson, whatever you call yourself, this is absurd. The whole thing is absurd,' she said.

I sat up in bed and she came and sat next to me. I couldn't see her face but I knew it well. She took my hand, kissed it, and then guided it between her legs. She moved it gently against her thick pubic hair. She was moving my finger to find the cleft and the bud at the top of it. She moved her thighs slowly apart to accommodate the rhythm of my strokes and I felt the immediate swelling and wetness under my finger. Then she draped her arms around me and dug her nails into my shoulders. Her clit began to swell under my touch, a tight hard nut. There was a current between my fingertips and her clitoris and as it spread through my body it must have electrified hers because she suddenly leaned forward and kissed me passionately, her tongue instantly in my mouth, hungry and searching.

Then she was upon me. I hugged her body to mine. I was erect and throbbing and she held my prick, brushed it against her clit a few times and then tucked it into her moist, warm and salivating cleft.

✦

I was still dozing when the phone rang the next morning. At first we ignored it but it rang persistently, knowing that we were there. Eventually she got out of bed and went to the front room to answer it.

'Who else would it be?' I heard her say. Then she kicked the door to my bedroom so I couldn't intrude on the call. My father. I could hear her through the door.

'Why did I take time to answer? You guessed it. Because I was fucking him, and he's better at it than you any day of the week,' she was saying in unconcealed and deliberate tones. She didn't care that I heard.

'So come and get them, come and get them, daughter-fucker,' I heard her say in Hindi.

Then she banged the phone down and came back to my room.

In the dawn light I could see the thick bush of her crotch, the brown skin, the lined loins and the neat hollow belly button. Her squarish shoulders were the only thing that may have prevented her being a model, selling soap on Indian billboards. Don't they all have delicate sloping shoulders and vulnerable-looking collarbones?

'We are getting out of this flat. We are in business, Govind.'

'I don't think we should fight with my father,' I said. 'And there was no need to tell him...about us.'

'Us?' she mimicked. 'I didn't think of this fuck as "us". But, oh well, maybe. Sweet.' She kissed me gently on the mouth holding my face with both palms.

'But seriously, Ravina, you can sell these gems, and then what? He controls the markets and knows the mafias of Bombay. They'll never let us buy another consignment.'

'We won't need to,' she said. 'I am having a shower. Your father has ruined our fuck. Or our "usness" for the moment.'

She had a shower, changed into a smart suit, and went out and found another flat, an address where presumably my father wouldn't find us.

'I can't run away from my father,' I said. 'Why would we do that?'

'If he double-crosses us, we triple-cross him. He doesn't kill people, not like you. The worst he'll do is come after us for his gems. But they belong to me too. And you may have annoyed him by fucking me, but what does he expect? Sending you off alone with me. Maybe he doesn't care. You know your father has three wives?'

'No,' I said.

'He's got three families and he treats them like dirt – like people he's bought or people who work for him. That is, when he sees them. I am just his partner and even me – he thinks he can use me as he likes.'

'Why do you want to be used by an old man?' It was the first and the last time I asked such a question.

'Because, Johnson, I was a very poor girl and I wanted to get rich fast. Not slow and steady. I told myself that after I got rich I'd settle down with a husband and three or four kids, or whatever the average is, and lead a bourgeois life. But first I'd get rich.'

'You're on your way then,' I said. 'What are we going to do with the stones?'

'You are going to sell them to tourists,' she said.

Later, meditatively, over a cup of coffee in a street café, she said, 'Your father likes to give the impression that he chews people and spits them out, but he is the one who has been betrayed again and again. He trusts nobody. The gem trade is like that. His brothers cheated him, his sisters' husbands cheated him. His servants robbed him. The trust ebbed away. He doesn't trust me, that's why he sent you with me.'

'I thought it was the other way round,' I said.

'No, he still has this thing about blood being thicker than water. He talked about you every time he was betrayed, you know. "I have a son, I'll find him," he used to say.'

'He never made any effort to find me.'

'He suspected you'd find him,' she said.

'What about his other children?'

'Your sisters? They hate him.'

5

The flat at 15 Rathchparaya Street was on the first floor. It had three bedrooms and two bathrooms and a balcony overlooking the huts and shanties before the harbour. Bangkok was booming in the late 1970s with people on the hippie trail who came from a richer class than the earlier generation of hippies. These were travellers, backpackers from every corner of the West, who were passing through Bangkok on various missions of unspecific quests and adventure.

I bought a car so we could get to Phuket and roam around the country on our own steam.

I was getting to know the town, spending time walking by the sides of the canals, hanging around the bars and outside the malls, observing people. I watched the stalls selling junk in the markets to tourists and marked the varieties and types of buyers as they came and went.

Then we targeted the jewellery stores and I chose my first victim. He was a young Greek who seemed to be travelling alone and who seemed uncomfortable with it, lonely.

The fellow tried to put on an air of self-sufficiency. I followed him from the jewellery shop where he bought a ring, to one of the canal-side bars where he ordered a cocktail and sat watching the girls in their tight dresses and absurd shorts come and go. He would stare hard at them, hoping the stare would turn into an invitation that at least one of them would understand. He was no good at picking up women. In half an hour, he gave up and went back towards the jewellery shop. I followed him in and pretended to examine the handicrafts. He was buying another ring and the shopkeeper seemed most interested in him, having picked up the fact that this Greek with the broken English had money. He bought a twin ring to the one he had bought earlier.

I waited for him to step outside the shop. He was clearly a man without a mission. He looked this way and that deciding where he would go next and willing his luck to change.

I made sure it did. I went up to him.

'Are you interested in buying genuine, clean gemstones? Diamonds, rubies, absolutely authentic and at real Eastern prices. Not the rip-off of the shops?'

He fell for it.

'It must to depend on the price,' he said.

'Sure, everything depends on the price,' I said. 'Judge for yourself. You can sell them in Europe for two, three times what you pay here. If you want, I'll show you.'

'Yes, show me something,' he said

I asked him to follow me to an isolated bar nearby. We sat on the high stools and I took out the three diamonds I had casually wrapped in a piece of old paper. I wanted to make it look as if I traded in these things every day and that I didn't need to afford the courtesy of a setting to these familiar objects that passed through my hands.

'You know something about gems?' I asked him.

'A little,' he said.

He examined them and when he picked up the biggest one, he whistled.

'You have dollars?' I asked. 'It's better for me.'

'I can get dollars,' he said.

When I quoted him the price I was asking, his eyes darted from me to the gems. He couldn't believe he was getting such a bargain.

'Three thousand?' he repeated.

'I am selling them at less than the trade rate. They are not stolen.'

'No, no, you are doing strictly business,' he said. 'This is good but I have to arrange for the money, is not in my pocket, eh?'

'Of course. You can meet me later.'

'Tomorrow, in this place?'

He said his name was Nikos and asked for mine. I told him. The next day I left him waiting for twenty minutes, letting him sweat it out with his money in the leather pouch on his belt. By the time I reached the bar, it was filling up with women in their bikinis and their sunbathing gear, and the Greek couldn't keep his eyes off them, preoccupied though he was with not getting mugged.

We walked out by the side of the canal. The boats were furiously taxiing tourists around the Venice of the East and onto the river. He was wary.

'I will make a bargain with you,' he said.

'Let's hear it.'

'You're stranger for me, so I must get some verify,' he said.

'I understand that.'

'I will go with you to a jewellery of my choose and we will ask him for see the gems and say if it's good.'

I was ready for this.

'Then you must give me three thousand and three hundred – for my time and the verification.'

Not trusting me was going to cost him and he weighed up the odds now. He had been talking to someone about the gems and the asking price was still far below what he could sell them for, even in Bangkok, and they would make his fortune if he carried them to Europe. I could see the calculator clicking behind his eyes.

I appreciated the touch about the jeweller of his choice. It shouldn't be one I took him to and could be in league with to swindle him.

We walked into town. He had already spoken to the jeweller and I went into the shop with him. The man was expecting him. The jeweller was a four-foot dwarf. He fixed his glass to his eye and looked at me with the other one, giving me a careful once-over when I took out the gems. I had them in a proper gemstone velvet bag now.

He took them behind the counter and rolled them on the gem tray.

We watched him as he took a few seconds to examine each. He came back with the tray, shaking his head, Indian fashion, to say that he approved, that yes, they were genuine.

I took up the stones and the dwarf asked, 'You have some more?'

'These are his. I will come back another day,' I said.

The Greek led me into the street and we walked into a park. We found an isolated bench where he handed me the money and I gave him the gems. He was wearing a ring with the constellation of the crab on it in green gems.

'Where are you staying?' I asked.

'The Peninsula,' he said. That was one of the most expensive and oldest hotels in town. He must have money.

That evening, Ravina and I sat in the car and waited outside the Peninsula. Nikos came out and walked towards the seafront. We left the car and followed at a discreet distance.

Nikos went into the Romeo and Juliet bar off the Sukhmuvit Road. We waited for ten minutes and then followed him in. He was being accosted by the girls. He looked as though he couldn't handle it. I walked up to him with Ravina behind. The girls immediately fell away. The bar was too smart to encourage blatant touting. His face brightened with recognition. I had told him my name was Eduard.

He couldn't take his eyes off Ravina in her tight Chinese dress.

'So this is your hang-out?' I said, and introduced Ravina as my partner. 'My business partner, strictly,' I added, to forestall his disappointment and leave options for flirtation open. Give him hope and lead him by the nose.

Ravina smiled, openly, flirtatiously. 'I hear he gave our best stuff away for a song this morning. I was angry with him.'

'Look, Nikos is not a customer,' I said, 'I can see he is a Cancer and we will be friends.'

'How did you know I was a Cancer?' he asked. My eye went down to the hand around his beer glass. He wasn't wearing the ring this evening.

'Kindred souls, a feeling. I am a Cancer too,' I lied.

We chatted for an hour. Nikos was obviously lonely in the foreign city. He told us he was going round the world and his next adventure would be to cross the Australian desert on a camel. His friend had done it the previous year and written a book about it.

He talked about Greece and told us he had given up his job in a bank in Athens.

'Why?' Ravina asked.

He said he wanted adventure, but he looked into his beer as he spoke.

'Someone broke your heart,' Ravina said.

He looked up as though he'd been prodded. An accurate guess. Ravina was looking hard at him trying to convey sympathy mixed with curiosity, as though it was her wish and duty to hear more and to offer solace.

He fell for it. He invited us to dinner at the hotel. I could have pleaded other business and left Ravina to work the snare alone, but it was too soon and it may have aroused in him the suspicion of a honey trap. And Nikos had demonstrated that he was no dupe, he had wanted the gems double-checked even though he was confident that he knew his diamonds.

We didn't talk about gems or trade at dinner. We went to the Indian restaurant of the hotel. He asked the waiter for the hottest curry he could have.

'A Malay curry can be even hotter,' Ravina said. 'You should try Mussaman curry – it's just a Far Eastern perversion of Mussalman, meaning Muslim, because it must have been introduced by Indian immigrants.'

Nikos was obviously fascinated by Ravina and at the end of the meal, as he paid the bill, not by signing it to his room, but by pulling out currency notes from one of the two money pouches he was now wearing on his belt, he asked us when we could meet again.

'The bar where we met? The Romeo and Juliet bar?' he asked.

'It gets crowded in the evenings, but we go there a lot. That would be okay,' Ravina said.

'Great stuff,' Nikos said, grinning.

'One warning. Don't carry too much money or anything valuable. That part of town is notorious for muggers and thieves. Our friend is the police commissioner and he told me that last year there were a hundred thefts a day reported in Patpong market.'

So now we were citizens of Bangkok familiar enough with police chiefs to have casual conversations? Did she say it to make Nikos feel safer with us?

'I don't have any cash. It's all in the bank in…' he hesitated, 'in Europe,' he said. 'I phone for it and collect the cash when I need it. Safest.'

'Good arrangement, smart boy,' Ravina said. 'People wander about the East as though it was London or something. Mind you, I suppose London is also full of thieves with all the immigration.'

Was she hinting that we too were globetrotters? Or people with international business? We hadn't mentioned India even once in the evening, but he must have known I was French because I sometimes groped for the English word and had to use the French one that sprang to mind instead.

'This is very good night,' Nikos said as we parted.

We met at the bar the next evening and then again the evening after for dinner at a restaurant I named. He told us he intended to stay in Bangkok for an indefinite period now. It was an exhilarating feeling to make new friends and to have no schedule to keep, with no one expecting you anywhere in the world. It was new to him. His work in the bank had meant regular hours and endless meetings and now he felt a sense of absolute liberty.

'Staying at the Peninsula indefinitely will eat into your fortune,' Ravina said.

'I was thought of that. I come in there because it was recommend to me, but I go to cheaper hotel, I think, and stay for more longer. Especially if you peoples are going to continue here.'

'Oh yes, we are continuing here,' Ravina said. 'We've got work. And we live in a very convenient big flat, you know. It has three bedrooms and I am sure that Eduard would be just as happy as I am to invite you to come and stay. If you need to. It'll be a gas. You won't have to pay us anything. And then with the money you save you can buy more diamonds from us. Good business move.' She smiled.

He couldn't believe his luck.

'You mean this? Come to be your guest? Really? You are able to do this?'

'Of course I mean it, why would I say it?' Ravina said.

'This is too good,' Nikos said. 'If you are sure, I come tomorrow.'

'Come tonight,' Ravina said. 'Eduard can fetch the car and we can drive your luggage round.'

'I have not much luggage. Just small bag. I think I buy clothes as I goes along,' he said.

'Then go to the hotel and bring it along. We'll wait in the lobby.'

'Just give me the address and I pay the bill and clear

up everythings and then come to your house by taxi,' he said.

'It's not that far,' Ravina said. 'We'll wait and we can walk. It's a nice night.'

So that's what we did. She hadn't asked me or prepared me for this move.

When Nikos went to fetch his things and check out, she said, 'Go and get your stuff out of my room and get into the small bedroom. He mustn't know we are "us". Get your toothbrush into your own bathroom and make it look like strictly business.'

I hurried to the flat and did as she had asked. There was nothing much to move. I had a few clothes and my male cosmetics, a luxury of aftershaves and creams and skin-softeners I had picked up in Paris and had felt crucially deprived of in jail.

Nikos loved the flat. He oohed and aahed about it and about our kindness in letting him stay. He now felt sure that he would soon be moving from the second bedroom to Ravina's bed. Why else was she being so familiar?

And yet there was some lingering suspicion in his mind because he never left his money pouch lying about. At night, he kept it under his pillow and Ravina said she knew he kept the diamonds in it.

Poor suspicious loser.

The next day, we drove out to Pattaya beach.

We didn't eat in the flat and our fridge was deliberately kept bare.

Ravina now told me the core of the plan. We had the

money Nikos had paid for the diamonds. Now we wanted the diamonds back and were going to keep the money.

We walked into the Khao San road with its fake Rolex watches and Louis Vuitton bags.

'If you're hungry we could eat here,' Ravina suggested.

We found a little restaurant with a tidy menu posted on the door. We asked for beer and predictably, Nikos said he would eat the hottest curry on the menu.

'It's called lamb, but it'll be goat,' Ravina said.

When the steaming plate of curry came, I looked at it with curiosity. 'Look,' I said, 'there's a stomach bug going around the city. I think we should be careful.'

'The place look very fine and clean,' Nikos said.

I pulled out two small plastic packets from my pocket.

'My doctor friend gave me this herbal thing, tasteless, but it'll stop any stomach bug from infecting your gut. Ancient Thai remedy,' I said, and sprinkled the powder on my curry.

'I have some too,' Nikos said.

'Why save just yourself?' Ravina asked.

I sprinkled the yellowish powder on Ravina's curry, then opened the second little bag and put a generous portion on Nikos's food.

I tasted my own.

'He's right, only the taste of the food. The herbs have as much taste as spring water.'

'Yes, hmm, very hot. Very burning and plenty trouble in morning times,' Nikos said.

He devoured the food. Ravina and I ate heartily too.

At night, I heard him get up and go to the toilet a few

times. The third time he went I could hear him retching. I was to stay in bed. Ravina got up and I could hear her cross from her bedroom to his.

'You've been sick?'

'Are you perfect?' Nikos asked her.

'I am fine,' she said. 'Eduard's powder obviously didn't work its miracles on your goat curry. Seems to have worked on my veggie dish.'

'I will be perfect,' Nikos said and rushed to the toilet again.

Ravina stayed with him for half an hour or so till his retching subsided and then she went to bed again. I stayed in bed pretending I heard nothing.

In the morning, Ravina asked me to take Nikos some tea. This is how we planned events, without planning. It was an instinct. I knew what she was thinking and she knew what I would do and which instruction I didn't need to be given.

She'd made the tea and now gave it to me with a grim face, taking the spoon with which she was stirring it and washing it thoroughly in the sink. I took it in to him. His face had turned pale. He ran to the toilet again. He was clutching his stomach and was obviously in pain.

'Try some tea,' I said. 'I am not feeling too good myself. But the tea helped.'

He drank the tea and immediately rushed to the toilet. He didn't make it and threw up at the door.

Ravina was on the phone to the doctor.

A doctor arrived an hour later and asked what the symptoms were. He took Nikos's pulse and we told him that Nikos had had a hearty meal of goat curry in a market restaurant. The doctor shook his head. He asked how many times Nikos had vomited and how many times he had emptied his bowels.

Nikos had lost count. The doctor wrote out a prescription. He could hardly talk. I paid the doctor in cash at the door and he left.

Ravina said she would go out immediately and get the medicines and I was to look after Nikos. She came back with one bottle of mixture and two little phials of pills. Nikos was to take a dose of the liquid medicine mixed in water and swallow two lots of pills. In four hours he was to repeat the dose.

Nikos took the medicines as he was told, and sank back into bed. In a few minutes, he was asleep.

Four hours later, before noon, Ravina woke him up again and though he was dozy and groggy with the medicine, she forced some more into him.

By the time the sun set, he had gone down. He passed out and then his heart and pulse stopped. He was dead.

I took the leather purses off his belt. They contained his passport, the bag with three diamonds he had bought from me, a few thousand Thai baht and some dollars. In his bag were his clothes and what we presumed were love letters from the girl who had broken his heart, and a swimming costume.

'We are driving him to Phuket,' Ravina said. 'Take his clothes off and bundle them up. Put his swimming trunks on him.'

We carried the body to the car. It was already beginning to leak fluids. We held him upright between us as though we were walking a sick friend. No one was about at that time of night.

This was our second body in the boot of a car. We drove

to Phuket beach and got there by dawn. Before the sun rose, we left his bundle of clothes on the beach and floated his stiffening body as far as we could to sea. We held it down till it had absorbed or swallowed water and was heavy with it. It felt as though it wouldn't float and we let it go. We walked for half a mile in the water so as not to leave any tracks and then emerged along the beach, found our way back to the car and drove back to Bangkok.

Two days later the newspapers carried the story of a late-night bather drowned in Phuket, a lone swimmer whose identity the police were still attempting to check.

Ravina saw the newspaper article and behaved as though it had nothing to do with us. She was eating a jam sandwich. She put the paper down and, holding me by the wrist, led me to her bedroom.

'Make love to me, now,' she said, unbuttoning my shirt.

'What was in the bottles?' I asked.

I knew that she had planned to make him sick, but I didn't know what Ravina had fed him to kill him. The herbal powder I sprinkled was something she had brought me. She said I should invent some patter about insulating ourselves against the lethal stomach bug. Tourists in the East were always grateful for remedies against stomach bugs.

'Doesn't matter about the bottles, concentrate,' she said, unzipping my trousers and pushing me into sitting on the bed. She pulled my trousers off. Then she took her own clothes off and kneeling at the side of the bed, sucked me erect. When I was aroused and hard, she got on my lap and put her legs around my hips. She was very wet and leaked onto my thighs. She closed her eyes as I manipulated myself into her.

'Kiss me. Pretend you love me,' she said.

I kissed her and gently tried to move her into lying on the bed. She had splayed her legs out behind me and I felt her resisting changing positions. She was undulating back and forth on my thighs with me inside her and moaning softly.

She had been in control of the game up until now. I stopped kissing her and pulled my face away. She didn't stop her frantic rhythm, undulating on my lap with her eyes closed. She whispered, 'You love me, say you love me.'

'I love you,' I said and looked at her face.

She had her eyes closed and she smiled. I forced her body to fall next to mine on the bed. Though her breasts were tiny, they fell away to the side, revealing the lines of her ribs. I climbed on top of her and thrust myself into her hard, counting the strokes in my head to prevent coming straight away. She appeared to climax when I hit a hundred and twenty and though I was banging away clinically, her moaning as she came brought me rapidly to eject into her.

It must have been a sort of catharsis, a way of relieving herself of the immediate preoccupation of the body we had drowned. But why did she want me to say I loved her? It came from deep inside her, another voice, and yet it was not like the practical commands or demands she issued. It was a pleading voice, a need like a vapour that had leapt out of a locked, rusty locket that she had long ago cast into a deep well inside her.

The case was reported again the next day but the police were no nearer identifying the body, which lay in the morgue. There were other deaths, other murders.

'Are we going back to Bombay now?' I asked.

'No, my love,' she said. 'We are staying in Bangkok and

selling the diamonds again.' This time the word 'love' was sarcastic, thrown as a challenge. Yes, she remembered begging me to say I loved her and recalled me saying it and now she was ashamed of having exposed that little wisp of need and called me 'love' to prove it had been a game all along, even in the throes of passion.

But had I spoken from the heart? Was I in love with her?

6

I met Harry in the bars of Phuket. I could see he was on something because of the circles under his eyes. I was drinking in the beachside bamboo bar and he came in and went straight to the toilet. He looked around the bar when he emerged. The guilt was written all over his face. He was new to the game of dodging into toilets to snort his cocaine or inject himself, whichever he was doing, unnoticed. The idiot was drawing attention to himself.

I was sure the bartenders knew but they didn't seem to care. He walked out of the bar without ordering a drink of course, happier as he emerged from the toilet than when he had gone anxiously in. I followed him out and shouted at him. 'Oi, have a drink.'

He stopped and I knew he was thinking of running in panic.

'I've got stuff,' I said. 'I know you well. I am a head myself.'

He came back and I introduced myself as Pierre. He didn't take my hand or tell me his name. 'I just needed the bathroom,' he said. 'I was caught short.'

'I don't care, you can shit, you can shoot, I don't own the place. I came out after you to see if you needed anything.'

'How much?' he said.

'I can get you the best deal on junk you've ever had,' I said. 'Interested?'

'Nah,' he said. He was still suspicious and walked away.

The next day at about the same time I was sitting in the same bar and he came looking for me.

'Pierre?'

'That'll do,' I said.

'You wouldn't be deceiving me?' he asked.

I smiled. 'Would I tell you if I was? You are English, and stupid, eh?'

'You are a French immigrant, aren't you?' he retaliated. 'You are not really Pierre. You're probably Abdul.'

'You'll find out if you stick around. Let me buy you a beer,' I said.

It was a hot day. I was dressed in a patterned bush shirt and khaki trousers and he was wearing shorts and a long-sleeved shirt. To cover the marks. Obvious. He was a new junkie and the veins in his arms must be still operative and raw from fresh woundings.

'You're not a user,' he said.

'Of course I am,' I said. 'If I was a dealer I wouldn't be talking to the punk likes of you. I'd be chasing real money.'

'So you're not a dealer or a policeman?'

'I am a gem dealer. I have an income and I use drugs for recreation.'

'What gems do you deal in?'

'Diamonds,' I said. 'And anything else you want.'

'I'd be interested in that,' he said.

We walked around the beach and he said he would like to

see just one stone, a real diamond. He wanted it for his girl; they were going to get engaged.

'They are cut but they are not set. You can get a stone set in the markets in Bangkok. Just be careful they don't substitute your rock for a piece of plastic.'

'You think I'm a fool?' he asked.

'I'm gathering evidence,' I replied.

We met the next day and the next and he did buy a stone from me for a few hundred dollars. He asked me again for the heroin.

I said I didn't have any on me but I could deliver it.

He said I should bring it to his hotel room.

I went that afternoon with a bottle of champagne and the cocktail of drugs I had got from Ravina. This was my operation and I didn't need her for it. I had asked Harry for his room number earlier, and went through the crowded hotel lobby straight up to his room. I took my shoes off, held them in my hand and walked in wearing just my socks. He might have thought this was strange but was so anxious to get at the junk that he said nothing about it. Instead, he enquired urgently whether I had the stuff.

I gave him the liquid and he immediately took out a syringe. He injected himself in the vein, striking his arm to induce faster absorption in his blood. In ten minutes, he was almost unconscious, as Ravina had assured me he would be with the dose she had prepared. He faded away and his eyes turned heavenward, the gesture of a ham actor praying. He staggered.

'Here, take these,' I said. I curled his hands around the bottle of sleeping pills – only his prints would be on it – and forced him to pour a quantity of them down his throat. I opened the champagne and hearing the pop of the cork he regained a moment of consciousness. I poured a single glass, which I fetched from the bathroom, and put it to his lips, holding the stem through a tissue. I forced it down his mouth. He was gagging because the pills were choking him but after spluttering, he got them down. He dropped the bottle of pills and the glass fell to the ground. He tried to get up with a final effort, staggered and fell next to the bed. The champagne glass smashed. I went through the wardrobe and recovered my diamond. I decided to leave the passport and the spare cash he had. It mustn't look like a robbery. I listened at the door till there was no movement in the corridor and went down the lift, into the lobby and out into the street.

I drove back to Bangkok and to the flat. Ravina was waiting for me. I didn't describe the 'experiment' as we began to call these encounters. I just showed her the retrieved diamond and handed over the money. She was the treasurer.

I felt nothing. Junkie Harry was dead. In a sense, he had killed himself. I am not stupid enough not to realize that I had hastened the process, but left to his own devices, injecting himself with the nasty and adulterated drugs that they peddled in the East, how long would he have lasted? He would probably never have gone back to the girl to whom he was going to give the ring. And wasn't she better off without a junkie? Hadn't I done her a favour?

The newspapers reported it as an overdose because that's what the hotel doctor diagnosed. There were no poisons involved, just an overdose of heroin mixed with half a bottle of sleeping pills. The hotel wouldn't go for a post-mortem and more publicity. They would pay the papers to hush it up. The British embassy would be handed the body and the report and record of the hotel doctor's autopsy if there was one. The body would be flown back to England perhaps and there would be no case to answer.

I felt I had been more efficient than Ravina. The business with Nikos was messy and had lasted too long.

'So what do you think I did before I joined your father in his smuggling ring?' Ravina asked, looking at the diamond in her hand.

'You were a doctor?' I said.

'I was a pharmacist. I trained in college in Bombay and then in London for a year.'

For several weeks, we sold gems but failed to lure the customers back into our orbit. Some Arabs bought a few diamonds from Ravina at a hotel and immediately left the city.

'We didn't even make much of a profit on them,' I said.

'Profit? We never paid for them,' she said.

'You chose the wrong people. The gems are now irretrievable.'

I was implying that I ought to take more control of our schemes. Harry was my untraceable success. It was my skill at having spotted his vulnerability that had delivered him.

The next ploy would be to hang around the lobbies of the five-star hotels and see who entered the jewellery shops.

✦

An American couple called Abe and Abbie. They were dressed in expensive but casual clothes and both had hippie hair, his down to below his shoulders and hers down to her waist.

They were looking at gemstones. The trader had brought out a tray.

These are my people, I thought and as they emerged from the shop, I went up to them.

'I couldn't help noticing, sir, that you were in that tourist trap of a shop.'

They both seemed surprised at being addressed in this fashion.

'We didn't buy much,' Abe said.

'I have a much fairer trader friend who sells real high-carat gems,' I told him.

'Where's the shop?' Abbie asked.

'She is a private trader and doesn't work out of a shop. No overheads, and quality gems at prices you won't find anywhere in the world. Certainly nowhere in the markets of Bangkok and certainly not in five-star hotel lobbies. If you are interested I can introduce you.'

Later that day, Ravina and I went up to room 404. She had bought a small gem box and had arranged the best stones we had left in good professional settings. She carried the jewellery box in a plain lady's leather bag so as not to attract attention. She was wearing a sari and I wore a grey suit. We passed through the lobby. There was a delegation of Chinese businessmen sitting in the lobby and more Chinese men were coming and going from the restaurants. We took the lift to the fourth floor.

She showed Abe and Abbie her collection and he examined the stones as a professional would. I could tell he knew about stones. He was examining the colour against the light and checking the crystalline structure.

'These are worth a lot. I hope I'm not giving my own game away when I say that,' he said.

They talked prices for three or four of the stones. Abe was visibly surprised. 'That's very reasonable. You're sure they're clean?'

'Sir, we wouldn't boldly show these to customers if they were not.'

'I guess,' said Abbie.

Abe went to the safe in the cupboard, the small safe that hotel rooms have for their guests' personal belongings. I thought he was going to fetch the money. He punched in the four-figure code and the safe opened.

He took out a pistol and went straight to Ravina, and standing behind her, pointed it at her head.

'Okay, stand clear away from the stones,' he said.

Abbie immediately became active. She brought out two long scarves that she had rolled into gags and came towards me. I had my hands up.

'Just be cool or she gets it,' Abe said. 'We're going to leave you here with your lives intact. We don't want you, we just want what you've got, so play ball and I won't shoot. This thing's got a silencer,' he added.

'Don't do this,' I said. 'You can't do this.'

'Can't I?' Abe said.

'No, you can't, bud, bad luck, you're fucked,' I said. 'Look out of the window. These gems don't belong to us. The owners are waiting downstairs. They know what you look like. You think we walk into traps like this? We've got twenty guys in the building.'

Abbie was about to bring the gag to my face when Abe got curious.

'What are you talking about?'

'The Triads. Chinese. We are just runners for them. They put me on to talk to you. They've got two guys right now in the lobby and they have targeted you. If you try and get out of the hotel without us, they'll get you, wherever you go. They are killers.'

'You're a fucking liar,' Abe said.

I remained cool. 'Okay, try it.'

'Suppose I take you or her with me?'

'You think those guys give a shit about her or me? We work for peanuts for them. Well, they give us a percentage. The Dragon even had the idea that you may not have the money, but that you may be useful to them in different ways.'

'Tie him up,' Abe said. 'This is bullshit.'

Abbie brought out a pair of handcuffs and yanking my arms to behind my back, she clamped them on. She went to Ravina and did the same.

'You're playing with your lives,' Ravina said. 'They'll punish us for losing gems. Maybe break his knees or something, but they'll kill you. There'll be no escape.'

'What do you do for these guys?' Abbie asked. She was wavering, on the verge of believing – maybe.

'Sell things, not just gems,' I said. 'And we look out for people who can work for the organization. Talent scouts. You can look out of the window. They should be waiting for us.'

Abe indicated that Abbie should look out. She went to the window. Their room looked out on the front street over the hotel's entrance. I don't know what she saw. I was relying on there being some Chinese drivers hanging around in the street with the conference delegation.

Abbie came back from the window and nodded. Abe looked confounded now. What were they to do? Were these Triads waiting for them? Was it bullshit?

'Some Chinese men came in,' Abbie said.

This was going my way. 'They don't have to know what went on in this room. What you tried to pull on us. Sometimes when we don't make a sale, we recruit helpers, agents. You are perfect.'

'How perfect?'

'You are bad and you think fast. And you're Americans. Perfect cover.'

'They will believe people like you. Maybe you'll need a haircut,' Ravina said.

'I didn't cut my hair for my dad,' Abe said.

'Maybe you can do it for the Triads?'

'This is real confidence, man. You're fulla shit,' he said. But there was the hint of a doubt in his voice. 'Tie 'em and let's go. Gag the fuck, Abbie!'

'No, hang on, these guys want to make a deal. They can't do it if they're gagged.'

'Are you contradicting me?' Abe asked. 'It's horse-ass. Chinese in the hotel! There's Chinese in every hotel. Look at them, I don't trust them.'

He didn't see that it was a funny thing to say. He had a gun pointed at Ravina's head and he didn't trust us?

'Look, we'll prove it. You can keep a few of the gems till we deliver the introduction and the commission,' I said.

'They'll kill you,' Ravina added. 'No questions. If we go missing, you are dead.'

'Then we'll leave you not just missing, we'll leave you dead,' Abe said.

'You'll leave the gems?' Abbie asked. She was buying the ruse.

'One or two. Till tomorrow morning,' I said.

'We can talk to them on the phone, that should convince you,' Ravina said.

'You think I'm crazy?' Abe said.

'Then let me go personally,' Ravina said.

'Let her speak on the phone,' Abbie said. 'I can listen on the extension and if she says anything wrong, the first wrong move, we shoot this bastard. Give me the gun.'

She was quite domineering. She took the gun from Abe and held it to my head. They undid Ravina's handcuffs. Abbie picked up the extension by the bed.

Ravina dialled.

'Hi, it's me,' she said. I could guess whom she was calling. 'Yeah, he's here. Sure, we'll pass it all over to your guys. If you send them over. We are working with two friends… And yes, we'll wait for them.'

Only Abbie could hear what my father was saying at the other end.

'No, it was just the flu and it passed. Yeah, the doctor says it's a variant on the old Asian flu… Yes, it takes three weeks. Look, I can explain that later.'

She cupped her hands over the receiver.

'Sorry about that, the boss is always worried about my health. Can I get an escort out of here?'

Abbie nodded and Ravina went back to the phone.

'It's room 404 at the Planet Thai hotel… Yes, of course… everything.'

Abbie was nodding. She obviously approved of what the voice at the other end was saying.

'Tell them to come unarmed,' Abe said.

Ravina shrugged.

'We are all friends here. You two could fool the marines.'

Abe smiled at the joke. 'Yeah, we could pass,' he said.

'I'll call after,' she said and put the phone down, then turned to us. 'The big boys will be here in half an hour. They can make deals.'

We waited. They let us sit down. We watched each other, Abe still holding the pistol. Within the hour, there was a knock at the door.

Abe looked through the peephole.

'Put your hands on your head,' he said to me. Ravina looked at him in horror.

'No. Don't alienate them! We are friends, you are the new agents,' she cried out.

'Okay, come and sit here then. I'll keep the gun hidden but it'll be aiming up your butt.'

I did as he ordered and sat on the bed. He sat behind me, the gun out of sight, scraping my tailbone.

'Let them in,' Abe said. 'Let's see 'em.'

Ravina opened the door and two Chinese men walked in. One about sixty and the other maybe in his twenties.

'Hey, pleased to meet you, come and sit down,' Abbie said.

'Yes, the business. JJ tell us come quick, you have something for us,' the old man said.

Ravina handed him the box of gems. She turned her back to us and undoing the front of her blouse, took out a money pouch she kept inside and handed it to the old man.

'All JJ's,' she said. 'And he said you would have plans for us. For my friends here.'

'These your friends, very nice. You American?' The old man smiled.

Abe looked at Abbie.

'Yeah,' she replied and smiled.

'We need you if you are friendly,' the old man said.

'They are very friendly,' I said.

The Chinese man with the fixed smile introduced himself as Hua.

'JJ told me you would call, but you never call,' he said.

I got it. Ravina had been in touch with Papa. All that stuff about sex with me and abandoning him, was it all theatre? She seemed to have got Hua's number from my dad and had obviously promised to call him. Or was he so smart that he picked up a vibe from her voice and was doing what was needed? And what was all the stuff about the Asian flu? And three weeks? Code? I asked myself what was the worst that could happen. To me.

Sweet Papa. Orphan Ravina whom he had taken in. Back to his paunchy pleasures and his three wives.

'We have plenty plans, plenty plans,' Hua said. 'JJ said if you are right you are going to Malaysia for us. These two friends,' he indicated Abe and Abbie, 'you meet us at Dragon bar near the floating market early next morning.'

Abe and Abbie looked at each other. Hua took an assortment of gems out of the box Ravina had handed him and gave them to Abe.

'We are leaving now. Then you leave after five minutes,' Hua said. He bowed his head and they left.

Abe looked at the gems.

'Mr H. is now in charge. If you want to take those gems and disappear tonight, that's up to you. We can't stop you. But my advice is turn up tomorrow and play for higher stakes,' Ravina said. Then she motioned to me. 'They'll be there,' she said as we walked out of the room.

'So you've been in touch with Papa?' I asked.

'It's none of your business,' she said.

'And you've given away everything? All the money, everything?'

'Not all the money,' she said. 'And it was his in the first place, wasn't it?'

'So what about the Asian flu?'

She turned to me. We were now out of the lift and in the hotel's lobby.

'Where had I been for three weeks?'

'So when did you last call him?'

'Are you jealous of your father?'

'Jealous? Look, Ravina, if we're playing blackjack I'm not asking to see your cards. I just want to know who else is at the table.'

'You are such a clever boy,' she said.

Ravina slept in her own bed and I in mine, but she came to me in the dark and made love. She was silent, turning me over onto my back, and the only sound that escaped her was 'Oh maa! Oh maa!' as she called for her mother in the dark.

Abe and Abbie turned up the next morning. Hua came with two other men. He was wearing a bush shirt and not the heavy grey suit of the previous evening. I could see his ribs through it. In the sunlight, his face looked heavily wrinkled but his smile hovered as before on his downturned lips. If there exists an art to read lines on faces, his would have been a complex study. He talked to Abe and Abbie in direct and simple terms. They had a compartment of gems to transport and being Americans they would be ideal. It was a car journey to Malaysia. They would have a fake American diplomatic car with facilitating border passes. No Thai or Malay border police or customs ever stopped American diplomats.

I too had a purpose. I was told to pick up the car with the secret compartment that afternoon. Its Corps Diplomatique and the American credentials for Abe and Abbie were being fixed even now.

'What you think of haircut?' Hua asked, still smiling.

'Now you look like a vice-presidential candidate,' Ravina said.

'In the US they say running for office. In England they say standing. That's the difference,' Abe said. He winked at me.

Abe and Abbie were told they'd be paid on delivery, all the talk conducted in a sort of made-up gangster code. Hua's smile remained fixed.

A car with an imitation Louis Vuitton suitcase, the type you could buy in any Bangkok market, was delivered. Only, this suitcase had a hidden compartment with black plastic packets in it.

Abe and Abbie would drive the load to Kuala Lumpur and check into a hotel. The stuff would be collected and they would get their cash. It was the coolest buck they had ever made. They thanked me genuinely. And maybe, Abe said, there was a continuing partnership in it, especially as they had genuine American passports.

I opened the suitcase and showed them the genuine gems.

They were mugs. Amateurs. Of course there were two suitcases, one carried by Ravina from the lobby to the car. I left the one with the gems in the lobby in a row of tourist suitcases by the bellboys' desk and she substituted the empty one into the car that Hua had provided.

Abe and Abbie drove into the sunset, smiling, happy.

Ravina picked up the suitcase from the lobby. Were we going to make a run for it from Hua?

'They'll kill us,' I said.

'No. They'll kill them first. Then they'll come after us. So we have time.'

Four days later the national newspapers reported that the bodies of two Americans had been found dumped in a hotel car park in Kuala Lumpur. They had been shot. The newspapers said it was probably the work of thieves. The police were trying to identify the bodies.

'Time to phone Hua,' Ravina said.

She called him.

'They tried to get us involved with double-crossing you,' she told him. 'But we recovered the gems and want to return them to you.'

Whether Hua was deceived or not I never found out. Ravina returned the gems to him. She said he was grateful.

'Amelicans, bloody clooks,' he said, according to Ravina's report. I hadn't noted the way he spoke. Did he really say 'l' for 'r' as a comic-book Chinaman would?

In the days after that incident, I noticed a Chinese man following us around the city. Two days later, this man approached us. Hua wanted a meeting.

We went to the back room of a huge grocery emporium to meet Hua who sat, wrinkled as a prune, in an old wicker chair so large it made him look like the naughty boy on the high dunce stool. There was another oldish Chinese man with him. He was introduced as Jing.

'Your father want the other gems,' Jing said to me. 'No esclooz. His gem. What you take flom him.'

I looked at Ravina.

She looked penitent. She said we were going to bring them that very day, return them.

'I also look into the future and see leturn of all gems,' Jing said. Was this guy a proverbial Triad? An ultimate nasty?

Ravina said they were as good as on their way.

'All a' them. We do pijness. You go,' he said, pointing at me, and then turned to Ravina, 'you stay and have some tea.'

I went to bring the gems we had taken from the suitcase. I returned with them and handed them over. Hua took them into another room and came back and nodded. The permanent smile was gone.

'You can go. I will call you for more business,' Hua said.

Back in the flat, Ravina phoned my father demanding to know why he had put the Triads onto us. Did he think we were so stupid that we would try and keep the gems we had rescued from the Americans? He replied that he thought the Americans were part of our gang of thieves. Yes, she said, that's why we didn't trust them. We got the gems off them by deceit and were going to return them to Mr Hua and take our cut.

'Let me speak with Govind,' he said. Ravina handed me the phone.

'Hullo. I hope we are partners again, my son,' he said, clearing his throat.

'I think we are,' I said.

'Nothing should come between a father and his son. How can I lose my only son for the sake of money?' he asked.

'Why didn't you get in touch with me in Saigon or in France?'

There was a long silence. Had I betrayed any hurt in my voice?

'I thought I had lost you. I lived in mourning, I promise you. But I knew somewhere the path of your karma and my karma would meet. I was sure. My daughters have been poisoned by their mothers, you know. They aren't women of the world like our Ravina. You are the colour of my blood. You must work with me and treat me like a father. No more beyimani,' he said.

I should have said 'How can I treat you like a father when you treat me like a rival for a woman's love, or at least for her body?' – but I didn't. And he was reading my mind.

'Ravina is our trusted partner. She must have told you she is a poor girl. It is all lies. She is the daughter of a general in the army. You ask her.'

I did ask her.

'He can say what he likes,' she said.

'Anyone will understand why I am as I am. But you? If it's true, why did a nice Indian girl like you associate with this dirty world?'

'I'll tell you. You have one life and your job is to defy destiny in that one life. Now your father, he is capable of having us killed. Son, lover, mistress, nothing matters to him except his own survival and winning. You think they killed those two without asking him?'

'So you're scared of him. You think he'll kill you!' I said.

'Us. Remember "us"?' she countered.

'No, I don't remember. You've been calling him. What for? But I suppose it's fine. No stones. The business is over. Should we go back to Bombay and beg Papa to give us some more?' I asked.

'He has plans. He knows we are lovers. He is a jealous man. He thinks I was his woman, even though he was never my man.'

'But you never wanted a man to be your man,' I said. 'That's too normal. That's following destiny, not defying it.'

'Yes, it's defeat,' she said.

She looked at me for a long time and maybe there was just the hint of sadness in her eyes. 'No, how could I want a man to be just my man? It wouldn't happen, would it?'

I wasn't going to say I would like to be her man. Did she even want me to say it? She'd despise me if I did. Another defeat, another giving in.

'Okay, so what do we do?'

'We experiment.'

7

In the next few months, we performed several experiments. Our luck brought us Bagchi, an abortionist. He had made some malpractice blunders in his Indian medical career and been struck off the medical register for incompetence and corruption, but he knew medicine. He washed up in Bangkok and had set up a yoga and ayurvedic clinic.

He ran classes for yoga in the afternoons and evenings, and supervised a medicinal clinic, calling himself Dr Bagchi, something that Thai law allowed him to do if he was practising herbal medicine and not using his medical qualification. The flat below ours was vacant and so he came to live below us. He said he had gone from five- to one-star status in the few months in which he lived in hotels.

'I am now looking for a place where the bugs and the bills won't bite,' he said.

He was a young man with black hair that looked as though it was constantly standing on end. He had high cheekbones and large eyes and was quite handsome in his own way.

'The yoga keeps me in contortionate solvency,' he said. He fancied himself as something of a man of words. 'But the rent in the centre of town blots it up and the balance between income and endeavour is constantly defeated by the nature of the beast. These itinerants learn to meditate and then bugger off without paying for the sessions. I get whole classes of them absconding.'

'Charge in advance,' Ravina suggested.

'I tried for two months. My rivals undercut me and nearly ran me out of business. I can only gather part as a deposit. But these bastards take all sorts of cures and disappear. This is the disappearing footprint of this city of passing souls, this monument to shifting sands, this metaphor for the human condition. Even the police can't trace them to recover my cash. Where they come from, where they go and what their real names are, only the eternal energy, which some call God, knows.'

I think his little speeches gave Ravina ideas. She put up a notice in his yoga class about cheap accommodation to let.

It brought us the next guinea pig for our experiments and then the one after.

We used the method we had used on Nikos. We sublet them the spare bedroom and bathroom and gave them the run of the house.

The first tenant was called Ikey. He was Jewish and from France. He was a yoga freak and a vegetarian. Ravina gave him the room saying that she thought he seemed as though he was rich but didn't want to spend too much money. He said he had renounced possessions and was trying to own less and less of the material world and was now down to a couple of shirts and two pairs of jeans for cleanliness.

'We'll get nothing out of this fellow,' I said.

'He has a fat wallet and he never loses sight of it. He takes it into the bathroom when he's showering or shitting,' Ravina said. 'I go and do his bed when I hear the bathroom door, but there's never a wallet about.'

The tasteless crystals with the amoebic dysentery dose were mixed into the opened pot of yoghurt he had bought himself from the health shop and stowed in the refrigerator. It worked as it was supposed to. He returned from his morning meditation class dizzy and sick. He emptied his gut and vomited. We sympathized and Ravina offered to call a doctor.

'Get Bagchi,' Ikey said. 'I don't trust doctors. Bagchi will sort it out with ayurvedic cures.'

We went to fetch Bagchi from his yoga clinic and told him what the matter was.

Bagchi hadn't lost his doctor's manner and asked the appropriate questions, feeling Ikey's pulse and asking him what he had eaten. Ikey told him that he had bought some fruit and eaten yoghurt and nuts and a salad for lunch. Ikey looked frightened, shaken. For the first time he left his trousers with his wallet in the pocket on the floor of his room as he rushed to the toilet in his underpants.

'The water in the salad,' Bagchi said. 'Bad stuff, bad cess,' and he asked him to stay in bed, saying he would send him a herbal mixture which would settle it tomorrow if not as he slept in the night. Ikey was reassured but still sick.

I went back with Bagchi to his clinic. He gave me two lots of pills ground together with some herbs in a mortar, and asked me to mix it with water and make Ikey drink it.

At home, Ravina had her own powders ready. She poured some liquid into a glass, mixed it with water and asked Ikey to swallow it.

'Foul things,' he said, as he tasted the medicine.

'Doesn't matter, now get to bed,' she said.

Outside the room, as we shut his door, I asked what it was.

'Get the car ready, it is fast acting, but it can be detected in the body for years afterwards.'

Ikey was dead in an hour. Ravina removed his wallet from his pocket and we carried him to the boot of the car. Bagchi would return home after his night classes and would no doubt enquire after the patient.

We cleaned out his room and stowed his scant possessions in the car. We drove out of town on the road towards Nakhon Pathom and fifty miles down the road, turned onto a dirt track and into the jungle.

Ravina drove the car away while I went into the underbrush carrying a spade and found a spot to dig. In an hour I had made a hole deep enough to bury the body and perhaps to keep it from wild animals digging it up again. Ravina returned to the deserted dusty roadside and we carried the body to the shallow grave. We threw his stuff in and covered it up. Ravina helped me drag two fallen tree trunks over the grave and then we hurried back to the car.

It was only now that we examined the wallet. He had the equivalent of four hundred dollars in francs and in baht. There was a French identity card with his signature. Not a great haul.

Bagchi came up an hour or so after we had returned. 'How is the patient?'

'You worked a miracle for him,' I said. 'But not so good for us. We were out and he's cleared off without paying the rent.'

'Ah, this is what these bastard foreigners do. You should have taken at least half in advance.' He knew he was being ironic. He didn't display the slightest hint of suspecting what had happened. 'He might have gone out for a night on the town, a stingy binger, but he'll come back.'

'He took his toothbrush and the shampoo and cake of soap and the toilet roll, the son of a bitch,' said Ravina.

'That doesn't sound like a great night out on the town,' Bagchi said. 'Did he pay you for my medicines?'

'We called you, so we should pay you,' she said.

'On the house,' Bagchi said. 'Let us suffer these tribulations together – partners in loss, like the human race.'

✦

Ravina and I never talked about our experiments. She didn't discuss her past either. Her present was censored too. She would talk about films we went to see or wanted to see, discuss their stories endlessly. She called them 'pictures'. We saw Hitchcock dubbed in Thai. We watched any and everything. We went almost every afternoon. She liked to drink and to eat and to sit in coffee bars and look through glossy magazines. She wasn't interested in spending the money we were gathering. And yet when she looked at the glossy magazines she would look carefully through the real estate, in America, Europe – wherever that particular edition of the magazine originated. She would leaf through the fashion pages, through the household hints and recipes. She wasn't interested in the travel sections or the fast cars, but much more in the decor of country houses or urban flats.

She wouldn't ever be drawn out on her past.

'Did you go to a posh school?' I would ask. 'Did your mother teach you to cook?'

'My mother taught me to not answer stupid questions,' she would say. I would leave it be.

✦

But once it burst from her.

'We have no friends,' Ravina said.

People like us don't have friends, I thought to myself. And yet I knew that lumping us together was not right. We were not both the same. Ravina, somewhere inside that bravado, was someone who wanted friends, who wanted to live a boring bourgeois life and visit friends and call them to dinner and to treat me as her boyfriend and wait till someone, not me, proposed marriage and then make children. Of course she looked the opposite of all that and was proud of seeming so.

But life had taken this peculiar twist for her and she had fallen into the patterns of one kind of escape and then another and now into this experiment. She was the furthest one could think of from bourgeois fulfilment. She was a serial murderer.

It was different for me. The experiment seemed to be what my fate held. It was my natural way of being, even though the bourgeois-minded femme might have done it unwittingly herself and led me into it.

'Why do you need friends?' I asked. 'You have me here. And now we can never be separated, because I will be suspicious of you and you will be suspicious of me, so we will never let each other go.'

'Very different from Romeo and Juliet,' she said.

'They died in the end, didn't they? And anyway you always laugh and make fun when I say "Us" or anything like that.'

'I do. And we all die in the end, but we should have love before, like R and J,' she said.

'You can't have friends now,' I said. I knew that she had launched into this train of thought because from the experiment with Nikos, who was dying to be our friend – dying without being our friend – she knew that every potential friend was also a potential victim.

'But like dogs who meet in the park, we can wag our tails and play with the people we meet for a while and then we part and we never have plans to meet again. We must be like the dogs. Only feeble human beings plan to meet again for no reason,' I said.

'That's not exactly friendly,' she said.

I don't suppose Bagchi was what anyone would call a friend, but we pulled him in to become part of our experiments after the incident with Bruno.

Bruno was a Frenchman who followed Ravina on the beach where we were consciously parading her as bait. She was wearing her emerald-green bikini and walking along the water's edge when he spotted her and began to chat her up.

She brought him back to where I was sitting on a mat in my shorts. We made it plain that I was not her lover, but the person who shared her flat. She even told him I might be moving out and that she was looking for someone to share the place and the rent. It was as though he couldn't believe his luck. Here was a brown-skinned, long and black-haired creature of his dreams offering him a bed. Her bed? He was so puffed up with the idea of his own charm, that he thought that moving from his bed to hers would be like water flowing downhill – there was no other course.

Ceremony required that he come to see the flat before moving in, but he made it very clear to us that he wanted to take Ravina out to dinner that evening without my being there. He was going to work his charm on her.

And she, quite taken by that charm even as he moved his luggage from his hotel room into our flat, made rapid plans with him to go to Chiang Mai and show him the temples and the palaces in the next few days. They had to book plane tickets, they said, but the agency was closed so they went to dinner. Ravina took the packet of crystals from me before she left.

They came back from dinner and Bruno kissed her on the doorstep. He had made his conquest and they were going straight to bed and locking me out.

They went into Ravina's room and slammed the door behind them. After ten minutes, a naked Bruno ran out of Ravina's room and headed for his own bathroom. He saw me and must have panicked, searching his blown mind for an explanation, something to ameliorate the blow to his dignity.

'She is occupying her own bathroom,' he said.

'She takes ages to make ready for love,' I replied in French.

I could hear him throwing up. He flushed the toilet once and then again after an interval.

Ravina stuck her head out of her door. She was fully clothed. We heard Bruno come out of his bathroom and he emerged again, still naked. He looked shocked that Ravina was there and not in her bedroom.

'But you are changing. For me,' he said.

'Yes, sure,' Ravina said and Bruno, shouting an excuse in French, clutched his stomach and rushed back to the toilet. He couldn't explain his condition in English. He was reluctant to say he was sick and abandon his amorous trajectory. But the compulsion was too strong.

'Stomach spasms. That bloody food,' he said.

'I told you it might not be good, but you wanted to show me your favourite restaurant,' Ravina said. She spoke as though they had shared the tense banter of lovers for years.

He looked at Ravina. 'Come to your room in your bed,' he said. Then he rose slowly. The spasms must have passed.

'Not if you are going to fart and shit all over the place,' said Ravina.

'How do you know shit? Who said shit?' he grabbed her by the wrist.

I made the mistake of grinning. He caught a glimpse of my face and it turned him mad.

He started to drag Ravina to her bedroom. She broke loose, jerking her wrist from his firm hand. He tried to grab her again but he was cramping again. He crouched and clutched his stomach.

'My God. Oh God.'

He rushed to his own bathroom.

'Is blood, is blood,' he screamed. 'Ah, the death!'

Ravina nodded to me and got on the phone.

She made five or six dialling feints. She spoke and shouted down the phone. Why did she have to act for him? He wasn't going to report it. Was she acting for herself?

'I can't find a doctor,' she said. 'They won't come out.'

'Hell is now. I am dying,' Bruno screamed, loudly enough to have alerted the neighbouring flats.

'Call Bagchi from downstairs.'

'I am poison,' Bruno screamed. 'Is blood in my shit and hell in my belly.'

I didn't have to call Bagchi; he was halfway up the stairs. As luck would have it, no other tenants emerged from their doors.

'Some trouble, Govind?'

'We need you – a doctor.'

He followed me into the flat.

Ravina had managed to make Bruno lie down on his bed. He was clutching his gut and writhing on the bed.

Bagchi took one look at him, felt his pulse and went into the toilet, possibly to examine the toilet bowl. 'Bad gastro,' he said. 'Wait a minute.'

He went downstairs to his own flat and came back with a doctor's black bag. He pulled out an injection capsule, which he stuck with a needle and began to suck into the syringe.

'This will relax your spasms, young man, and maybe you can sleep. Another injection against the infection,' he said. He took out another injection and a clean syringe from its plastic packet and looked for the vein in Bruno's arm.

'You save me, doc,' Bruno said.

'You'll be okay,' Bagchi said.

Bruno curled up in a foetal position on the bed. Ravina covered him with the Indian cotton quilt we had on the bed.

'Sleep,' she said. 'Try.'

Outside the room, Bagchi said he couldn't write prescriptions, so we would have to get the antibiotics on the illegal market, which of course wasn't an issue. Any chemist would hand us antibiotics. He said we should also get some Flagyl.

Ravina poured him a drink. There was no sound from Bruno's room.

'I knocked him out,' Bagchi said.

When Bagchi left, I tiptoed into Bruno's room. I wanted to see whether the 'experiment' was going to be worth it or whether we should abandon it. His induced dysentery had been calmed by the drugs. When he woke up, we could pretend the overdose of sleeping pills were the prescribed medicines and complete the experiment, but now I wanted to know what we would get. I hated disposing off bodies and Bruno was a particularly muscular fellow. I would have to lug his body down the stairs and then wherever we were taking it. Ravina said she would go out and, for Bagchi's sake, in case there were any questions later, actually go and fetch some antibiotics from the night chemist's.

I crept into his room. He was fast asleep. I looked in his suitcase and searched all the compartments. Nothing much. A silver cross on a chain. Clothes. Then I remembered that his jacket and trousers were still in Ravina's room. His wallet would be too.

I found his wallet. It had a wad of baht. I found his French passport and was looking through it, when I heard Bruno say, 'So you are a thief.'

He was standing behind me in his underwear. He grabbed the passport from my hand and his eye fell on the wallet I had left on the bed. He took hold of me by the throat. 'Bastard,' he said. 'You rob a sick man?'

His grip on my throat choked me and I tried to get his hand off my gullet with both my hands, pulling his thumb and twisting it back. His other hand smacked me in a karate chop on the side of my neck and his knee went into my groin.

The pain that went through me must have given me a burst of strength or resistance, because I tore loose of his grip and tried to get away. He jumped on me from the back. The lamp in Ravina's room came crashing down and the wire pulled her table with a vase and flowers down as well.

I got out from under the brute and ran to the living room. I wanted to head out of the front door but again he jumped on me. In the struggle, we knocked over the television from its stand and as he came at me, I pushed it at him.

I ran into my room, slammed the door and bolted it. He started banging against it and then using his shoulder tried to break it open. Pushing the bed or anything else against the door wouldn't help. I had a few seconds before he would smash it down. I rushed to the window and climbed out. I dropped to the ledge outside, gripped it with my hands and swung down my body as gently as I could, pushing my feet against the wall to slow down the momentum of the drop. I was hanging from the ledge and, kicking away from the wall, when I let go. I fell to the ground and both my ankles twisted with the impact. It was agony. I couldn't get up.

Then the headlights of a car caught me where I had dropped and Ravina got out of the car.

'What happened?'

'He woke up, he's gone mad.'

Ravina grabbed a shovel from the side of the garage and I limped with one very damaged ankle behind her. We went to the front door, which was open. We went up the stairs and found Bagchi coming down them. Our door was ajar.

I struggled up the stairs.

The flat had been trashed. I was not sure if it was the damage we had done when we fought, till I saw that the glass of the crockery cupboard had been smashed and the paintings on the wall slashed with a knife.

'Is he…?' Ravina began.

'No, he's gone,' Bagchi said. 'My one and only patient has fled.'

We put things roughly back as they were. Bagchi looked a bit quizzical.

'You demanded double rent, eh?'

'No,' Ravina said. 'Nothing like that. He tried to rape me and I didn't want to play.'

Bagchi didn't look too convinced by that.

Ravina continued, 'We have to move out. And you have to move out in case he comes back with complaints to the police or army or whatever. And we shall go too, so we don't get questioned and lead them to you.'

'You think he'll come back? And why are we afraid?' asked Bagchi.

'He was vicious. He might. And God knows what he'll say – that you poisoned him?'

That was a stroke. Bagchi was getting convinced that he had to move. We knew we had to go. If he was interrogated the game would be up. Bruno would be sick elsewhere and they would analyse the poisons in his body and come looking for us. So we packed our things, put them in the car and headed out of Bangkok for the coast. Bagchi said goodbye and assured us he too would make his escape.

First we thought we'd go down the coast to the border, but Ravina argued that if Bruno had turned vindictive and complained to the authorities, we would be less conspicuous if we used the different passports we had acquired in our travels and experiments, and stayed in some crowded tourist resort.

8

'These fragments have we shored against our ruin,' Pradhan said, walking into the cell. Thhat was bent over his exercise book, writing, and made no reply 'When can I see the continuing masterpiece?' Pradhan asked, looking over his shoulder. 'When it's done,' replied Thhat.

'And all this is true? What about Kathmandu, will you tell the truth about that?'

'You have to wait and see,' Thhat said. 'I haven't got to that. I am still in Thailand, trying to remember everything, man.'

'This might assist your memory,' Pradhan said. He pulled out a folder with a dark brown cover from his shoulder bag.

'For me?'

'Yes. I got it for myself, out of curiosity, some years ago, and now that I have made your acquaintance, perhaps you should read it.'

Thhat opened the document.

'My God,' he said. 'Where did you get this?'

'I was a policeman, remember? I wrote to my counterparts in Holland. They had this on file together with other things, which you may not find as interesting. I think they got these letters from the Thai police. Maybe you can fill in the gaps.' Pradhan said. 'And I want to watch you as you read to see how cold-blooded you really are.'

✦

10th April

My dearest Jop,

I was completely, absolutely, flatteringly stunned and surprised by your letter and your proposal on the phone and yes, yes, yes, yes! I will say again, you have made me the happiest girl in Rotterdam. My flight: KLM 267, at 9.30 on Wednesday. And I shall not sleep through the night and I'll knit you a sweater like a good fiancée should. I still can't believe it. Why not two years ago, my darling?

You know breaking someone's heart is excused if you can stick it together again.

And no, it's not too late, I don't have anything serious to break off here.

xxxxx,

Desiree

17th April

Dearest Jop,

I didn't mean to fly into a temper. I just wanted to be close to you and I'm writing this because I can't say it on the phone. I am a stupid girl. I live for you, you know that, and I wanted us to lie together and to talk and to kiss and to sleep together and fuck and sleep again and wake up and fuck again and then for me to make breakfast and then come back to bed with you and have a shower together and then go to the beach and sip cocktails in a bar and talk and tell you my dreams and hear yours and I know the dinner with the Korean ambassador was important and I am really sorry. I messed it up.

And yes, you are right. A few days here, away from you, despite the ache in my heart will make me sober enough to have what you call a 'real relationship'. The hotel is great and the beach is lovely and please, please call me every day and every night – I am afraid to bother you at the office and even at home by calling you. The question is on my lips and leaping out of my heart, when do you want me back? I so want you.

Your,

Desiree

21st April

Dear Desiree,

What the hell was all that crying on the phone for? I didn't mean to put the phone down, but really you are wasting whatever time we have with this hysteria and nonsense. We agreed that with the Trade Agreements coming up I am completely snowed under. You hear the phone calls, which come all night. People are in different time zones and they call and out of consideration for you I haven't been answering the phone – I said let them wait till I wake up and get to the office tomorrow. Please be reasonable. You got a taste of life in the Service at high diplomatic season.

Try and understand who we are. In Bangkok, when you are back we shall buy you some evening clothes. There is a long list of dinners and occasions, including state functions, which I have to attend, some of which you must accompany me to as my fiancée.

Please, just relax and go out and make friends. We should fix a particular time of day to call. Let's say 6 in the evening every second day?

That should sort things out.

Lots of love and a x,

Jop

22nd April

My darling Jop,

Yes, it's good to hear your voice every day, but you sound so remote and you are so remote. I can't stand this any longer. I know that deep down you are still the person I fell in love with, the man who would be King and make me Queen of whatever and wherever, I don't mind… But I started thinking today maybe you need a break too, maybe the Ambassador knows that you work the hardest and longest and are the most dedicated and talented diplomat the country has and will give you a few days off to get married and go on a honeymoon. We should get away from this country for a while and maybe go to India and see the Taj Mahal and not have trade deals hanging over our heads and the Chinese delegation to look after and ALL THAT CRAP. Am going to call the Ambassador myself and tell him you brought me here on false pretences and show him the letter you wrote me before I came out. I am sure he fucks his wife and doesn't keep her in a resort three hundred miles away so he can have time to think.

Forgive me. I love you,

Desiree

23rd April

Desiree,

Don't write that stuff again. It's ungrateful and unnecessary. Yes, we will get married and of course I'll ask for short leave. We must discuss the dates.

Jop

STATEMENT OF JOP VAN DER KAMP, SECOND CONSUL, EMBASSY OF THE NETHERLANDS, APRIL 29, TO INSPECTOR PREM THANARAT: Address: 57 Tanao Rd., Bangkok. Desiree Bergen, my fiancée, is suspected missing since the 24th of April. She was last seen by the receptionist and the concierge of the Ocean Lodge Hotel, when she left the premises on the night of the 23rd of April and did not return. She has not been seen by anyone I know since then. She is unfamiliar with Thailand and is on a visit here to be married. Her permanent residence in Thailand is the same as above.

29th April WHY WHY WHY WHY
WHY????????????? Why call me, why destroy me?
Are you the devil?
?????????????????????????????????????

Desiree,

I don't know where you are or I would explain. I have gone through hell and am still in hell. Nothing matters to me now but to find you, and I am writing this in the hope that the person who delivered your last frantic note will call again. I have nothing but regret for what I have become. Please, please, please, let me send you back to Holland where you can forget that I or the nightmare ever existed…

✦

'That note never got to her?' Pradhan asked

'I don't know what you mean,' Thhat replied.

'Jop Van Der Kamp insisted in his statement that the man who delivered her first note came again and delivered a second one, typed, and in exchange took away the letter he had written. But it didn't go to her. It was mysteriously sent to the Bangkok police. After she died.'

'Could be.'

'I don't understand what you have to hide now. You said you'd come clean,' Pradhan said. He looked at Thhat.

'I did,' Thhat said.

'So did you send all these letters, at least the ones you could gather from her side, to the police?'

'Yes.'

'To strengthen the case for the suicide theory?'

'The suicide theory. Or for the murder option – by the boy.'

'The boy didn't kill her,' Pradhan said.

'He was a suspect,' said Thhat.

'That's not what I asked. Did he kill her?'

'No. He took one shot and he missed and then he ran. He bought the gun.'

'You showed him where to buy the gun?' Pradhan asked.

'Yes.'

'Tell me. The whole thing. How it happened. Have you already written it?'

'I am way past that incident. I'll tell you. I came across her on the beach. She looked as if she was going to wade into the water and go as far as she could and never come back. I could spot the desperation, the weariness with the world, the loss of the will to live. I waded in after her, called out to her, swam out, took her by the hand and dragged her to waist-high water where she could stand. We stood exhausted, both of us, and I didn't let go of her hand and pulled her to shore and she was crying all the time.

'Remember, Ravina and I were on the run. Our experiments in Bangkok had ended and we were thinking of making a getaway, but we needed some more money. I swear I only meant to save the girl. My eye didn't fall on her pouch with the money till I had brought her out and helped her dry herself. I got her talking. She said she was fated to die. I told her she wasn't, that I could read palms and could I look at hers. She held her palm out and I told her, "There you go, it isn't your day to die."

'She laughed.

'"But you will die one day," I said. I put her hand to my nose. "Yeah, I can smell it. You smell human, you are bound to die one day. That's it."

'That made her smile.

'"You will talk to a fascinating stranger today," I told her. And she pulled her hand away but agreed to come for a drink.

'I told her she had had bad man trouble and she said she had. After three drinks, it all came out. She said talking to a stranger was easy. She had come to Thailand to marry Jop. They had known each other at university and though they had never slept together, she had gone out with him and enjoyed a deep intellectual relationship with him. She was sure she wanted to marry him, but he seemed nervous of commitment and never asked. Then he was recruited by the Dutch foreign service and sent to Thailand.

'He was very ambitious and she thought she had lost him to his ambition. So, like the letter said, she was blown out of her mind when he wrote saying he wanted to marry her. She came to Thailand full of romantic dreams. But she seemed to do everything wrong and get on his nerves and she felt inadequate and got hysterical and was so disappointed she started behaving badly at a diplomatic function. He sent her away.

'She couldn't take it any longer and didn't want this relationship to be monitored by remote control, living in a tourist resort. He didn't seem to want her back in Bangkok, but one night she defiantly went back, not letting him know. She got to their flat at night. She had a key and let herself in. She heard noises and went to the bedroom and found him in bed with the boy Sarin.

'She ran out of the house. She got to the coast and didn't go back to her hotel. She walked several miles up the coast, thinking, crying, hating, forgiving, hoping and all the time dying inside. I didn't kill her, she was already dying inside.

'Then she stayed in my hut. She had a lot of money that Jop had given her, in that pouch. And of course, that gave us ideas. Ravina had done the disappearing trick and moved into a hotel and I stayed in the beach hut with Desiree. I told you she was dying inside. If I had asked her for the money, she would have handed it to me. But that's not the way we operate. People who give you things can change their mind. Getting has to be final.'

'It's only the outside that counts in law, Thhat. If you killed her on the outside, you killed her. The statement to the inquest was in the package,' Pradhan said.

STATEMENT OF JOP VAN DER KAMP
BEFORE THE CORONER, BANGKOK, MAY 24:

I met Sarin in a beach bar when I first came to Thailand to take up my position in the embassy as second consul. Yes, I was fully aware that he was twelve years old. Yes, you can call it love. Yes, I admit I proposed marriage to Desiree as a cover, but not deliberately and cynically. I hoped my desires would change. I was actually ashamed of the business with Sarin. It was getting dangerous for my career and my social life. I met Desiree in Amsterdam and had then known her for two or three years and we were close. I met her in Amsterdam, and in Paris we became good friends but nothing more. In order to get on in the foreign service I needed a wife, not a young Thai boy companion. But as soon as she came here, I realized I had made a mistake, one that I couldn't admit to or retract. What was I doing? How could I be unfaithful to Sarin now that she was here? She started showing her frustration with me because I had no feelings, sexual or emotional, towards her, only guilt that I had messed up this girl's life through the needs of my ambition. No, morality was not what bothered me. It was that I found her body undesirable. I hadn't been with a woman before and thought at first I could get over it, but our urges are stronger than us and believe me they are predetermined by our genes or our blood. I liked her in every way, except naked and close. She sensed it and I pleaded tiredness and busyness. She wanted contact and reassurance but I couldn't even bring myself to give her that.

(The witness breaks down and the Coroner calls for a recess. The inquest resumes after ten minutes.)

She appeared without warning. I thought she was away at a resort where I had sent her but she stole back to Bangkok and surprised me. She ran into the night when she found me in bed with Sarin. I went after her. I went to the taxi rank, to the railway station. Nothing. Sarin was waiting for me when I returned at dawn. He began accusing me. I had been false to him and had promised that we would go to Europe and live a life there together. Yes, I had said those things. He said he would kill himself. I hadn't told

him about Desiree. I thought he would find out and
go away. I thought all men with young boys promised
them these things and the boys were mature enough
to understand that it was just the talk of foreplay. But
no! Sarin said he wanted to marry me. He would kill
this girl, he would stab her, shoot her, drown her – and
we could be rid of her and together again.

*(Disturbance in the public gallery. Coroner calls for
silence.)*

The police know; everyone knows he didn't do it. Yes,
the gun has been traced to him because he bought it
with the help of the mystery man…

*(The Coroner interrupts Mr Van Der Kamp, saying this is
not what he is here for; others will determine the cause of
death. He should give competent evidence and that is all.)*

I am sorry, sir. I am in a state of complete despair,
breakdown. She is dead and my career is finished.

(Witness breaks down again.)

'So why didn't the inquest conclude it was suicide?' Pradhan
asked.

'My stupidity,' Thhat said.

'You mean you should have waited till she was nice and
ready to actually do it? Surely it wasn't far away.'

'She wouldn't have done it. People commit suicide to t
ake revenge on someone or on the world. She was coming
to the conclusion that Jop and the world weren't worth it.
And then the boy Sarin appeared. Furious, crying, vowing
revenge.'

'And you showed him where to get the gun?' Pradhan asked.

Thhat looked at the policeman in the face to see if he was adding to what he already knew because this wasn't a confession, the facts were known.

'And you told him where the girl would be and when she would be alone?' Pradhan continued.

'Yes, the beach. A little strip of sand hidden behind a cliff. You had to wade out to sea and come back through the shoulder of the cliff to find it. It was a secret place where she'd take the sun in a bikini.'

'So you told him where she'd be and led him there. But when he came back to kill her, he couldn't do it, so he dropped the gun and ran?' Pradhan asked.

'Exactly.'

'And then… She died of a gun wound.'

'Yes.'

'So how did they get you?'

'She was left-handed. I didn't realize. The bullet entered her head from the right temple and came out under her left ear. It would be very difficult for a left-handed person to hold the gun to the right temple and shoot inwards to the head.'

'And they pronounced it murder and got to you?'

'Just bad luck, old man. The boy Sarin led them to me. This son of a bitch miser Jop had noted down the number of every big bank note he gave to Desiree, and of course I was carrying these and tried to change them into Indian rupees. They had an alert on the numbers. They took me in for murder. This fellow Inspector Prem started looking into the other deaths also.'

'How many?'

'Eleven murders, old man. A bit of an exaggeration, but the police don't care.'

Pradhan smiled. 'So how many are you owning up to?'

'I don't know, but it was not eleven. They just have unsolved cases they want to pin on innocent people, you know.'

'You are so diligent about the truth of numbers, Johnson Thhat. So they tried you?'

'Inspector Prem, very honest man, wouldn't take a bribe. I offered him diamonds. He said blood will have blood and they put me in front of a military tribunal and would have sentenced me to death by firing squad. By that time they had brought witnesses from everywhere, mostly false.'

'But the cases, the murders, were true. How many of them were real Bikini Murders, as the press started calling them?'

'A bastard American journalist in Thailand. Not many. It was just sensationalism, man, cheap tricks to sell papers. As I told you, old man, if you play ball I will tell you...'

'When you got away free the whole world knew about it. It was reported in the Nepalese papers. I have the cutting.'

'What did they say?'

'The old Sydney Carton treatment, from *A Tale of Two Cities*, or was it *The Count of Monte Cristo*? I can't remember. I brought it for you,' said Pradhan, taking out a yellowing newspaper clipping from his pocket.

BEAST BECOMES PRIEST SERIAL KILLER
Escapes Justice in Bangkok

Johnson Thhat, notorious Bikini Murderer convicted of eleven murders and about to be sentenced to death by firing squad by a Thai military justice tribunal, has escaped from his prison in Bangkok by impersonating a Buddhist monk.

A friend of Thhat, posing as a Buddhist monk in dark brown robes and with a shaven head was admitted by police to Thhat's cell on the day before his sentencing. The friend exchanged clothes with Thhat and, pretending to give him a lesson in final meditation, shaved his head to resemble himself. Thhat left the jail dressed as a monk while the friend remained behind, ready to take the consequences of assisting Johnson Thhat to escape but obviously not facing the death penalty.

It is one of a series of bold impersonations carried out by the notorious Thhat who is half-Indian and half-Vietnamese by birth…

'When I read that I was just a young police officer. I said to myself that my path will cross that of this fellow one day,' said Pradhan.

'You believe in fate and all this?'

'No. I believe in deduction and detection. I knew that you preyed on backpackers and wanderers in search of what they think in the West is spiritual truth. And I knew there were thousands of those people headed this way, to Nepal, in search of some bullshit dream. And I knew if there was a flood of them, the sharks would come in on the flood. And maybe you'd be among them. And I was right. You were.'

'I don't know about that, old man. You believed the newspaper story, eh? About shaving my head and coming out of prison and walking free as a monk.'

'That's what you did. I admired you for it.'

'Because you're an idiot. Of course, that's what I did. The policeman who let me out of the jail needed a story and that was it. Things don't work like that in real life, my friend. You just said it was some fellow in *A Tale of Two Cities*. But those two cities weren't Bangkok and Kathmandu. Here you have to pay. I didn't fool the policeman. The Chinese Triads, under instructions from my father, paid them off. In diamonds. They told me to ask for a priest and one came in and they suggested shaving my head themselves – the police – they brought hot water in a bowl and two razors and took the shaved hair away on a newspaper. And I did wear the robes and walk out past the police receptionist and then ran down the road. A car was provided for me, again with my father paying heavy money, man. That's how real life works. Not the stuff in books, fooling people with disguises. These were diamonds that came out of a Nigerian smuggler's arse. Five Thai cops were paid off and the rest knew what had happened but they had to stick to the story we planted about the miraculous disguise and escape.'

'I didn't know you'd turn up this soon. I had memorized your features and after the murder in Kathmandu I was sure this had the hallmark of the killer I had read about. I sent for the details of the Thai police reports even before you got here.'

'That's very disturbing. I came for a holiday, you know,' Thhat said.

'Don't make me laugh. Murderers don't take holidays.'

'I heard the policemen were the stupidest in the world – a good place to live.'

'Tell me, Thhat, if you had all these diamonds to bribe these policemen, why did you need to kill this Dutch girl. How much did you get from her anyway?' Pradhan asked.

'I had to give the diamonds away. My father bailed me out. I didn't know whether he wanted me out so he could hire me or kill me.'

'But he did bail you out? And he didn't kill you?'

'Ravina. She told him she would go back if he helped me to get out. And he is a sentimental fool. He said he could only be sure of her loyalty if she went back while I was still alive, not if I was dead and she had no alternative.'

'So she went with him?'

'She was bullshitting him. Yes, she went and when I got to Kathmandu, she got in touch. My father is a cool customer, but he allows his feelings to dominate. Listen, Pradhan, I can still get in touch with my father. He can arrange something for you if you want to help me out.'

'First of all, I can't and then, Thhat, you ought to realize that you can only bribe people who want or need something out of life. I am old, I need nothing, I am becoming the Buddha and soon you as a Buddhist can worship me and forget about trying to buy me.'

'I know what you mean. That's good. So do it for friendship.'

Pradhan ignored the remark. 'And the story is convincing as a confession, so far, but I looked at the next chapter and you've left something out, haven't you?'

'I gave you the whole thing,' Thhat said.

'No, all the chapters after this one are renumbered. One missing. Why?'

'You are the policeman.'

'Because it contains the bit about Kathmandu, about Smolinsky and her murder?'

'Maybe.'

'What did you do with the paper?'

'I ate it. Very short chapter,' Thhat said and smiled.

Pradhan did not know whether to believe him or not.

'Put it this way,' Thhat continued, still smiling, 'I am not writing it down, but I will satisfy your curiosity.'

'Your accomplice?'

'Yes, Bagchi. He is the real Bikini Murderer, you know…'

9

About twenty miles from Pattaya along the coast, some Indian fakirs and fakes had set up a shop to sell spiritual nonsense to foreigners who wanted to be enlightened. They were making good money, man, off all the rich and stupid Americans and other westerners.

They wore beards and beads and long white shirts, all following some fellow from Madras who called himself Guru Satdev. I met some of them in a bar in Pattaya market – they didn't mind drinking. One of the guys said to me how every minute of the day, every second, he was meditating even when he was talking to me. He gave me a lecture about all humans wasting their potential. They said this fellow was opening up their minds and spirits. I pretended to be so interested, man. I got the address. I could make out they had cash. So in a few days I went along to check this hustle out – and found that that was not all that their guru was opening up.

I got to their ashram by bus and stayed in a nearby shack on the beach. I tried to visit their ashram and get in on the meditation lessons but whatever those guys said, they wouldn't let me into the ashram because the ashram security fellows at the gate said they could see 'from my vibes' that I was a sex pervert and wanted to get in there to meet white girls. It made me laugh, man. But you and I know Indian guys and Thai guys like that, who want to pick up meditation girls.

Then see the luck, eh? As I was turning to go away, I met this young American girl who was giving out leaflets saying the guru had fucked her in every hole of her body and all this rubbish. I read her leaflet and then approached her. She was crying and shouting to nobody, like a mad woman. The guys at the gate weren't even listening. But I got talking to her and then when they shut the gate and there were no more people to give leaflets to, I said we should go to the beach and she could tell me the story. She came with me. Her name was Poco. I think she might have had Red Indian blood, Native American kind of.

She drank milk in the bar. She told me she had no place to stay now because they kicked her out of the ashram when she started to cause trouble. The guru had used her as a girlfriend saying he would release her 'kundalini' and all this mumbo-jumbo talk. She had good times with him for a few days, she said, and then he got tired of her and moved on to some Danish girl or Australian man or someone.

Poco hadn't conquered her ego with meditation by that time so she started making a big scene and a fuss and abusing the guru so they threw her out. She was sleeping on the beach, she said, and then she told me something she shouldn't have – she wanted to get back into the ashram because her money was hidden there. Nobody knew it but she had thousands of dollars in American Express travellers' cheques hidden in the large hollow false heels of some shoes she had left with her belongings in the ashram.

I asked her to come to Pattaya with me that evening. By that time we were walking hand in hand down the beaches. She said she wanted to borrow money from me and write some more leaflets and expose the guru. I said we could have the leaflets typed and printed at my hotel. Of course she didn't want to sleep on the beach that night and she took the bus back with me to Pattaya.

Ravina had gone back to Bangkok. At least that's where she said she was going, but I think she had gone to India to negotiate something with my father. Poco stayed with me and we went everywhere together for a few days. I told her I was a diamond merchant and I was waiting for a big shipment to reach Bangkok so I was spending my time in Pattaya. I found out a lot of details from her about how she had been travelling in India and Thailand and how her father sent her money when she phoned him. She told me about the ashram and how she had been hypnotized by the guru and believed everything he said.

That was when this idiot Bagchi found me. He was sitting on a bench outside my hotel, man. He gave me a scare. He said he was desperate and could I lend him some money, he needed it for drugs and equipment. He had moved to Pattaya and was now lending his freelance services to a private clinic as an abortionist, but they wanted him to carry his own equipment and he had left it all in Bangkok. You see, he didn't want to travel in a bus with medical equipment. He was scared the police would search him and identify him as a doctor or a medical man. He said he wanted me to pay for the equipment and keep it with me. Just one case of stuff.

That, my friend, gave me the idea. Of course. A new experiment. This time with abortions.

I made an excuse to Poco and caught the bus to the ashram. I told the fellows at the gate that I was Poco's fiancé and that their guru had made her pregnant and we were carrying out blood tests and we would launch a paternity case against him.

There were some girls at the gate, and they just looked at me with wide eyes. They said nothing to me but one of them went inside to consult and then this older American guy came out. He said his name was Swami. He was wearing their uniform of flowing white kurta and a long beard.

'What you say is impossible,' he said. 'Guru Satdev has retentive powers and never expends his energy into a woman.'

'The blood tests will prove what he expends,' I said. 'And my fiancée Poco and I will get a court order. We will also go to the American embassy and apply for a passport for the baby. Her father is rich and influential, you know that.'

He looked very worried. He asked me if I could give him half an hour to consult further.

I said he should bring out all of Poco's possessions.

He went back into the ashram.

I returned an hour later to find Swami waiting for me at the gate with another white guy. They looked relieved to see me. Swami handed me a suitcase. 'All her things, I think,' he said.

I knelt by the roadside and opened it. There were three pairs of shoes, two of them with high heels. Yes, this must be the payload. I shut the suitcase again.

'Can we talk to Poco?' asked the other guy.

'No, you talk to me. Look, I am marrying this girl. I love her. I don't want her to have some bastard's baby. I can come to some arrangement with your guru or your ashram.'

The two of them looked at each other as though this was what they expected from me.

'Think about it. Would you want to start your marriage this way? Even if we sue the ashram and get millions of dollars from you, what kind of life will I have bringing up the child of some fraud? What would we say to the child?'

They again exchanged glances.

'He doesn't have millions of dollars,' Swami said.

'Why do you say that? I haven't even started bargaining yet,' I said, grinning.

'What do you propose?'

'That we come to some arrangement and then I will go back and persuade her to have an abortion straight away. You will have proof of it. Look, her passport.' I showed them the passport. 'Then you will never hear from us again.'

The other guy was obviously in charge. 'How much?' he asked.

'Ten thousand.'

He hesitated. 'Six. Three now, three with the proof of the termination.'

'Four each way,' I said, and put out my hand to seal the deal, but he ignored it.

'And you say nothing to anyone about anything and neither does Poco?'

'That is part of it. I can sign a contract if you like.'

Swami looked at me as though to say any contract I signed would be beneath contempt. They both clearly thought I was a worm, but they had brought the money.

I took the money and the suitcase to Pattaya. Poco asked me how I had got hold of it and I told her I had posed as her fiancé and even showed her her passport. She was curious about who packed the case and who delivered it to me at the gate. She seemed excited. I was her hero. She unscrewed the heels of the shoe and found the traveller's cheques intact. She would countersign them and withdraw the money. She wouldn't have to phone 'Pappy' for more.

I gave some of my money to Bagchi and he gave me a pill to dissolve in Poco's food or drink to make her miss a period.

Two weeks later she approached me with a very serious expression. She said she had missed a period and perhaps she was pregnant.

We were lovers and it was perfectly possible that she could have been carrying my child, but that was not a chance I was willing to take. Her pregnancy test had to show up positive whether she was carrying my child or not.

I took her to the clinic from which Bagchi operated. It was a back room in a small hotel. Neither he nor I gave her any indication that we knew each other. I said he had been recommended by a friend.

Bagchi took a urine sample, did some tests by the sink and turned to Poco and told her that she was definitely pregnant.

She turned pale. Her lips turned thin and white.

'I can't afford to have the baby at this point either,' I said.

'I never asked you,' she snapped. 'You think I'd have your child? You fucking lied to me. You said you'd been snipped.'

'Why can't I lie to you? Are you a goddess or something?' I said and turned to Bagchi. 'Are you sure, doctor?'

'The tests don't lie,' he said.

'But women do. You've been sleeping with someone else or maybe you were pregnant before we met,' I said.

She made a quick mental calculation. 'That's impossible. You are a bastard! I fucking hate you!'

It was working.

I shrugged. 'I'll pay for it,' I said.

'That's not the question, you snake,' she said and slapped me hard.

I stood there holding my cheek and Bagchi intervened. 'Look, I can recommend a chemical termination. I can give you an oral dose and it will, with any luck, clear out, like a late period.'

'Yes,' she said. 'I don't want anyone's filthy hands or filthy gloves inside me.' She wanted to sound tough but she just sounded scared.

'My sweetheart, I'll do whatever...' I started to say.

'All I want you to do is fuck off. Hit the road, Jack! I don't want to see your fucking chinky face again, you son of a bitch.'

I shrugged again.

Bagchi went and got his pills. He told her how she was to take them and in what sequence. 'Stay active, don't sleep or lounge about. Go for a run, swim, do something vigorous until you begin to bleed,' he said.

I walked with her to our hotel room.

Without a word, she went into the bathroom. She came out wearing her bikini and carrying a towel.

'Do you want me to go with you to the beach?' I asked.

She didn't answer, just walked out.

I followed her to the beach. Bagchi had told me what might happen.

Poco was swimming some way from the shore while I waded in the shallows. Then she called out to me. 'Johnson, cramps…please help!' she shouted.

I swam out to her and helped her to the beach. We spread both towels. There were a few people about but at some distance from us. They couldn't have seen what was going on. She lay down holding her stomach and the blood was trickling out of the sides of her bikini bottom down her thighs. 'A whole fucking tennis-ball-like thing fell out,' she said.

'It's expected,' I said. 'Can you make it to the hotel?'

She was convulsed with pain and could hardly speak. 'C…cramp… inside…' she stammered.

'I'll get the doctor, just wait and lie quietly,' I said and ran. I got to the hotel room and took her money and my clothes. Bagchi was waiting for me in a hired car downstairs. We went to Bangkok and decided to split.

When they found her the next morning on the beach, some distance from where I had left her, she was dead. The newspaper reports said that the girl who had died of internal bleeding on the beach was wearing a bikini.

But it was only after the Desiree business that the journalists really picked up the bikini thing and began that nonsense.

✦

'So it was Bagchi's medicine and your little plot that killed her?'

'Since she was American they did very thorough tests on her. And they found out she had been given a heavy dose of something to make her bleed to death but at that time nobody connected her with me at all.'

'Was she pregnant with your child, then, Thhat?' Pradhan asked.

For once, Thhat's eyes flickered. 'How do I know?'

'Didn't you ask Bagchi?'

'No. Why would I want to know?'

'So you went back to the ashram and claimed the rest of your money?'

'Are you mad? They must have read about it but kept very quiet because they didn't want any murder scandal touching their holy hoax. Later on, after they captured me for the Desiree thing, they started asking about Poco also.'

'And Bagchi?'

'He disappeared. From Thailand at least.'

'And then you bribed your way and came to India?'

'When I got away from Bangkok myself, I went again to Bombay. I didn't call my father or Ravina. I swear I had given up the experiments. I thought I would go to tourist places, because of my face, you know. People may recognize me, but in places where there were hippies and travellers, people wouldn't notice. I grew my hair long, man, and I went up to the mountains to Simla, where there were thousands of tourists. I thought I could lose myself in the crowd. I met people every day and in those days the hippies, everyone treated everyone like a friend and brother, you know. All fake, but the idea was that you could go up to anyone and ask for a cigarette or food or sometimes even for money, as long as you looked like them and called them "brother" or something.

'I found out after a few weeks there that the hippies had a favourite doctor who was handing out LSD and marijuana and uppers and downers on prescription. I had a feeling about this doctor and one day I went in to meet him with some "brothers" I had picked up. You guessed it. It was Bagchi.

'He took me to his room and told me he was prospering there. He used to go to Delhi every now and then to pick up supplies. There was no need to do anything to these fools, they volunteered vast sums of money for his concoctions.

'But he got into trouble when one of his clients overdosed and the police came looking for him.

'He phoned me to tell me where his money was hidden. He couldn't wait a minute longer in Simla, he said, and I was the only one he could trust. I was to meet him in Delhi with the money.'

'A lot of money?' Pradhan asked.

'Huge. Buried in the garden of his dispensary in plastic bags.'

'So why couldn't you take it and run?'

'He blackmailed me. He said he would phone the police and tell them who I was.'

'So you helped him out?'

'Yes. It was his idea to come to Kathmandu.'

'You came together and because selling drugs had become risky you started the murders again?'

'I didn't say that, but I will tell you that he was here and he was fucking your Mary Ann Smolinsky, whom he picked up in a bar. He is the bloody Bikini freak!'

Pradhan searched Thhat's face, now lit up with a serene smile, like a Buddha statue.

'Do you play blackjack, Inspector?' asked Thhat.

'No, but I know the game. Eleven in Thailand – that we know of. Mary Ann makes twelve, so nine to go, and then you have to stop,' Pradhan paused, then continued, 'or, as in blackjack, you go bust.'

10

Now I was back in Delhi. Ravina came to join me. She had told my father she was travelling on his gem business and sure enough she got in touch with some fellows in the capital. But she was with me. Maybe he was suspicious but didn't ask.

We were moving as a French couple on false passports. We decided to go to the Taj Mahal. Have you been? Always a sea of coaches and taxis, hundreds of them.

We were there looking for opportunities, man, not for romance, and we spotted this coach full of French tourists. We could hear their chatter and we followed them into the courtyard in front of the Taj where there were all these touts and fraud jewellers.

The Frenchmen and girls, mostly in their twenties, were all heading for these. There must have been sixty of them on that coach. A group of them headed straight for the Pathans who were selling fake gems. I knew the Pathan game. A notorious network that preyed on tourists and idiots, dodgy guys. And dangerous. If you interfered, they could knife you.

I hung around till the Pathans were about to make a kill with the Frenchies, and the money was being counted.

'These are fake gems,' I said in French. 'Don't fall for it, my friends.'

One of the Frenchmen came over to talk to me. The transaction was halted. 'You speak French?' he asked in English.

'So what were you hearing, Greek?' I said.

'Pardon,' he said. 'It's unexpected in India, huh?'

'Don't touch the stuff. The gems will turn to dust in your hands. They will show you one or two genuine ones and sell the company fifty duds.'

'Shit. Who are you?'

'Just a friend. I was brought up in Paris. If you want gems, I can direct you to genuine cut-price traders in Delhi. You are going back to Delhi?'

'How did you know?'

'The sign on your coach, my friend. It's a Delhi hire firm.'

'Of course.'

He turned to his friends and said they shouldn't deal with those guys. The Pathans began to glare and shouted 'sister-fucker, daughter-fucker' at me.

'Call yourself Mussalmans?' I shouted back in Hindi. My few months in India had revived the language I had learned as a child. 'Your souls are damned. Now fuck off or I'll follow you all day and warn your customers off. And I know the head of police and I'll have you deported back to Pakistan. Fucking crooks.'

The Pathans conferred among themselves and then slunk away to look for other victims.

The French girls giggled.

'You are a hero,' one of them said.

'My hero,' Ravina said, as though she was naturally possessive.

'Of course, yours,' the girl said in French. 'For now! I can claim him later.'

The others laughed.

The young man who had heeded my warning came up to me. 'We've only got tonight. We fly back tomorrow morning. Your gem dealer, can he come to our hotel later?'

'I will see about that, mon ami. Which hotel are you in?'

'The Taj Mahal. We are only one night in Delhi. It's very expensive.'

'Of course it is. With sixty of you, they should charge you one third of the price.'

'Ah, I wish. How to find such a place? We would love to save the money and stay a few days more and shop in Delhi.'

'Which airline are you on?'

'Air France.'

'I know a lot of travel agents, they will change your tickets. And I can save you your hotel charges. Look, I will phone from somewhere and book a whole hotel for you. How many people?'

'We need thirty rooms, or thirty-one.'

'You go and see the building and come back here, I will arrange it all and I will free you from the Taj also. You didn't leave a deposit?'

'No, the French embassy checked us in, they trust them.'

'They are rip-off merchants, man, don't feel guilty about them. They are rich like fuck. They won't go empty.'

'You have descended from Valhalla.'

'No. From the Fifteenth Arrondissement.'

He left smiling. I looked for a shop with a phone and called Santosh, the owner of the hotel that we were staying in. It was in Paharganj, the old part of the city, a three-star joint with a lot of hippies and Indian travellers coming and going. It was called the Kohinoor.

'Santosh, this is Mr Deauville. I got you a big fat deal. I want thirty rooms for the night.'

'I might have ten rooms spare, but then again I might not. The Bombay train comes in at seven,' he said.

'Look, I know your dirty clients barely pay you anything. Just kick twenty of the freeloading hippies out.'

He hesitated for a moment. 'Tell them they can move to the Paradise and other backpacker joints,' I said. 'You can't miss this opportunity. And listen, Santosh, I don't even want a cut. I am doing this as a favour to you. And they will buy plenty of booze. I'll take a cut from the profits of the bar. But one thing, I am checking out tonight and as a return favour you must never tell anyone that I and Madame Deauville were here. Okay?'

'Whatever you say, boss.'

'I am bringing them by late evening, early night. Keep some dinner ready.'

The next thing to do was to find some gems. I asked Ravina if she would phone my father and ask him to send some of his traders or goons round.

'You call him,' she said. 'He loves you.'

'You're the one in touch with him.'

She shook her head.

'You are saying you haven't called him since we came to India?'

'I haven't said it, but it's true. Tell him we don't sleep together.'

I waited for my call to Bombay to come through. The old man was on the phone.

'It's Govind,' I said.

'Where are you?' he asked. 'In India?'

'Yes. Delhi. Look, Papa, I am sorry if there's been any misunderstanding, but you know I thought I ought to prove myself to you. Do something myself and then come to you.'

'You are being a child,' he said. 'I had so many plans for you. You and that she-devil, you just disappeared.'

There was a pause.

'She is nothing to me, Papa, a business partner,' I said.

'Govind, Govind, let's talk about other things. Let her go to hell. You know, I wanted you to be rich, my money is your money. Maybe money can't buy you love, but it can buy you freedom.'

'Maybe,' I said. I didn't want to hear any more platitudes from him.

'Not maybe. If you can, you must come back and spend some time with me.'

'You have other sons, other families,' I said.

'They are not important. Look, if a labourer had money he wouldn't be tied to his work, would he? If a wife had money, she wouldn't be tied to her husband and household, she would be free. I am not tied to any family. I can give them a roof over their heads and enough money and so I am free.'

'Is that why your other children hate you?' I asked.

He didn't reply for a few seconds.

'The bitch has been talking to you? You know she means

nothing to me. You can use her. You have my permission, Govind.'

'Thanks, Papa, but that's not the favour I called for.'

I told him what I wanted. He said he'd send the men over.

'Good, good, good, now we can be partners. I have longed for this day of reuniting in business,' he said. 'I will look after you, never doubt that.'

After I rang off, I dialled the Taj, put on a French accent and said I was from the embassy. I then said the coach of the French party for whom we had booked had crashed and several people were dead and several more were injured and obviously we were cancelling the booking. The manager came on the phone and said he was very sorry and of course he understood and was there anything he could do to help? I said we were attending to everything and obviously I had no time, I had to call Paris. He said again that he was very sorry and hung up.

When the Frenchies came back from their sightseeing trip, their eyes misty and their film exhausted, the fellow who was their leader came up to me.

'You have rooms at the Kohinoor,' I said.

'I don't mind if it's the Gorilla,' he said. 'How much?'

'Quarter of what you pay at the Taj and they are charging you as if you are Indians and not foreigners. I have influence there. And the gem dealers are coming. I have cancelled the Taj. There's nothing I could do about the plane tickets. They won't change a block booking.'

'Ah! I knew that. Tant pis!' he said.

He was happy.

Ravina and I rode back to Delhi on their coach and directed them to the hotel through the crowded streets of

Old Delhi. They told us they were all engineers who had graduated together and were having a reunion after a few years of working. They loved Delhi architecture, they said, and wished that the French had fought harder and not allowed the fucking British to colonize India. They would have liked to own all this, they said.

As we were on the road, I noticed two motorcycles staying pretty parallel to our coach as we travelled from Agra on the highway to Delhi. They would go ahead and then stop or fall back and follow again. It was something my eye and brain registered but not something I thought about at the time. I just noted the bikes. I should have paid more attention.

When we got to the Kohinoor, the French party got out and took their luggage to their rooms. Santosh had his whole staff in attendance and they had changed their uniforms and were wearing laundered, crisp shirts. Santosh was ready for a big haul of cash and was laying it on.

Ravina and I waited in the bar for the party to come down from their respective rooms in this warren of a hotel and meet the gem dealers who had already arrived – five men, dressed in old bania fashion with the traditional moneylenders' black felt cap and carrying velveteen gem cases.

In the bar, I asked Santosh's barman to set up glasses of whisky, rum, vodka and gin. The drinks would be free, I said. I was going to pay for the first few rounds in celebration of my new friendship and new gem business.

The Frenchies came down and we started the gem exhibition. The dealers spread their boxes out on the billiards table in the room next to the bar and began their sales patter. The Frenchies crowded round and Ravina and I noted who was buying what. The gems were genuine and very reasonably priced, much lower than anything they would have seen anywhere else in India, and they were going fast. Several of the guys bought diamonds, set and unset, and the girls bought necklaces.

And the drinking started. The drinks that Ravina and I had prepared were handed round. She asked each of them what they would have and what they would like it mixed with. The bar, I announced, would shut at twelve. They would, we hoped, trickle up to their rooms after that to get something of a night's sleep before catching their plane back to France the next morning.

We had timed the doses so that they would be unshakeably, unwakeably asleep between one and two o'clock. They may have woken up with headaches later in the morning and they would put this down to the free, filthy Indian booze.

And then the guys on the motorcycles came in. They wore scarves around their faces like masks, to shield them from the wind while riding, and now these hung loose from their shoulders. The four Pathans. They looked me over. They greeted some of the Frenchies as though they were long-lost friends and indicated that they should go out into the reception area and see what they had brought them as presents.

They spoke in Urdu, but I understood them. Santosh certainly did. And now there was shouting and arguing from the reception area outside. Santosh hurried out, following six or eight of the Frenchmen. I followed them to see what was going on.

In the reception hall were twelve painted prostitutes, dark-skinned girls in gaudy skirts with their faces painted white and their lips bright red, with spots of pink on their dark cheeks over the white powdery paint which made them look like the ghosts of circus clowns. Some of them had high foreheads and hairlines, like men, and looked square-jawed like eunuchs. They were smiling at the Frenchmen and some of them were making bold to approach them and caress their cheeks to demonstrate that they were admiring and willing. The receptionist and his assistant stood by helplessly. They had resisted the entry of the girls into the Kohinoor but the Pathans had forced them in, saying the guests had called for them.

'You can't indulge in these things in this hotel,' Santosh said, above the din.

His objection was met with a torrent of French abuse and laughter from the girls. One Frenchman, accommodating the youngest-looking prostitute on his arm, a Nepali girl who must have been all of sixteen and was less made up than the rest, walked her into the bar holding up a finger to Santosh. Others followed and one of the bold Pathans emerged from the doorway of the bar and asked the rest of the girls in crude Urdu what they were waiting for, and didn't they know that they couldn't get any action or money in the hall and they'd better grab a Frenchman for themselves from the bar and take them upstairs.

'This is illegal. There is no licence for these person, police will coming,' Santosh shouted.

The Pathan came up to him menacingly. 'You want to say no one ever fucks in your hotel, son of a bitch?' And then pointing at me, 'This bastard ruined our business this afternoon, we are now going to ruin his and yours.'

Now there was shouting from the billiards room. Male voices and the sounds of a fight. Santosh and I both rushed in. Our gem merchants had packed their boxes as soon as they heard the row and now they were being assaulted by the Pathans. They had knocked the black marwari caps off their heads. The traders were offering no resistance. One lay on the floor in a foetal position with his arms protecting his face, lying on his box of gems. One of the Pathans was kicking him in the stomach and groin. The trader screamed for help from God and anyone else. Santosh and three Frenchmen pulled his assailant off. The trader scrambled to his feet.

No one knows who called them, but all of a sudden the place was full of police. Their commander had a whistle, which he blew persistently for no reason as though the piercing, rolling sound would restore order. The place was full of khaki-uniformed cops.

Santosh rushed to the receptionist. 'Did you call these fuckers?'

The receptionist said he hadn't, nor had his assistant. No one in the hotel had been near the phone, they added.

I knew precisely what had happened. These traders, out on the town with precious merchandise, must have had an alarm system and some arrangement with the police who came straight to their rescue. They wouldn't wander out with gems without such a system or support. And they had resorted to it in this emergency. They had taken loads of money and still had a stock of gems.

One of the boxes of gems had been scattered during the fight. The traders had held on to the others through it all.

'No one leaves the building. We have arrested some dangerous fellows, illegal immigrants. Maybe Pakistani agents,' said the whistling commander.

People were waiting to see what he wanted us to do.

It was after twelve o'clock now and in front of the police Santosh made a great show of shutting the bar. The Frenchmen howled.

The whistling commander walked into the bar, looking around self-importantly. His men were posted down the corridors and at each exit. There was no escape.

'What are these doing here?' he said, seeing the painted girls.

One, bolder than the rest, walked defiantly and coquettishly up to him making kissing sounds with her lips. 'Captain sahib, what are you asking what we are doing here? You have put me to use so many times. You know, better than any man, how to get pleasure from a woman's holes,' she said in crude Hindi.

The others began to laugh and the commander himself broke into a boyish grin, which he immediately suppressed. 'Who brought these bitches here?'

'The illegals,' Santosh said.

Then quite unexpectedly, 'Do you like our girls?' the commander asked the Frenchmen. 'These are very bad girls.'

'That's why we like them,' said one engineer. 'No Frenchman likes good girls.'

The rest of them laughed. The commander joined in.

'I might have to delay your flight. You have all been in touch with potential foreign spies. I don't know when I can release anyone. I have to find out all facts. How you came here, why you are choosing this hotel, all these stones you are buying, if these transactions are legal, everything.'

Ravina looked at me. I knew what she was thinking.

'I have to get back to the hospital, Commander sahib, I am a doctor and I have a night shift,' she said.

'Madam, I don't care if you are Indira Gandhi and have a country to run. Just now you are staying here till I am finished.' He was quite pleased with his own wit.

'She is much prettier than Indira Gandhi,' said one of the Frenchmen.

The Pathans were handcuffed and led out by a horde of cops. They had found knives on them, one of the constables said.

'So that's sorted, let's have a drink,' said one of the French girls in French.

'How you are allowing these naughty girls to mix with your good ladies?' the commander asked. It was a genuine enquiry. Some of the Frenchmen were sitting on the sofas of the bar with the prostitutes on their laps or with their arms around them.

'If it's not illegal, it's okay,' another French girl said. 'We know these silly boys from studying together and living in the same apartments. They know that we know what men are like. Why don't you have a drink, Captain? You must need one after this heroic battle.'

The whistling commander just smiled.

'No, no, not for me on duty, but if you want drink, go ahead, you are personal guests of Mr Santosh here and the law is okay if he is not charging. It becomes private party and I have nothing to say except to keep the party going.' He wanted their approval. He was playing soft cop.

Ravina whispered into Santosh's ear. Santosh nodded.

'I think the party is finished, everyone should go to bed,' Santosh announced.

'No, no, they can't leave this floor,' the commander said. 'Very sorry.'

I looked at the bar clock. Soon it would be one. The drug would start taking effect.

I went to the reception area and looked out of a window. There were two policemen posted outside.

I went to the receptionist.

'Can you show me any way out of here? I'll pay well,' I said.

'No, sir. The police are at the front and back door and that is all there is. They are covering the windows and the alleys where the windows lead. They are holding guns, sir.'

I could see that those guarding the doors were armed.

Then it struck me that if the traders had an arrangement with the cops, maybe they could get us out of here. I approached one of the traders, who was still clutching his gem box. 'Did you alarm the police?'

'I came for business like I was told,' he said.

'Listen, I am not a Frenchman, I am Indian. I know you got the police alerted and they came here to see you weren't looted. If you have any sort of communication or deal with them, just tell them to let me and my missus go, right now. We have urgent business. You will definitely get a reward.'

'Sir, I believe that rewards don't come in heaven, they come here and now or they don't come at all,' he replied. 'That is my motto.'

'Fuck your motto. I tell you I'll pay. You know my dad. Look, I have a Rolex watch I can give you here and I'll get you much, much more. Just call the police chief or whoever and get us out.'

The fellow examined the watch, which I had taken off my wrist and handed him. He peered at it with one eye, shutting the other.

He handed it back to me.

'Our police contact is secret,' he said. 'Only our boss deals with it and he is sleeping.'

'You woke him up when you were being beaten,' I said.

'No. We woke him when his gems were in danger. He doesn't care if we are kicked all the way to Lanka as long as his gems are safe. I can't wake him up for you or the queen of England.'

'Then speak to the commander yourself.'

'Commander doesn't know what is happening here. His superior told him he is raiding a suspect spy operation and to keep everybody here till morning and the idiot believes it. He feels important,' the trader said.

Even if he was willing to help me, it was too late. Ravina rushed up to me looking frantic. They had started dropping. I nodded to her, indicating that she should remain calm and we walked to the bar. Two of the men sitting with the prostitute girls had fallen asleep. One fellow, standing at the bar with a drink, suddenly slumped and slipped off his stool to the floor with a thud. Others ran up to support him. I caught Ravina's eye and we left the bar and went to the stairs. There were two armed constables seated at the bottom and one halfway up on the landing.

'Everyone stays on the ground floor,' one of them said in Hindi.

Before I could turn back I felt a hand on my shoulder. It was the Frenchies' leader.

'They are dropping like flies. What did you put in the drink? Who are you?'

'What are you talking about?' I asked.

The commander came and addressed Ravina.

'You are a doctor? Some people are falling and fainting in the bar. You have to help them,' he said.

Ravina went into the bar. Yes, they were dropping by the dozen now and were laid out on the floor. She bent over the nearest person and took his pulse and then felt his heartbeat and, lifting one eyelid after another, looked into his eyes as though she knew what she was looking for. She then turned to the whistling commander.

'I think they have all been mildly poisoned. I must pump out their stomachs. I can only then tell if it's urgent. My stomach pump and my doctor's bag, some injections I could use, are all in the car round the corner.

The commander thought for a moment.

'Your stubbornness could kill them,' she said.

He nodded to a constable next to him. 'Take madam doctor to her car. Help her fetch some things,' he said. And as she was going he clutched her elbow. 'Thank God you are here.'

It didn't occur to him that she was with me and that we had together brought the tourists to this hotel. He didn't think to ask.

The Frenchie captain had by now figured it out. He had definitely worked out, long before the clueless commander, that we had timed it so that we could take the gems they had bought from their rooms while they were knocked out, and disappear before dawn. But he was himself in no state to put two words or thoughts together. His eyes were rolling upwards as he made the effort to stay awake, but he too finally fell.

The commander kept looking at his watch. Fifteen minutes passed and there was no sign of Ravina or the constable who was sent to supervise her and bring her back with her medical kit. Twenty minutes later he sent two more cops to look for them. He couldn't wait. He called his superiors and told them that he had a coach full of fainting Frenchmen, a fugitive female doctor and a missing constable, four illegal immigrant terrorists on his hands, all in one hotel in Old Delhi. He didn't mention the prostitutes. That would have been one complication too far.

I suppose headquarters decided to deal with all these emergencies at the same time and said reinforcements and better brains were on the way.

With most of the Frenchmen horizontal, and the ones who were still standing in no mood to play, the prostitutes parleyed with each other and asked the commander if they could go.

'There is no "action" here,' they said, using the English word.

The commander nodded. The cops 'searched' the girls, feeling up their breasts and bums shamelessly, and then, before a higher authority came in, bundled them out. Some of them demanded pay for the night from the standing Frenchies, but got a kick in the arse from the cops as a send-off at the door instead.

Still no sign of Ravina or the constable. Had she made him some offer he couldn't refuse? Had she knocked him cold and run off? Where had she led him? There was of course no car and no equipment. Neither of them returned. It was now morning.

I only found out what happened to Ravina that night years later. Many years later.

An hour after the whistling commander's call, with paramedics and doctors pumping out the fainted Frenchies, using every bathroom in the hotel, the detectives came. They took charge of the Pathans and took them away. One cop, a lady, assigned herself to me.

'I didn't know we'd find you here, Mr Thhat, the Bikini Murderer himself,' she said.

'I am Patrice de Deauville. I have my passport,' I said.

'I am Officer Chandrika Nath, Mr Thhat. I am sure you have a hundred passports and a hundred identities and the very bad luck to have encountered someone who is in the international branch and has received your whole record from the Thai police, who asked us to be on the lookout for you. When we send you back, they'll hang you. Or is it a firing squad there? I can't remember.'

'I don't know what you are talking about, Officer. I am known at the French embassy. In fact, only today I have been making arrangements for this party. You can phone up the Taj and ask them. I phoned them after hours from the French embassy, they will have a record of my name.'

'Cut out the bullshit. What are you doing here, Johnson? That you would turn up in India on the run from Thailand was a good bet. The Nepalese police also put a few queries through a few months ago. You were there, weren't you? But that you'd walk into our very backyard and poison French tourists comes as a complete surprise.'

'It seems you are gripped by some fantasy, Officer. However much you know abut this Mr Smart or whoever it is you mistake me for, I am Deauville. I own two houses in France, I am in education and specialize in expanding the horizons of our young people. Fortunately I was on another assignment in India when I came across these people. It is unfortunate that they have been taken ill, but they were fed something by these prostitute girls who were brought quite illegally to this place. And as for Nepal, I have never been near the place.'

'Where are the prostitutes?'

'They were released by your commander, the fellow with the whistle.' I pointed to him. She went up and had a word with him and came back. He had, no doubt, denied their presence.

'So no confession, Johnson? You want us to go all the way with you?'

'If I am not charged with anything, I think I can take your leave now. I have important work. I have wasted enough time,' I said and stood up as if to go.

'I am sorry, but I am arresting you pending further investigation.'

'Under what charge?'

'I'll make something up for the front desk,' she said. Then she turned around and shouted in Hindi, 'Grab this fellow and take him to the central station. Book him as my suspect.' And as I was being taken away, 'Bonjour, M de Deauville. A bientot!'

Chandrika, Chandrika!

11

Then began the mind games with her. They put me in a cell in the central police station, an old brick building with lime dashed onto the cell walls so the brick and the cement sealing showed through. The police cells had no toilets and you had to rattle the cage and shout to the cop to take you out. The drunks and pickpockets in the other cells didn't seem to bother and the place stank. Then they began removing these fellows one by one and for some reason they left the cells around me empty. Had Delhi ceased to produce drunks and pickpockets?

Chandrika came on the second day. She wore trousers and a loose short kurta and could have been a modest young college lecturer. The only thing that may have indicated that she was a cop was the tightly tied back, long, black hair. A stool had been brought for her, while I sat on my bunk.

'Time to think, Johnson?' she asked.

I knew then that it was her intervention that had left these normally crowded cells empty. She wanted to give me a taste of isolation.

'I don't know why you continue with your game. Have you bothered to check my passport? Or with the French embassy? I tell you I am Patrice de Deauville and all this Johnson business is wasting your time. If you are after someone, go find him.'

'I don't think I will find him outside this room,' she said. 'Now let's get down to business. I am going to accept that you are M. de Deauville. Or can I call you Patrice? I want your story. Why were you in the Kohinoor? Did you poison these people? Are you going to ask how they are? Or don't you care?'

'Of course I care. They are my compatriots and my friends. I made friends with them and gave them advice on buying gems. I do this as a hobby, but this lot I just came upon on my holiday sightseeing at the Taj. And yes, I hope they are well.'

'Suppose I tell you that some of them didn't recover from the poison?' She was watching me.

'Don't tell me! That is tragic. That is murder. How many?'

'But you know they wouldn't die. The dose wasn't lethal. Just a deep, convenient sleep, eh?'

'I don't know. I am just sorry if anything like that…'

'Good. The persons who gave them the heavy dose of tranquillizers knew what they were doing. The risk is small. The drug would have to interact with severe heart conditions or something else for it to be fatal.'

'I know very little about drugs, Officer. Aspirin for headaches and clove oil for toothache is about as far as I get.'

'And your mystery companion, the doctor?'

'Yes, where is she? I last saw her go out of the hotel in the company of one of your people.'

'Yes, a uniformed constable. He too has disappeared.'

'But you must find her. She is my wife.'

'I know who she is, er…M Deauville.'

'Is she in custody? Why? What kind of country is this?'

'I have asked myself that question throughout my life. I have no answers, except that it is a country where people sometimes disappear because they choose to, and sometimes because they don't choose to. You must know all about that.'

'I am being kept here for no reason, Officer. I refuse to speak to you unless you fetch me a lawyer. I can secure my own lawyer.'

'You are entitled to under law. But I don't follow the law.'

'You shouldn't say that sort of thing to me, Officer. I will report it to the authorities when I get out of here. I have some knowledge of how India works. The powerful talk to the powerful, you know. Some judge, some superior will get to hear of your attitude.'

She grinned. The only blemish on her beauty was the fact that she exposed her gums when she smiled. She had long gums and her upper lip pulled over them.

'I am not an idiot, Johnson – I mean Patrice – I have political protection. You know how I got it? I hold the evidence in three cases against very prominent politicians. I make friends with them. I tell them the evidence is our little secret. I tell them it's no use having me bumped off by one of their mafia contacts or goons, because I have placed the evidence at the disposal of other people and getting rid of me would trigger a chain reaction.' She was smiling and her eyes reflected the smile.

'You blackmail politicians?'

'There's nothing else you can do with politicians here, M Deauville.'

'So, truthfully, how are my countrymen?'

'The truth is none of them died. They have all handed us statements and we've released them and they've gone home to France. They have said some very bad things about you, Monsieur D. They were not happy with you at all. Some of them even thought you and the person you call your wife had drugged them in order to loot the gems they had just bought from your henchmen. Tch, tch, tch. Libel.'

'I don't believe it. They can't say that. I was doing everything to help them.'

'How did you enter this country, M Deauville? There must be a record at an airport or passport checkpoint…'

'I told you, we can make small talk, but I won't speak officially to you on any matter till I have a lawyer.'

'That's it, then. For today,' she said abruptly, and got up and left.

✦

She was back the next day, this time with a file. She opened the file and thrust it towards me, again sitting on the stool that the policeman brought into my cell. She was wearing a sari and her hair was loose. She looked very good, man.

'I owe you an apology, M de Deauville. I looked at the files last night and again today very carefully and at the stuff the Thai police sent me, and the picture of the person I thought you were is in there. And of course it isn't you. That man had dark circles under his eyes and his bone structure is different. He is thinner than you are.'

I opened the file. There was a mugshot of me from the Thai cells with my hair much longer and brushed back and my face haggard and thin and without glasses.

I casually leafed through the other pages in the thick file. There were police photos from the morgue of the body of Desiree taken from different angles. And there was a picture of Jop in police custody.

'This case. I remember it now. I read something about it in the French newspapers. We always thought that being homosexual would assist the career of a Dutch diplomat, not hold him back,' I said.

She didn't acknowledge the witticism. Perhaps she didn't get it. She held her hand out for the file and I gave it to her.

'But you must admit, there is a resemblance,' she said.

She seemed to have nothing more to say to me and she left after asking if I was being fed adequately.

'You can order whatever kind of food you like,' she said. 'I have told the fellows to get you tandoori chicken if you want it. After all you are not even under trial yet, so you have to be treated like a guest.'

'If you are not charging me, you have to let me go. What about habeas corpus?'

'We don't speak Latin here. A bit of Sanskrit, maybe.'

She walked off. I shouted after her. 'What about a lawyer if you're going to charge me?'

'All in good time,' was what she shouted back.

That afternoon Santosh was brought into the cell next to mine. The police deposited him and left us alone. We could talk by standing next to each other at the bars, even though we couldn't see each other's faces.

'You mother-fucking son of a bitch!' was his civil greeting. 'They are questioning me about you and your bitch wife poisoning those bastards. They slapped me and didn't let me sleep for twenty-four hours. You and your fucking snake-woman have done for me and my business.'

'You shouldn't have got your barman to poison them,' I said.

'You served the drinks,' he said. 'I didn't know what you were up to.'

'Listen, Santosh, I am a French professor, not a child from the bush. I know the police have planted you with a microphone to get me to talk. All I will do for you is give them a recitation of French poetry.' I began to sing:

> *Frere Jacques*
> *Frere Jacques*
> *Dormez vous?*
> *Dormez vous?*
> *Sonnez la matin,*
> *Sonnez la matin…*

'My lawyer is coming now,' he said, shouting above my singing.

'Great for you. I can sing him a song too,' I said.

He was quiet now.

We said nothing more to each other till his lawyer turned up. I stopped him as he was walking past my cell escorted by a cop.

'Excusez moi,' I said, 'you are a lawyer? They haven't allowed me a lawyer, even to talk to one, so will you act for me? It's the same Kohinoor Hotel case.'

I think he was genuinely surprised to see me there.

'I am Deauville,' I stretched my hand out through the bars.

'I am Sethi, how do you know I am a lawyer?'

'You look like one,' I said and grinned.

He spoke to Santosh. Then two more cops turned up to take Santosh out of the cell. He was getting bail, Sethi explained, and said he could come back and listen to my case.

'Only if you want,' he added.

'I really want,' I said.

He came back that evening accompanied by Chandrika.

'Voila, Monsieur, your lawyer,' she said and showed him into my cell. The policeman brought the same stool. Chandrika left us to ourselves.

'She speaks French and knows a lot of things for a cop,' I said.

'I did not come with her. You mustn't get wrong impression. We met on doorstep.'

'I was wondering,' I said.

'But I know her. Very strong reputation she has. These girls are damned smart. They sit for the Foreign Service exams, get selected and then decline the Foreign Service, the diplomatic corps, and ask to join the police so they can stay in the country and their parents can get them married.'

'Surely a diplomat has a better marriage prospect than a policewoman?'

'People have strange ideas. Husbands don't want to move around with wives who get posted from Beijing to Lagos and then to Outer Mongolia.'

'This one seems to enjoy being a cop,' I said.

'Now I looked into the case. They haven't got a statement from you, but the statements they have from eyewitnesses are pretty damning. I must tell you, most of them blame you and your partner, a lady, for drugging the drinks.'

'Nobody saw us doing any such thing,' I protested.

'That's true, they have no eyewitness to the act of adding drugs to the drink, nor has any drug been detected on you, but you did try to close the bar and get everyone to their rooms before they started dropping.'

'Look, I don't know how things work here. I thought I was assisting the French party and didn't want them to stay in a bar after legal hours. I was looking after them.'

'This is a good point,' Sethi said. 'And the lady with you? Your wife?'

'I have no information.'

'That she has run away is not good for our case.'

'She would never run away. One cop is missing with her. Maybe he did something to her. Who can say?'

'But she lied about being a doctor?' he asks.

'I didn't hear her say anything about being a doctor or anything.'

'But she isn't a doctor?'

'Not as far as I know. I met her four years ago and we were married. What she did before that, I thought I knew, but I could be mistaken, old man.'

He wanted my side of the story and I gave it to him and he took notes.

'Was your man Santosh working for the police?' I asked.

'I don't think so, M Deauville.'

'Well, if he was, they have a unique tape recording of *Frere Jacques* and they have my permission to use it for French lessons in the police academy.'

'I am sure there was no tape recorder, but in case there was,

I shall convey your generous offer to the police commissioner himself.'

I liked Sethi and decided he wasn't a plant.

✦

The first day in court was just formal. I had to wait four hours before the case came up, sitting in the cells in the basement of the New Delhi courts from whose high windows I could see the lawns and the gardeners mowing the borders by hand.

Sethi came down to the cells and told me they wouldn't give me bail because I did not have an address in Delhi or anywhere in India. He would ask for the case to be immediately heard and he said he would threaten the judge with publicity in the press. The story, he said, would inevitably be picked up by the French press and the judge would be quite proud of being in the international spotlight.

Chandrika turned up with two government lawyers and they read out the indictment in the name of Patrice de Deauville, being charged with administering a potentially lethal drug to the named individuals. Then they read out the names of the Frenchies who had collapsed, one by one, as though they were separate cases: 'That you did on the night of…July,' etc.

Sethi told me to plead not guilty to all counts and I did. I exaggerated my French accent as much as I could.

They mentioned Ravina in the indictment without knowing her name. They didn't ask me who she was.

Of course I didn't expect Ravina to get in touch with me and put herself in danger. I was waiting for her to make her move to help me out, but couldn't think what she could do. She had, if I knew her, made good her escape. I thought I might ask Sethi to call my father and see if Ravina was there, but I didn't want to tell Sethi anything really. He was representing Deauville and I should let him get on with that.

I was no longer in police cells now. They moved me to the remand wing of Tihar jail.

Sethi came to see me two days running and went through the evidence against me. He said it was circumstantial and we stood a good chance. And I insisted: no one had seen me drug the drinks. That they were drugged was certain. They had analysed the pumped-out stuff from the stomachs of the Frenchies and taken blood tests. They had statements from the bartenders, statements from the Frenchies and damning statements from Santosh who was now a witness for the state. Chandrika had dropped all charges against him.

The day before the trial Chandrika came down to the cells with a briefcase full of papers. 'Here are all the statements against you,' she said. 'If I were a judge, I'd send you down for a lot of years. But look what I am going to do.' She took the statements, divided the pile into manageable stacks and then theatrically tore the papers to bits. She threw the bits on the floor. 'Here you are, M Deauville, I have destroyed the evidence against you. I had the damning statements. Now they don't exist.'

I was astounded.

'I find you very interesting, M Deauville,' she went on.

This was the last thing I thought I would ever hear from a police officer. But of course she wanted to see if any shock or surprise registered on my face. Perhaps it did.

'You are now wondering why I am doing this. Because we can come to some arrangement,' she said.

'I don't understand,' I said. But I did, even before she continued.

'I am after that bribe I am sure you can give me. Find your so-called wife and get me some of those diamonds and you can go back to France. I have to trust you on that, n'est ce pas?'

'I don't know about diamonds,' I said. 'I earn a salary in France and I can send you some cash from there.'

'I can even help you get back to Nepal if that's what you want,' she continued. 'But trust only goes so far. I can take you to a phone and you can call the people you have to call. We have eight days till your next hearing and by that time some good stuff ought to be in my hands.'

'Ah, but this phone business…'

'It won't be tapped. Think about it. And while you are thinking, don't take me for a fool. That evidence is truly destroyed and there are no copies – but is that all the evidence? You didn't read any of it. I might still be holding some cards. Think,' she said.

'Are you?'

'You'll have to rely on me. You have no alternative, I don't think. Indian courts don't take poisoning very lightly. It's part of our tradition. We don't like poisoning guests.'

'Maybe I can get my lawyer to call a third party from a phone which he knows is not tapped.'

'Tch, tch. You don't trust a woman who is offering you your freedom? Well, suit yourself. I don't mind how you get hold of the materials. Let me know.'

'How can I let you know?'

'I shall not be far. I have to stay close to you. I shall be back. I think about you a lot.'

Then she left me.

This game has no science to it. You move by instinct and observation. I saw the look in her eyes, and I read it like a book. These weren't the eyes of a greedy woman. They were the hesitant, doubting eyes of a predator wondering whether the prey is hovering near her trap, wondering whether he will fall in. I hadn't admitted to anything.

'Get me a book on Thai law, find me anything you can about treaties between Thailand and India, on extradition and things like that,' I said to Sethi. I wasn't prepared yet to give him my father's phone number and inevitably reveal to him that I wasn't who I had said I was.

He was puzzled but went away agreeing to do as I asked.

He brought me two international law books and some papers on the South Asian treaties. I didn't sleep that night. I was reading.

If that was her game, it was the sneakiest thing I had ever encountered.

Chandrika came to the jail again, and simply asked, 'So?'

'It just takes time. The stuff will be with you tomorrow.'

'How will it be delivered?'

'If you give me a phone number, someone will phone you and tell you where they will rendezvous with you.'

'You are a sensible man, M de Deauville. You are in the remand wing, but you must have seen the wretches who have been sentenced. Some of them have been here forty years.'

'I haven't seen them, but I hear them getting instructions for yoga in the morning from the yard.'

'Well, you can thank God and me that you won't see them. Provided you keep your part of the bargain. I am taking a risk and I want it to be worthwhile, you understand. And of course after this is over I should like to see you again.'

'I will make sure I invite you to Paris.'

'Paris?' she asked.

'Look, this is a dodgy business. If my fellows can't deliver by tomorrow, they will definitely do it by the day of the trial.'

'That might be too late,' she said.

'So what will you do?' I asked

'I don't know. You'll have to wait and see. I am used to making deals and that means both sides keep the bargain.'

'Can't you see I am stuck here, man? I can't push and pull from jail.'

'I sympathize, Monsieur D., but I really can't see that as my problem. It may be that I feel generous and then I can wait for the delivery. I can always grab you after you leave the court. This is not France, you know. Here the police don't work for the law, they are the law. You have heard of "encounters"?' she asked.

'Yes, you shoot people in the back of the head and say they were trying to escape from police custody,' I said.

'Criminals,' she interposed.

'So they deserve to die?'

'Who on earth can decide who deserves to live and who deserves to die? I take it you are a Christian, Monsieur D.?'

'I was brought up a Catholic. In a country where they guillotine people.'

'I am a Hindu. I believe in karma – as you sow, so shall you reap. The men we shoot in encounters have been asking for it. Sometimes one has to make that sort of judgement. Is the world well rid of a person? Is a person dispensable?' she asked.

'I don't know how anyone can make such a judgement or take such a decision about some fellow human being's life,' I said.

Now I was watching her to catch any twinge or change in her face. Yes, it was there. In the eyes again, the little candle of triumph. And then I knew what she was after.

I finished reading and rereading the books and the paper that Sethi had brought.

'I don't know how I shall pay you, my friend,' I said to him.

'I don't want payment from you, Mr Patrice. I will be happy if I can do my bit towards getting you off this terrible charge. That will be my reward.'

I put my hand on his shoulder. 'You know, I begin to suspect the woman I was travelling with. I have a confession. She is not my wife actually. I hardly know her. I met her the same day as I met the Frenchmen, at the Taj. And she probably did the dirty work and disappeared.'

'Why didn't you tell me that before?' Sethi asked.

'I didn't think you would believe me,' I said.

'But of course I believe you. This changes everything. I will go for her in court tomorrow and challenge the police and the prosecution to prove that you had anything to do with her or with her crime. Because a crime was committed, but you were totally innocent of it. That's it. The stranger woman did it.'

'I didn't think you could prosecute someone in their absence, that's why I kept quiet.'

'My dear Mr Deauville, this is not prosecution. We are coming up with your defence. Someone else did it. You saw them do it.'

'I didn't know what she was doing at the time, but she certainly had a handbag with stuff in it, a brownish-white powder which she said she was drinking herself for her stomach problems. I can say I saw her putting it in the soda.'

'Yes, yes, yes. I was beginning to think it looks bad, but it looks good.'

He went away happy. I fell into a thoughtful sleep.

✦

'Pradhanji, I had to take the biggest decision of my life that night. If I asked you when you were thirty years old what you would be doing in twenty years' time, would you have an answer?' Thhat asked.

'I may have had. It could have even been accurate. I would have said I would rise to be a middle-ranking officer in the Nepalese police force and would have a few more children and buy a car and have a house in Kathmandu to retire to,' replied Pradhan.

'That's true of most people. And then there is the chance that things could turn out different. That Chandrika, she told me that Sethi was right, she did do an exam for the Foreign Service and she passed with flying colours as they say, but then she joined the police by choice, which is another service to which you can be transferred inside the Indian civil services.'

'When did she tell you this?'

'Later, much later.'

'And what happened in court?'

'She turned up and sat with the prosecution lawyers and they began the trial. I was watching her…'

✦

Sethi had prepared himself to blame the mystery woman who had fooled the whistling commander and absconded with one of his constables. He told me, before the proceedings began, that he was going to make mincemeat of the police in the witness box for letting the culprit get away.

The prosecuting lawyer said openly in court that he only had circumstantial evidence of my guilt.

I looked at Chandrika and she flashed a very quick smile, a Mona Lisa downturn of the mouth.

God, she was clever.

The prosecution called Santosh and when Sethi asked him if he had seen me administering any drug at any time to anyone, he had to say he hadn't. He tried to say that I was near the bar, but had to admit that so were twenty other people.

Chandrika looked steadily at me. No bribe had been delivered.

The judge asked if the victims were to be produced in court and the prosecution had to say that the police were powerless to stop them boarding a plane and returning to France.

'Then where are their statements?' the judge asked.

The prosecutor said he could produce two statements but they weren't a useful part of the case.

The case against M de Deauville was melting away.

The poor whistling commander was called to the box. He was in his uniform and sweating. His face was wet and shiny.

He told the story of how he had been called to the Kohinoor when his superior called the station where he was on duty to get a force down there. He was told a fight had broken out and it could end in fatalities. He said he cordoned the place off because the miscreants were possibly Pakistani nationals and possibly spies.

The judge was astounded. He hadn't gathered any of this from the previous proceedings. He took his glasses off. 'Hold on, hold on. What are you saying, deputy sahib? That you were called into an incidence of spying?'

'No, sir, that case is going on separately. They are bad hats.'

'Oh, bad hats,' said the judge. 'But you said spies.'

'Suspected, sir.'

'I see. Well, proceed.'

'The accused was not giving drinks when I arrived on the scene at Kohinoor. In fact as per hotel laws, the bar had been foreclosed.'

'I am glad to hear it,' said the judge.

'And people began to collapse one by one. The foreigners.'

'What do you mean by "collapse"?'

The judge was interrupting the defence questioning at random and taking notes.

'They fell down and into sleep straight away,' said the whistling commander.

'You did not see my client, the defendant, going near any drink or offering any drink?' asked Sethi.

'Mr Sethi, we have established that this is happening after drinks are exhausted. Now people are collapsing. Proceed,' said the judge.

'One woman was identifying herself as a doctor and she

started examination of the fallen. She said she must go and get her medical kit and I was agreeing that as many lives as possible should be saved. I was not in the knowledge at this particular time that basically she was the one who was under suspicion of tampering with drinks. I thought she was the house doctor.'

'Have we noted this doctor before in the records?' the judge asked.

'Yes, sir, she is the same lady who appeared at the same time as the accused and was living with him, as the learned counsel for the defence said, in Kohinoor hotel,' said the prosecutor.

'So what did you do with this lady who said she was a doctor?' the judge asked.

'I sent her with a police escort to fetch her tools and injections from the car.'

'I don't know about any car,' the judge said.

'She said the tools were in her car, sir.'

'Can that be noted? There was an alleged car.'

'But she never came back, sir.'

'Absconding?' the judge asked.

'We have no knowledge,' said the whistling commander.

For the first time the sleeping press benches stirred. Reporters began taking notes and one or two left the courtroom.

The prosecution concluded by bringing on the whistling commander. Chandrika mostly avoided my steady gaze, but now and then glanced in my direction. Was she trying to read me to see if I had caught on to her game?

I hadn't made any phone calls. Now what would she do? I was going to push this to its limit. I had made up

my mind. Diamonds or no diamonds, she was going to let
M de Deauville get away with it. He would be found innocent
because she would throw in the towel.

So when Sethi rose to cross-examine the whistling
commander, she actually smiled and I knew that I was going
to win this match. She could smile, but I had her little game
worked out.

Sethi attacked the poor commander without mercy. His
opening question was, 'So you let the real poisoner go just
because she said she was a doctor? You let her escape?'

'I didn't know who she was.'

'She was a confidence lady who had met my client a few
days before and you let her escape after making a big show of
arresting the whole hotel!'

'There were people dropping like ripe mangoes from a
tree, sir.'

The commander was sweating. The judge came to his
rescue. 'Hold on, learned counsel for the defence. There
has been no evidence produced that this absconding lady in
question had anything to do with the poisoning. Nothing at
all. I cannot allow this piece of fabrication to enter the case in
this manner. You understand?'

Chandrika looked at me and then immediately spoke
to the prosecutor who went up to the bench. 'Sir, we have a
sworn statement from one of the victims that he has seen this
lady tampering with the drinks and adding some substances
to them thinking she is unobserved. We have this statement
and it can be read out in court.'

'Then why was it not produced before?' the judge asked.

'Because the lady in question is not on trial, your honour,

and this statement has nothing to say about the defendant whom we are prosecuting.'

'But now it has become material,' the judge said.

Sethi was beaming. This was collaboration beyond anything he could have expected.

Chandrika handed the prosecutor a paper and the prosecutor took it to the bench and offered it to the judge for examination.

She was going to win. She was sure. The bitch didn't realize, even then, that I knew what she was up to. I would destroy her trap with the necessary sacrifice.

'Your honour,' I said, clearing my throat. 'I wish to make a statement.'

'You will have time for that at the end. Your counsel should explain to you,' the judge said.

'He won't,' I said. 'The fact is that my name is not Deauville at all. I am travelling under false papers. My name is actually Johnson Thhat and I did plan the poisoning of those tourists and carried it out. I plead guilty to all those offences.'

I looked at Chandrika and smiled.

Panic.

'Mister Defendant, you must say that again for the record,' the judge said. He, too, was fazed.

Sethi sat down slowly.

'I said my name is not Deauville. My real name is Johnson Thhat. I am travelling in India on a false passport and entered the country illegally. I entrapped those sixty French citizens and put sleeping doses into their drinks in order to rob them of the diamonds they were buying and of their passports and anything else I could take. The plan went wrong and I was trapped and captured. The police have treated me very well. I plead guilty.'

Everyone in the room heard what I had said and there was a moment of stunned silence, then a babble of voices.

The press benches went wild. Reporters shouted out to me, sensing a scoop.

'You are Thhat, the serial murder fellow?'

The judge banged his gavel as though he was in an American film. He knew he had something on his hands and he moved swiftly to consolidate his position.

'Take the prisoner below. We must reopen this case with the recorded statement of the accused and the changed guilty plea. I will consider the charges of contempt of court and of perjury as part of this case. As for the illegal entry and passport, I would urge the police to take note of the admission and act accordingly. Court adjourned till the afternoon.'

They took me down to the court cells.

Chandrika came down to see me. It was cards-on-the-table time.

'Son of a bitch,' she said. 'Murderer!'

'Tell me, why do you want me deported and dead?' I asked.

'Because you killed all those people!'

'Then I'm sorry. Indian law says that if I am found guilty of an offence here I have to serve my time before I can be extradited to Thailand to face a sentence.'

'For how long, Thhat? You'll get six or ten years for this poisoning business. Then we'll send you back to Thailand to be shot.'

'We shall see. In ten years' time, who knows?'

'I was trying to get you off.'

'No, my sweet. You were trying to get someone called Deauville off. The poisoning case would be closed and then I would walk free and you could arrest me, no doubt prove that I am Johnson Thhat using photographs and Thai fingerprints, and deport me to Thailand to be shot. So fuck you, baby. I got there first.'

'I don't know what you are crowing about. I can wait. You need twenty years away from Thailand for the statute of limitations to take effect. You need nineteen more, Thhat. How are you going to stay in jail for twenty years? And is that worth it?'

'Maybe. To stay alive. Where will you be in twenty years?'

'I shall be inspector general of police and I shall have an eighteen-year-old daughter and a seventeen-year-old son. I'll encourage the daughter to take up politics and I'll send my son to Oxford to study psychology,' Chandrika said. She had consented to play my game.

'All this without a husband?' I asked.

'I'll get one along the way. But I am not forgetting you, Thhat. I hope you rot in jail. You come out in five, six years and I'll be waiting to send you to hell. I am a bad loser.'

'You are prettier when you're angry,' I said.

She spat in my face.

✦

The judge gave me eight years. He said he was being lenient despite the fact that I didn't seem to have a care for my victims and had wasted a lot of police time. Sethi waited around in court and made some half-hearted plea for a lesser sentence. He seemed like a broken man.

'I am afraid of you' was all he said to me as he left the court after I was sentenced.

'What about the forged passport and entering India illegally?' I shouted as the judge was dismissing the case.

'Don't worry, Mr Thhat, justice will come to you on every count. We will revert on those matters – in jail,' the clerk said.

The whistling commander, whose name I now knew as Vasudev, came to me in the cells as I was awaiting transportation to jail.

'No hard feelings, Mr Johnson. I was doing my duty and I enjoyed meeting you, sincerely.'

'No hard feelings,' I assured him. 'Perhaps we will meet again. Good luck with your career.'

He looked startled, but thanked me.

They did 'revert' on the other matters while I was in jail. I was transported to the court several times to answer them. Six times, to be precise, and after they heard the depositions to which I pleaded guilty, they added two years to my sentence. Chandrika turned up on the last day of sentencing for the illegal entry into India from Bangladesh, an offence I confessed to as described.

She and I were the only ones who realized why I was smiling with every year's increment of my sentence.

PART 3

1

'Jhowson, Jhowson!' the murmured distortion spread through the prisoners like one of their yoga class mantras. A man with a reputation for eleven known murders and poisoning a busload of tourists is a natural magnet for respect from thieves and criminals. Even the murderers were one-time crime passionelle fellows or robbers who had blundered.

I refused to smile at or talk to any prisoners. If this was to be home sweet home, I had to either adjust to its ways or get it to adjust to mine.

I shared a cell with Roy, a Bengali swindler and forger, who told me as the days went by that he was a Doctor of Philosophy.

'Indian stuff?' I asked.

'No, Western philosophy. I used to teach at the university, but I fell into bad company and the money was attractive so I started printing bank notes. I had bad luck.'

'What happened?'

'My partner was duped by a rival forgery gang in Calcutta. We were ruining their business so they wanted us out of the trade. The bastards printed and passed off a load of twenty-pound notes on my idiot partner. Perfect looking. Absolute ink blocks, colour, false watermark, everything.

If you keep to small denominations of dollars, you can sell them to the black market money changers. What happens is fellows come with rupees, trunks full of rupees, and want them changed into foreign currency. Most of them don't know what a dollar bill or a fifty-pound note looks like and they accept stapled stacks of them. The black marketeers exchange them and then disappear. It goes on all over India. Most of the foreign currency doesn't go through banks, so people like me can move in and publish a lot of foreign currency.'

'Sounds like a good racket, man.'

'Sure it's a good racket. We made millions on the deals. Then these bastards passed off these twenty-pound bills to my man. On one side is the picture of the queen and on the other side is a musician called Edward Elgar. On the real ones. We had never printed twenty-pound notes before, but these bastards, instead of Elgar had printed a special wad with George Bernard Shaw's picture on it. It looked completely authentic and was the same modernized design.

'We printed thousands of them in replica and passed them off on to a black marketeer who was very pleased with them. When he tried to sell them on, he was caught. The buyers knew their notes and wouldn't accept George Bernard Shaw. The black marketeer or "two-number" as we call them in India, was a bastard. When he got hauled in by the police he gave them our names and everything and they raided our place.'

Roy had a pile of books he was reading in the cell. I looked at the covers. One of them was the complete plays of George Bernard Shaw.

'It's very good, very socialist. If we had a proper communist society, fair to everybody, I wouldn't be a crook. I would just be a professor.'

He was an analytical fellow and was very curious about me, though he never asked about my crimes.

'You know, you are like Neatshare,' he said to me.

'What is Neatshare?' I asked.

'It's the name of a German philosopher. He was proclaiming that God is dead and if God is dead, all the rules he made are also dead, so it is legitimate to forge notes or do anything else to people. I don't believe it, but I can see, Johnson, that you believe something of the kind. He then wrote some books called *Why I Am So Clever* and *Why I Am So Wise*.'

'He prescribed some diet?' I asked.

'No rubbish, man, this was philosophy: epistemology, ontology. I read them. Very great mind. Like you.'

I asked him how he'd got hold of these books in Tihar.

'You can buy anything here. I gave them packets of cigarettes and they allowed my wife to bring in these books. This play of Bernard Shaw is new, but the others are all my old books from home.'

'I have no cigarettes to give them,' I said.

'Give them anything. They will take your wristwatch.'

'I think I need to keep that chained to my wrist.'

'Time is chained to you and you are chained to time,' Roy said, smiling and revealing the fact that his front teeth, top and bottom, were missing.

'How did you lose your teeth?' I asked.

'My dear fellow, in Bengal, philosophy is a dangerous profession, you get beaten up.'

Roy was also on remand. He had been found guilty of forgery and of swindling, but was awaiting his sentence.

A few weeks into my residence in Tihar, the four Pathans who had started the whole ruckus in Kohinoor were brought to the prison and put into the cell next to ours.

I now took the trouble to look them over. One of them was quite old, maybe sixty, and he seemed to be their leader. Another was probably in his early twenties. They had all been badly beaten up by the interrogating police. They glared at me and shouted and spat as they came in.

'It is that infidel Jaansingh,' said the young one. 'I will kill him for you, Daddy. I will eat his liver and feed you his heart. Don't worry.'

The young one referred to the leader as 'Daddy'. We heard him through the cell walls. He was in with the old man and the other two were further down the corridor. In the night, Roy drew my attention to strange sounds.

'They are loving,' he said.

I strained my ears. There was the sound of heavy breathing and the young man said 'Daddy, Daddy' in a low whisper. Roy was right. There was something going on. There were clear sounds of men groaning in sexual climax.

'This misfortune will soon leave us, but I will never leave you, Daddy,' the young fellow said.

The next morning the four of them were hauled off by the prison guards and a police escort was waiting for them in the yard.

Roy and I and some of the other remand prisoners had been allowed to walk in the yard and we could hear the clatter of the regular convicts in their wing adjoining it. There were a few barred windows to their wing and some of the convicts were pushing their faces to the bars, crowding them, to catch a glimpse of the big forger, the serial killer and the four spies. This was the daily news of the prison, the concerns of a small, enclosed world.

Their curiosity was rewarded. As the Pathans were led out they swore at me in Urdu.

The prison guards pushed them along. And the police used batons on their backsides to urge them into the covered, black prison van.

'They are not being taken to court. You see those civilian fellows outside the car? They are being taken for interrogation and more beatings.'

'How do you know?'

'Those are people from RAW,' Roy said.

'Jaansingh, your days are numbered,' the young Pathan shouted.

'Then it's lucky for me that you can't count,' I shouted back. This brought a cheer from the detention block convicts.

'You are becoming their favourite murderer,' Roy said.

'I better not see you again,' the young Pathan shouted.

'I have a feeling you won't,' I said.

✦

I meant nothing by it, Pradhan sahib, it was just a response to his nonsensical threat, but that night only three of the Pathans were brought back to the jail and thrown into their cells. The young one was missing.

'Where is the young gandoo, the arse lender?' Roy asked the warder of our wing.

'Dead. Killed in an encounter, trying to run away,' the warder said, grinning.

The news filtered through the jail. Somehow my name was associated with the elimination of the cocky young Pathan. The prisoners recalled my threat. And now it seemed my will had been done. There was no logic connecting my word to the police encounter, but trapped creatures become cynical and superstitious.

'Don't do anything to us,' one of the warders said to me the next day.

Two days later the old Pathan was found hanging in his cell. He had made a rope out of the bed sheet and choked himself to death hanging by the bars. It couldn't have been a clean hanging with the snapped spinal cord, more a slow strangulation.

We heard nothing till the warder who came to give him his food screamed for help.

'Jhowson has killed another of the Pakistani fellows who swore to get him. The remaining two are pissing in their pants with fear.' The word spread.

The two remaining Pathans didn't threaten me again. In a week they were, at their own request, transferred to another prison. It was never proved that they were anything other than disappointed, diamond-dealing Pathans.

There was a change in the attitude of the warders towards me. They would come and ask me if there was anything I needed, whether I was comfortable. I said I needed a phone. There were no mobile phones in those days, but one of the chief warders on our block took me at night to the deputy governor's office and allowed me to make my calls.

I called my father. He said he'd read about me and he had also read about the two Pathans who died. I asked him if he could help me. He said he was under surveillance himself and I was not to call him, but that he would see that I had visitors who brought me presents on a regular basis. I told him I was determined to stay in jail for as long as I could.

I didn't ask him about Ravina. Maybe the phone was tapped and though nothing worse could happen to me if it was, the police might still be looking for her. I was sure she must have gone back to him or got in touch with him at some point. Where else would she go?

At my last trial Sethi was there again pleading mitigation of sentence. A man turned up in the public gallery and gave Sethi a matchbox. I had got my two-year extension and was being taken down to the cells to be carted back to prison when Sethi gave me the box.

It had five gems in a little plastic bag, the sort used to carry dope. I put the tiny bag under my tongue. Matchboxes would be confiscated and I thought it unnecessary to take the trouble to shove it up my arse. I could still manage a few words with it there.

The deputy governor came to see me. I was being treated as someone special even then. He said I would now be transferred to the general wing and would have to eat and exercise with the rest of the prisoners. I said I didn't want to. I had a ruby in my hand and I opened my fist.

'For your wife,' I said.

He took it without a word. Then he said: 'I think you are a danger to the other prisoners, Johnson, so we will have to keep you in isolation.'

'What about Roy? Can he come into a cell next to mine? I need his philosophy and it is very dangerous for the other prisoners to hear it.'

'How is that?' he asked.

'Deputy sahib, Roy says, "There is no God, there is only the police!" Things like that.'

'Oh, no! I'll see what I can do.'

We were both moved to the special wing where prisoners who were awaiting transportation to a mental institution or to hospital were sometimes kept. The deputy told me that because of overcrowding, the rules governing who could be kept where in the prison had to be flexible and that he had used his discretion to move us both to adjoining cells. There was also an empty cell in the block.

This was to be home for a long time.

A fraction of a diamond, its value converted into currency by Roy's delighted, roly-poly wife, who was allowed to visit once a month, over the years bought me a refrigerator, an electric typewriter, a desk, a mattress, an electrical wire extension and an electric kettle for instant coffee and tea, and four takeaway food menus. There were three Indian restaurants and one Chinese. We could order food when we wanted and the warders on particular shifts would fetch it. This bought-in food was all we ate.

2

The years went by with the fortunes of the prison not worth noting. I was writing my story, slowly, on the typewriter.

Then one day, I was interviewed, you know. French TV was very interested and a documentary-maker named Virginie came to see me. She had permission from the Indian foreign ministry and then from the home ministry and she said she had been following my case from the time I had turned 'assassin' in Thailand.

The word she used was strange. It was like murderer with high heels. I had been elevated to an assassin. It's what one calls a killer of presidents, not of punks.

The governor called me to his office and asked me if I wanted to cooperate with French television. The request had come down to him from the Home Office with details of what the programme-makers could and could not shoot in the jail. I said I was busy with my law studies and other things, but I would talk to the producers.

Virginie arrived with a French fellow who was her cameraman. She introduced him as Fernande, but I always called him Camera. Though we were all French, the governor said we had to speak in English. There was no real reason, because the warders who were sitting outside the cell hardly spoke any English and we could have been plotting to escape from Colditz for all they knew.

Virginie explained her project. It was about me as an assassin and criminal mind, and I had to agree to this angle. She already had interviews with the French engineers who remembered that afternoon and night more clearly than any other day of their lives. They had seen the Taj Mahal, bought fake gems, bought real gems, got drunk in Delhi, caused a fight to the death between gem dealers and been guided through the day by a serial killer who had tried to poison and rob them: they were not likely to forget.

'Some of them are very kind to you on camera, Thhat,' Camera said. 'They say you are the most fascinating character they have ever met.'

I kept a straight face and stared at him, saying, 'They were easy. Idiots. Not because they fell for my drug, but because they were going to buy cheap gems with expensive money.'

'Bravo! That's what I want you to say on camera. So you will agree?'

I agreed.

This Virginie had long red hair, which fell over her face. She flicked it back from her heavily rouged cheeks in a coquettish way. She spoke with her hands. I had not seen a woman for a year. She said she'd come again the next time she could get permission. I said I could get her permission for the next day or any day. She raised an eyebrow. 'Watch,' I said.

I told the warder that I would like to see the deputy governor or at least send him a message if he was too busy. The warder took the message and went out, leaving the three of us locked in my cell.

'He can do anything he wants in this holiday home,' Roy shouted from his cell. 'You want to make a TV programme on philosophy of crime?'

'That is one of your fans?' Virginie asked.

'One of many,' I said.

'So am I,' she said. 'That's why I am here. I look in your eyes and see that you are even more interesting than the stories about you.'

'I am not interesting to myself. I lived with myself too long. You must come tomorrow and you can start the interviews.'

'Of course we are doing this for commercial TV, so we pay you, yes?'

'That's good,' I said. 'The money I collect will gather interest by the time I come out.'

'Can't you escape?'

'Now that is the sort of talk that the deputy governor was trying to discourage when he told us to speak only in English,' I said.

She turned her head to catch a glimpse of me as she left.

She returned the next morning, alone. 'I thought I would set up the interview, and gain your trust. That is essential.'

'You already have it,' I said.

She sat down on the chair in my cell. I had furnished the cell with three chairs and I sat opposite her and leaned forward.

'Shoot.'

'You've had a shave since yesterday and removed the shadow. The shadow was very intriguing,' she said.

She was pretty and she wanted to show it. She had worn a tight blouse that morning which accentuated the shape of her breasts, long rather than round and voluptuous, but still sexy, the open blouse showing hard bone between them. She had a very short red skirt on.

My eyes strayed to her legs. She was deliberately sitting with her knees apart.

'Yes, I've shaved. And you've come in a tight skirt and without knickers,' I said.

'Yeah, I don't like them, especially in India, the sweat, you know.'

She put her legs together, not out of embarrassment at my observation, but slowly, deliberately.

'Or would you like me to keep them open?' she asked.

'I haven't been with a girl for over a year now,' I said.

'That can change, if you want,' she said.

She looked towards the bars.

'I can tell them to get lost,' I said.

'Then tell them,' she said.

I went to the bars and called out to Dilawar, the screw.

'Don't bother us for an hour,' I said.

'You won't take an hour, not after one year, will you?' she asked. She took her skirt off and sat on my bed in the darkest part of the cell.

I could see the reddish triangle of her crotch above her thin but muscular, shaped thighs. I went and sat next to her. I didn't take my clothes off, but I kissed her and as I held her she undid the buttons of my trousers and pulled me towards and over her as she lay down and spread her legs.

I felt her heart beating against my ribs. She wouldn't shut her eyes, she wanted to watch me as we fucked and she held my face in both her hands.

I couldn't hold myself for long though I tried, attempting to distract myself by thinking of the dinginess of the surroundings in which we were venting our mutual lust. But when I looked into her face, her mouth open and her eyes full of surprise, it made me flow.

She clung to me and moaned.

I felt light, and light-headed. She went for the towel in the toilet corner of the cell. I wanted to watch her as she cleaned herself. I couldn't get enough of her body, even though I had come so fast and was unable to make the most of it.

She zipped up her skirt and looked in the wall mirror I had and grimaced. 'Not one hour then?' She laughed.

'I am sorry. Your attractiveness caused the impatience. Not of the head, just of the blood,' I said.

'So you haven't forgotten the bullshit,' she said.

'One never does. Even though I don't know after all these years which bullshit works and which doesn't,' I said.

'Try poetry. Can't lose, even if you get a dumb French bitch who doesn't understand a word.'

Dilawar looked her up and down as he let her out of the cell. He allowed me to walk her to the door of the block where I turned back. She gave me a peck on the cheek and said she'd see me the next day with her crew now that she knew that she had my confidence.

✦

The next day, as the crew were setting up their equipment, lights and the sound boom and camera, I asked Virginie who else she was interviewing in India.

'I started that yesterday afternoon,' she said.

'Whom did you speak to?'

'I've put the story together. We'll speak to the commander who made first contact with the group at the Kohinoor and then we'll speak to Mr Sethi, your lawyer, and to Mr Santosh, the man at the…'

'I didn't ask you that, Virginie. I asked you whom you spoke to yesterday afternoon.'

'Chandrika Nath,' she said, and looked straight at me.

'I thought you might. What did she say?'

'Did you have anything to do with that woman, Thhat?'

'Chandrika? I had a lot to do with her,' I said.

'I mean in that way,' she said. 'Did you fuck her?'

'You are crazy?'

'No, I'm not. She spoke about you in a very strange way. And I…we had been together in the morning and you had said one year and she said she hadn't seen you for over a year. She used the same words as you did.'

'You really are crazy.'

'No, you don't owe it to me, one half-hearted fuck doesn't give me the right to know, but did you?'

'What do you think?'

'I think she was so coy about you. Like she's a policewoman and you are a convict and she's telling me that she wants to get inside the brain of a serial killer and she is sounding like she wants to get inside the pants of one…'

'Oi, Virginie, relax. This woman was trying to frame me and send me to Thailand to be shot. Not much love there, yeah? But I beat her at her own game.'

'Suppose she did her best to let you win?' she asked.

'No, no, no. She still wants me dead. I outwitted her. She

pretends she wants to "understand" and all this. Would I sleep with a woman who wanted to do that?' I asked.

'Yes, I think you would. But I think the camera's ready now. I'll send the crew off after the interview.'

Virginie asked the questions from behind the camera. She went through what I could remember of that night. The only thing I kept a mystery was the identity of Ravina. I said she was a French Mauritian whom I had met. None of the others had identified her definitely as an Indian.

The shoot finished and the crew packed up and Virginie sent them away out of the jail.

'Why did you tell that bullshit story about Ravina?' she asked.

'Who told you about Ravina?'

'Guess?' she challenged.

'Chandrika definitely didn't know who she was when my case ended. She must have been working hard since. What did she say about her?' I asked.

'Only that she was your accomplice in Thailand and that she is probably out of the country now.'

'Thanks for that. I am sorry, but I don't want you to use the Ravina bits in the film. Not even Chandrika saying it. Otherwise no deal.'

'They are interesting bits. Everyone speaks of her as the mystery woman and suddenly Chandrika knows who she is and has some history. Great editing surprise.'

'Leave her as the mystery woman,' I insisted.

'What's it to you?'

'I think she may be useful some time in the future. Please.'

'You trust me to edit it out? You'll have to. I can see you really want me to edit it out.'

'Yes,' I said.

'How badly?' she asked

'As badly as you want me to.'

'Okay. Can I stay a night with you?'

'They count visitors carefully. Too many checks and different people checking,' I said.

'Then can you come out for the night. I thought you had clout here.'

'Not that much clout,' I said.

The flicker of a doubt passed through my mind. Chandrika. She wasn't a rule-book player. Had she put this girl up to tempt me out of prison so I could be bundled off illegally?

No! Paranoia. I could see that Virginie had some perverse need to be my lover.

'You could come in as a working woman with the maintenance cleaners,' I said. 'Only one warder counts those in and out and I can fix that person.'

Oh, that appealed to her. I called Dilawar and told him to see to it. He made an appointment to meet her outside in the evening a few days later when he would be on night shift. The prisoners did all the cleaning in the prison, but once a month these outsiders came in. He would see her in past the staff registration.

I had two more interviews with Virginie, one with me walking around the yard with the other prisoners looking on. The other, with me joining in the yoga exercise of the prisoners, which I never ever attended except for Virginie and for Camera's camera.

And Virginie, behind the camera, would look at me as though I was telling her how I saved the world or won the battle of Waterloo or single-handedly built a commercial empire when all I was telling her about was how I avoided being sent to my execution in Thailand.

Then the appointed night arrived, and she was brought in by Dilawar. She was dressed in a worker's salwar-kameez with her head covered and the flap of the dupatta about her face, hiding her hair and complexion. She replaced one of the cleaning women by arrangement with Dilawar. The woman would return to the gate to be registered when the others left.

Dilawar was happy with the arrangement. He would allow us complete privacy and he would move Roy, who volunteered, to a cell round the corner.

The arrangement worked. I had some beers in the fridge and we had a drink and ate the Chinese food I had ordered by the light of two candles. It was a proper date.

She wanted to know why I didn't want to know about her.

'Why would I want to know? You come as an angel and you will fly away as one. Why should I bother with your histoire?'

'I bothered with yours.'

'Did you talk to anyone outside of India and France?'

'Okay, I spoke to Jop. He is in Amsterdam. He is out of the diplomatic service and works as a labourer. But I don't want to talk about them. I want to know you.'

'There is nothing to know.'

'Yes, there is. The equation between money and life. If you did what they say you did, then you did very huge things to people for very little gain.'

'You can speak straight to me. I don't need the softening of a code. I live with myself all the time. What you mean is why take a life for fifty or a hundred dollars? There are other ways of getting fifty or a hundred dollars?'

She looked long and deep into my face, lit by candlelight as hers was. The shadows fell, making her eyes look hooded. She said nothing for a while.

'Yes, you got it, that was the question.'

'It's an obvious answer. Suppose I ask the same question about flies. You swat flies. They bother you, they sit on your food, someone has told you they eat shit and vomit on the rim of your glass when you are drinking. You swat them. They are bad for you. Their lives are not what you are thinking about. You might or might not gain something by their deaths. You see what I am getting at?'

'But these are human beings. There's no camera now, Johnson, so tell me.'

'Maybe I don't value myself. You know Jesus Christ said treat other people like you would have yourself treated? I know that the rest of the world will swat me like a fly. I mean nothing to them or to time or to the future or the past and that means I don't think very hard about other people's lives. They should be like me. The same injustice, the same indifference. If they don't die today, they die tomorrow, tant pis.'

'Then why are you fighting so hard to preserve your own life? It shouldn't matter.'

'Instinct. And because there's nothing else to do.'

'Yes, there is,' she said and stood up, pushing the chair behind her and taking me by both hands and pulling me to the bed.

She sat me down and knelt and took my shoes off. She unbuttoned my shirt like she was my mother. She bent down and kissed me and when I tried to put my arms around her she started unbuttoning my trousers, which she pulled down together with my boxer shorts. I was naked and still sitting upright on the bed.

She lit another candle and by candlelight undressed and hung her clothes up on the back of a chair. For the first time I saw her fully naked. I didn't want her to approach me. I wanted her to stop and to turn round and I wanted to look at every curve and crevice of her body. She sensed this and lifting her arms to her head, did a slow step, a dance that got her to rotate.

'Beautiful,' I said.

'You could never get yourself to say, "You are beautiful, Virginie," could you? That would be personal. You are just making an aesthetic comment. But hush.'

She got into bed with me and held me so that her breasts were hard against my chest and then her stomach was on mine and our legs were entwined. She could feel me hard against her and she turned me from my side onto my back and was on top of me. She held my prick with one hand with a look of girlish concentration on her face, and fitted me into her. Then she smiled and relaxed and I could feel her weight as she began to hold me inside her and squeeze me as she moved.

She determined the length and rhythm of the strokes as we fucked, but I knew I was in control and could last as long as I wanted. And then I put all thought of control out of my head and I kissed her and got lost in her kiss.

I had my hands on her ass and could feel her pumping at and above me. Her breasts, which seemed small and firm when she was standing, swung away at my chest, the nipples stiff, long and brown.

We fucked for two hours. There were sounds outside in the prison. Whistles and the sounds of the changing of warders and the watch.

The jail would wake up early. I had arranged for Dilawar to smuggle her out while it was still dark. Then the hymns and bhajans would start and it would get impossible for her to leave unnoticed.

'We shouldn't fall asleep,' I said after she came, softly whimpering as she lay on me, shivers running all down her body.

'No.'

We rested in each other's arms for a few minutes, and then she shook herself awake.

'What will you do when your time here is up, Thhat? Have you thought about it?'

'Yeah, I've thought.'

'Can't you apply to Thailand for some sort of pardon or something?'

'I don't think so,' I said.

'I think they've got a king and he can hand out pardons,' she said.

'That's in the movies. This is the real world.'

'Is this the real world? You and me making love by candlelight in an Indian prison?'

'It's the only reality open to me.'

'What would you like my film to do for you?'

'Nothing.'

'Your wish is about to come true. It will do nothing.'

I saw her once again, but with her crew. She said that she wanted to have one more encounter before her return to France but I told her I couldn't face it. I couldn't trust my emotions and would rather deprive myself. I implied that I was falling in love with her and that it would be too painful for me if I allowed myself to fall further and inextricably in love with her.

She didn't suspect that the night was delicious, demanding, fulfilling, but quite enough. I didn't want her desperately any more. Her red hair was no longer luscious. It looked dry and artificial. Her body was not attractively muscular, just oddly developed and her legs were too long for a short torso. Her eyes, though, her eyes were alluring, and staring at them and holding them in focus seemed to alter her other features. She was beautiful again.

But she had to go.

✦

She wrote a few times and when I didn't reply, when I even stopped reading her letters, hers trickled off. One of the letters I read told me that the documentary had been shown and had made me famous, internationally.

Letters from other people poured in. There was a fan club out there. Roy read the letters, which had been read and censored by prison clerks. Dilawar told me that they didn't give me the letters from ladies, some young and some not so young, mentioning their ages and offering themselves, saying they wanted to sleep with a killer and be his lover.

Sick people, old man.

✦

The governor and deputy governor were changed several times. Each time a new one came he or she (yes, there were women in charge) would come around to visit me.

Except for Razia Gaznavi. She was high profile, a Muslim woman who had been promoted, the newspapers hinted, above her station and abilities, because the ruling political party wanted to appoint Muslims to seemingly commanding positions.

Razia thought my privileges should be taken away and I should be sent back to the main block. On her first day there, followed by the press, she came to visit our block. The papers reported it: 'Governor Gaznavi didn't speak to Tihar's most notorious prisoner, Johnson Thhat, or the other prisoners on the separation block, but examined their cells. She did not look pleased.'

They came and took away everything – the refrigerator, the typewriter, the furniture, the soft mattress, everything.

'We are going to store it, sir,' Dilawar said. 'You just wait, it will come back.'

She ordered my move, together with poor Roy, to the main block. They took away our civvies and put us into the homespun cloth uniform of the rest. The beds were just boards and the toilets were holes in the ground in the cells, which we had to clean ourselves.

The food hall and the food itself stank. The prisoners sat on wooden benches to eat potatoes, sawdust chappatis and daal, day after day.

The warders were all extremely apologetic. They seemed to hate the new governor and her tightening regime and routines, and brought Roy and me some of their own food.

'I can get through all this, Jaan Senji,' Roy said. 'All I need is my Spinoza.'

'I doubt if they can smuggle Italian food in,' I said.

'It's a philosopher, a book, Jaan Senji, not pfeeza-pfaasta!' he said.

The book was retrieved from the store.

As it happened, there was an election in Delhi and the people elected a party that the left wing and liberal press referred to as 'fascists'. I never bothered with Indian politics but I gathered that this new chief minister, or whatever she was (yes, a woman) of Delhi was not as sympathetic to promoting Muslims as the last government.

Then Razia made her false move. She quarrelled with the instructors who came in to put the prisoners through their yoga routine. Razia wanted to move the yoga classes to later in the morning and the yoga instructors, who wanted to be free to get on with other jobs outside the prison during their day, objected. The four instructors said they would go on strike unless she reconsidered the new routine. Razia declared to her staff that she wasn't going to be kicked around by a team of yogis. If they didn't want to work there, she could get other yogis and they could go.

The yogis went on strike and the prisoners were locked up in their cells in their yoga hour and they didn't like it.

Coincidentally, Virginie had returned to India to make another documentary on some river and dam dispute somewhere in western India and she made her way to Delhi to see me. She had to wait till visitors' day and had to ask special permission as a foreign journalist. But she had by then made many political contacts in Delhi and she got the passes and came to see me in the visiting area.

'No home comforts or privacy here,' she said.

Not a word about why I hadn't replied to her letters.

She enquired what it was like.

'Not so hot. The yoga teachers are on strike and the prisoners hate the new governor.'

'Then get rid of her,' Virginie said. 'Yoga is a Hindu thing, isn't it?'

I didn't understand what she was saying at first.

'I hate her too,' Virginie said. 'I have been a week in Delhi trying to get into this fucking place to see you.'

'Alas, it is no longer a fucking place,' I said.

'No,' she said. 'But the city is alive with political talk and Hindu revivals and all this bullshit.'

'So?'

'So use it.'

It was her plan. The next day at yoga time when we were locked into our cells, the prisoners began a hunger strike and started rattling the tin mugs they used to wash their arses against the bars of the cells, making the most awful din possible. The warders came round scraping their batons threateningly along the bars.

Razia turned up to have a look and retreated immediately. She made the wrong move again: she issued an order cancelling all privileges and visiting times that afternoon. Some of the prisoners, who relied on their relatives to smuggle tobacco, cannabis and other indulgences once a month into the prison, were not at all pleased. The tactic spread across the prison. No cooperation.

The prison gates were assailed by reporters and TV crews.

The first headlines were 'Tihar Prisoners on Strike'.

The strike went on for days with the prisoners refusing to leave their cells.

The next week the headlines were worse: 'Religious Protest to Reinstate Yoga in Tihar'.

The prisoners asked Roy to lead Sanskrit prayers and they sat up all night reciting prayers and singing holy songs. The TV crew gathered outside the walls to record them.

It had the desired effect.

The more rabid publications came out with 'Muslim Governor Attacks Hindu Practices in Tihar Jail'.

Virginie had been active. Several foreign TV channels asked for access to Tihar to report events and the Home Office swiftly moved to deny the requests and even to cancel some of the journalists' visas.

It had become a national incident.

The poison spread in the prison. A Muslim prisoner was beaten up and, though it may have had nothing to do with the yoga and the strike, Razia moved swiftly to isolate the Muslim prisoners from the rest.

Again this was the wrong move: 'Religious Apartheid in Tihar by Governor's Decree'.

Dilawar reported that politicians had turned up at the gates and Razia and her deputy had been called in for consultations. For days now she had hardly put in an appearance at the prison, she was with politicians, arguing her case.

Other senior police officers turned up and came through to inspect the strikers of the main block. Some of the prisoners started shouting slogans. 'Reinstate visits, reinstate yoga!'

The officers left.

Dilawar said he had met Virginie at the gates. She was with a horde of other foreigners. There was a lot of police. She went up to him and told him that if they couldn't film inside, they were filming outside. She sent me a note.

'International news. Razia refuses interviews. Chief of Delhi says prison policy will be rethought.'

The next day, C. P. Singh, who had been a popular deputy governor, returned to the prison and was greeted with cheers by the prisoners and warders. He gathered everyone together in the exercise yard and addressed us. He said that he was now acting governor of the prison and that Governor Razia Gaznavi had taken indefinite leave and the prison could now go back to normal. He also announced the reinstatement of the yoga team and the allowance of extra visiting days.

The prisoners cheered and cheered. You would have thought he was Mahatma Gandhi declaring Independence.

He must have been very busy but he came to me that evening and asked the others whom I lived with to be taken out.

'How are things, Johnson?'

'As you see them, boss. You are a big hero.'

'I have to go cautiously. You must be patient. I will have to wait till press attention dies down and then you can go back to your old quarters. How is Roy sahib?'

'He is reading Spaghetti,' I said.

'Very good, very good,' he said.

He was as good as his word. In a few days we were back to normal. I returned to the sequestration block with Roy as my neighbour and my furniture and stuff followed.

3

JOHNSON THHAT IN DARING
ESCAPE FROM TIHAR

Johnson Thhat, convicted fraudster and poisoner, the big daddy of Tihar jail, has staged a spectacular escape after eight years of detention. In characteristic style, Thhat, who befriended the jail staff, staged a birthday party and in a widely criticized move was allowed to bring sweetmeats into the jail to celebrate his thirty-seventh birthday. The sweets were offered to the inmates in his private wing and to the warders of the jail.

What they didn't know was that the sweets imported into the jail on Thhat's behalf were heavily drugged and soon the entire shift of the jail's governors not including Governor C.P. Singh who was off on a day's leave, were fast asleep.

Thhat, it is believed, then extracted the keys from the jail's central office and left the sleeping citadel by the front door. It is not believed that he allowed any other prisoners to escape or took anyone with him.

The home minister is expected to come under

severe questioning about the escape of this notorious prisoner and about conditions in Tihar jail, which allow prisoners to import sweetmeats without any check as to what is being brought in. There will no doubt be questions asked about security at the jail and the laxity of relationships between the staff and the convicts.

Thhat was convicted of poisoning a party of tourists in order to rob them of their possessions and now, in this extremely daring and unprecedented move, he has repeated the crime on his warders to the great shame of the particular correctional facility.

Thhat had one more year of his jail term to serve as he was given additional time for entering India illegally and for possessing a false passport.

Police say that a nationwide hunt for Thhat is in progress and that all exits from the country have been put on alert as this master of disguise is bound to try and leave the country.

A good story. But of course it wasn't true. Only a child and a childish nation like India was ready to believe such garbage. I wrote the play, the whole drama, the story – exactly what I wanted the papers to say. I had no idea that they would fall for it without a murmur of doubt.

Yes, it was my birthday, and yes, I did get Mrs Roy to make some sweets, enough pedas, laddoos and barfi to fuel a wedding. Roy knew where to get hold of a crooked chemist and he supplied the dope. The sweets were brought in by a stranger who said he was Roy's nephew and had brought the vanload of stuff for a surprise party for me.

Yes, the warders and prisoners were fed the sweets and some of them did feel drowsy and some of them did drop, but the key warders on my wing and the deputy and the governor, who had absented himself as I had warned him, knew exactly what was going to happen and I was actually escorted to the gate and let out to where a car was waiting.

Eight years and I was up for good behaviour and release. I read in the papers that Chandrika was now a superintendent. She was the fastest-rising star in the Indian police force and she was one of the officers controlling the military-like move against the Sikh separatists in Punjab. The thought crossed my mind that she was preoccupied with a much more important job than seeing that justice was done for eleven stale murders in Thailand for which she had no official responsibility. Why would she pursue me through time?

But then that look in her eye when I had frustrated her intent came back to me. I can still picture it, man. I have betrayed women and know how they howl and scowl, but this was different. It had become her religion to have me shot in Thailand. I would meet her again.

I still had the last of the gems concealed in my cell and I put it to use.

✦

Governor Singh had returned for the third time to Tihar and now he was promoted from acting to full-fledged governor of the prison. It was delicate discussing the matter with him.

He started the conversation. He visited my cell when I was typing.

'All police work is being done on computers now. The latest thing, imported from US. Knowledge systems,' he said.

'I've seen them. I don't think I can use them. This electric typewriter is fine, as long as you can supply me ribbons and paper.'

'What are you writing?' he asked.

'My memoirs,' I said.

'What about a game of rummy, Governor sahib,' Roy shouted from his cell. 'If I win you take my place and I take yours.'

'Not now, I am busy,' Singh replied.

'I think the library needs a Western philosophy shelf,' Roy shouted. 'I can do it for you and start classes. Think of the publicity you will get in the newspapers, Governor sahib!'

'I will think about it, Roy. Are you getting commission on the books? And if not, why not?'

'Don't insult me, Singh sahib, I am not small-time. I am big-time, like your favourite man Johnson Thhat there.'

'I came to ask for his help,' Singh said.

'What sort of help?' I asked.

'A point of law, Johnson. You read all this stuff and I can ask police lawyers but I think they are playing some tricks on me here. Can you come to my office and we'll discuss it? Come after dark. I will tell Dilawar. I don't want the whole prison to know we are having a tea party.'

I was taken at night to his office. There was more than tea on offer.

'You might remember those Pathans who came in with you after your incident?'

'Yes, two of them died,' I said.

'One of them died, if you remember, in an encounter and the other old fellow hanged himself when I was in charge of the prison as the deputy.'

I said I remembered all that.

'Now some politicians are trying to help the old man's relatives, who are not Pakistani – they were all Indians it turns out – to sue me for negligence on that count. You see, these fellows were detained without due judicial process.

Your bloody Chandrika. They were being held here because the RAW, the Indian secret service, wanted to interrogate them. Apparently they turned out not to be anything of the sort. They were just swindlers and petty thieves. Nothing to do with terror or spying. The politicians are embarrassed by this so they want to put the blame on someone else. Me. A case for negligence or something like that will shift the focus of their illegal detention.'

'I don't know about it, but I can look it up for you,' I said.

'Let me call Sethi if he is still around and he can bring me the right books.'

He found Sethi for me and I had a conversation with him and got the books.

C.P. Singh came round a few days later looking worried. 'They are going to court,' he said.

'You have to hit them first,' I said.

'Not the relatives, the politicians.'

'They have moved on,' he said.

'Then use a diversionary tactic. The old man killed himself, I remember, because he was mind-blown after the young Pathan was shot in the encounter. You see, I watched them. At least heard them. They were lovers, the old man and the smooth young fellow without hair on his cheeks. The old man had left his two wives and a lot of children and went chasing this boy.'

'So what about that? He did kill himself.'

'His family doesn't want big publicity and exposure of the reason for suicide. Even in their community it would be a big disgrace and they will want to hush it up. The papers will be most interested in that aspect, though. For them that is the story, not whether you issued a bed sheet legally to him and whether he was being watched and could have been stopped from hanging himself. Call the papers and give an interview saying you recall the case – it was a homosexual-love suicide.'

Singh looked at me, all admiration and gratitude.

'And the other thing you can do is hit the officer who carried out the encounter.' I continued. 'We know whom we are talking about. There were other ordinary constables, who must now have retired, on that transfer mission of the young Pathan. You can look up police records and find them. If you pay them they will be ready to reveal the truth or even just to hint that Chandrika ordered or actually carried out the shooting – pulled the trigger – into the back of his head after releasing him and asking him to run for his life from the van.'

'What? Attack Chandrika? She has solid influence. She will crush me like a worm.'

'No, she won't. First find the old cops and then just let her know that if this case is opened against you, hints will start reaching the press that the old man hanged himself because his lover was shot in a dodgy encounter, murdered by Indian police and their commanding officer. I know her. She has influence, and doesn't want to be bothered with this rubbish so she will herself have the cases crushed.'

'You are mad and you are marvellous. I thank God I am your friend and not your enemy,' he said.

'Singh sahib, I will soon have to tell you how to be even more of a friend by pretending to be even more of an enemy,' I said.

'I'm waiting. But meanwhile I will set out looking for the old policemen.'

It worked. Singh called me two weeks later and said he had subtly let Chandrika know that the case might explode in her face and, as if by magic, the negligence charge had been withdrawn. The family had been paid off by persons unknown, and threatened with exposure of the old man's motives. They had gone away, off Singh's back.

'Chandrika has good, heavy, clunking political clout, old man, the favourite woman in the service, even though you may mistake her for a man,' I said.

'Yeah, but I've made an enemy of her,' he said.

'Wrong. A friend can be someone who doesn't want you as an enemy,' I said.

'What can I do for you, Thhat?'

'You can make sure that you are not directly in charge of the jail on the twenty-third of this month. In fact take leave and have an acting governor and give Dilawar gate duty and permission to do as I say.'

'What are you doing?'

'Don't worry, I'll be back, Singh sahib. How could I leave you and your hospitality?'

I didn't tell anyone what I was planning, but I asked Roy to tell his wife to get me a car and some money. He knew exactly what I was doing.

'Take me with you,' he said.

'Look, you have four months left with good recommendations. Stay here and finish it. Otherwise you'll be on the run and may be back here for a long time. Reading bloody philosophy.'

'I know, but I will miss you,' he said.

'Not for long,' I assured him.

✦

I fixed it and Dilawar led me out to the waiting car with the keys on the left front tyre for me to drive away.

I had a panic attack in the night when I found myself going round in circles in north Delhi. I couldn't read the signs and I must have lost six hours just going along one highway in the wrong direction, trying to find my way to another and losing myself in the warrens of the city. If the police had started looking for me, now was the time they would find me. I didn't want to stop and ask for directions.

I finally found my way out of the city, heading south.

I got to Agra, the city of the Taj where my adventure had begun, and abandoned the car as dawn was breaking. I knew there was a train to Bombay in two hours. I went into the town, bought a Muslim cap and a long shirt, pyjamas and a furry cap. I changed into the Indian clothes and threw my own away. With a pair of glasses bought from a street vendor, I looked very different. I bought a suitcase to avoid looking suspicious, tested my disguise on the ticket clerk, and boarded the train to Bombay. I found a seat with no one next to me. I kept my fingers crossed. The ticket inspector greeted me with

'Salaam aleikum.'

My disguise was working.

When I got off in Bombay the day after, the headlines of the morning papers were about my escape. They had a picture of me with dark glasses and a full crop of hair, the mugshot from the police station.

I discarded the shades.

I made my way down to the harbour with my suitcase and booked a ticket on the hovercraft to Goa. I had an hour. I went to the phone booth outside and called Virginie in Paris.

'If you want to see me, get a plane or planes to Goa,' I said. 'I will be on the Taj hotel beach every day for three days between two and three in the afternoon.'

She knew better than to ask me where I was or how I had got there. 'I'm on my way,' is what she said.

In Goa, I checked into a small lodging house with a fat landlady who seemed already drunk by mid-afternoon when I approached her house. Not the sort to read newspapers.

On the second day, I made my way down to the Taj beach. I walked about as I had said, between two and three. Nothing.

The next day, Virginie was waiting for me. She had taken the first plane out of Paris to Bombay and then on to Goa. She had her suitcases with her on the sand. She had money and I sent her to book herself a double room in the Taj and then thought better of it and ran behind her. I would boldly go in as her escort. They wouldn't expect me here and of course, I had no special fear of being caught.

I just wanted a few days.

✦

We spent six nights of eating, drinking, fucking , walking on the beach, taking boat rides, going around the old Portuguese churches and letting Virginie point out features of the architecture, hiring a car and riding around the islands of Goa fantasizing about buying an old derelict Portuguese bungalow with lots of character and doing it up and living happily ever after, throwing and going to local champagne-and-lobster parties.

All that week she didn't ask me what I was doing or how I got there. We just enjoyed it.

Time and her absence had made me fond of her body again. The T-shirts and shorts she had bought suited her. I too bought myself holiday clothes: bush shirts, cotton shorts, very large dark glasses and ridiculous hats and caps to cover and disguise my face. She swam in a bikini and when we went to relatively isolated beaches, took it off and swam in the nude.

One morning on an isolated northern beach she threw off her bikini and, spreading the blanket we'd brought from the hotel, lay down and held her arms up to me.

'Now, here, with the sound of the sea in our ears! Back to when we were creatures of the deep. Come, Jean.' This was the name she had adopted for me.

I slipped out of my trunks and sat on the blanket and she took my hand and rubbed it on her tummy. My hand automatically descended to her tuft of red hair.

'See how wet I am for you. Make love to me, now.'

Of course I was aroused and I lay on top of her supporting my weight on my elbows. The sand ground into them and cut me so I put my arms under her. Sand there too, on the blanket I shook out before laying it down.

'Lick me,' she said.

Sand got on my tongue and I had to repeatedly interrupt myself as she gyrated and moaned under me. The sand on the tongue, trapped in her hair, was a much harsher irritant than the single strand of hair that persists on the tongue and that you have to try and pinch and scrape off when you go down on a woman. 'The sand,' I said.

'Fuck the sand. No, fuck me. 'Come on.'

She was on her back and thrust up towards me as I entered her. I could feel the grains of sand cutting the thin skin on my hardened prick. It must have been cutting her too, inside or on the surface, but she gave no sign of noticing the pain.

I withdrew, sat up and picked up a towel and cleaned the sand off, but I couldn't brush off all the grains. I could feel them. They were in my pubes and some came off the towel.

I found a clean patch of towel and looked at her crotch to clean the grains off it.

'Just wipe it off, come on,' she said.

'It comes back as fast as I can clear it.' I could feel the sting of a couple of gashes on the side of my prick where the sand and friction had cut it. 'We'll damage ourselves.'

'Ohhh!' she said, exasperated and standing up, gave me her hand to lead me into the water.

'Come and wash it off, we can make love in the sea.'

She led me into waist-deep water and the salt stung my cuts, but we weren't going to give up.

She wrapped her legs around me, holding my neck. The water lifted her and made her delightfully light. I manoeuvred myself into her, ignoring the stinging and she flung her head back, in pretence of ecstasy. She wasn't play-acting; she was anticipating a surge of feeling and posing dramatically for it to come on.

I tried moving her on me, up and down, with both my hands under her, but the salt water had completely washed away her lubrication though it couldn't get rid of the stubborn grains of sand. Fucking was abrasive, cutting, painful and not the primitive joy she expected in the water.

'You don't like it, do you?' she asked, untangling her legs from behind mine, standing in the water and ending our embrace.

'The chemistry is okay, but the physics is no good.'

She laughed.

'Then let's go back to the hotel,' she said. When we got back to the blankets and towels she saw the gashes on my half-erect prick and held it and, kneeling down on the offending sand, kissed it.

'I am sorry, Jean Valjean,' she said to my prick. 'Me and my romantic notions have got you injured.'

Back in the hotel room she generously said she wouldn't insist on making love until my sand-cuts had healed.

She had a few cuts too.

The books say women want sex to get love, but what love was I offering her? What love could I ever have offered Ravina? No, they didn't want me for love. Their lovemaking was compulsive, as though they wanted my body to prove their attractiveness to themselves. And beyond that proof they wanted to cocoon themselves in the shelter of my wickedness.

We drank rum with ice and I said I had to do something before our money ran out.

'Let's escape to France,' she said. 'There are so many boats in the harbour. We can buy ourselves places on one that goes to the Gulf, say. Get one of your forged passports and then get out.' There was a pleading edge to her voice.

'I could move from one place to another, but if I don't get back into Tihar, Chandrika will put an international contract out on me, and from France or from Dubai if I am recognized I can be sent back to Thailand in chains. They don't have the same regulations as India where I've got to serve my sentences before I can be moved.'

'But your time is nearly up.'

'I know,' I said and then picked up the phone and dialled.

'What are you doing?' she asked, grabbing the phone from me. I grabbed it back and held my hand up to urge her to relax. She resigned herself and waited.

I called a Delhi police station and asked for Inspector Vasudev, the whistling commander. He came on the phone and identified himself.

'Call this number from another phone outside. Ask for room 412. Just do it.'

He asked, 'Who is this?' just once. Then, a pause. I repeated the number and my demand and he didn't ask again. He knew. He put the phone down.

Virginie knew who Vasudev was. She didn't ask what I was doing. She too knew and she sat down on the sofa of the suite and let her hand holding her drink drop to the carpet and spill it. Her pretty red brow was knotted and she scowled into the distance.

The phone rang.

'Yes, I can speak now,' he said.

'You know who this is?'

'Yes, I know.'

I hadn't spoken to him in eight years.

'You take a holiday and bring your family to Goa. When you arrive get a cheap hotel or lodge in the police holiday home or whatever and call this number again. I see you are still an inspector and your Chandrika has become a big shot, man.'

'I'll come,' he said. I hung up.

Two days passed and then the phone rang at night.

'I arrived this evening by train. I have spent a lot of money. I brought my wife. This is Taj number, right?'

'No detective tricks with me, Vasudev, I am going to make you the most famous policeman in India. Tomorrow afternoon you carry a police revolver and come to…'

I was about to tell him when Virginie came up from behind me and with a blow knocked the receiver out of my hand. When I went to pick it up from the floor, she wrenched the phone wires from the wall and stood challengingly over me.

'Let's get out of here, please. You can't do this, Jean.'

'I have to do what I have to do. There's another phone in the bathroom. Are you going to wrench that one out too? You want to see me dead? Blindfolded and shot so you can make a documentary about it?'

She was crying. She let herself go and sobbed.

'I am sorry,' she said in English, and then in French over and over again.

The phone rang again in the bathroom. I picked it up.

'At the Rainbow bar on the beach behind the Taj. I shall

be there at two in the afternoon. You are going to come with your wife, make it look casual. Then you recognize me and arrest me,' I said and put the phone down.

'Why?' Virginie asked through her tears. 'You don't give a shit about me!'

'Do you wish you had a camera? You could record all this. Good stuff, good TV.' I pretended that I thought she was being dramatic and self-indulgent.

'I asked you why you are doing it,' she shouted.

I sat on the bed.

'You know, when I was in France as a boy we used to go and see American films. And some of them were cowboy films in which people got shot and dropped dead. That was like good, clean fun. And then there were other films about prison and death row and fellows condemned to die by the rope or by the electric chair or gas chamber or lethal injection. Somehow the guillotine seemed to belong to the French Revolution and the age of equality and romance and all that shit. But the American films terrified me, with the condemned fellow sweating and walking down to where his life would be ended by the throw of a switch after he was strapped in. I had nightmares about those films.'

She wiped her tears and listened intently.

'And sometimes I think if I was condemned to death that way and I had a last wish I wouldn't ask for a cigarette or a drink or a meal. You know what I'd ask for? I'd ask to be played six hours of Ravi Shankar's sitar music.'

She suppressed her crying.

'You like it that much?'

'No. I can't stand it. And if I had to listen to six hours of it my will to live would disappear and I would go humming an Elvis Presley tune to the electric chair.'

'Why do you think that's funny?' she shouted, enraged. 'Nothing is funny. You just called a man to give yourself up and go back to jail!'

'That's what's funny. This fellow the whistling commander will become a general if he captures me.'

'You need not keep the appointment. We could stay on the run in India until they capture you by themselves. We could get weeks, months, years together. Maybe they'll never capture you. And we'll grow old and die natural deaths.'

'They will capture me. Chandrika? Remember? And then the new sentences will start from that day. It's better it starts tomorrow and I can finish my twenty years and then roam the world, free. I will come to France to you if you can wait. And anyway if I am lucky they will send me back to Tihar where I am fixed up as the uncrowned king and you can visit me most times. We are together. No despair, ma chérie!'

'That's not like living a real life.'

'What real life are you talking about? You come after a guy like me and then you talk like some bourgeois college girl wanting to live in the suburbs of Paris with a Citroën and two-and-a-quarter kids and a nine-to-five job selling insurance? Then why me? I am a killer!'

'No, I don't want that. I want you. As you are. Sorry,' she said and came up and closed her eyes and held her face to mine for a kiss.

I kissed her indifferently. I was thinking of other things.

We didn't fuck or sleep that night.

She kept me from dozing by prodding me with questions.

'Suppose we went to a place where the Indian police don't go, like Afghanistan?'

'Just let me try and sleep, okay? I might have a hard few days ahead.'

✦

We sat in the Rainbow bar sipping Virgin Marys 'to celebrate Virginie and the pure taste of her', I said. We wanted to stay sober. Vasudev, the whistling commander, turned up on the dot, wearing a tasteless yellow bush shirt with large prints of the monkey god Hanuman on it, white trousers and white leather shoes. He was carrying a small revolver in his trouser pocket and he sat down with his wife at a table and looked round the bar at the customers. He had already spotted me but wanted a little drama.

The bar was just a bamboo enclosure covered with thatch with tables and chairs under it and a bamboo bar towards the back.

I was wearing dark glasses and Vasudev ordered his snacks and then theatrically turning around, recognized me, doing a number out of Hindi films, opening his eyes wide and drawing back, his face struck with surprise and horror. Then he whispered to his wife. He obviously hadn't told her why they were in Goa, as she was clearly puzzled. Vasudev got up quickly, walked over to me with his hand in his pocket and as he approached our table he said, 'I am a police officer. I am arresting you, Johnson Thhat, because I recognize you. Put your hands above the table and up. Drop the glass.' Loud enough for all the people in the bar to hear. I did as he said – literally, and the glass smashed on the floor.

Everyone in the bar was now looking at us. I had my hands up.

'Take my glasses off, Virginie,' I said, and she did it.

'Don't panic. I am a police officer,' said Vasudev. 'Phone the police station immediately to come here,' he said in the direction of the bar, keeping his eyes and hand steadily on me as though I posed an immediate danger.

The bartender began to dial.

'There is a police jeep on the road at the back, always cruising,' said one of the waiters and he dashed out.

Vasudev instructed me to stand.

'I remember you,' I said out loud. 'What are you doing here, superintendent?'

'Doesn't matter what I am doing. I know what you are doing. You are escaping.'

The spectators were impressed.

The patrol jeep that the waiter had gone for arrived before three other police jeeps. They parked on the beach and rushed in. Six of the cops were armed.

'Inspector Vasudev, Delhi Police. This is Johnson Thhat whom I have recognized and arrested,' he said.

Two cops pointed their machine guns at me.

'Easy boys, I am not going anywhere,' I said.

Vasudev took his police identity card out and showed it to the cop in charge, who nodded. Vasudev was his superior.

'Who is this lady?' the Goan cop asked.

'I know her. She is an interviewer from England,' Vasudev replied.

'France,' said Virginie.

'You will have to come with us also, madam,' the other policeman said.

'What's it got to do with me?'

'This is notorious criminal. You may have helped him to escape in which case it has everything to do with you,' he said, and then asked me, 'Do you acknowledge that you are Johnson Thhat?'

'Yes, I am,' I replied.

'We require you to walk to the police vehicle,' he said.

A crowd had now gathered outside the Rainbow bar. People had come running from all corners of the beach. Everyone knew that I had been captured. I walked to the police car and felt like one of those film stars walking through a crowd of fans to the Oscar ceremony. Only, I had my hands on my head and they don't usually proceed like that, but that's just a detail, Pradhan sahib.

✦

Vasudev, the whistling commander, was in all the papers. He was the hero of the day. He gave statements saying he needed a quiet holiday with his wife as she was getting very stressed at her work. He was nominated for a special award for vigilance from the Delhi Police involving cash and marked for immediate promotion.

Constable Ribeiro, who took charge of me, was nice enough. I was to be taken back to Delhi by plane. I asked after Virginie and was told that she had been released because she proved that she just came into the country and met me by accident, just as Vasudev did. When Ribeiro told me this, I could see that he didn't believe either fact. He was a seasoned old owl with huge saucers of dark beneath his eyes like burnt wrinkled skin. Things don't happen by chance. He suspected, rather knew, that there were appointments and rendezvous in both cases.

His last words, as I was taken from the station by the CID officers who were to escort me, were, 'I hope you enjoyed Goa. Come again.'

I liked his face. His cheek.

✦

They gave me six years more for the successful escape, which involved the drugging of prison officers. C.P. Singh was transferred from Tihar to some obscure jail in central India, a definite demotion. But he told me when I got back to Tihar and he was clearing his things that everything had worked out for him. With the money he now had he had built a house in his village and hired people to put his land to productive use. Also, his son had invested in an import-export business to sell things to Canada. That would surely make money. He said we would most probably meet again. And soon he would, with his investments, be rich enough. All because of me and the lump sums in diamonds, he would soon have enough money to bribe politicians to make sure he advanced in the service. 'So demotion is the path to promotion,' he said and he grinned at having thought up his first irony.

✦

Back in Tihar, Roy greeted me with a grunt. He said he knew I'd be back and had even worked out whom I'd call to rearrest me. He said he had moved on from Spinola to someone called Soap-and-Hire and this one was even more like Vedantic philosophy. I agreed that one day he would tell me all about it.

The new governor had been round to his cell, having been given the appointment while I was still on the run, and asked him a lot of questions about me. He was a friend of C.P. Singh's and he suspected that Singh had done well out of his acquaintance with me – and he didn't have any plans to upset me. He had told Roy that we were welcome to stay on the sequestration wing as C.P. Singh had designated it, even though there was no such thing in the rules. In fact, he said I would scare the other prisoners if I mixed with them.

'I would scare them too, Governor sahib,' Roy said.

'You are a mild fellow,' the governor said.

'But my words are harsh. I can prove with Bishop Berkeley to these prisoners that they don't exist,' Roy said.

'That would save a lot of trouble,' said the new governor.

On the day I got back to Tihar I had chalked up nine years, three months and three days of what I called my exile from Thailand. For the statute of limitations to expire in Thailand I needed ten years and one month. I was sentenced to eight years more for my escape. Two years short. Shit!

I had spotted Chandrika in court when my hearing for the escape was in session. She came, stayed for five minutes and then was called away by a fellow in uniform who whispered into her ear and she left the courtroom glaring at me. She had, through even this brief appearance, confirmed my fears. She was still interested in my fate even though she was now advising governments on policing policy and subduing large political uprisings.

It was said that she personally shot a lot of Sikh separatist suspects in Punjab when she was a senior officer in charge of the troubles there. The newspapers had begun to compare her to the goddess Durga: beautiful, fearless, a final judge and ruthless executioner. She had said to me that I had killed at least eleven people. I would have liked to ask her what her score was.

4

The newspapers called him Haji Ghulam and this was the name he wanted to be known by. He was hunted down by the Indian police for masterminding the bomb attacks on the Indian parliament. Three trucks had been driven against the concrete barriers and exploded. Two suicide bombers died in the debacle and took twelve passers-by and four security guards with them to hell.

No parliamentarians were killed and no damage was done to the parliament building. The third truck was either driven by a ghost or the driver dived out at the last minute unobserved and disappeared.

I was living on newspaper and TV news. Poor Roy, due to leave prison two years previously, had had more cases of swindling laid against him.

I now had a television set in my room. In the nine years, the last part of my sentence, I had made great strides. I had changed the electric typewriter for a computer at which I had become pretty good. I had two mobile phones and could call Virginie or anyone I wanted any time. In fact we would order our daily meals over the mobile phones. When the credit ran out, Dilawar or one of the screws would take the money and recharge them. We tipped heavily.

The news that day was all about the arrest of Haji Ghulam. The TV reports said that he was a Pakistani national and the head of a terrorist organization called the Army of the Universal Caliphate (ATUC). They had pictures of him without a big beard when he was a student and he looked very ugly. No wonder he was hiding behind the bushy hair he now sported. His real name was Ehsan Battiwalla. His family was originally Gujarati but had migrated to Karachi when Pakistan was formed. He was captured by the police in a suburb of Delhi with equipment, which they said could be connected to the truck bombs used in the attack on parliament. He would be tried for murder, for terrorism, for spying, for conspiracy and be hanged. There was only one place he could land up. He did.

There was a lot of shouting across the yard that night. We heard screams as we slept but were too far away to make out what it was. It isn't terribly unusual in prison. Then it went quiet.

In the morning I asked Dilawar what the noises had been.

'It's that son-of-a-bitch terrorist fellow. They brought him in last evening and they let the other prisoners loose on him.'

Dilawar had brought me the morning newspapers as usual. As Roy and I ate breakfast together, I read the papers. The headlines were all about the capture of Haji Ghulam, the mastermind of terror.

A small item on the foreign pages caught my attention. The conference of Asian nations was on, and among other things, the participants were to negotiate the extradition treaties between themselves. Sethi came that morning to see Roy about his case. I called him aside. I wanted him to get to the top treaty lawyers in the country and ask them what the foreign ministry was planning vis-à-vis treaties with Thailand about extradition.

He brought news the next day. He knew what I was concerned about and had asked the right questions. It was conceivable, he said, that the foreign ministry was talking to all South Asian nations about terrorism and about law and order. There was a clause in a possible treaty which would allow countries to render wanted or convicted terrorists and also criminals to the country where they had perpetrated an act of terror or a crime or were wanted for trial. There could be new extradition laws in India arising from this treaty. It was really all about security from terror, but it could have consequences for ordinary killers.

'Could it mean they send somebody to Thailand if the Thais request it even if that person is serving a sentence in India?'

'It could mean that, sir,' Sethi said.

Pradhan sahib, I will never say I didn't know what to do. You know enough about me now to know I have never given way to that. Only death is a dead end. This was a political threat; it would have to be dealt with politically. I had to enter the game, but I had no cards.

I called Dilawar.

'I don't want lunch ordered. I will go to the dining hall today and eat with the other convicts.'

'You can't eat that stuff, sir,' Dilawar said.

'Just tell me when it's time.'

He knew from my tone that I meant it. This wasn't a whim, it was part of some scheme. He conducted me to the dining hall on the hour.

I walked in with him and surveyed the scene. The convicts had taken their seats and there was an awful din in the hall with their tin plates rattling and their voices raised as they had been given time for free association.

As I stood framed in the doorway I was noticed.

'Jhowson!'

The hall was hushed. Everyone was looking at me. At the corner of one bench, isolated by a long space from everyone else, slumped over the trestle with his hair long over his prisoner's tunic, was Haji Ghulam.

I walked over to him and lifted his head with my hand. He was only half conscious. Everyone, prisoners and screws, watched.

His eyes were black and protruding like golf balls and his face was badly bruised, bleeding and filthy. I don't think he knew where he was or what had befallen him. He had been beaten nearly to death by these patriots of India – thieves, gangsters, murderers, arsonists, child molesters all. They had stood up for India and faced with inferior numbers, one against a hundred, had battered this fellow to near death.

He let out a cry of pain, of fear or begging for help, I don't know.

'Ghulam, it's all right,' I said in English. 'They won't hurt you any more.'

I turned to the hushed hall, which was watching.

'You bastards, you daughter-fuckers,' I said in Hindi. 'Were you giving this fellow a taste of Indian justice? Is that what you want for yourselves, you sister-fucking sodomites? If any one touches so much as a hair of this fellow's head, they'll be answerable to me.'

A murmur passed like a tremor round the room. 'It's said that he is a terrorist. Let the government prove it and if he is guilty let him hang and his soul rot in hell. That's what I believe. But you and I have no right, you less than me, you sons of pigs and bitches, to decide.'

The hall was quiet. This was the first time in my nearly eighteen years that I had spoken to the assembly. I turned to Dilawar and the screws behind me. 'Take him to my block and put him in my cell. Please tell the deputy sahib that I would like to see him and that the prison doctor should come to this man straight away. Take him.'

I turned on my heel as though I was some Pharaoh, and walked off. Behind me came a tide of noise.

They laid Ghulam on a mattress on the floor of my cell and the doctor came. He said the fellow had lost a lot of blood, had broken ribs and a broken collarbone, endless bruises and perhaps brain concussion. He gave him several shots and said they would ensure he didn't die in his sleep.

The deputy came and thanked me.

'If the man had died I would have been in for a very high jump. I didn't know, these bastards didn't report that he was being beaten up. Like the convicts, these warders also feel patriotic and believe terrorists should be bashed up. Especially a big catch like Haji Ghulam.'

I told the deputy that returning Ghulam to the block would be risky and that he should be moved into our wing. He agreed and gave the orders. Ghulam was now our neighbour.

The doctor sent for a nurse and a drip feed and they attached an apparatus to his arm in the night. Over the next few days the doctors and nurses came to him, bandaged him, cleaned the bruises and gave him more shots. Slowly he recovered and gathered where he was.

I introduced myself.

'I don't believe in terror or in your religion, but I believe in justice,' I said. He reached out for my hand and kissed it, not subserviently, but proudly as though he was offering me a benediction.

As he recovered, he began to talk. He wanted a Koran brought to him. He said his prayers and read the Koran the rest of the time. We stopped ordering Chinese food because he said it was not halal and he couldn't eat it. I used my mobile phone to order tandoori from the Muslim restaurant and shared it with him. He said he had had his teeth knocked out and his jaw was slowly recovering. His eyes were on my mobile.

We didn't discuss the crime or activity that had brought him here but we discussed the past. He had been a schoolteacher in Kashmir, he said. He could read Urdu, Arabic and Persian apart from English, of course.

He looked at Roy's books. He looked at my computer and refrigerator out of which we took fruit juices and lemonade.

'Just like a Pakistani jail when politicians go in,' he said.

'We shouldn't discuss Pakistan or India or politics,' I said.

'Then I have to keep quiet. I don't know anything except the word of the Koran, the acts of the Prophet and politics. Otherwise I am dumb.'

'No, sir,' said Roy. 'Every human is a walking culture, a walking etymology, a mobile metaphysics and ethics.'

'Why is your name Ehsan Battiwalla?' I asked.

He was a bit taken aback. 'That was my old name,' he said. 'Now I have my jihadi name. You see, gentlemen, I live for it, but the discussion of jihad may trouble you.'

'Discussion? Words? None of that scares me, old man.'

I caught him looking at my computer again.

If this guy was interrogated, his body language would give away a lot of things. He might be a terrorist preacher but he wasn't much of an operative. No wonder they caught him.

As the days and weeks went by, we made friends. He realized that I had undoubtedly saved him from a slow mutilation and death. The Indian government and police had no evidence that would hold up in an international court of law. Yes, he was a Pakistani, yes, he had entered the country illegally. It could be proved that he belonged to a radical mosque and had preached sedition and death to the infidel, but the much-touted connection to the parliamentary bombers of Delhi was, I thought, pure speculation. He was a likely suspect. If he wasn't masterminding terror, what was he doing in a suburb of Delhi? He said he was visiting relatives. He was. The people in the house where he was hiding were relatives and they too had been taken away for questioning. Why didn't he apply for a visa and come in legitimately? He would never have got one. He had openly spoken against the country and called for India's defeat in Kashmir through armed struggle.

Roy believed he was a terrorist and I was in my heart of hearts hoping he was. The more dangerous, the better.

He would be admitted to my cell to watch TV. We would eat together.

One day there was a news item of a kidnap plot by Kashmiri terrorists foiled by the Indian border police. They had gone into a nest of terrorist kidnappers and rescued three hostages, one Britisher, one Australian and an American. The terrorists had surrendered when they realized they were outgunned. Weapons, ammunition and two computers were recovered in the raid.

Ghulam was extremely agitated by the report. He started scratching himself under the chin; he straightened his eyebrows a hundred times.

'Something troubling you, chief?' Roy asked.

'No, no, no, nothing,' Ghulam replied.

Later that night I walked to his cell. He wasn't asleep. He was lying awake on his mattress. The warder opened his cell door. They were still wary of him and would only do that if the two external doors to the wing were securely locked. He came with me to my cell, sat on a chair and held his head in his hands. He was visibly distressed.

'If I can help in any way I will, you know,' I offered.

'They will now get my family and all my contacts. Those stupid boys have kept all the information and now the Indian police have it. Bastard English boys, they think they own the earth and they don't change and give up arrogance even if they join the jihad – because they get everything there. It's like paradise on earth, with loose white girls and sharab and filthy pictures and dancing.'

'The boys who were caught?' I asked.

'Yes. My boys. Or at least one of them is a British Pakistani who joined us. I am not worried about myself, but my house and my wives and children and…other things.' He sighed.

'I tell you, old man, if you want to use my mobile phone, no one will know, yeah? You can dial abroad,' I said.

He jumped at it.

'Can I? Allah lay his blessings on you,' he said.

'Just keep your voice down,' I said, fetching the phone. 'You must go in your own cell and do it privately,' I added.

He took the phone with both hands. It was as though I was handing him a benediction or the Holy Grail, not just a mobile phone.

I didn't bother to hear what he was saying. He talked in muffled tones for fifteen or twenty minutes. I knew the battery was about to run out.

'Yohan,' he shouted.

I went over to his cell. 'This thing is dead. It's gone dark.'

'Oh shit, battery!' I said. 'I am sorry. Did it interrupt your call?'

'No, no, no, no. You have come like an angel. I got my work done. You have earned yourself a place in paradise, brother. Now I must convince you to embrace the faith and obey the book.'

'We will talk about that,' I said and smiled. 'When I recharge the phone you can use it again.'

'Later, later, later. My work is, inshallah, done for now.'

I think he went to sleep more at peace. I charged the phone for a few hours, resting it by my pillow and then switched it on. In the call registry I found the seventeen different numbers he had dialled. I hate to boast, but that's the sort of thing I can remember. I memorized all seventeen. Some of them were Pakistani numbers beginning with 0092. Some of them were

British with 0044 and others were, I assumed, American or Canadian with 01 prefixes. I revised them a few times and tested myself before erasing the numbers.

The next afternoon I held my stomach and collapsed in pain. Both Roy and Ghulam were most concerned as I groaned and writhed on the bed. The prison doctor came and I pointed to where the pain was.

'Appendicitis,' he said and poked me here and there in the abdomen and I screamed in agony.

He ordered me to be removed straight away to the guarded wing of a public hospital for an operation. The governor came and signed the papers. I handed my mobile phones to Roy in front of Ghulam and said they weren't to be used.

They took me in a prison van to the hospital and I was admitted to the emergency operation theatre without delay.

A young doctor came to examine me.

'Where's the pain?' he asked.

'Listen, doctor, do you know who I am?'

'I have heard,' he said. He wasn't impressed by my credentials. 'Tell me where it hurts.'

'It doesn't hurt,' I said. 'It's a bluff. I had to get out of the jail and speak to someone like you. I have vital information about international terrorism and I want to speak to someone high up in government. The home minister or the prime minister himself. If you don't act on this and arrange it, you will make the biggest mistake of your life.'

He looked at me sceptically. He was wondering whether this was a ploy to escape prison. I could read his face.

'I doubt if the PM will give you an appointment,' he said. 'So no pain at all?'

'Look, doctor, I have found out things in the prison which could be a matter of life and death for more people than you can count. There is no way you can ignore me. You must make a call now.'

'I don't know how. Why would they listen to a junior surgeon in a Delhi hospital? Whom can I call? The PM's office? They'll think I am mad and lock me up.'

'I know what you can do. Can you find a policewoman called Chandrika Nath for me? The Delhi Police will know her. Say Johnson Thhat has information for her. If you don't, you will regret it for the rest of your life.'

He looked at me curiously, called the orderlies and the armed guard and instructed them to wheel me into an office. We passed the operation staff, the nurses and the anaesthetist's assistant who were waiting for the operation. They looked puzzled, but the young doctor told them that there had been a change of plan.

They wheeled me into the office and he immediately picked up the phone. The hospital had a hot line to the police.

I said the orderlies and the guard should leave.

He was still nervous. Might I yet spring off the trolley, knock him unconscious and try to escape? I told them to go and he motioned them away. He knew I was serious.

He asked for Chandrika by name. He was given another number. This went on through four or five calls.

'There is no such person,' he said finally. 'They don't know any such person.'

'Then get me someone in the anti-terrorist department. Please. I have information about bombings.'

After an hour or more someone called back.

A voice at the other end said, 'We know who you are, Johnson, what have you got?'

'Whom am I speaking to?'

'We ask the questions,' the voice said. 'What have you got?'

'I have shared a cell with Haji Ghulam for months now. I know things.'

There was silence at the other end of the phone. Then he said 'okay' and hung up.

I was put into a secure wing by myself with two armed policeman by my bed and one at the door.

Within half an hour, three men walked in.

'I only want to see a minister,' I said.

'I am Das Gupta, senior secretary in the home ministry. That's as high as you'll get, Thhat, so you better make up your mind. No ministers make contact with criminals. These are my colleagues from the foreign ministry.'

'You are from RAW?'

Neither of them replied. They were.

'We can take you to a safe house and you can talk to us or you can go back to Tihar and go to hell,' Das Gupta said.

'I'll take the safe house,' I said.

'We are promising nothing, Thhat,' he said.

'Neither am I, Das Gupta.'

✦

The safe house was a bungalow outside Delhi. I was in a room on the first floor with two grilled metal windows. There were plain-clothes police about and they kept their arms out of sight.

'No childish nonsense like trying to run away, Thhat,' Das Gupta said. 'The chief will be here to talk to you.'

The RAW men had stayed silent throughout the journey. They let me rest for an hour or so. It was late at night. Then one of the silent ones came and took me to the room downstairs and I could hear the policemen talking outside and a vehicle drawing up.

Chandrika walked into the room.

She greeted me as though I was an old friend. Das Gupta remained with us and the door remained open.

'How are you, Johnson?'

'How are you, superintendent, or is it chief or something by now?'

'As you see, I have shifted departments.'

'What are you now?'

'That which dare not speak its name,' she said.

She sat down.

'So you have information that can convict Haji Ghulam in a court? Did he confess to you about the bombing?'

'No, I don't,' I said. 'I have much more than that.'

'What have you got?' said Das Gupta.

Chandrika raised her hand to motion him to restrain himself.

'So, Thhat, what do you want in return?' Chandrika asked. 'We know each other, you can come out with it or even trust me with the information you have.'

If I had been anyone but myself I would have laughed, but I kept my blackjack face.

'Before I tell you anything, what I want is an assurance from the foreign ministry.'

'The foreign ministry? You are getting quite fancy,' said Chandrika. 'What would you want with them?'

'This treaty that they are working on about anti-terrorist cooperation between Asian countries, the one they will sign at the South Asian Nations Conference.'

'Yes, we know about that,' Chandrika said and as she said it, it dawned on her. She knew what I was going to say. 'I see, I see, I see, I see,' she said now pacing the room. 'You don't want them to include ordinary serial killers?'

'If you want to put it that way,' I said.

Das Gupta was struggling to keep up.

'You want to make sure they don't send you to Thailand under a new extradition treaty and – what did we decide when we last spoke – hanging or shooting by firing squad? Do you like it in Tihar?'

'For two more years after this, I do,' I said.

'You think I can influence foreign policy? Make deals with the government?'

'For what I can give you, yes, you should be able to.'

She kept pacing the room.

'Enough games. What is it?' asks Das Gupta.

'I want a guarantee.'

'Are people in immediate danger? Do you have some info about a terror plot?' Das Gupta asked.

I looked at Chandrika

'A fair question. Go on,' she said.

'Not immediate danger. You can have till tomorrow to see if my deal is agreed upon. Then you can debrief me. Short and vital. And as you say we know each other so you know I am serious.' I was taking charge now.

Das Gupta looked at Chandrika. It was now two o'clock in the morning. He said we should adjourn. She nodded.

'Let's see what we can do for you. Are we in any danger of losing lives or property if we extend the talk till tomorrow?'

'No. It's long-term and more important information, not just one terror assault.'

She understood.

I heard her vehicle departing. I slept well and they gave me breakfast in a civilized way in the dining room downstairs. Das Gupta was not there and RAW One said he'd gone with 'the chief' to consult in Delhi.

They came back by the afternoon.

'We can't obviously give you anything in writing, Thhat, but you have to trust me,' Chandrika said. 'We will make you an exception to any treaty we sign with Thailand, depending on how vital your information is.'

'Not good enough,' I said. 'Suppose you decide my information is not vital enough, even if I have proof of the second coming of Christ.'

She smiled. She was still pretty even though there were lines around her eyes now.

'We wouldn't do that. We are all honourable people,' she said. 'I guarantee that you will complete your twenty-year holiday in Tihar, one way or the other. We can work out some extension of sentence for you and I give you my word that the government will accommodate you. Is that good enough?'

'Yes,' I said.

'We'll even buy you a return ticket to Bangkok after that. How's that for a deal?'

'Thank you. That's a good guarantee.'

'Now tell us.'

'Get a pencil and paper,' I said.

She turned around and one of her attendants handed her a pad. RAW Two got his own pad and pen.

'I am going to give you a dozen numbers that Haji Ghulam used to phone abroad. They are, I know for sure, the numbers of his terrorist contacts in Pakistan, the UK and, I think, Canada.'

Both the RAWs looked extremely eager. Chandrika and Das Gupta looked at each other.

I began rattling off the numbers from memory. First the ones beginning 0092, then the 0044 and then the Canadian ones.

RAW Two read them back to see if they were correct.

'All right, Johnson, what do you want for the rest?' Chandrika asked.

'The rest of what?'

'The other numbers you have. Come on. Play fair.'

'I am playing fair. What you mean is, keep no cards in my hand?'

'What's the price?'

'That you negotiate with the French embassy to get me a passport. India has given me a very bad name and they will be reluctant unless the foreign office puts pressure on them.'

'You think I have any say in the French embassy?'

'Get some.'

'How many other numbers? The truth!'

'I've got five more. All abroad. Maybe even one or two in France and Algeria.'

'How are you going to save yourself from Ghulam's

network?' Won't they know that you informed us?' Chandrika asked. 'Otherwise you won't want to leave Tihar at all, ever.'

'Let me worry about that.'

✦

'No operation. Bad infection. Six antibiotics. The doctors didn't know whether I would live or die,' I said to Roy, Ghulam and the concerned warders gathered when I got back to the block. The RAW men had got me a battery of pills, which I used to impress them.

Ghulam didn't even have the whiff of a suspicion that I had betrayed him. In the weeks that followed Chandrika must have acted upon the information I gave them because there were reports of swoops on British houses in Slough and Birmingham and reports of the roundup of terrorists in Toronto, Vancouver and Buffalo, USA.

Men had been taken in for questioning and they were pictured on TV being taken away. Ghulam, Roy and I watched the reports and though Ghulam's face was drained of blood as the news hit him, we didn't discuss the matter. No word escaped him. No suspicion crossed his mind. I suppose he thought it was the will of Allah.

Ghulam asked to use my phone again. This time he told me that he had to shift resources from one location to another. It was the closest he had come to admitting that he was involved in the transfer of 'resources'. I didn't know then whether he meant men, guns or money. He was naïve about technology. He asked whether mobile phones could be tapped and I reassured him that they could be intercepted but that I had set up a system whereby my number was on a temporary purchased card and this could be changed every day. He didn't know that dialled numbers were stored. He had called the Middle East and Dubai, but I didn't need the numbers, my bargaining was done. Still, I memorized them – just in case.

The Indian justice system didn't put Ghulam on trial. They left him to rot. Every now and then he would be taken from his cell to an interrogation room in the prison or outside. People from the police and the secret services would interview him. Once he returned to say that a woman had interviewed him and seemed to know a lot about his networks. I didn't blink or indicate that I may know this woman. He said he gave away nothing. Roy asked if he had been mistreated and he said he was treated formally and courteously.

'The police don't like anyone associated with Kashmir killings or Islamic groups,' Roy said. 'If they treated you well, it's only because you are a friend of Thhat's.'

PART 4

1

I was released two days before the dawn of the new millennium. Dilawar brought his wife and children to say goodbye to me at the gate. The convicts knew I was leaving and they banged their shit-mugs as I was brought into the yard and taken to the gate. The prison rang with the clanging. The governor said his farewell at the gate.

Roy had arranged for his nephew to pick me up by car and take me to their house till I could make my plans. I didn't know where I was going, but my twenty-year waiting period for the statutory time to expire in Thailand was over. I was free but I had no passport and nowhere to go.

At the gates of the prison, as I walked out to take my lift, there was a car with darkened windows, waiting. There were TV cameras and reporters. I had been given a denim jacket and jeans to go out in and I now shielded my face against the flashing camera bulbs.

'Johnson, this way,' said a young man grabbing my elbow.

'I have a car,' I said.

'Chandrika,' the young man said.

I followed him to the car with dark windows and he opened the door and urged me in.

She was in the back of the car.

'I am sorry, Thhat, but you are under arrest,' she said.

'For what?'

'For your own protection. I made a deal with you that I'd get the French embassy to issue you a passport and entry. I have your details but the bastards don't want you. They say they don't want a convicted serial killer!'

'I could have had a French passport before, only I never got a genuine one. My mother is Vietnamese, born under French jurisdiction and I was born before the French gave up the country formally.'

'They are at liberty to take away your papers,' she said. 'We have to take you in because you are not a citizen of anywhere – you are stateless, which is illegal – and we shall now determine where you should go.'

'I have friends waiting for me,' I said.

'Don't talk like a child. You are a non-person without a passport,' she said and tapped the driver to move on. 'You realize, I have better things to do than try and help you, but I gave you my word, I remember.'

'What are you now? Are you the head of the secret service?'

'Oh God, no,' she said. 'But I'll tell you. The information you gave us helped me a lot.'

She drove me to a remote police station. She said she wanted to avoid the reporters. I had to go along with her. There was nothing else I could do.

'In return for the breakthrough you gave us, I will find you a country that will take you,' she said. 'It may be some African country or some obscure island nation somewhere, but I will see you are all right. I'll keep as close to my word as I can.'

Before she left, she said, 'There is one more thing you can do for me. You can confirm the identity of the person who was your assistant at the scene of the crime. Think about it.'

'What do you mean, confirm? Do you know who it is?'

'Look, Johnson,' Chandrika said, 'I am not dead. I am alive and alert and have been following the case. The one big possibility, though we don't know what happened to her, is your father's sometime mistress Ravina. The general's daughter.'

Now this was not news to me. My father had told me that Ravina was an army brat from the higher echelons, educated in good schools, who had run away from college, fascinated by crooked money.

'The most dangerous kind of woman, eh, Thhat? Attracted to criminals to get away from her crooked father who got rich by swindling the military and milking army contracts. You know the big scandal, starving the troops under his command by making deals with the ration suppliers. If I had got hold of that case, he would have been in jail all those years. Instead he died a very rich man. And a national hero.'

Again, she was looking at my face and I put on my mask. She smiled.

'What makes a girl like that go with your wreck of a father? She went to the best boarding schools, then college. I suppose she knew her father was a crook and had possibly been responsible for the deaths of soldiers through his manipulations. And he got away with it. But that's India! Then she runs away first with petty crooks and ends up with your father and then with you. So where is she now?'

'I don't know whom you are talking about,' I said.

I had heard nothing from Ravina or my father except for the occasional scandal or scam concerning the gem trade which I read about in the newspapers. The scandals never contained his name, but when they involved thefts and smuggling and big illegal deals I thought of him and her and could see their dark hands in it.

The whistling commander came to see me. He had been promoted several ranks and was now seen as an expert on catching escapees even though the world and its uncle should have known that in the story we concocted he caught me by complete coincidence on his Goan holiday.

I stayed six days in the cell at the remote police station. Chandrika wasn't in touch. She was probably still exploring the embassies of some remote and drug-courier countries and making deals with them to accept me as a citizen. And then there was a report in the newspapers that the military police had arrested two Frenchmen and a Frenchwoman taking photographs of the thorium sands processor in south India. It was to do with a nuclear installation. The Indian press said they were spies acting for Pakistan. They were two miles inside the perimeter fence of the plant, which was out of bounds and military land. It was an open-and-shut case. The three Frenchies would be put on trial as spies and the sentence for espionage against the Indian state was death.

The papers were full of it – in India and in France.

Chandrika brought the papers to me.

'Your friends in the foreign ministry are still grateful and they are working for you,' she said.

The next day the deal was struck. The three Frenchies were in fact eco-warriors against nuclear power. They weren't

Pakistani spies. The French ambassador represented their case to the Indian ministers. These were stupid idealistic kids interfering in places they shouldn't go. They were not spies; they were campaigners.

The ministers understood this, but it was a propaganda coup to have bagged some European 'spies'. And yet, the foreign office negotiators told the French embassy, a deal could be struck. The Indian government would release the French spies if the French would give Johnson Thhat his French passport and take him as part of the package.

The uproar and anxiety in France had to be alleviated. The French made the deal.

Chandrika came to break the news. She was triumphant. She had delivered, she said. I didn't want to remind her that her concern with me began with delivery to another fate. I asked for my mobile phone, which they had taken off me in the cell.

I called Virginie.

'That's great. I will wait for you at Charles de Gaulle. You must be exclusive to me. See that no one takes your pictures, okay?'

I was taken to the airport and put on a plane to Paris a day after the French prisoners were released and packed off. I was accompanied by a man from the French embassy for no reason whatsoever. The embassy in Delhi said they had to take me to France and control any backlash that might result from my being accepted as a citizen. I would have police protection from the airport to a safe house until they could make arrangements for me. I said I could make my own arrangements. That I still had a mother living in France and a stepbrother and besides, a woman who was willing to marry me. He was very surprised. He treated me as though I was a prisoner he was taking home, only there were no handcuffs and I could walk around in the plane and go to the toilet as I chose.

The world didn't look strange to me. I remembered the story of Rip Van Winkle who fell asleep and woke up after many years and found the world had changed. For me, there was nothing I didn't know about this world. It had been waiting for me.

Only the traffic. Everywhere in Delhi there were cars, and big concrete roads and flyovers were being built.

'The reporters are waiting for you,' my escort said. 'But the Delhi Police will help us dodge them. We have made arrangements to go by a back door and check in as diplomatic passengers and go straight from the lounge to the plane.'

I didn't see any reporters while boarding the plane. Other passengers looked at me and whispered to each other.

'There is no way you can escape attention in Paris. The press will be waiting for you. Those ecological idiots reached yesterday and the country is now expecting you.'

'They will be disappointed,' I said.

Before we got off the plane, I asked the attendant to give me the largest plastic bag they had for their duty-free goods. She brought it to me and I made two holes for the eyes with a ballpoint pen and as we were getting off the plane I put it over my head.

There were photographers inside the terminal building. They started clicking at my masked head. One or two lunged forward to take the bag off my shoulders but I dodged them.

Outside, Virginie was waiting with a camera crew amongst a crowd of others. As we emerged with a police escort, I was still wearing my bag. I had to take it off for immigration and for customs inspection but I put it on again.

Virginie came and spoke to the police. She was telling them that they could verify the fact that her channel had exclusive rights to my pictures and to an interview. They gave her their phone number but wouldn't let her speak to me there and then.

'Bravo, Jean,' she shouted at me and I waved as I was taken away. 'I will come to you. I spoke to the police. They will tell me where.'

We had to elbow our way to the waiting police cars. It was a grand public reception.

The papers published pictures of my arrival with an Air France duty-free plastic bag over my head. The headlines were unkind. One said: 'Trash Exchanged'. Another: 'The Indians should have hanged all four – good riddance.'

✦

The Paris police took me to one of their safe houses and debriefed me. Whom did I know and what were my plans? I said I would get in touch with my relatives. Was I in any danger that I knew of? I said I wasn't.

'I have friends. I am contracted to one of the top TV directors and they will pay me for exclusive use of my story. I am a writer. I already have a book and the publishers will be lining up to buy it. I have to get an agent,' I said.

The police interrogator seemed unimpressed. French police are not imaginative like the Indians.

Virginie turned up with her crew. She looked just a bit nervous at meeting me. She took my hand and said, 'At last.'

She gave me a light peck on the cheek and then seemed to get down to business.

'That bag was a stroke of genius. We want to talk to you exhaustively. We can start right here. They are processing your papers and they will let you go.'

'I have a passport,' I said.

'Now they have to give you identity papers and residence papers and all sorts of shit. While you were away the bureaucracy has taken a stranglehold on la belle France.'

The cameraman – the same 'Camera' of old – chose a pose by the window.

'Shall I put on my bag again?'

'You were on TV earlier with the bag. It looked like the fliques had captured a Ku Klux Klan man.'

She began by asking me what I felt about the French citizens who had been held as spies.

I said I never met them and didn't know who they were, but in India everyone they don't like is a Pakistani spy. And maybe if it hadn't been for me they would have been put on trial and fitted up. Indian politics is very volatile. Unlike our country, in India justice depends on politics. Maybe I saved their lives and they should be grateful.

I thought I would work my way into being and sounding French without ever saying 'I thank you for allowing me back.'

After a few questions of that sort, Virginie suggested that we go and film me against the sights of Paris.

She assured me that I was free to go. A policeman came and gave me some papers. I had only one light suitcase with clothes that the embassy had bought me in Delhi. We drove in Virginie's car with the crew following behind in a van with the recording equipment. She put on a pair of specs to drive. I hadn't seen her in specs before. But of course it had been ten years. Her red hair was cut short now.

When we got into the car and were alone, she turned to me. 'Let's have a look at you,' she said. 'They've been feeding you, you've put on weight.'

'Not really, it's the Indian tailoring, they make the jackets very baggy,' I said.

Then she leaned over and kissed me passionately.

'I have been looking for flats for you. Not too luxurious, but a bed and a shower and kitchen.'

'That's good. Have you found one?'

'The agent has marked out three. We can finish with the interviews for today and then go and look. I would like to take footage of you choosing a place to stay in Paris and talk about your plans.'

I sat on a bench in the Tuileries.

'Can you tell us about the book?' she asked.

'It's about prison life, a kind of fictional account but based on my experience and the suffering and the injustice of India. You see, in writing like that one has to have a theme and the poverty of India, the fact that the poor are not given justice and the rich get away with everything, that is the kind of thing I want to expose. It is a metaphor for the whole of life.'

'And are you the hero of the book?'

'I wouldn't say exactly it was me, but the main character does rescue people from the cruelty around them. If you have read André Gide, books like *L'Immoraliste*. Or Jean Genet. He was the fellow whose writing is most impressive and it comes out of a life like mine, you know, a kind of existential way of finding oneself. You must have read *The Thief's Journal*. It's a bit like that. Or like Camus in *L'Etranger*. I'm essentially questioning the values of life and death.'

'You have quoted a few French writers, but you are half-Indian yourself. Were there any influences from the great Indian cultures on your writing?'

'Well, I very consciously read the philosophical works of Hinduism, you know. I have a friend who is a professor of philosophy and he made me acquainted with a lot of philosophy. And I had time, you know, time to read into the ancient texts even. Now the Bhagavadgita, which is the great religious text of the Hindus, says that there is no death and life, there is only illusion and the mind playing tricks. So where does that leave human law and let us say the act of murder? You get my point?'

We moved to the Eiffel Tower, and then Virginie wanted shots of me walking on the bridges across the Seine.

We finished shooting by late afternoon. She said the light would get dull so we had better pack it in. Camera hadn't seemed at all pleased to see me. He did his job sullenly. Then the crew went home. Virginie and I sat in a brasserie and had a drink.

'I have a cheque for you, but you have no bank account so I can give you some cash now and we'll see about a bank account tomorrow. But first let's get you into a flat. I want to be inside somewhere with you. You understand? This is so frustrating.'

She called the estate agent. He was a young man with a long face, like a dog. He brought out the leaflets describing the flats he had earmarked. I asked for a map of Paris and for him to show me where these flats were located.

One was very far north, nearly in the suburbs and he said he thought it as very nice. The landlady lived downstairs and there was one flat on the first floor but it was a very polite house.

Another was in the Fifteenth, where I had spent years as a boy in my stepfather's house, and where there would perhaps still be people in the streets who would recognize me.

The third flat was the one I would go for. It was in the Chinese district on the seventh floor of a large building. I imagined those large buildings even though they hadn't been built in the Paris of my boyhood. I said that would be ideal. It would give me a base of anonymity from which to plan whatever moves I wished to make. At that time, I tell you, I was sincere about writing and being a writer. I had this whole manuscript and had practised writing a few hours a day. I knew I had seen the world through my eyes and I thought I could make a fantasy out of what I had seen.

Now, Pradhan sahib, in this predicament, rotting in Kathmandu jail where you and fate have put me, I am finally telling the truth.

No, I haven't become religious. I have realized that the only person I can't fool is myself. So when I write for myself it is best to tell the truth. This is part of it.

✦

Virginie, Dogface and I went to see the flat. It was a concrete bunker on the seventh floor. The metal lift was clunky and made a big noise going up. There was a car park below the building and other identical high-rise buildings all around. Below, the streets were full of Chinese shops, restaurants and shopping malls with massive Chinese supermarkets.

This would be good, I thought, and told Dogface that this was the flat I would take. We went in. There was nothing except a telephone on the floor in the flat.

'The landlady's flat in the north is fully furnished,' Dogface said.

'I'll stick to this one,' I said.

Virginie agreed.

'You'll have complete freedom here and won't have to be quiet at nights,' she said. 'Living with a landlady will remind you of another place you've been.'

I signed some papers and Virginie wrote a cheque for the deposit. Dogface handed me the keys. There was even a card to open the garage doors and a space reserved there for me. I didn't have a car of course.

When Dogface left us in the empty flat, Virginie opened my suitcase and put all the clothes I had on the floor. I didn't know what she was doing. She made a pillow out of some clothes, spread the rest as a mat and sat on them and held her arms out to me.

'I want you now,' she said.

She unbuttoned her shirt and bra and pulled them up above her breasts and when I sat next to her, my bones awkward on the hard floor, she held my head and thrust her erect nipple in my mouth. She saw I was uncomfortable, hesitant.

'You can lie on me, I'll be on the hard cold floor, and I've got your clothes under me – that's how much I want you, Johnson.'

She hardly ever called me 'Johnson'. She lay on the 'bed'. We made love, or had quick sex, and then she got up and pulled tissues out of her bag and cleaned herself.

She took charge. From the streets downstairs we bought a second-hand mattress and table and three chairs from a junk furniture shop. It was closing down but Virginie told the Chinese owner that we'd only buy these things if the man had them delivered straight away. He didn't want to pass over the business. We gave him the address and Virginie paid him half the money as a deposit.

Later, we drove to Galeries Lafayette and came back laden with bags. A houseful: sheets, towels, curtains, dishes...

Within hours, I had set myself up. I was a householder.

'Not as comfortable as your cell,' she said.

'And your flat?' I asked.

'Tiny,' she said. 'And my flatmate is a crazy and very curious girl and from the day before yesterday, reporters have been calling and camping outside on our street because they expect you to turn up. I'm happy to leave them disappointed.'

I agreed. She said she had to go back to her edit studio but would be with me first thing in the morning. I should go out and get coffee and milk from the shops which stayed open late. She left me some money saying that she was keeping an account and would take it all back when my cheque was cashed. I kissed her on my doorstep and waited till she had gone to recall the lift and wander into the streets of Chinatown.

I wasn't going to call my mother or even try to trace her. Ever since I went to India, she and her family had not bothered about me. They must have seen the news items in the press from time to time over the years. The French embassy knew of my mother's existence because when I had to fill in the form claiming citizenship I had to give her name and last known address and they had checked on the fact that she existed and had given birth to me all those years ago.

The next day Virginie came to my flat with Camera and the rest of her crew. They made me rehearse and repeat entering the empty flat and made me pretend to bring the mattress and the furniture up myself. She said she wanted shots of my adjusting to French life. She asked one of the crew to bring the computer up. She had brought one from the TV station to lend me so I could be filmed beginning my career as a writer. They set it up on the table and I was filmed working on it.

After the shoot, we went out and bought Persian carpets for the flat and we put them down and made love and Virginie took me out again in the evening and bought me clothes, dressing me as though I was her living doll, saying which jacket suited me and which dark glasses I could wear.

As the flat got furnished, we filmed some more. She introduced me to a literary agent, a Russian Jewish Frenchman who had been educated in England. We had a drink together and Gerrard said he would be very flattered to take on my book. I said I was privileged to have him read it.

Virginie had told me a story about him. He was an operator. He could sell most things and the story was about one trip to the Frankfurt Book Fair where he arrived with a briefcase and sought out the biggest gossip bar. He sat on a stool next to a publishing girl, a big mouth.

'What have you got for us, Gerrard?' Big Mouth asked.

'Nothing that your outfit can afford,' he said.

He wanted Big Mouth to persist, Virginie said, and of course she did. So he tells her he has the autobiography of Sean Connery in his briefcase. She whistles, she buys him drinks. He says she is to keep it secret, knowing that that's real temptation. She waits for him to turn his back and she's on her mobile. He moves from bar to bar and everyone wants to know him. He goes back to his hotel room wined, dined and pursued by every publisher in town. At two in the morning from his hotel room he dials a number in the States. 'Mr Connery, you don't know me, but I am a literary agent. My name is Gerrard and if you write your autobiography I can get you four million dollars.'

There's a pause at the other end of the line.

'Well, Gerrard, I am not thinking of writing my autobiography, but that's a very generous offer and if I ever do, you shall be my literary agent.'

That was Virginie's recommendation of Gerrard and I liked it.

✦

Virginie would never take me to her flat. There was always an excuse. We met in mine, almost every day. Sometimes she would drive me out to places, to Versailles and frequently to the coast. We stayed five nights in Normandy in a cottage she said belonged to a friend. She said she'd been there many times and had brought the keys to all the cupboards and the wardrobe and wore her friend's clothes and swimming things because they were the same size.

We walked on the beach. It was a celebration of sorts of the end of the project. The documentary that she was making about me was ready and it had been scheduled for transmission the next week. The publicity around it would put me on the map.

Did I want to be on a map?

When the day of transmission arrived, I said she should come over to the flat and watch it with me, but she said she had to see it with her bosses at the studio. It was weird watching it on my own with a bottle of beer and some Chinese noodles I had bought. She had used the footage from Tihar and then the pictures of me in the Ku Klux Klan plastic bag arriving in Paris and settling into the flat. She had cut it in a sort of surrealist style with my talk about being a writer and my recollections of the prison and other random thoughts, made now to seem deep and wise, running onto the pictures of the Tihar cell and my empty flat before I furnished it; then over footage of me walking across the bridges of Paris and back again. The whole effect was of a lonely, meditative man. I had never seen myself like that.

James Bond, with a licence to kill – yes! A kind of murderous, sad monk – no!

And Ravina, so long out of my life, hadn't seen me like that either.

2

Then Canal Plus sold the documentary to PBS in America and they transmitted it there and Camera brought me a note:

Dear Johnson,

The secretary at Canal Plus told me on the phone that she couldn't give me your address, but that if I gave her a name and a phone number she would give it to the documentary department and they would get you to call me back if you wanted to speak to me.

But yes! You are wondering who this is and where the hell did she come from? I am in Paris. No, not on a trip. I came especially for you, to see you again. Please see me. For everything we did together, you must say yes, even if it is only for a glance and to tell me to go away again. I mustn't say more, Govind. It breaks my heart. My phone number is 00331547393837. Please call. So much water, so many bridges…

Your own,
Ravina

The envelope was torn open and there had been a crude attempt to reseal it with sticky tape.

'What is it? Why is it open?'

'Because she read it,' he said. 'Then she put it back and asked me to give it to you.'

I opened it, quickly took it in, looking at the signature first. It wasn't a surprise. Had I been thinking of Ravina? If I am to tell the truth, I had thought of her, not as Ravina but as the idealized form of a woman of my dreams. But here she was and she would be older. Undesirable. What did she want?

I asked Camera to have a drink.

'What did Virginie say? To this?' I asked.

'She gave it to me to read, eh? Old friend. Some heavy business, eh?'

I stared at him.

'Heavy?'

'I mean we know a lot about you, everything you told us and Virginie thought I should see the missing piece. This is some girl from the past who shared some actions, maybe, yeah?'

'No. But Virginie, what did she say? Was she disturbed?' I asked.

'Virginie is always disturbed,' said Camera.

'I mean did she seem to care? Did she start asking who this was?'

Camera shrugged. 'Johnson, a little note like that? What's it to her? Virginie only cares about what she does. She doesn't care about too many things. Maybe her children.'

'Children?'

'And her husband's money.'

I wasn't going to betray any surprise.

'I know you don't know and maybe she sent me with this letter to say goodbye to you. She could have burnt it,' he said. 'It's her way of saying she wants you to go. Enough.'

I put the letter down and then lifted it again.

'Virginie has a husband and many lovers,' Camera said.

'Including you?' I asked.

'That's an old story,' he said.

'But like a willing dog, you carried the letter to me because she sent you?' I asked him.

'She will always go back to her husband. She has never left him. He doesn't ask her anything. He has five or six houses, one on the beach in Normandy. No doubt you went there and she told you it was her friend's. She doesn't have to work for television. She can buy the channel if she wants.'

She had lived with me for days at a time pretending to have a flatmate and room somewhere. I have never been a faulty judge of character and I didn't want to admit that I had completely mistaken Virginie. I didn't want to get any more information from Camera, though he appeared to be burdened with information he wanted to give me. He wanted to see an end to my romance with her.

'She has other men right now,' he said.

I didn't answer. I went to the phone and dialled.

Ravina was waiting as she said she'd be.

'I just got your message,' I said.

'I sent it four days ago,' she said.

So Virginie hung on to this note for four days? And she had come to the flat and spent the night with me after she knew that Ravina was in Paris and looking for me? And I read no signs? Maybe she didn't realize who this was. Had I ever given away the name of the woman who brought me into the game? I couldn't remember. I knew I never intended to, but I had told Virginie everything or almost everything and I had said it wasn't really me that had physically killed anyone; it was this woman I was with. But the name?

I arranged to see Ravina straight away. I didn't say I would pick her up. Camera gathered I was going out and he left, wishing me luck.

Ravina had aged as I had, weathered rather than altered. She had lost the thin, lithe look. Perhaps it was the tweed skirt she was wearing, but from below the waist she looked perfectly rounded, her hips and stomach not flat any more.

She was in this little hotel and she took me by the hand, crammed me into the lift and took me upstairs. She couldn't stop saying my name. She said 'Govind, Govind' as though to convince herself that I was really there.

The hotel room was tiny but clean. I sat on the bed.

'It's so, so, so good to see you,' she said. 'You. You haven't changed.'

Why was she making small talk? I had said nothing except hello. She had only touched me once to direct me to the lift. I thought she was dying to embrace me. There were tears in her eyes. 'I want to talk to you before we go out, if we go out. It might take some time.'

'Take your time. It's been twenty years anyway, a few minutes or hours don't matter.'

'You are not disgusted by me… I have grown old and fat?'

'I don't see these things. I only see Ravina,' I said gallantly. She smiled and shook her head and now she burst out crying. I didn't touch her or want to comfort her.

'So why are you here?'

'For you,' she said. 'I have left everything for you. You don't understand, it's like coming out of a dark tunnel and suddenly seeing the world and the sunlight.' She would use this silly picture again and again.

'So where have you been? I can tell you where I've been,' I said.

'I know all about it.'

'Sit down and tell me your bit.'

She sat on the chair near the window, which looked out on an alley.

'Everything?'

'Everything. Think that we are in a cinema in India or Bangkok and the film begins.'

She smiled at this.

'Yes, the film begins,' she said. 'You need the whole story and I need to explain myself. I have to tell you, not just what happened, but how it happened. Understanding is forgiveness, they say…'

✦

When I left the Kohinoor that night, I knew I had to get away. Returning to the hotel would not have helped you in any way. Besides, I had told them that I was a doctor and was going to fetch my medicines. I had to think of a way to shake off the policeman escorting me. There was no way I could release you as well. I knew that you would want me to get away, and then help you from the outside. It's what you would have done if the roles were reversed.

I fled into the depths of Old Delhi that night and caught
a rickshaw to the ends of the town and then got on a state
transport bus. The next day I hitched a ride from a lorry going
to Nasik. I wanted to get to Bombay. I had to…to lend myself
to the lorry driver and was desperate enough to do it.

I got to Bombay and went back to my flat and found that
the servant I had trusted to look after it had rented it out to
some very rough people who said they didn't know who I was
and asked me to get lost. I said it was my flat but they didn't
believe me. They said they were sitting tenants and I could
go to the police if I chose.

So I went back to see your father. I didn't want to turn to
him, but there was nowhere else and no one else.

He wasn't at first pleased to see me. He still wanted this
connection with you but he hated the fact that I had run away
with you after promising to return to him. Even after all the
phone calls I had made from Bangkok – you know about
those, you caught me when those Americans held us up with
guns – didn't help. I had hurt his ego. But he has the kind of
ego that forgets insults if you go crawling back.

He kept asking about you and I didn't tell him. He would
find out from the papers. I just told him I wasn't with you and
that was enough for him. He took me back. I knew he would
ultimately take his revenge. He would make me feel what he
thought I was – a whore.

I swear on anything, Govind, each time I slept with him
I thought only of you. I am going to tell you everything as it
happened.

He did read the papers and find out about your arrest.
He boasted he would help you. He said he was planning to

groom you to take over his contacts with the Triads and other organizations of that sort that he had carefully won the trust of through his crooked life. His money would one day be your money, so why did you have to start an independent life of crime? His crooked cash was there for the taking.

Crooked – the word might surprise you coming out of my mouth. But living with him and listening to his deals and his double-crosses I began to get disgusted even with his business. I had long been disgusted with his body. His hair coming out of his ears and nose and his farting loudly in bed.

He would boast that he was involved with the elimination of powerful warlords and gang chiefs, politicians, judges, policemen and that you were a punk, a cockroach who kept crawling back to him, even after having stolen his whore, to beg for favours and money. He tried to convince me that he had enough influence to get you out of jail, and I never challenged him to fulfil his boast though I felt like it.

I followed your case as it was reported and thought for a moment that you would be free when they started putting the blame on the mystery woman in court and so I was determined never to be caught.

I was very surprised when you gave yourself up, but I instantly worked it out, believe me, I knew what you were doing, Johnson, and I was full of respect and wonder. I couldn't come and see you or make any kind of contact. I wondered if I would ever see you again. Twenty years, my darling!

I know that you phoned your dad from jail and you never asked about me. He was quite pleased that you didn't, and he didn't volunteer any information about my whereabouts or even that I was alive and in his bed. He boasted for days that you had to come crawling back to him. He was happy to send you precious stones. It made him feel he was still on top. Buying people is all he knows. Stones? He has enough of those. Sons? He says he has only one. And begging sons? Yes, the same one and only.

And when he got drunk and demanded that I sleep with him and found himself unable to perform, he would get out of bed and curse me, abuse me, call me names.

I began to work for him again. He sent me one day with a box of diamonds to the Oberoi hotel to do a deal with some Russians. They asked me up to their room and I gave them the gems and they gave me the money. There were two of them. One of them began talking on the phone and I couldn't hear what he was saying. Then he came over and handed me the phone. It was your father. He said he knew they were pleased with the deal and now they wanted to know if I would sleep with them.

'What are you talking about, you bastard?' I said.

'It will be good for business and good for you,' he said.

'Come and be fucked by these pigs yourself, I am sure your flabby arsehole will do,' I said and banged the phone down and picked up the moneybag and was leaving the room when one of the Russians came and grabbed me by the wrist.

'Your boss said it was part of the deal,' he said, looking genuinely surprised that I was leaving.

'Fuck off, let go of my wrist,' I shouted and wrenched my arm away.

'Bunny wants to play rough,' he said and grinned. I don't know if he thought I was saying 'no' when I meant 'yes'. I could see he was going to rape me.

'I'll scream the place down,' I said, and began screaming.

He put one hand over my mouth and then he slapped me. I pulled his hand away and screamed again. No words, just screaming. He tried to push me further into the room and asked the other guy to help him and get a pillow.

'Shut the bitch up,' he said.

Someone in the corridor was banging at the door. There were voices outside. The Russkies looked worried.

'If you let me go I won't tell them and I'll walk straight out,' I said. 'I'll tell them it was a mistake. Otherwise you'll get hanged for rape.'

They looked at each other and said something in Russian. Then one of them opened the door. There were three hotel guests outside. They had heard the screams and gathered.

'Nothing, nothing, bhai, nothing. Sorry, just a misunderstanding,' I said. 'These men are my friends.' I slipped past them, clutching my handbag with the money in it.

It was only when I got out of the hotel, out of the air-conditioned nightmare and walked into the hot sea breeze of the Bombay seafront, that the tears burst from me. I felt my burning cheek. The left one was bruised with the mark of the slap. My knees felt weak at the thought of it. I felt faint. I got to the pavement and staggered towards the parapet that separates the land from the sea on that beautiful bay in Bombay. I must have fallen to my knees and half passed out, because I remembered a voice asking me in an American accent if I was okay.

That terrified me, because the Russians also spoke in American accents, and jerked me into consciousness again and I held my arm up and screamed.

'Hey, it's all right, I'll help you. Please, it's okay,' the voice said and I looked and could see it wasn't them.

This man reached down and helped me up. I stood and then sat on the sea wall. There was a coconut-seller watching this drama and the young man turned to him and got hold of a coconut and had its head chopped to open a hole in the green orb. He brought it for me to drink.

He saw the finger marks on my cheek and let out a low whistle to indicate that he knew I was in pain. I drank the coconut water. My eyes were still wet.

'You better now?' he asked.

'I think so. Shaken.'

'I can see,' he said.

'Can I get you a cab or something?' he asked.

'No, just let me sit here.'

'Will they come back, whoever it was?'

'I don't know.'

'Do you want me to hang about in case they do? I'll keep my distance, I won't bother you.'

'No, no, it's all right, please go. Thanks for the coconut water.'

He nodded and went a little distance and then sat down on the pavement. He was pretending not to watch me, but he was keeping an eye.

After a while I shouted to him.

'What are you doing?'

'Sitting. It's a free country.'

'You said you wouldn't bother me.'

'Am I bothering you?'

'Yes,' I said. 'You should sit on the parapet if you want to sit, not on the pavement like a dog.'

He nodded. 'Guess you're right.' He sat on the parapet.

I had decided not to go home. I didn't want to face your father, the pimp, and fight him. That felt like it was over. I turned and sat with my legs dangling out over the tetrapods.

When I glanced his way again, the American had moved six feet closer to where I was. I looked at the gulls and the sailing boats out at sea and when I glanced right, he had again moved a few feet closer. He knew I was smiling.

'Trying to find the right spot,' he said aloud.

'For what?' There was no harm in him.

'To start a conversation with you,' he said. He wasn't smiling, but when he looked at me he had a softness in his face. 'Tell me what happened there. I'd like to sort your problem.'

'Nothing much. Just the usual. Theft, smuggling, pimping, whoring, entrapment, rape.'

'Doesn't sound like my kinda fun,' he said.

'Or mine,' I said.

He now turned his face towards the sea too and came closer to me.

'Morgan,' he said, stretching out his hand.

'Ravina. Thank you for rescuing me, Morgan.'

'I'd like to do more. If there's any risk, I'll show you home safe,' he offered.

'I'm homeless,' I said.

He looked me up and down.

'That's a trick statement, isn't it? But if you really are, that makes two of us.'

'But you are American, aren't you?'

'Lucky me.'

'So what are you doing in Bombay?'

'Believe it or not, I'm checking out mosquitoes.'

'Mosquitoes?'

'Yeah. I was doing a project out in the lab in north Mumbai but some idiot let some viruses out and now the whole tropical vermin shop is in quarantine till it's decontaminated. I've come downtown and moved into a hotel. Not that one,' he said indicating the one I had run out of. 'A cheap one.'

'Show me your hotel,' I said.

Morgan Sands was very tall and very nice-looking, about my age. He wore his hair long and was in blue dungarees which he called 'science clothes'. He was a biologist and was at the time looking into the genetics of mosquitoes so that a scientific project, out of his university in the USA, could work at a cure for malaria. They were coming at it in a funny way, which he explained. They weren't looking for drugs to kill the filaria germ. They were going to eliminate the female anopheles mosquito which carries the malarial infection by genetically eliminating the possibility of females being born.

'Like parts of India where they kill girl babies,' he said. And then, 'Sorry, that's a nasty joke. Not like that. We don't actually kill anything. We just stop girls being born.'

I went with him to his hotel which was not dingy and horrible, but a smaller, nineteenth-century building overlooking the harbour. I said I'd take a room there too and I booked myself in. I wasn't even going to tell your father that he could go to hell.

Your trial was over and you were in jail by this time. Your fate was sealed. Nothing I could do.

Then something happened – it's time you knew and sorry to break it this way. Blame me for everything.

I stayed in the hotel several days. I saw Morgan every day and spent most of the days with him. We went on a boat to the Elephanta caves and we took another cruise to Alibagh on the mainland, across from Bombay harbour.

And I was getting more and more anxious in those days because my period was late. Very late. I went to a doctor and had a pregnancy test. I was pregnant. The doctor said she could arrange for an abortion after a certain period, and I went away with that possibility. There was no one I could talk to.

Morgan asked me why I looked worried. We were just friends then. There was nothing I could say to him. He didn't know who I was and had never asked me what I did. I had volunteered that I used to work in the gem trade, had made some money and was staying away from work for a while.

The Frenchies whom we drugged had reached France and had sold the French newspapers their photographs. There were photographs of you and me at the Taj Mahal standing with them next to their coach. The Indian newspapers published one and called me the mystery woman and were virtually asking anyone who could identify me to go to the police.

I panicked. I didn't even want to pass through the reception area of the hotel in case someone recognized me. All I said to Morgan was that I had to get out of the hotel and possibly out of Bombay. I hinted that the trouble he had witnessed had returned.

He was an angel. He didn't ask any questions and one

night, having hired a car, he paid both our bills, smuggled me, wearing his Texan hat, out of the building. He still had the keys to the hostel flat for scientists that the mosquito foundation had given him and we could stay there as long as we liked and no one would bother us.

We stayed there, isolated, for a month. Morgan was a good cook, amusing, considerate and he played the guitar and sang. He slept on a divan in the front room, an arrangement he suggested when we got there so that I could have the bedroom. He bought me clothes.

'Why are you being nice to me? You know nothing about me,' I said one evening as we sat on the balcony of the hostel flat swatting mosquitoes, drinking vodka and lime.

'Because I am comfortable with you, and yes, I do, I know quite a lot about you.'

'You don't. And if you did you wouldn't like it,' I said.

'I know for instance, that you are pregnant,' he said.

'And how do you know that?'

'I cook your food and have been noting the flow of your tastes.'

'Good guess,' I said.

'And are you?' he asked.

I didn't reply.

'And would I be right to say it's Johnson Thhat's child?'

'You saw the papers. The Frenchies' photographs?'

'Yes,' he said.

'Then why didn't you say anything?'

'I wanted to wait till I could really claim that it was some of my business,' he replied.

'And how would it become your business?'

'Suppose, just suppose, for instance that I was in love with you and you… well, you sort of cared for me, then it could be a little bit my business.'

'Could be.'

Then after a pause and looking at the first star of the evening, he said, 'And suppose we were both getting away to America to escape your being recognized here and that you had to marry me to get a visa to the United States, just a marriage of convenience, with a lot of trust thrown in, and you became my wife, then it would be a little more my business.'

'That too is true,' I said.

'And if you said you loved me or could love me, then that would make me very, very happy and it would be a lot my business.'

'I have thought of getting rid of the child, you know.'

'If we were together, I wouldn't want you to,' he said.

I bit my lip. I had never met a man as gentle as this. Take you. Interesting and exciting you are, but gentle you are not.

'So will you think about it?'

'Yes.'

We had some sparkling wine with our meal that evening and it was when I was alone in bed and thinking that my feet started moving on their own and I found myself going to the front room and creeping under the sheets of the divan with him. I cuddled up and we slept together. Just slept.

I thought about it. Morgan would talk about mosquitoes and worms and bring back fascinating stories from the laboratory, which had now been decontaminated and was operating again.

I started reading again, something we never did together.

Your father's house had no books and on the trail with you, it was difficult to get through more than a woman's magazine.

And then there was no way out of Bombay, India, except to apply for an extraordinary visa.

We were married at the American consulate. Morgan wore a suit and cut his hair and played the respectable American and fooled them. They gave me my visa on the Indian passport and assured us that it could be converted to an American passport when we got to the States. The happy couple kissed each other at each hurdle crossed.

The police weren't watching the airports for me. Morgan did a clever thing and booked a flight on Aeroflot to Moscow and then on to London, New York and then Houston. The Russian girl at the desk wouldn't have read the English Indian papers and she wouldn't have an eye out for me. My name hadn't appeared anywhere.

And then? Shall I go on? Please, Govind, hear me out, I have to tell you all of it.

✦

We lived in a house on the campus in New Mexico. I don't want to bore you with the life of an academic wife. The fact that I was an Indian counted for me in some circumstances and against me in others. Everyone was curious. About my customs, my religion and my culture. For the first time I settled down in the library and read a history of India, books on Hinduism, the Mahabharata (abridged) and the Ramayana (abridged) and I bought coffee-table books on Indian art, ancient Indian sculpture, the Indus Valley Civilization, modern Indian painting and ancient Indian architecture. And of course *The Illustrated Kama Sutra*.

It meant going to faculty parties and meeting the faculty wives and talking about tenure and who was close to finishing which book and who was being poached from one campus and who was hoping to be poached but was unwanted and stuck. It meant cooking curries for research students, keeping the lawn mowed and learning to play poker and bridge. It meant shopping for food and learning new languages of American politeness and not saying what you think.

Govind, I can see from your face that you don't understand, you can't understand. But please believe me, after your father had shown his hand, that his revenge consisted of turning me into the company whore, this was salvation. I had been martyred and come to heaven and maybe deep down, like my mother, who hated my father's rich lifestyle and absences, I wanted to be a typical bourgeois. After your father, Morgan was like coming out of a dark tunnel into the sunlight and seeing a landscape for the first time.

And in all that jigsaw, the pattern that put it together was the life and the future of the baby. Our baby. Bringing her up safely was the first concern. It overrode everything else.

She was born six months in. Our daughter. She is called Samara. She is now twenty years old, Johnson, and she looks like you with slightly curled ends of the eyes and cheekbones from her Vietnamese grandmother. Morgan brought her up as his own with never a word to her, even though when she was a year old she had a brother called Paul.

I'll show you the photographs in a minute, but let me

finish. When she was eight she was teased in school about her eyes and her colour and she came home asking if she was Korean. Morgan sat her down and explained that he wasn't her birth father but was her 'real' father and her birth father had a mother who was Vietnamese and he went to the library and showed her pictures of Vietnamese people and told her they were her distant cousins. She grew up knowing that he was not her natural father but never asked about who the 'birth' father was till she was fifteen and then I told her he was in India and we had agreed to separate. She wanted to know if he was dead and I had to tell her he wasn't but that it was best she forgot about him because she would probably never see him, or if she did it would not be with me.

Morgan cracked his bit of the mosquito problem and there was a huge party. I can see myself at that party, almost like the last reel of the film, Johnson. I see myself serving vol-au-vents to the faculty wives, wearing a low-cut dress, for God's sake! The last reel of the film. And I was trapped in it. Captured, as if on celluloid, to repeat the same gestures forever, like others who follow that script. Forever.

Morgan has moved on to proteins in viruses. I respect his work and have grown to admire his kind of life to an extent. But it means being stuck on campuses and singing Neil Young songs to a badly strummed guitar year after year and doing the unpredictable things in predictable ways and never seeing the real world. Everything has to be safe. And then as he grows into middle age he has grown in weight and tries to disguise his baldness by wearing a ponytail and is more into gardening than anything else.

To me it's an acceptance of withering away, of getting old with grace, whereas I, and I think you, are determined to 'rage against the dying of the light'.

Forgive me, my darling, my love, my only love, for all this. I have a question at the end of it because I have taken my life in my hands and am placing it in yours.

I saw an announcement in the TV schedules one day on a French documentary on the 'Serial killer, notorious escape artist and con man Johnson Thhat'. It was on a satellite channel and my eye fell on it by chance. It was transmitted with subtitles at two in the morning.

Of course I couldn't sleep that night and came downstairs and turned on the TV and watched you. They said you'd been released. I had been calculating the weeks and months and years. There you were in jail and then walking free in Paris and across a park and bridge and you looked sad. My heart was in my mouth. You know one takes the wrong turn in life and then one is stuck, walking that road till you die!

You said you wanted to be a writer. Then the Eiffel Tower behind you and you were talking and every room of my memory echoed with your voice.

Then steps on the wooden staircase and Samara came down the stairs in her dressing gown, rubbing her eyes, and I heard her and panicked and switched the TV off. She was suddenly wide awake.

'What were you watching?' she asked.

'Nothing, just some rubbish, I couldn't sleep.'

'Why are you lying, mom? Your cheeks are wet. You've been crying.'

She picked up the remote and turned on the TV. It was still on your programme and she stood there watching it, watching you for maybe three or four minutes.

An Indian policewoman was being interviewed about you and how she wanted you to be sent back to Thailand to be shot for the eleven murders you had committed. The interviewer was asking her why she had changed her mind. Did she now condone serial killing and think it should be excused? She said something about being a policewoman and not dispensing justice but implementing the law, which is all that society could do.

Then you came on again and you were being asked if you had any regrets and you said you had none.

Samara's mouth was wide open. She turned to me.

'No! No! Not him! Please, not him! It isn't, is it? Is it?'

She screamed and threw the remote control in my face. Then she screamed again. 'Noooooooo!' and before I could stop her, she was running out of the house.

I ran after her. Morgan and Paul came running down the stairs. Samara had run to Morgan's car and started it. I ran to stop her but she revved the engine and drove off into the night.

'What the fuck is going down?' Morgan asked.

'We had an argument,' I said.

'What? At this time of night?'

The TV was still on in the house.

'I'll get my keys,' I said.

I switched the TV to another channel, got my keys, grabbed some clothes and my wallet and ran to my car before Morgan could stop me.

There was one road from our house out of the campus,

but a quarter of a mile down the road was a crossroads. She could have gone any which way. But I wasn't chasing her any more. I was going to the airport.

I called Morgan from New York as I was boarding the plane for Paris. I told him I still loved him, said I was sorry, but I needed time because my life was in a rut. He listened patiently and asked me where I was. I said I wasn't telling him, not out of viciousness, because he was blameless, but because it didn't matter. He asked me to come back in the gentlest of tones. For Paul and Samara's sake. I said I'd be no good to them in the mental state in which I was. He didn't even know what I was talking about. He would only find out if and when Samara returned.

He started pleading again and I think he was crying. I put the phone down. I couldn't take it. I had made my decision. I had to see you, to be with you, to feel you, to cry over you, to be wanted by you, to fuck you, to see the world through our eyes, to be together again.

3

'Samara when she was born, at two, at three, at six, as a teenager, Samara graduating.'

Ravina had them ready in her bag in case I suggested walking out and now she produced them: photographs of our daughter. She handed them with her commentary, one by one. She had weeded out the pictures and presented me with only those without Morgan and Paul in them.

'Do you have one of Morgan?' I asked. 'And one of your son?'

'Why would I want one of Morgan?'

But she dug in her bag and found the photograph of a thin boy who looked very much like he was Samara's brother.

'My letter was delivered to you?'

'Of course,' I said, and told her what she was really asking. 'I live in my apartment. Alone.'

'You must have made plans for the future?'

'I am thinking about it. I have only ever had a future. My past is not worth thinking about.'

She looked at me. She wanted me to hold her and claim her. It was too early for that.

'You've had a very full life, with two kids and the university and mosquitoes and everything.'

'Yes. It was busy but empty.'

This was too direct. I didn't want to fill out anyone's emptiness. She sensed that I was getting shifty and the old pride returned.

'I want to stay here, in this hotel – by myself. I don't think we should rush into anything,' she said. 'You have a woman, I suppose?'

'No, no, I don't,' I said. Then, 'This is a good hotel.'

'Yes, very comfortable. Let's talk about hotels. Very central,' she said.

I liked her sarcasm. She had switched on the small-talk mode in perfect bourgeois pitch and it made me smile. I was going to throw up my hands and discuss the future, but my mobile phone rang.

'Where are you, mon cher? I've been calling your studio.' It was Virginie – as though nothing had happened.

'Why do you want to know?'

'Because I am going to Aix and Arles on a research trip and thought you might go with me. It's lovely there and we have a car and several hotels.'

'When?'

'Now. In an hour. You can meet me at the station. I'll get the tickets, just come to the platform. You don't have to go home, I'll get you some spare men's shirts.'

'Your husband's?' I asked.

'What?' She perhaps didn't catch the words because she wasn't expecting them. 'Yeah, I've got two already. Are you coming?' She meant shirts, not husbands of course.

'No,' I said and put the phone down.

She rang again and I didn't answer and then she rang again and I switched the phone off.

'Woman trouble?' Ravina asked.

'Offers I am in no mood to accept. Get your things and check out. Let's go to my place,' I said.

'Just like that? It takes you one phone call and fifteen seconds to decide?'

'No, Ravina, it has taken me twenty years.'

I got up and took her in my arms and she began to cry. 'I have already packed. I hate this room,' she said.

At the flat, she looked all over for traces of Virginie, found them and threw them in the garbage bin. I let her do it.

We opened a bottle of Sancerre which she'd bought. She nattered on about the wine, showing off like an American about grape varieties.

'Could you still make love to me?' she asked.

'Of course.'

'Do you want to?'

'That can't be a serious question.'

'I want to wait till it's dark,' she said.

'Why?'

'I want to do it in the dark, so you can't see me and the cellulite and the rolls of fat on my tummy. Two kids, Govind! But we switch the lights out and you can imagine we are back in Bangkok.'

'I don't want to imagine I'm in that place. Ever.'

'But I don't want you to see the stretch marks and my thighs.'

'I don't give a fuck, man,' I said. It was the wrong thing to say. 'As long as it's you, I don't care. But we can wait and play in the dark. As you please.'

We did. And in the next days she bought a dim reading lamp and put it on the floor and we made love by its 25-Watt effulgence.

'But I wanted to see you – with me. And the risk is worth it.'

We made love by candlelight and then suddenly as though she had got over the hump of the crisis of confidence, she changed. She brought the full-length mirror which I had stood against the bathroom wall and altered the position of the bed so she could prop the mirror up horizontally against the wall on the bed lengthwise and watch ourselves making love. It was now as though she wanted proof that it was happening and I caught her glancing at it whether I was on top of her or behind her as she crouched on her elbows and knees. Her eyes and face were triumphant. We were at it; she could see it.

She bought things for the flat and in a few days established a lived-in atmosphere with flexible meal timetables and menus. We played blackjack.

Virginie rang a few times and I switched the phone off. I had to admit that the domesticity with Ravina was like a holiday. I had never had either properly in my life.

Then Virginie rang the front doorbell and Ravina answered. I was behind her.

'Who's this?' Virginie asked.

'Ravina,' I said.

'No, who is she?' Virginie persisted, still confronting Ravina on the doorstep.

'The woman whose letter you read,' I said.

'What letter? Why do you never answer my calls? Where have you been? I sent Camera round and he said he'd tried you ten times but you must have left town. I was getting worried, Jean.' She tried to push past Ravina who stared at her and then turned and went inside leaving me to deal with Virginie on the doorstep.

'Why should you worry about me?' I asked.

'Who is this dump of a woman?' she asked, still from the landing. 'Are you going to explain what's going on?'

'It's my wife. And I'm not sharing myself out between lovers, so fuck off.'

'What's come over you?' she asked, pleading. Then she shouted to Ravina.

'Where did you come from, bitch?'

'Get rid of her,' Ravina shouted back from the kitchen.

So she had sent Camera round and he had lied to her.

'Are you with Camera?' I asked.

'Jean, have you gone mad on me? You bastard.'

Ravina came back from the kitchen with a plastic bucket of water and flung the water at Virginie.

'Ohhhhhhh! You fucking whore, you two-bit crook and murderer. You think I don't know who that is. She's the serial murderess. Your accomplice whom you wouldn't betray.' Virginie kicked the door a few times, then left. We heard the lift door bang. She didn't ring me again.

Two weeks later she wrote a bullshit story in *Le Figaro*. They gave her two double pages. They had shots of her and me and even one of Ravina surreptitiously taken as she went shopping below our apartment. The headline was 'Dregs

Seek out the Dregs'. In French it was some pun on nostalgie de la boue.

Virginie used her own name in her story and used ours. The story had everything. She was confessing that she was fascinated by my murders long before she went on the assignment to India. She was in confessional mode as though she had reverted to being a serious Catholic and was letting it all hang out in the blab box. Maybe the French public understand that. My stepfather was the sort of person who would read it.

She told the whole story: the sex in the jail, escape to Goa, how she said she helped me get released, and the documentary. She wrote about why I had stayed in jail and how I had kept in touch with my co-murderer whose name she had only heard me say once when she confronted me after I ended our relationship by betraying her and going back to the murderer. Nothing about her own husband, her children, wealth, Ravina's note, intercepting it jealously and nothing about what Camera had told me – her serial affairs with other men.

Virginie's story concluded with her cheap analysis about 'evil being essentially banal'. She had fallen for the slim and slant-eyed allure of the yellow-skinned devil. She said I was hypnotic, that women would find it difficult to resist me, that I could turn on a charm, which was like a magnet to the spirit. She was talking French rubbish. She said she'd been deeply deceived, but sincerely in love with evil. Until she discovered that the human shape of evil was weak, a failure of a life and a failure of a human being.

And all this time, after she made a scene at the flat, I began wondering what I was doing with Ravina. She said she

had come back because this was her life, that being restricted
to being Morgan's wife and the mother of children who had
now left the nest was never what she wanted. It was not even
the dark tunnel, it was the grave. And for her my life and my
future and being with me were open territory, creativity, 'being
in touch with the energies of the universe', which were good
and evil and interwoven.

Pradhan sahib, did I love either of them? Look at me.
Have I ever loved anybody? But I chose Ravina, the returned
Ravina because she 'believed' and made me believe she
believed.

I read Virginie's newspaper story over and over. It came to
me. I hadn't been wrong about Virginie. She hadn't deceived
me. She had been straight with me.

Camera! He had always wanted Virginie, had watched me
with her, had burned when he saw the hypnotized fascination
for me in her eyes. Then Ravina's contacting note gave him
his chance. Virginie never saw the note. He intercepted it and
made his little plan. There was no rich husband, no children,
no lovers, no lies. The first that Virginie knew about Ravina
was when she turned up at my door.

Virginie gave no address in the newspaper, but the
photograph of the Chinese supermarket and her mentioning
that Ravina was 'boldly going shopping in her apartment
complex' was enough. The press camped downstairs. They
were baying for blood. Two proven serial killers and poisoners
were living in the neighbourhood. There was no way out and
no one to call.

Except, there was. Ravina said, 'Call your father. I know
he knows influential Chinese people in Paris. Tell him where

you are and what you need. Say nothing about me. He knows nothing about me. He lives in a world of telephones and commands from a distance.'

'What the fuck am I? I run to him every time like a rat. You know what it makes me feel? That I have done a lot of desperate, individual, crazy things. But the power is still with the system, the organized syndicates. I'm a mug, a loser.'

I dialled the number. My father was very happy to hear from me. He didn't know where I was but had been waiting for this call for years, he said. Then cautiously, he asked if I had traced my mother in France and I said I hadn't. He was happy with that. What was I doing in Paris? I told him I needed help. Yes, he would see what he could do. He sounded almost grateful to be asked. He was at the centre again.

In a matter of hours after the phone call, with the paparazzi banging at our doors and sitting on the doorbell till I had to disconnect it, three Chinese gentlemen called at the flat. They shouted and I opened the door to their accents.

Only one of them, who introduced himself as Wing Kee, said he had taken stock of the situation and since very many Chinese people lived in our building and in the complex and these people, his people, felt threatened, intimidated and inconvenienced by the media scrum outside and downstairs, the 'Chinese Universal Welfare Association' would send its representatives to the reporters, photographers and TV people and present them with convincing arguments as to why they should go away and never come back.

Mr Kee said this persuasion and debate were even now under way and we could see the results by looking out of our bedroom window.

I looked. In the parking lot between the buildings a van was disgorging young Chinese men in leather jackets carrying short batons. Another van drew up and opened its doors.

Mr Kee said he would make sure that the results were satisfactory. He left me a phone number and said I was to call him if I needed any assistance in the future.

The media crowd seemed to have dispersed by the time I went downstairs. They never came back.

Pradhan sahib, did I want Ravina to stay? Creatures like us don't have tradition and culture planning their relationships and lives for them. People like you do. You are a policeman, a Nepali Hindu. You look forward to marriage, children, a house and old age, to promotion and exciting assignments and then retirement with stories to tell. Criminals in gangs look forward to the day when they will have their own gang, when they can kill their leaders and take over or pull the biggest heist ever. But the lone snake has only the lair it has presently made. There was no plan and couldn't be. I began to think of Ravina as home. It was an idea she planted in my head. She said, 'Johnson, you are my home and I am yours.'

In all the while we were together we never discussed Bangkok or what we had done there. It was a movie we had seen long ago. I only wondered how she had known that I would join her in her schemes and experiments, but then that first death, the taxi driver hadn't died because we wanted to kill him. He died because he wanted to abandon us. It was almost an accident and it was so easy.

No, Pradhan sahib, no amateur psychology or criminology please. You think about it – you want an omelette, you break an egg. You don't think about any possible fertilized chicken in the shell. You are hungry, the egg is there. That's all I will say about it. That's how it is for me. I knew it was true for her too.

Yes, once, only once I asked her whether she had told Morgan about our life in Bangkok. She just looked at me with contempt.

If I didn't know the answer to that question, I didn't know her.

✦

Three days after the paparazzi had been dispersed, Ravina went down to the supermarket. I had forgotten to ask her to bring me razor blades, so I went down too. The shop was in our complex in a glasshouse construction between two residential buildings. I went in. It was huge, with twenty shopping aisles and arches and enclaves so that one could lose someone in there.

I bought my blades and went towards our lifts. I could look out onto the car park and as I waited for the slow lift, a car passed me with three men in it – and Ravina in the back seat. I didn't believe it. It must have been someone who looked very much like her in profile.

I went and looked round every aisle of the supermarket. She wasn't there. I looked in the shops nearby. No luck. Had the wretched reporters kidnapped her? But what could they do to her? I waited a while. Had the journalists kidnapped her? Interpol? There was no one I could appeal to.

She returned with the shopping bags before I made any calls.

'Where did you go?' I asked.

'To the supermarket,' she said.

'Who were those men?'

'I didn't want to worry you. They were not press.'

'Who the hell were they?'

'It doesn't really matter. They were Americans, from the embassy. They had read the papers and someone from India had called them, the Indian police and told them I was an American citizen. They asked me a few questions and I said I had no plans to return to the USA. They wanted my passport but I said I'd lost it. Would you like cassoulet for dinner?'

I said I would. If she didn't want to come clean, I'd drop it.

The next day I called my father in Bombay.

'Has anyone come enquiring about Ravina recently?' I asked. The mention of her name must have given him a shock.

'The police came. I told them she married an American and ran off,' he said. He again wanted to know if I had seen my mother and hummed with pleasure when I said I hadn't. The satisfied humming of an old man.

'You should now start giving me grandchildren, Govind. Get a nice French madam,' he said.

I wasn't in the mood for chit-chat so I said I had to go.

The police had called. Of course they'd called. Chandrika! So she hadn't given up. Not as far as Ravina was concerned. She must have traced her journey from New Mexico to Paris. She would have read Virginie's article on the Internet and put two and two together and started sniffing around again.

4

Gerrard the literary agent did come back to me. He was not tactful, he was not kind. I picked up the phone feeling as though I had been called in by a teacher for unsatisfactory homework.

'You are half-Indian and half-Vietnamese,' he said.

'Yes,' I said.

'You should write in Hindi or better still in Vietnamese and invent some kung fu stories, because you can't write English for toffee. And even if I got a ghostwriter to straighten out your illiterate prose, you don't know the difference between the truth and lies and you wouldn't know an autobiography from an automobile accident. That being said, can you collect your rubbish or send us the postage?'

I was stunned.

'Does he like your book?' Ravina asked

'He says I am too much like Sean Connery in a movie,' I said.

That was the effort of years.

I told Ravina that we should go to London, I wanted to track down an Indian writer who would get me a proper agent. She didn't seem to want to go. She had already made a date, she said, with friends on the Riviera whom she wanted to see.

'Riviera? Not Morgan's friends! Or are they millionaire marine biologists?' I asked.

'No, no, a childhood friend from school in India. Her husband is French.'

She said she'd spend a week with them because they'd been on the phone and pestering her. Then we'd meet back in Paris. It was the first I had heard of any such plans and the fact that she had mentioned it only when I said I wanted to travel to London got me thinking. But what was there to think about? She wanted a few days with friends. It wouldn't matter to me. Jealousy was for mugs and idle minds.

In London the big news was that the terrorists who had kidnapped the mountain-trekking trio of British, American and Norwegian climbers and held them hostage had been presented for trial. One of these terrorists was called Omar Sheikh and he was a British citizen – a fellow from a Pakistani-British business family who was educated at a public school and then went on to the London School of Economics. He ended up in India as a man from Haji Ghulam's outfit, the Army of the Universal Caliphate.

The newspapers were full of profiles of him and his school and teachers and his life in Britain and one news item said he had been moved to Tihar jail awaiting sentence. The trial had been pending a few years.

I knew he'd be with his boss Ghulam and they'd have no access to a phone and no protection unless Roy could handle it. I had no way of knowing and it was strange that I was even curious about their fate. They'd possibly be beaten till they were near-dead.

I hadn't told anyone about the phone numbers and the double-cross I had to pull off to make a deal with the Indian government. I hadn't informed the Indian writer that I was turning up to see him but I knew he'd be in London because his latest book was being launched and it had been announced. He would be signing books the next day at a bookshop. I was going to buy his book.

Murad Sultani is a very special writer because he predicted terrorism before it happened. He had travelled in Iran and Saudi Arabia following the publication of his book predicting a nuclear attack by jihadis, he had been interviewed by a hundred TV channels, condemned as a spy by Pakistani organizations, celebrated as a money-spinner by the publishing world, reviled as a publicity seeker by left-wing spokesmen, associated with a young Indian dancer in a gay partnership by the gossip papers and nominated for the Booker Prize.

At the bookshop, I bought a copy of his book and joined the signing queue. When it was my turn, I held out my hand. 'I am Johnson Thhat.' A young woman from his publishing house was keeping the pile supplied and re-pronouncing some names for him.

He had no trouble with mine.

'Ah, the serial killer,' he said, looking up. So damned cool.

'Good, you read the papers,' I said.

'But we must talk. I'll sign your book later. Will you wait till after, just a few minutes? Have a coffee; the publicity...er, person...Deirdre will get you one.'

'I can wait. I have driven down from Paris to see you.'

We went to a bar after his signing was over. This was his third book, he said, no one had heard of his first one which was the best, but the second one had become famous. He had written the book just before the first attack by truck on the World Trade Center and he had predicted worse – the terrorists may be losing, but they were relentless.

He asked how I came to be there and I said I had especially come to see him and give him my manuscript. He said he had a meeting with the Indian high commissioner later that evening, but he gave me his number, took down mine, and said we should be in touch.

I had checked the hotels in Earls Court. They all wanted credit cards or cash deposits. I had money for a week and a budget for the ferry across the Channel and for petrol to return to Paris. I was buying a Lebanese meal from a takeaway on Edgware Road when I saw the casino's lights: '21' in neon.

That night I parked the car in the casino basement and went to the blackjack tables.

By ten-thirty that night I had converted my five hundred pounds into five thousand. My instinct was good. But from then onwards I started to lose.

By two o'clock I was down to my last twenty-five quid.

Ravina should have been with me. I would have sent her to draw out more cash. I had no way to get any more. But I know that when I am down and out I am luckiest, so I continued.

I lost the £25.

I had nothing now.

I had to get off the table.

I stepped out into the cold London night. The old Merc I had bought from a trader in Paris was parked in the public car park and couldn't be retrieved without paying.

I called Murad and woke him up.

'I'm sorry for the late call, but I've been mugged and my wallet is gone and I'm stranded. I can't even get my car out.'

'But you must be in your hotel,' he said.

'I was in a fancy hotel, but they were racists and I had a fight and got thrown out,' I said.

He agreed to come out as I knew he would.

He was intrigued by me. Maybe he thought he could be like that writer fellow in America who talked to some killer and wrote a bestseller about all of that. I would play along.

He paid for the car to come out of the park and gave me some spare cash. He said he couldn't take me home because his partner was nervous of 'new people'. I said I would sleep in the car, not to worry. I knew he wouldn't want me in his house, but also that he would go to dinner parties and boast about how he was friends with a serial killer who couldn't be that smart because he had been mugged on London's streets. He wanted to know about the racism fight and I made something up about one drunk calling me a Chinky-Paki and then the management taking his side because he was rich.

I parked the car in a side street with free parking and slept till the police woke me, tapping at the window at dawn.

'I am from Paris and got mugged yesterday so couldn't go back to the hotel,' I said. They looked me up and down and then left me alone.

I called Murad. He said he'd meet me around lunchtime.

I left the car, bought a coffee and a newspaper and sat down to pass the time.

The headlines were startling: 'Indian Airlines Plane Hijacked'.

The article said that the Indian airliner on its way to

Nepal had been diverted to Kandahar airport in Afghanistan by a group of hijackers calling themselves the Army of the Universal Caliphate.

Ghulam's boys.

I read on. They were holding twenty-two men, women and children and threatened to shoot them if their demands were not met.

The Taliban government of Afghanistan, while condemning all hijacking, said it had surrounded the airport with its troops and was facilitating communication between the Indian government and the 'freedom fighters'. The hijackers were demanding the release of three of their people 'illegally held by the Indian government'. They named them as Haji Ghulam, commander in the Army of the Universal Caliphate, Omar Sheikh and a third member of the Army captured with Omar in the abortive kidnapping incident.

I called Ravina on her mobile. I asked where she was.

'The Riviera,' she said.

'What town?' I asked.

She said she'd call me back immediately.

She did. She mentioned some town but said she was in a village nearby. There are no villages on the Riviera, it is one continuous strip of development, but I let it pass.

I read part of the article to her and said she should get a paper.

'Why? I am far away from any newspaper shop here and don't have a car,' she said. She sounded strange, making up excuses for nothing.

'Because, honey, I can speak to Ghulam. He trusts me,' I said. 'The hijackers are under his instructions.'

'Why is that good for us?' Ravina asked.

'The Indian government is in a fix. The American government tells them never to give in to terrorists. Their own population will want the hostages safely returned. They can't do both. I can.'

I sat with Murad in a Bangladeshi restaurant for lunch. I gave him my manuscript. He gave me enough money to pay for the ferry and petrol back and I said I would send him the money as soon as I got to France.

'You know people in the Indian government?' I asked.

'Yes, why?' he asked.

'This hijacking. I know the guy Haji Ghulam, their leader. He trusts me with his life. I can talk to him if the Indian government will bring him to the phone in jail. Listen, Murad, do you know the Indian foreign minister? He is negotiating.'

'Not him, but the high commissioner can always talk to him. So what will you do?'

'This guy trusts me. I saved his life. If they connect me I can tell him that the Indians will take him to a provincial prison near the border with Pakistan. Then a few weeks later he can escape from there; I can arrange it. In exchange he releases the plane and the twenty-two hostages and he can make some big statement for the world press that being a Muslim he knows that the Koran forbids any attack on caravans of travellers, which means, in today's world, passenger planes. That way he and his friends get free and the Army of the Universal Caliphate wins a huge propaganda victory. Same result but much better for him.'

Murad looked impressed. He called the high commission on his mobile and stood up and walked out so people in the restaurant wouldn't overhear.

'The high commissioner knows who you are and believes you know this Haji character. But he said I shouldn't get involved in this. I have to keep out of it. For one thing, I was born Muslim, because of my fiction I am suspected in certain circles of having subversive connections and if we do this my name will get on some Indian government file as a friend of Haji Ghulam and of yours and some bureaucrat will be chasing me years down the line.'

'So no go?' I asked.

'Yes go. I gave him your mobile number. He will convey your proposal to Delhi's incident room and they will assess it and be in touch with you.'

I waited till that evening and then set out for Paris. I had nothing more to stay for in London and no cash anyway. As I was coming in to Dover, the call came.

The voice said he was a Mr Bannerjee and he was the friend of my friends. Could I get back to London, please?

'I don't have enough money to stay in England,' I said.

'We will accommodate you.'

I turned the car round. 'Bannerjee' had given me an address in Tooting. It was a furnished flat with very few personal effects in it. I rang the bell and a young Indian man let me in.

'Bannerjee?'

He shook his head but indicated that I was to go up to the first floor. No Bannerjee was waiting for me but there was Chandrika.

'You are looking fine. I flew in just for you.'

'You now deal with terrorists?'

'Thanks to you. Since our little clean-up in Delhi. No time to lose, tell me what you said to the incident room.'

I told her my plan.

'You take him to a prison in Punjab and I tell him he will surely be allowed to escape in two months, but anything can happen in two months, can't it? And sometimes in India people who try and escape don't make it.'

Chandrika listened without taking notes. Another man came in. Chandrika introduced him as 'Bannerjee from the Visa Section'.

He sat down. 'Things are developing fast out there,' he said. He took Chandrika aside and spoke to her privately. I sat perfectly still.

'They are going to try and connect you. They know the plan,' Chandrika said. 'You talk to him as you outlined to Mr Bannerjee, but we will have to listen and to record the call.'

'You know me and know what I want. The government knows I am trying to help because I am Indian by birth and spent so much of my life there, but there has to be some return,' I said, looking straight at Chandrika.

'The government can't bargain just now, Johnson. The situation is serious. But I've never let you down,' she said. 'Even getting you to Paris.'

'I know, Chandrika. I am not asking for money, but maybe some facility to publicize my role and a favourable attitude if I ever apply for citizenship.'

'I can promise nothing, these are political decisions, but we'll see,' she said.

Bannerjee was now on the phone and he motioned to me. He said Ghulam would be put on directly.

'Salaam aleikum, Ghulam sahib,' I said.

He was happy to hear from me, he said. He sounded confident, like he was suddenly in charge.

'I am speaking with the full authority of the Indian government. Ghulam sahib, you remember your readings in the Koran and your explanations to me and Roy? They were very instructive and I have thought of them a lot. Now at this moment I was reminded of the passage you translated – that a true Muslim would never interfere with or harm travellers in a caravan, but always protect them and be hospitable. You said it meant travellers on their private business. If you, Sheikh sahib, interpreted this for the world on TV as the correct moral behaviour according to the Koran and released all the hostages, the government will give you a guarantee of release in a short time for yourself and all freedom fighters. They will shift you to a low-security jail and then release you. I give my word as a Muslim. The victory will be yours, ours and Allah's, Sheikh sahib.'

'Jaan Sen, this is not an unworthy thought, my friend. You are a Muslim? You are convinced? Allah be praised. There are plenty of talks going on just now. My main problem is trusting the Hindu government. I will soon be free and I will find you, my friend, in Paris. Thank you for everything you are doing. I will seriously consider. Khuda Hafiz.'

The phone was taken from him, I thought.

If Chandrika was puzzled by the brevity of the call, she didn't show it. It was morning already. I left for Paris and was home by afternoon.

The same evening, the news report on TV said that one hostage had been taken out of the hijacked plane onto the tarmac and brutally shot.

That left twenty-one hostages.

My luck kicks in when I am at the lowest. I now realized that the 21 Casino was not the lowest point. I had to reach lower. But how low was this lower?

Ravina rang and said she was coming back by car and would go straight to the flat. She would be dropped so I was not to bother about coming to the airport.

'I thought you went by train,' I said.

'Yes, yes, but they also have a private plane,' she said.

She was lying, and getting tangled in it, but I couldn't be bothered to question her. What was it to me? Then I realized that to be lied to by Ravina was probably the final deterioration my luck was looking for in order to kick in.

Twenty-one hostages. Fate itself had committed murder to descend to my own lucky number.

The next morning I rang the High Commission and asked for Chandrika at Operations, but was told there was no such person working there and no such department.

Ravina returned. I didn't question her though she tried to tell me about the beautiful house and the view from the cliffs.

On the third day of the hijack, we heard that the Indian foreign minister was personally escorting Haji Ghulam, Omar and the other released prisoner to Kandahar to secure the release of the hostages and the Indian Airlines plane.

My plan had not been used, but Ghulam was back in Pakistan and was my friend and, I said to Ravina, could be useful. I had further plans for him and myself.

5

My entry on the world stage. Ghulam got in touch with me. He was back home in Karachi, and showered Allah's blessings on me. I don't know how he found my phone number. He said a man would come and see me, his 'Little Brother', and pay me off for all I had done. I gave him my address and then regretted it.

I got to thinking that my intermediary plan was perhaps not refused by the Indians but by Ghulam himself. Did Ghulam talk to the Indians about my plan? Was there a soft-cop/tough-cop approach to these talks and did RAW tell him that this same friend of his, Johnson, had betrayed him and the Army of the Universal Caliphate by selling its phone numbers? Was he in touch with Chandrika who could have betrayed me by telling him that I had betrayed him?

Or had Omar Sheikh, out in the field after Ghulam was arrested, begun to put two and two together when the Canadian, British and Pakistani police seemed to have simultaneous information about their organization?

Had he made Ghulam suspicious?

Was his man coming to kill me?

✦

I didn't know what to expect when the 'Little Brother' found me. How could I stop him? I couldn't explain to Ravina. She didn't know about the bargain with RAW or Chandrika and the betrayal of Ghulam. She could see, though, and asked what I was worried about.

'We'll run short of money,' I said.

'I can work,' she said. But it didn't come to that yet.

Little Brother came. I sent Ravina out first to be sure he wasn't armed. He wasn't. He had come not with a bullet for my head but with a wad of dollars.

'Salaam aleikum! Sheikh sahib said we should give you these,' he said. He didn't stay. He handed over the naked notes and 'Sheikh's contacts' – 'Careful! For you alone!' – between two salaams.

Was Ghulam biding his time? No, I decided that he was not that clever. He still believed I was his friend and on his side. I would get in touch when I had more to say than thanks.

My father phoned.

'Are you settled?'

'Yes, I am,' I said.

'I hate to see my boy wasting his life on petty crimes. Do something to make a father proud,' he said. 'Make a baby.' This was becoming an obsession with the old man. I didn't tell him I already had a grown-up daughter.

'I am not your boy and never was,' I said.

'You have Indian blood and respect for your elders flows in it, so shut your fucking mouth,' he said.

'Right, tell me what to do,' I said.

'Phone Winky,' he said. He meant Mr Kee, his Chinese mob man who had chased the paparazzi away for us. 'They need someone who speaks clean English and whose French accent is not a joke, someone who doesn't say "flied lice".'

They were not Mr Kee's words, but I got the drift and made the call.

He invited me to see him in a Chinese supermarket. I was conducted to a back room, a sort of office with three desks and ten or twelve calendars, all but one in Chinese, on the walls. The Chinese mafia seemed to conduct their business from the back rooms of groceries. Was it a metaphor?

Mr Kee was waiting for me.

'Velly glad to have your coopelation,' he said.

They needed a spokesman and negotiator who could speak Hindi and cleaner English than they did. My father had recommended me.

I was to go to Brussels and enter the antique furniture trade with a couple of people they would put me in touch with. I was to understand that I was not my own boss, that he, Mr Kee was the boss, but that the 'Belgian tlash' with whom he was putting me in touch had to be at all times treated with suspicion and circumspection. He explained some details and gave me some money.

'You have fliends in Pakistan. I know. Next step is under my hat,' said Mr Kee.

✦

I met the 'Belgian tlash' in Brussels in the person of Hugo Flandermann. He was a tall, attractive Belgian, perhaps thirty years old, and said he was an antiques expert.

We sat, on three consecutive nights, in an art café and bar just off the centre of town and a few doors down from my hotel. The café specialized in chess and the patrons played and watched each other play.

Hugo invited a stream of people and talked constantly on the mobile phone and intermittently to his guests, some of whom brought him files, brochures, notes and plans which seemed, from the glimpses I caught of them, to be in a variety of languages including Chinese. Hugo introduced me to them as his partner and them as 'antique dealers'. Most of them, I was thinking, wouldn't have known an antique if it crumbled before them.

Four days later, Hugo, another Belgian called Charles, who wore a red scarf in a navy knot round his neck, and I, drove to England in a large white van full of old furniture.

We crossed the Channel on the train which accommodated our van and then took the motorway to London. Hugo drove, muttering abuse at the left-hand driving lanes and British laws. He hated Britain and its ugly girls, he said, and its dull warm beer and its assumption of superiority.

He turned off the motorway into the park of a large mock-Tudor building, an inn with which he was obviously familiar. Once we stopped, he asked me to call my English acquaintance. We had already discussed the deal and I had mulled it over and agreed.

We each had our separate rooms on the first floor of the inn. I called Murad, the Booker Prize fellow. I told him where I was and said he was to come over as soon as possible, I had a great deal for him. He protested. It was nearly midnight.

'So it is. Come early morning and have some breakfast,' I said. 'There's more money than the Booker Prize.' Which I knew he hadn't won.

When he came, I embraced him as if we were long-separated brothers.

'How's it going, Shakespeare?' I asked.

'I haven't had any answer from the agent on your book,' he said.

'Never mind that, I am into a new business now,' I said. 'And you are part of it.'

'What is it?' he asked.

I gestured to him to follow me into the car park and I showed him the van. I opened the back. The tables, the Louis XIV stuff, the Art Nouveau vases were all stacked and covered. I uncovered a few.

'Antiques, international trade,' I said.

He looked puzzled. 'I know nothing about it. I am a writer,' he said.

'You don't have to know anything. As a resident of the UK with a passport, an address and a bank balance, we need a few things from you. First of all get us a shopfront for the trade. They won't let us foreigners sign a lease, but you, they will compete for. Then help us open a bank account and if you can, get me a membership of the Groucho Club. You can say I am a French writer and Indian and Vietnamese and ethnic and all that. These British racists love that.'

'Why not do all this in Paris?' he asked.

'UK is the place, for several reasons. We will pay cash straight away. Five thousand pounds to you as soon as the lease is signed. You lose nothing. Just to use your name. Then my friend, the riches follow. A rain of thousands.'

He didn't reject the offer out of hand. He looked thoughtful.

'What's the matter? You don't look happy. Come and have a coffee,' I said, and put my arm around him and led him in.

'I suppose I should think about it. My book was badly timed. It was written before the terrorists went and drove a truck with bombs into the World Trade Center, but when that happened just after it was published, everyone thought I had taken important real events and needlessly fictionalized them. I had to take time writing them,' he said.

'Good foresight, bad timing,' I said. 'But everything is all right otherwise. You will be writing more prize books? This little packet, how do you English call it – wind-drop – could keep you alive.'

'Windfall,' he corrected me. 'Maybe. To tell the truth my boyfriend and I are splitting up and the little vixen is demanding half the flat. I don't have the cash and will have to sell it.'

'If you take my deal you will have cash to buy a bigger flat and buy him back,' I said.

'I have a counter deal for you. That's why I came in a rush. Listen, Johnson, my agent read your book. Frankly he didn't like it. But, and this is a huge "but", he said if I talk to you and you tell me the truth about your life, the whole truth and nothing but the truth and I write it up as a biography or as fiction, I can get an advance. I can pay you something from that and give you a percentage of whatever the book makes. But I have to have everything. Like what you did, the killings, the thoughts, the strategy.'

'That's a very tall order, my dear friend. I have to think about that one,' I said.

That too was a game, because I never think things over.

I am not a committee, I am a person and decisions come like lightning.

'I could do that with you, you know, tell you the story, but would my life be safe after that?'

'That's a very important factor, and your call. I wouldn't want the blood of my subject on my hands, so to speak,' he said, pretending that he gave a shit about my life and chances of survival. He just wanted confessions for his wretched book.

'After that I won't be safe anywhere. Except maybe, I am thinking the United States. I've always wanted to go there. Tell me something, Murad bhai, do you know anyone in the CIA?'

The question seemed to amuse him.

'How would I?' he said. And then, 'Hang on, I know a guy who knows a lot of people in the CIA. He's written a history of it.'

'That fellow will do. I'll do you a deal. You'll do my work, I'll do yours and give you money and take no cash for the book. I'll stay with you for some days and tell you the stories in a tape recorder.'

He was nervous but he shook on the deal and then we embraced again. I wanted him to feel I trusted him.

✦

Murad got us a lease on a shop on South Circular Road, just down from Forest Hill in the South East.

Murad didn't choose it, Hugo just made us stop as soon as he saw the first board, which said TO LET outside a derelict boarded-up property. We got out and he peeped into the shop through the holes in the boards. We were standing on the pavement. Hugo pulled out his phone. 'This is perfect, eh,

Thhat? Good for the British and visitors coming from Europe. Well placed,' he said. 'Get the lease, brother.'

'Who's going to buy antiques here? This is broken-down, second-hand furniture territory,' Murad said.

'You have to create the character of a district to sell antiques,' Hugo said. 'We could go to Portobello Road, but we want bulk orders, you know.'

The estate agent answered the phone and Hugo passed it to Murad.

'Use your British accent,' Hugo said.

'I have an Indian accent,' said Murad in his English accent.

'Fake it,' Hugo said. He had no idea who Murad was and was treating him like a servant now that he had agreed to be paid. I could see it offended Murad, who thought of himself as the Booker-nominated celebrity.

But he worked it. The estate agent could hardly believe that anyone wanted the shop and came immediately to show us around.

We stayed in the mock-Tudor hotel for six days and signed a document towards getting a lease and started the business of registering a company and getting a bank account, etc.

Mr Kee sent his London man to the hotel with a stack of money and we paid Murad what we had promised. He seemed to feel guilty taking the cash.

'Now I want to meet your other writer, the man with the Big American contacts, the history, you know,' I prompted.

'I'll take you,' he said, 'I want to get away from London. Blazing row with my partner. Told him to take the money and go, the bitchy boy. He won't shut up crying at home and he's the one who wants to have an open scene and bring this pick-up and rent trash to my flat.'

'You must kick his arse in the street,' I said. 'How far is it to where your CIA history friend lives?'

'It's Cambridge, fifty miles once you get to the other side of London. He knows you are coming to meet him and he's quite excited.'

'Does he know I want an intro?' I asked.

'Oh, yeah. I sort of told him, but you can explain. I warn you, he's quite curious and tactless. He'll ask you outright how many people you've murdered,' Murad said.

'That's good. I will keep him interested by telling him nothing. You watch the performance, my old buddy.'

'He's a mischievous bastard. He's not going to do anything with whatever you tell him. It's just a good story. Boast at dinner parties that he's met you and that you confessed. I told him I was writing the definitive book, your confessions – with you of course.'

'Maybe we could write as joint authors, man?' I was fishing. He obviously wasn't falling for that. Not at this stage.

We came off the motorway and drove a few miles in through an English village.

'This is Cambridge,' he said, not wanting to tackle the subject. I pretended I was interested in the view.

'That's the Fitzwilliam Museum and Peterhouse on the left,' he said, indicating the old buildings.

'Whose house?' I asked

'It's a college.'

'Very old place, eh? You came here to study, didn't you?'

'A long time ago.'

'They must have a big library?' I asked. The ride from London had been sort of silent. We were discovering that, apart from plans and strategies, we had nothing to talk about. I had to make an effort.

'Of course.'

'And your books will be there, eh?'

'Yes, they are compelled to keep a copy of all published books. By law.'

'Have you seen the copy? Of your book I mean. Standing there on the shelves.'

He shook his head. He looked at his watch. It was a small modest black one. Not like my large golden blob, a mini-goldfish bowl of a watch which can tell me the time in Singapore and give me compass directions and everything.

'Your friend has read about me, then,' I ventured.

'Oh yeah, he knows your antics well.'

'As a top criminal?' I asked.

'Maybe. He has formed his opinion from newspapers. He might see you and change his mind,' he said.

'He will think I am more handsome than the papers show,' I said.

'Sure,' he said.

He told me were passing Queens. We went over a bridge where he said something about Newton, then we drove out of town and into a village.

'This is Grantchester, the village which Rupert Brooke made famous with a poem which asks if the vicarage clock will forever stand at half past three and if there will be honey still for tea.'

'I don't understand poetry,' I said. Writers are so boring.

I don't know whether Murad thought of me as a friend. How would he introduce me?

'You know, everyone in the literary world says that Harry is a spook himself. I personally think he still works for MI6 and writes thrillers under a different name,' said Murad.

'That's good for me,' I said.

I hadn't told him exactly what I wanted from this Harry, but Murad is a sharp man. He must have been thinking, though he said and asked nothing.

We passed a house with a Bentley parked outside. Murad pointed at it. 'There's a frivolous Boy's Own side to Harry. Look at that old grey Bentley for a start. He's a character out of John Buchan, but thinks he can be 007. But he's not. He's the kind of guy who diligently counts the thirty-nine steps and makes sure there aren't thirty-eight. But we'll meet him in a pub.'

He had made a mistake pointing out the house. He had to cover up the fact that even the CIA or MI6 man didn't want a criminal as a guest. They might be official murderers and poisoners, but they didn't want to mix with unofficial ones.

We parked and went into this pub with low wooden beams. I said I'd drink sparkling water.

Harry came in and we were introduced. He was wearing a bow tie and a brown jacket. He said he was pleased to meet me. I got straight down to my business and said I wanted to talk to him about the CIA. He didn't respond to this with anything more than a nod.

The two writers then drank beer and talked about the blue flowers that come up in the woods while the serial killer kept quiet. Eventually Harry proposed we go and see his wife's horses being trained, so we walked a little distance from the pub to the farm where the horses were and, while Murad watched them being led and watered and put through their paces over the sticks, Harry and I walked into the fields to talk business.

Even before I said anything, he knew what I was going to ask. Obviously this guy was a spy.

We walked for fifteen minutes and I told him what I wanted and what I was offering in return as a trade and bargain. He listened, his lips set downward. He had realized that this was a serious game and not a jaunt, not that little something to dine out on.

He became shifty. He obviously wanted to be rid of us. But yes, he said, he could help. He asked me to wait; he was going to the farmhouse to make a call.

That must be his contact, I was thinking.

He didn't ask me in. I turned to Murad and the horses. Harry came out and said, yes, the man was still there and would talk to us.

'I haven't told Murad what we are doing,' I said, and Harry looked startled.

'I see, I see,' he said. 'Maybe keep it between us.'

'I will say something on the way back,' I said.

'Maybe you shouldn't. Let him stay out of it. Leave it to the professionals,' Harry said.

On the way back to London I told Murad just enough to stop him calling Harry and poking around.

'I have to thank you, you gave me the right fellow. The CIA will send someone to speak with me. In London. They can't even wait for me to go back to Paris. I spoke to the big man himself.'

'The president?'

'No, man, the CIA or DSIA fellow in Europe who gathers the information.'

Murad didn't ask what the DSIA was.

'I have to change all my phone numbers and give them one. I must buy one of them card-phone things. Only you will have that number. I won't give it to anyone,' I said.

The next day I asked Murad to come to the antique shop he had leased for us. It was now full of the furniture and pieces that we had brought.

'You must know by now that we don't make money from selling this junk,' I said to Murad.

'I didn't think so,' he replied.

He drove me to the hotel, the mock-Tudor affair, and I took him up to my room. I showed him the brochures, catalogues. Some in Russian, others in French, English and Arabic.

'What are they?' Murad asked.

I opened them. The brochures had photographs, taken from every angle, of anti-tank guns, of missile launchers, flame-throwers, armoured vehicles, tanks, machine guns of several sizes and then written specifications for everything.

'The ex-Soviet guys, Ukrainian, Byelorussian and Georgian mafia, they are getting rid of these things with the help of the new governments of the former Soviet Republics. Huge trade. Millions of dollars. We are actually based in San Marino and we need this London office for contact and to pass the money. How do you think I paid you five grand? From antiques?'

He didn't look shocked. He leafed through the brochures.

'So why the CIA?'

'These fellows, Hugo, Charles, the fellows in Paris and San Marino must never know anything about that. I want to keep the CIA in reserve, strictly for myself, and see if they want to play. You see, being a top criminal is dangerous and I think I should eventually retire to the United States and have some money and a new identity and passport and everything. Paris might become too hot,' I explained.

'You mean you'll betray your contacts. Sell your partners down the river?'

I smiled and said nothing.

6

Ghulam sent Little Brother round to me again to ask if I wanted to go to Pakistan as his guest. Little Brother said he could deliver a Pakistani visa instantly, that there would be no need to fill in forms or answer questions. Ghulam had clout.

Ravina wanted to know how much time I would be away. She said she didn't like me spending time on my own abroad. She said she was frightened of being alone in Paris in the flat and would move from hotel to hotel while I was away, so she wouldn't have a fixed phone number, but I must keep in touch on her mobile.

One night I asked her what had happened to the policeman who accompanied her out of the Kohinoor hotel. He had disappeared, just as she had and had never been seen again.

She hesitated for a long while before answering.

'I never told you,' she said.

'So tell me now.'

'Your father's men, the diamond merchants, had thugs parked outside. They saw me leaving. They knew me. They got hold of him as we came out and went towards the car park. They grabbed me too. They wanted to know what was going on, and when I told them, they manhandled the cop and threw him in their van.

'I had thought of offering this cop, my escort, some money, sex, a new life, anything to let me go, but now it seemed my luck was in. The diamond merchant's thugs got hold of him. I told them their guys inside were bruised but safe.

'"We will release you, madam, where you want," they said and I asked them to take me to Delhi station.

'Before I got out I said, "What about him?"

'"Don't worry about him," the youngest of them said with a twinkle in his eyes. He spoke decent English. "We do an international trade. The German medical colleges pay a lot of money for corpses to dissect. We will cut this cop's throat, shave his body, extract his brain, put him in formaldehyde and send him in a deep freeze with other candidates to Hamburg for medical students to dissect. He is a good specimen."

'He kept a straight face as he spoke. I just got out of the van. I don't think the constable, tied with barbed wire and prone on the floor of the van understood quite what was to happen to him. Maybe it was all nonsense. They might have induced him to desert the force and work for them or something. I don't know. I put it out of my mind.'

✦

There's no such thing as a free trip to Pakistan. Of course Ghulam was after something. He hadn't called me for a holiday. He had the visa and ticket delivered and had a car pick me up at Karachi airport.

This was an impressive place, man, not like India where

all the guys on the street look like they are just hanging about or waiting to start begging.

My escort from the airport in the 4x4 that Ghulam had sent, were three guys with machine guns. They wore little round hats, loose flowing shirts and baggy pyjamas under them with trainers or thick leather slippers.

The 4x4 drove through the streets with my bodyguard surveying them with an air of ownership. There seemed to be escorts for other people, dignitaries in other cars. Some of the bodyguards with guns even walked behind a boss on the pavement. This was the Wild West. And here everyone looked the same, unlike India, where my eye could pick out a hundred varieties of caste, class and region.

Ghulam was at the gates of the mosque complex to welcome me. It was guarded by four armed men. This Army of the Universal Caliphate was not messing about. Ghulam had once explained to me that they were aiming for a world with only Muslims in it. The rest would be given the option to convert or die. Muslim kingdoms and powers had made the grave mistake in the past of allowing the infidels and idolaters to live on. Not this time. He said the Caliph would be a universal ruler of a universal umma and would rule in the name of Allah.

I wanted to ask him if he had ambitions in that direction, but stopped myself when he told me that Osama bin Laden was being flattered by his followers as the future Caliph. He didn't approve of that. Only God would choose the Caliph, he said. Then the world would live under Sharia law in peace and perfection.

They had struck at the Twin Tower in September and

the whole world had felt their power. Killing a few thousand people in New York was just a beginning. The Army of the Universal Caliphate needed troops on the ground, for which they needed arms and ammunition. The network to which Little Brother belonged had made it their business to find out that I was in touch with Hugo and Charles, the antique dealers. The network had set them up as arms dealers and it was so fortunate that a friend, a proven ally, almost a member of the Army of the Universal Caliphate, was their partner and now an important member of this trade.

Ghulam wanted the arms brought to the borders of Kashmir and then into northern Pakistan. He knew the routes through Uzbekistan and small, hidden airstrips in the mountainous regions of Baltistan and thereabouts. There were, he said, two ways of doing it. One was to ask me for the arms on credit and the other was to pay the money up front and trust me to deliver the consignments.

Which one did he favour, I asked, and what did they want?

Everything, he said, from light aircraft, tanks, armoured vehicles, missile launchers, heavy and light artillery and combat weapons of all sorts. He said that money was not a problem.

I was given a room in the mosque complex and met every day with different people from Afghanistan, Kashmir and the Middle East. Each time he introduced me to these fellows whom he called 'commanders', he would tell them about our life in Tihar jail together. He had faulty and even fantastic memories of those times and invariably said we ruled the jail together like sultans. He wanted to share my heroism. He would mention Roy as a man with great philosophical powers who had predicted, through the teachings of Nostradamus, that the Caliphate would triumph in our times.

Roy had said nothing of the sort.

Ghulam would proudly recall the hijack and then, getting down to brass tacks, would impress them by making me give a recitation of the possible arms that were for sale from Belarus or Ukraine.

✦

While I was in Karachi an incident took place that grabbed headlines all over the world. A journalist called Daniel Pearl from the *Wall Street Journal* had been kidnapped by Muslim militants. The Pakistani police were on the trail of the kidnappers and Ghulam told me that President Musharraf himself wanted Pearl released in order to stay friendly with the USA, which he was visiting at the time.

Musharraf's police couldn't find Pearl even though they knew that a section of their own secret service were in touch with the people who had kidnapped him. The secret service was out of touch or out of sorts with the president and his government.

The incident was high drama with Pearl's wife featured on TV from her Karachi home, begging for his release. She had an Indian Muslim journalist girl with her. Ghulam, watching television with me, said they were all CIA agents, including Pearl. They deserved to die.

His boys would bring him hourly reports from websites about what the world was saying about this kidnap. It occurred to me that he might be masterminding it, because a few curious incidents took place. A vanload of police came to talk to him in the mosque complex and when they left, I could see his boys clearing arms and ammunition out of the mosque complex through a side entrance in an alley and loading them in their Pajeros.

Then another group of police came and searched the place. They were not at all respectful and kicked down doors and even some people. They manhandled Ghulam and his chaps. They found nothing. They knew Ghulam had been warned by their own people and had cleared the complex in time.

The TV in the recreation room of the complex was now on twenty-four hours a day, monitoring the BBC, CNN and Pakistani and even Indian news channels.

Ghulam would go into enclave night and day with a few of his boys who would then shoot off on scooters on different missions. They told me nothing.

Then the police reported on TV that Omar Sheikh, the British kidnap-merchant who had been released with Ghulam in the hijack, had been arrested in Lahore for the capture and abduction of Daniel Pearl. The paper said he had been caught with help from the FBI, who had come down to analyse data from the web.

There were a lot of different stories flying round. Omar Sheikh was threatened by the Pakistani police who said they would kill his wife and family if he didn't surrender. Another story said he was working for the ISI, the intelligence wing of the Pakistani armed forces who had sanctioned the kidnap, the part of the security service out of step with the government.

This Omar Sheikh, a tall, thin fellow with specs, wearing a white kurta and pyjama, told the police that he thought Daniel Pearl was still alive.

He was wrong. A video was soon circulated on the web showing the execution of Pearl who was tied up and had his throat slit. The executioners made him say, 'I am a Jew, my father is a Jew,' before they cut his throat. But he wasn't bothered at that stage and said something like he was proud of being a Jew. It was a kind of 'Kill me, fuck you' gesture. Brave guy, man.

Ghulam's boys played the video from the web on their computers several times.

'He was not to be killed,' Ghulam said to me. 'Too many people formulating their own strategy. This is not a good way to run an army. I gave no orders.'

There were huge public demonstrations all over the world, even in Pakistan, in support of Daniel Pearl and against this brutal execution.

Ghulam said Daniel Pearl and his execution had done huge damage to them.

'This Pearl man was after the financial networks through which money reaches our groups and is circulated. He found out a lot of facts and must have passed them on,' he said.

'So he was a CIA agent?' I asked.

'No, just a smart Jewish journalist. Omar had to catch him and find out.'

'They say they'll hang Omar,' I said.

'We'll hang Musharraf first,' he said. 'But it means that money will become tighter. Omar, under my instructions, went to see bin Laden after we were liberated and he has a lot of the systems and facts and numbers about financing the whole jihad in his head. He is like an unofficial finance minister to the jihad and that means some funds may be frozen for a time. You will have to extend credit.'

The main men in San Marino said that the only credit the Russian or East European mafia were willing to give the Muslims was a note promising seventy-two virgins in Paradise. I don't think Ghulam would have appreciated the joke, so I didn't convey it. They wanted money and after the murder of Daniel Pearl, Ghulam said their money had gone underground.

I had been a month in Pakistan. I had phoned Ravina to tell her which day I was returning to the flat. She said she was dying to see me.

7

The phone bill for our Paris apartment arrived and I checked it casually.

Calls had only been made up to three days after I left for Pakistan.

'I thought you were away in a hotel,' I said to Ravina.

'The phone calls from hotels cost too much so I came back to make calls,' she said.

'Only for three days?' I asked.

'Oh yeah, then I used my mobile. I got scared of coming to the flat. There were men hanging about, or maybe it's just my paranoia,' she said.

'Twenty-six calls to America? In three days?'

'To my son and daughter, your daughter. She was having a crisis. Boyfriend stuff, you know. But I had to stand by her,' she said. 'Any problem?

'And your husband?'

'Why would I speak to him?'

'Well, you called California and two other places in the States. I checked the dialling codes. Michigan and then to your home in New Mexico,' I said.

'Have you turned into a fucking policeman? Paul is at

university in Ann Arbor, Samara was in California,' she said.

'Yes, but you called New Mexico ten times.'

'So are you now a full member of the CIA?' she said. 'I am a free agent, Thhat, I can call whom I want.'

'I don't need this,' I said. 'Or you.'

'You want that painted French TV doll, then? I always knew it, you know, you are a dog with your tongue out for white pussy,' she said.

'They like my tongue out,' I said. 'Unlike you who can't decide if you want to turn the lights out or watch us in the mirror like some porn show you want to be in. You are a sexual cripple,' I said.

She slapped me. The sound echoed in the room. I touched my cheek.

'I could kill you,' I said.

She burst into tears.

'I was only talking to Morgan about getting a divorce and I had to speak to somebody because I was worried sick that you would get shot by the mafia people for double-crossing them…'

I grabbed her.

'You what?'

'Before you left, when you were asleep, I tried dialling that phone you carry and leave on all the time. It only has restricted numbers. It's some kind of police phone. CIA? FBI? I don't know. You never tell me. And then Pakistan. What are you doing with all these people? I came here just for you. I gave up everything for you and you share nothing with me!'

She was working herself into hysteria.

I tried to quieten her down.

'Okay, okay, stop, stop. I want to speak to you,' I said.

I told her I was in a legitimate business, which required secrecy to protect the governments that wanted us to negotiate spare parts for industrial and other plants.

'Selling arms,' she said. 'To the Taliban! Look!'

She pulled out the crumpled page of a French newspaper from her bag. It had photographs of arrested Taliban fighters being marched away as prisoners by helmeted NATO forces.

'You will be on the losing side,' she said. 'And then the losing side will turn against each other and you.'

'So what do you want me to do? Join America?'

'Yes,' she said.

'Calm down and I'll make you some coffee, ma chérie, and I'll tell you what you want to know.'

I explained about being in touch with Ghulam, about Hugo's business and finally about the CIA. Why not? My life had been in this woman's hands many a time before.

'You called me a sexual cripple,' she said. She was sitting at my feet on the carpet and I was on the couch. She was staring up at me with her large black eyes. With her tear-stained cheeks she looked sixteen years old and reminded me of the picture she had shown me of our daughter.

'I said it to hurt you. You are actually an athlete,' I said. I stroked her hair and she clutched my leg tighter. She was silently sobbing.

'You still like me and want me?'

'I think we should go to America together. But later. Let's go to the bedroom now,' I said.

The phone rang, the special one. I had not given any information to anyone yet. I was earning a percentage from the stuff Hugo sold in Africa and in Indonesia and to groups in the UK and Canada. Maybe, I was thinking, I should stay with the dealers and forget about America and the CIA and double-crosses. Ravina had made me think again. But of course the fact is that the CIA, with the full backing of the American state, may lose a few battles or even a few countries, but they would win the universal war.

The contact on the phone used the code words they had given me, 'Hey Bhagwan! What about Pakistan?'

They knew where I'd been.

I told this anonymous contact that I could tell him who came and went from Haji Ghulam's outfit and that Ghulam was certainly involved in some way in the Daniel Pearl kidnapping and murder.

'Yeah, and that the Pope is Catholic and coyotes shit in the desert. Come on, Malcolm, you can do better than that. Where did your last consignment from Ukraine go?'

He had arbitrarily decided to call me Malcolm.

'I don't really deal with shipments, but I'll find out,' I said.

'Iran? The Gulf? Which ship?'

'I'll find out,' I promised.

'Something soon, Malcolm, or we'll close the line,' he said.

8

I was now involved in world events, Pradhan sahib. A defeat in Afghanistan. Osama bin Laden was the world's most sought after fugitive. Mullah Omar, the leader of the Taliban, went into hiding.

I got in touch with Hugo who said he was despondent. The defeats meant that our arms trade would get slower and money would dry up. He was looking for new markets.

I got an email from a name I didn't recognize, asking me for a meeting in an Arab suburb of Paris. I met the guy in a bistro outside the railway station. He was Algerian, with a big blob, a sort of birthmark, on his nose.

He said he knew who I was through Little Brother.

'What can I do for you?' I asked.

'I can't say who I work for, but we want you to make enquiries about something called Red Mercury,' he said. 'Big money involved.'

He didn't want to say any more.

I called Hugo again and he came back the next day and said this Red Mercury was available in controlled quantities and could be delivered. He could get a price when the quantities were specified.

I called Murad. 'Listen, you know any chemists?'

'I used to be at university with a few scientists,' he said. 'And my brother works in a multinational drugs firm.'

'Do me a favour, find out what Red Mercury is?'

'Why don't you check the Internet?'

'I have,' I said. 'The Internet articles contradict each other. I want an authority.'

He took two days to get back to me.

'I'm sorry, I've got the same answer. The Russians, during the Cold War, said they had synthesized a substance called Red Mercury which is a thousand times more powerful than any known explosive and can trigger a nuclear bomb, which is a bloody difficult thing to do. It's nuclear stuff. Triggers for dirty bombs. Any good to you?'

'Yeah, great. I won't forget you,' I said.

'When are we getting together for the book?' he asked.

'You know I will keep my promise on the book, man. I have to make a little money first.'

What did he expect? About his fucking book – that I would go to London, pay for a hotel and confess to murders into a tape recorder? Had he got his head up his arse?

✦

I called the Algerian with the blob nose and said the stuff he wanted, Red Mercury, was available and I could quote prices, delivery and everything. He said he was not the end negotiator but just the contact man and that I would have to travel to Bahrain and meet a man there. He would give me his email address and the man would communicate with me. His email address was Goatee2121@yahoo.com.

Yessss! The numbers after the name were magic. I wrote to him and Goatee invited me to Bahrain straight away. I wrote back saying I wanted to know the scope of the deal or else it wouldn't be worth my while.

'My team awaits your input of the sports equipment,' he said in his next email.

'Bahrain is not, I assume, going to compete in this Olympic event,' I wrote back. 'So I must know what the prospects of a sale for this sports equipment are.'

He replied promptly: 'My dear, you are not dealing with some small club. Our plans and intentions are huge. Already we have entered into global dialogue with the main teams. You are now in with the likes of Brazil, France and World Cup, with Ronaldo and Zidane. Come and negotiate the transfer and we can score goals together. This is urgent as the whole final team needs to go into training straight away.'

He had caught on fast, this guy. I wrote back: 'RM is a very rare player and not available to Brazil and France teams. You must quote transfer price for such a guaranteed goal scorer.'

Goatee wrote back: 'Biggest coaches entering new team into world game. All top prices comparable to any transfer of world-class players. Come personally to Bahrain to discuss.'

My problem was that Hugo had the Red Mercury supply contact and when I asked him for it, he wanted to see the correspondence with Goatee. I had no choice, even though there was a risk he would cut me out. I sent it to him.

When I phoned him the next day in the London antiques office, Charles answered the phone. Hugo had already left for Bahrain. So he was trying to double-cross me?

I said I would inform Mr Wing Kee and I would call my father. He put the phone down.

I called Murad and asked him to go round to the shop. An hour later he called me back from London and said it was padlocked.

So Hugo had taken the only deal going and disappeared!

I put it out of my mind. The San Marino boys would still be there. If business picked up, I was sure Hugo would surface and I could settle scores with him then.

For several months, cash would have been scarce, but for Ravina. She got work with an agency with some cultural freaks to translate Bollywood films into English and, with the help of a friend, into French.

✦

Then, Pradhan sahib, the Iraq war came and, months into it, the papers were full of Weapons of Mass Destruction and the search for them after the defeat of Saddam.

At the time the connection didn't hit me. It didn't click. I am not into politics and perhaps I hadn't noticed the debate.

Months later, Ravina said she had to go to London to get some translations of old Bollywood films. I went with her. A British newspaper called *The Independent*, opposed to the war, was challenging the British prime minister and government to come up with any evidence that Saddam Hussein had nuclear weapons or even that he had plans to build them.

Then it hit me.

I called the Algerian and a child answered the phone.

'Hello, is your daddy there? I am doing research on Algerians living in Paris,' I said.

'We are not Algerian, we are Iraqi,' the boy said.

I had it now. So an Iraqi was trying to buy nuclear materials of sorts. Through me!

I called my reserve phone. It was picked up by my contact. I called him 'Malcolm' as he had called me. I told him about my scoop.

'The British and US governments can now say that they were right. The people who say Saddam was not negotiating nuclear capability will be wrong.'

'This is very good, but it can't come from the government, Malcolm,' he said, cool as a cucumber.

'What do you mean?'

'I mean that we don't control the press in the USA. The general public are suspicious of the papers we do control. And when the main press starts verifying the story, your name will have to be linked and who will want this kind of information from a convicted serial killer? The whole thing can be shot through with holes.'

'Hold on, Mr CIA, I can get another fellow who actually went to the meeting in Bahrain to tell the story. He is an arms dealer posing as an antique dealer.'

'Yeah, and he has a lower murder score?'

'I didn't call you to be insulted. This is a big story for you.'

'I know it is, but here's what you should do, Malcolm. You should take your antique man and go to the London *Times* with it. That's a paper the world will respect, and if the Brits blow it first it will count big time. Americans don't trust what they read. And you, Malcolm, stay off TV and don't front this story. Push your antiques man.'

In the end, I thought, it was good that Hugo had stolen

the deal from me. Now he could genuinely front the story. I had to find him. He would be the key. And for good money, which I would demand from the British secret services for giving them ammunition when they and their prime minister were being called liars. For cash, I knew that Hugo would testify against his mother.

First I called Murad.

'Writer boy, I have a scoop for you,' I said. 'Remember the Red Mercury I asked you about? We have a story.'

Murad said he knew the editor of a weekly for which he wrote reviews. He would call him.

The next morning we went to the house in Highbury together for a breakfast meeting. I told him my story. I said I was an arms dealer and had been approached over a year previously to sell Red Mercury to Saddam Hussein's Iraq. I had proof. I had to explain what Red Mercury was.

The editor scratched his blonde, floppy-straw head.

'Blimey! We've taken the view that Tony lied to the country. Now we change our view?'

He didn't want to let the story go, thought it wasn't a magazine scoop. It was front page of the dailies and would steer political opinion and change the course of events in the world if I could stand my story up.

'The papers, prints of the emails from Goatee2121 are in France,' I said. 'And the witnesses are in Belgium.'

He called another journalist and the interviews began in earnest, about having evidence that the Iraqis, before the war broke out, attempted to buy Red Mercury from me and my associates and correspondence was exchanged and meetings took place.

'That much I can tell you now, but if you want the concrete evidence and the complete details of the meetings in the Middle East, the delivery and everything, you have to come to a deal,' I said.

'You mean money?'

'Right.'

'We normally don't pay for information. It's a matter of principle.'

'Okay, the papers don't pay, but this is espionage, my friend. I am giving your secret service evidence which they told parliament they had – but don't have. You tell them you are coming in and writing it up big and they will pay. Your government will come wagging its tail. With bags of money to buy me out.'

'I can't do that kind of deal, Mr Thhat. I have to refer this, naturally, to management and our lawyers. But you must realize that any story that MI6 pays for is contaminated by that payment. If you just give me the evidence, then it is, as it were, disinterested reportage and investigation.'

'You are the journalist. I'm the serial killer and nuclear contraband dealer, remember. You – disinterested journalism. Me – hard cash. Savvy?'

'I see your point. It will take me hours if not days to get round this deal if there is to be a deal,' he said.

'It will be unfortunate for you and for Tony if there isn't,' I said. 'Can you get a knighthood for doing this story?'

He smiled. 'It will take you time to fetch your papers, won't it?'

'I can send for them. But another thing. You won't even have to say a serial killer gave you the story. The man who is with me in this is an antique dealer. He is a good front and in this case, genuine. He can describe the meetings in the Gulf states in great detail and the names of the Iraqi negotiators and everything. This will be big.'

'I get the PR. Now both of us should get going. I have your number and will call to meet next.' British impatience. He was closing the conference.

I took a train to the antique shop, just on the chance. It was empty. No lock, nothing. The door had been left loose and swinging. It had been cleaned out. I went to the Asian newspaper shop next door and asked them where the antique dealers had gone.

The woman behind the counter came out onto the street, gesticulating, and said that several men had come some days before and spent hours loading their vans and blocking traffic and swearing in an uncouth fashion, making a nuisance and then had gone. She fearfully asked me if they'd gone for ever.

She even made them tea, she said, though she didn't like them and they left her a flower vase. She showed me. A little silver vase as a present. I asked her to describe the men, but she was bad at description and only said they were white and one was an Arab.

'Did he have a thing on his nose, a blob?'

'Yes,' she said.

The Iraqi.

I thought it out. They must have taken the stuff back to Brussels. But why were they packing up the London front?

I took the Eurostar to Brussels and searched all the places I had been with Hugo – the chess café and other haunts. I was still thinking that he would do the deal if tempted with money.

I sat in the chess pub each evening waiting for him to turn up.

Ravina rang. 'Where are you? You've got to come back.' Her voice was urgent.

'What's happened?'

'Someone's raided the flat,' she said. 'I was at the hotel, but they've broken the door down and taken your computer and gone through your papers.'

I returned to Paris. I looked through my papers. The emails, all the ones dealing with Red Mercury, were gone. And the computer. They'd stolen the evidence I was going to sell to the British papers.

The Iraqi, of course.

But how did they know I was going to blow it? There was only one possibility. Murad. The great writer had double-crossed me. He must have called Hugo. Hugo then made a calculation. He would get more from the Arabs for not blowing the story than he would from me or the Brits for blowing it. He had held an auction, called the Iraqi, told him to get in touch with Goatee and see what was on offer.

And he must have calculated that I had nothing to sell but the emails and he got hold of those by burgling my flat.

The editor called me back but I didn't answer the phone. He persisted for five days and then stopped. They wanted the story, desperately, but I had no evidence at all unless I could get to Hugo. Even then he wouldn't double-cross the Arabs or Iraqis or whoever they were. They would shoot him and me.

They would by now know, through Murad, that I intended to blow the story and they might try and kill me anyway. In crime there is always a clear motive. They want your money or your silence. In politics and in madness, there are no clear motives. Mad people kill for no reason and political slaughter is hardly ever understandable. Terrorists choose targets that cannot conceivably further their aims. Hugo was a criminal and there would be no point in him putting himself at risk by killing me. He wouldn't bother.

The Iraqi blob, on the other hand, was tied up in some politics and he and his people could do anything.

'I think we should go to the USA,' I said to Ravina.

✦

Why would Murad have betrayed me?

I was going to tackle him. For the first time in my life I felt betrayed. A weakness. Still, I got to London and called him.

'You won't…hurt me?' was the first thing he asked.

'Don't be silly, man. I am not a revenge killer. I want to talk to you as a friend,' I said. We fixed to meet in Holland Park, in the open.

Murad was wary of me and seemed genuinely saddened by what he had done.

'I am not in your kind of world, Johnson. I shouldn't have got involved, but I thought I'd write a book, you know, about you. But you were too busy to give me time. This fellow Hugo kept in touch every time he came to London. Now I'll tell you the truth, I am not really scared of you. I don't think you'll kill anybody again, but I am scared of Hugo. He called me to the antique shop once.

'I told him you were enquiring about Red Mercury and then…he wanted to pull the deal off himself and cut you out. He met Wajed.'

'Who the hell is Wajed?'

'The Iraqi guy with the mole on his nose.'

'Yeah, yeah, go on,' I said.

'They met a few times with Arab guys right here in London. In your antique shop. And then Hugo threatened he would kill me if I told you anything.'

'So why are you telling me now?' I asked.

The grass was wet under my bum and the damp seeping into my trousers.

'I trust you,' he said. 'And they are actually afraid of you. Hugo says you are the smartest man he knows.'

9

Pradhan sahib, they have moved a fellow called Gurung into my cell. He is a murderer. One victim, a girl who wouldn't marry him, he says. I have made friends with him, a Gurkha fellow.

His case is going for appeal and I am training him to pretend he has gone mad for love of this woman. They can't condemn a mad man to death. They will move him to a psychiatric hospital. I am sure he can pull it off with the Nepalese police psychiatrists.

His one legal problem is he had a motive. Madmen kill meaninglessly – the motiveless murder, somebody whom their schizoid brain has identified as a threat. He should have killed somebody at random and made up a story about being haunted by this stranger. Maybe he should kill someone else to make his case plausible.

Every day I instruct him on how to answer the psychoanalyst's questions. We have sessions, man. I draw pictures for him to teach him how to play crazy in mental association tests. The guy is learning.

But back to my story.

✦

Haji Ghulam called me while I was still in London. He had to speak to me urgently, as I could do Islam and the world a great service. He wanted me to go back to Paris. He had been informed that all calls from Pakistan were monitored by the West and he couldn't trust any telephonic contact. He said this on the telephone.

I knew he meant that Little Brother would pay me a visit.

In Paris, I changed the locks. Ravina had been away a few days but now she was back, cooking and cleaning.

Sure enough, Little Brother arrived. He brought with him another, older man with very thick glasses, wearing a grey Western suit and cheap moccasins. He introduced him as Doctor.

'The movement has run out of money,' said Doctor. 'The temporary defeats are owing to ill equipment. The Americans and their Crusaders think they are winning, but our hearts are steady. We are Muslims. They are fighting for Ronald McDonald, we are fighting for God. 'Meanwhile we need money, big money. Now our brothers are regrouping and they have control of large parts of Afghanistan…'

'You mean Al Qaeda and the Taliban?'.

'These are just names. I mean the universal jihad,' he said. Another wretched professor! 'Every man, woman and child on the land is with us and what they produce agriculturally and process, we can sell. But we need the markets.'

'You want to sell heroin to the West?' I thought it best to be direct.

'Correct,' said Doctor.

'Isn't that against the Koran?' Ravina asked.

'Leave that alone,' I said.

'No, don't leave it alone,' said Doctor. 'You know that Islam says if a tribe is dying and there is nothing to eat but a pig, then eat the pig. Survival in the ultimate service of God is more important than rules of behaviour. But you are right. We cannot be seen to be selling it.'

He turned to me.

'We can control the whole trade. Haji Ghulam Sheikh sahib knows you can put us in touch with buyers. They will trust you.'

'The buyers?' I asked.

'The Chinese in Paris, Thailand, London and New York. Don't they control the whole heroin trade? They have the sales. We have the stock. You have the connections, my brother. Then we can afford the arms you are selling.'

Little Brother and Doctor said they wanted me to move as fast as I could.

I said it could be done. They praised God and left.

I called Mr Kee. We sat in the back room of the supermarket as before and I explained the proposal. There would be unlimited stocks if Mr Kee's 'business' could handle it.

He said he would have an answer by the next day. He didn't want to wake them up in Hong Kong. He thought that was funny. It was the first time I had seen him laugh.

I made no overt deals, but I told Ravina we would get our cut. This was bigger than any piddling deal Hugo could be making and even with that, at the back of my mind, was the idea of the floating continent – America. I didn't even say the word to myself, but the picture of it, through mists shrouding the Statue of Liberty, flashed in the back of my brain.

Betray and move.

I met Mr Kee again at our flat. He came with his henchmen. He said it had been fixed and a group of people from Chinese Universal Welfare would arrive in Kathmandu, Nepal, in a week's time. Doctor would send his Afghan delegates and the deal and the delivery routes could be fixed there and then. I had simply to go to Kathmandu and get the two groups together, introduce them and sit in on the meetings.

Mr Kee said he wanted me to observe and report back to him when I returned. He was only entering this venture because he trusted me. He didn't know Doctor.

One of the Chinese delegates of Welfare who would come to Kathmandu was from America, and spoke English. I said I didn't know if the Afghans would but certainly the Pakistanis would be able to converse in English and I was always there to handle the Urdu. Language problems solved.

But Kathmandu?

'Do you really want to go there?' Ravina asked.

She had gathered that I might have been there.

✦

I didn't see the danger, Pradhan sahib. I didn't know you or your memories were alive. I came naïvely.

I told Doctor about the plans and he was very pleased. He had thought Nepal was a brilliant neutral idea when he proposed it. I thought it over. Indians, Pakistani, Chinese or even Afghans in Nepal would draw no attention whatsoever.

And that, Pradhan sahib, is how I came to your town and have fallen into the clutches of your unscrupulous and unjust puppet government.

Epilogue

A year and two months in the central jail, Kathmandu. Pradhan comes to see me. I have been allowed lawyers and they have appealed to the Supreme Court. Virginie is in touch. She pays for the lawyers and says she will send the best French criminal lawyer to help. I accept her assistance without comment.

Now this whole account is in your hands, Pradhan sahib, all except this epilogue.

✦

On his visit he asks me, 'Why murders, Johnson, why not drug the victims, take the money and run?'

'Just think it out, Pradhan sahib. You must have built some psychological theory in your head about compulsive killing and all this. Nothing like that. It's just that if your client is still alive and robbed he can make endless trouble. He can turn killer himself and come after you. These fellows are unreliable. We never called it killing. The client was simply the subject of an experiment. In these countries people disappear and no one asks anything. It couldn't happen in Paris, but in Bangkok, Burma, India, it's easy.'

'And it's easy in Nepal also, eh? There's still nothing about Kathmandu in your account, Johnson,' Pradhan says. 'Whether you killed Mary Ann Smolinsky, but you know and I know the truth.'

'You have a policeman's curiosity, man. I am going to get a French lawyer and appeal to your Supreme Court. Virginie is helping me. There's more in my life than some stupid American girl who died here. Now that you've heard the rest, that is a detail, isn't it?'

'A mere stitch in the tapestry of time, but I don't know how time works. Only how the law works,' he says.

'You don't even know that, you fool! When I called you a stupid policeman all those years ago, what did you do? Started reading books! That doesn't make you smart. Being a policeman is in itself a dumb thing to do. I never read detective books, because they lie. It's an elaborate lie, a fairy-story view of how crime happens and how it is solved. Look at me, man, I am the thing itself, as Roy used to say about me. Me.

'If you had really got smarter, you would have worked out by now why I am caged here for life. I'll get to your Supreme Court. But I predict they won't let me go. Fuck your Supreme Court because your Supreme Court is not supreme, it is a slave to politics. American politics and global plans. You'll see, French lawyer or no lawyer.'

'I thought you might have calmed down,' he says.

'You are blind, Pradhan, I have told you everything and you still know nothing,' I say.

'Sure. For now we know in part and prophesy in part, but then shall we know even as we are known,' he prattles on.

'I got a letter last week. Would you like to see it, my dear and only friend?' I ask. He holds his hand out and I give it to him.

This is it, surprisingly written in pen and ink, rather than the US undergrad's favourite word-processed prose. Written in a round, clear hand:

The Kohinoor Hotel
Paharganj
New Delhi

Wed, 5 March 2005

Dear Johnson Thhat,

You don't know who I am, but you should. I am travelling for a year around the world and have got to Delhi now. You may recognize the address. I plan to come to Kathmandu in a few weeks. I guess you'll still be there and I've decided that I want to come and see you. That's, of course, if you want to see me after I tell you who I am. What the hell: I am Ravina and Morgan's daughter, only I found out that Morgan's not my real dad and that that dishonour belongs to you.

Mom's book about you comes out next month.

Ever since that TV programme about you being released, I have known you were my real dad. Me, Morgan and Mom watched it and I was appalled but at last I had to learn the truth. It gave me hell for a few days but I've come to accept that you can't choose your parents.

Well, as you know, Mom decided she would do a book on you after they saw that programme. Now that Dad's retired I think they miss the limelight a bit and Dad thought if she really knew a guy like you she should do it.

I believe she lived in hotels in Paris and debriefed you about your early life when she'd met you but even to her what you did when you were in Bangkok came as a surprise. We thank God that she knew nothing about your criminal life and was rescued from being with you by your arrest.

But of course now she knows and it makes her shudder and the stuff she told us makes us shudder too. The publishers couldn't believe she had access to you and even they are startled by the stuff in her book, but there you are, and thanks to you she can now be more than a campus housewife.

I believe the French newspapers ran some sensational stuff about Mom and you while she was doing her research in Paris and then the Indian police tipped off the FBI and they went chasing Mom. So she had to get in touch with the Feds and give them all the dope even before she wrote it down.

Dad is very proud that Mom's going to be a famous writer, something she's tried before and failed at. He didn't even mind that she only came home for a month here and ten days there, the briefest periods in all the time she was researching the book in Paris and London. She's fine and there'll be a party to launch the book in New York. Pity you can't be there but Mom says she knows you'll be supporting her because unlike the newspaper reports, hers will be a view from the inside, which you have given her.

I tell you, ever since Mom returned from her research and started actually talking about you, I have been fascinated by your mind and exploits. From her point of view it must seem like a narrow miss. She said that my granddad, the general, didn't approve of you.

My brother Paul and I think and talk about it. Suppose she had gone with you to Bangkok as you proposed and then got involved with the murders and your actions there, life would have been so different for her. As it is Mom and Dad are happy and now they'll both be famous. Shame about you and your French girlfriend, the documentary maker, never having the opportunity to make a life together. But, hey, maybe Mom's book will stir something in the Nepalese king's heart and he will pardon you and you can go back to Paris.

So that's all the news to bring you up to date.

The reason I want to see you is that I want some idea of where I come from genetically. I have been to see Mom's family for the first time and that was a tearful reunion.

But of course it won't be like that with you and me. I can never be anything to you or you to me. I've read what Mom's written and I am sorry to say that though she might think your background made you, I am a Christian and actually believe that evil walks this earth. I want to look into its eyes and see if it's true. What intrigues me is how you kept the knowledge of your true self from her, I mean when she met you, and after I was conceived by mistake. I don't have many of your genes obviously because I can't keep secrets at all.

Never from Mom. I must admit she is very good at getting the truth out of people. And she is always curious about the truth, that's why she took so long in Paris getting the entire confession from you.

I'll tell you about myself when we meet if I decide to. You can imagine that I didn't bargain for our relationship and though Mom says it was the result of a mistake, it's now a fact and both of us have to face it. I don't know if you are permitted a reply, but I shall be at the gates of the prison and just hope they let you know.

Your (genetic) daughter
Samara

P.S. Please don't raise your hopes about any further contact with your 'flesh and blood'. I don't ever want to be that and am putting the facts down so you can decide whether you want to see me this once.

Pradhan reads it. He stands up and sits down again.

'You can bear this?' he asks.

'I can bear anything,' I say. 'You got me in the casino because the fucking Triads, Mr Kee's man from America and his gang didn't turn up.'

'Why didn't they turn up?' he asks.

'Because my darling Ravina, playing her little game of having a cake and eating it, trades my truths for her immunity from investigation by the FBI. She blows the fact of my CIA contacts, my phone links and intentions to Mr Kee. She tells Mr Kee I am about to double-cross him and he pulls out his men. So the CIA and associated agencies get to know that my cover has been blown. I am not only no good to them on the loose, I am dangerous. They tell your government to put me away forever and there you are, they get hold of the dope – retired inspector Pradhan, the great hero with the great memory, ready and willing to do it in the cause of justice.'

'Ravina,' he says. 'Wow!'

✦

Six days later:

Page 4, Kathmandu Times, *23 March 2005*
YOUNG AMERICAN WOMAN STABBED IN
KATHMANDU JAIL

A young American woman, identified as Samara Sands, was stabbed to death yesterday by a mentally ill prisoner, one Pita Singh Gurung, who shared a cell with the lifer

*Johnson Thhat whom the young woman had come to
visit in Kathmandu jail.*

*The father and mother of young Samara have been
informed in the USA about the tragedy and are on their
way to Kathmandu to identify the corpse and see to the
last rites.*